SNOW
ON THE SUMMIT

ART BY
LINAGANEF

Acknowledgements

To the Sleet Team! To Emily of JD Book Services! To Ally, Becca, Marissa, Mika, and Stephanie!
To the ARC readers!
To my heart, Mr. Fortneaux.
Thank you, all, for believing in me. You are what keeps me writing.

For a list of trigger warnings and an Ærta world-building guide, please head to www.Fortneaux.com

To the queens.
To the mothers.
To the servants.

CONTENTS

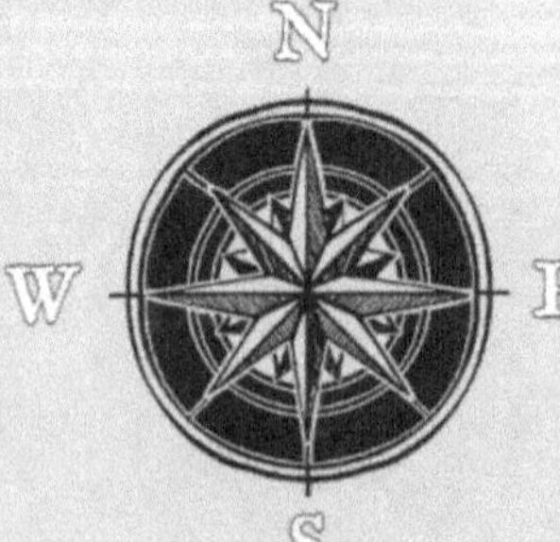

MONWYN
BASILIA
PENUM
COLPASS
CORDILLARIA
STORMRIDGE
RUINS
OF HAIN
LYK
N
W
E
S
BALDORVA

Silverstep
Snærshade
Nortia
Ruins of Inglis
Verus
The Rift
Mynder
Gaea
Ruins of Taleer
Solnna
Ærta

PROLOGUE

Ozius

"Welcome home, Scion. Gaea has felt the absence of its most treasured son and healer!"

Profound relief poured through me; his presence alone was enough to restore my strength and reinvigorate my fealty to this land. His smile warmed my soul and bolstered my resolve.

"Primus-King, I come to you deeply troubled and seek your wise counsel." I shifted my eyes, assessing the row of lesser queens and made note of an absence. "Your Lead Mate has gone to the Goddess. May her soul travel to Merrias swiftly. Most High Lord, I trust the babe she bore you is well."

A shadow passed over the Primus-King's eyes—this was the fourth High Queen he'd outlived.

"My newest daughter is a fine and healthy whelp—Mossius has blessed all of my children." He fanned his fingers, and his youngest mate rose from her seat, carrying two swaddled infants. "Brenlan provides an abundance of mother's milk and nurses the little one now. Show them both to Scion Ozius, little wife—let him lay his healer's hands upon them."

The diminutive woman smiled the weary yet pride-filled smile of a new mother and presented both infants. Laying my hands upon their perfect, round stomachs, I felt their futures on my palms. *Full cheeks and gaining weight rapidly.*

"Both will flourish, Primus-King. The girl's heart beats differently," I cocked my head to the side, felt the flutter in her chest, and watched as the same beat pulsed in the soft spot of her head, "but it will not stop her from living a full life."

"Because you say it is so, Ozius, I know it to be the truth."

The Primus-King grinned warmly and motioned for his wife to bring his children to the dais.

"What a lineage I have created. I truly am deity-favored." He kissed his little boy on the chubby cheek and rubbed the little girl's long-fingered hand softly between his thumb and index finger.

"Brenlan, doting mother, the babes have had their fill. Give the children to Mildrei and she will see to them—the healers have made me aware that you require another week of rest before you're fully recovered. You are more precious to me than gold and deserve the peace."

Brenlan nodded and bowed her head, her dark skin radiant in the light of the malachite chandelier that bathed the room in a warm glow.

"I am eager to return to my bodily duties, husband." She glanced up from under her lashes and smiled tenderly.

"And I am eager to find *your* bed again, ma'am." The Primus-King winked at his now blushing spouse, who giggled an airy laugh and turned to place the little ones in the arms of another beaming queen.

"You are a man of great wealth, my liege." I studied the tallest of his wives. "Mildrei bears another blessing in her womb, though it is early enough that she may not know it."

"How delightful! Another cabbage added to our patch." He looked at each of his wives with the eyes of a man who knew an abundance of love.

"Elderman Deekon, please approach," said the Primus-King.

I swiveled my head and acknowledged my former caretaker.

"Ozius, whom I love like my own son, returns from a mission of great import, as you know. I would speak to him privately. Send the younger Scions to the nursery and have them entertain my brood."

The man, who was like my second father, bowed and walked to the group of red-haired youth. He hugged each one of them in turn, before they shot off down the hall.

"My dears, you may retreat until this evening as well. There is no pressing business at the moment."

The lesser queens stood, one by one, and walked to the Primus-King. They laid their fingers in his palms and then raised their hands to their brows in a quick prayer. As they left, the room that was buzzing like a bee's hive quieted, leaving only the soft hum of a lone priestess at chant.

"Why is she not with you, Ozius?" The king stared at me with great concern etched on his face. "Speak to me of what has occurred."

I raised my head to my sovereign, who sat cross-legged on a throne of knot-worked wood inlaid with gold. I'd never hide the truth from him.

"They placed the Troth of Nortia and me together on the second day of the rite. We spoke at length, and, though the prospect of becoming the Lead Mate made her anxious, she was amicable to the idea. She was so moved, she blessed me with her own fingers." I allowed my lids to drift shut. Her holy hands upon me had been the most poignant moment in my life. "The Obligate was, at that time, pure... without the knowledge of a man."

"'Was?'"

The Primus-King dropped his feet to the floor, and his green, velvet robes dropped heavily around his ankles.

"The Monwyn Obligate defiled her, Noble One. He took her innocence and maidenhead. Our Queen... handled by th-that arrogant Scion. The thought makes me—"

"Ozius, control your rage. My anger matches your own, but I must approach this with a clear mind and ask the Goddess for her wisdom."

"I am fearful that your anger will only grow in measure. Our priest, healed by the Troth's lifeblood, made to spirit her away, but a Scion by the name of Evandr interfered. Scion Castor engaged him. During the ensuing melee, both lost their lives. In the end... the Protector of Monwyn absconded with our Divine Mother."

"Where is she now? Speak up!"

Dropping to my knees, I bowed my head contritely. I could sense the tension in his body as if my hands were upon him.

"Sh-she, High Lord, she is... I tracked them to a backwoods mountain town, wh-where she was forced to give her body to the men of the establishment in exchange for coin. There were too many for me to overpower, but know, my king, that I ended the lives of those who pushed her into such debasement. I will ensure that she has the proper cleansing when she is returned to us."

His Majesty's face contorted into a sneer. I'd never seen his displeasure displayed openly, and I cowered further, dropping my forehead to the marble floor.

"You have yet to answer my question, Scion. Where is my—?"

"Th-the Protector of Monwyn, he took her into the woods and used her body in ways I dare not repeat. He was a beast, my lord, an animal in a fit of rage. H-he took his pleasure as a wild creature would."

"And does *he* still *breathe*, Ozius?" Spittle from the Primus-King's mouth landed on the back of my neck. "He should no longer walk in this realm!"

His disappointment devastated me, and hot tears of self-loathing spilled from my eyes, wetting the feet of my sovereign.

"Forgive me, my lord. At Verus, he overpowered the Scions collectively. I hired a mercenary group to intercept them as they journeyed from Colpass to Cordillaria but he dispatched the band—all of them. Primus-King, he left no one alive. Confronting him directly would have meant losing my life and leaving her alone with no one to come to her aid, so I returned to you as quickly as I could—"

Another pair of knees settled next to mine.

"What, Elderman? What is so important you would interrupt me?" The Primus-King scolded.

"Primus-King, forgive my intrusion, but there is a missive, Your Majesty... from the King of Monwyn."

CHAPTER 1

SHIT, SHIT, SHIT.

"**I** am told you are quite fetching... daughter."

Not Cato. That's not Cato!

Fear ripped through me; the blood in my veins froze like the ice swells along the Penumbrean sea.

Move, Eira. Move now!

I flipped off the covers and scrambled to find a weapon in the dark. I balled my fist around the wooden pen I'd left on the bedside table—its small metal nib would have to be blade enough. My banged-up knees hit the floor, and I crawled my way to the far wall, seeking to distance myself from the shadow sitting on the bed's edge.

"Gammond's grace, not the manners I expect from a high-born Obligate," the figure said in a voice that rumbled like a rolling clap of thunder. "Your name is Eira, is it not? That is a pretty name. And soon you will wed my boy, Ambrose. I have missed him very much."

His son?

Cato's father. The King of Monwyn.

The conjurer.

"Here, daughter, where have you gone? Let me see you."

In the dark, my hand met the side of the fireplace, and when I looked to the left toward the chamber's door, I could *just* make out a soft glow in the distance.

He'd left it open.

I pivoted hard and shot toward the room's only exit, crawling as fast as I could, ignoring the tug of the carpet's fibers on my scabbed knees.

All at once, light surged throughout the room, filling the space with a glow brighter than the afternoon sun. The wall lamps roared as their flames leapt higher than the edges of their glass chimneys. Just as quickly, in tandem, they dimmed to a soft glow.

I skidded to a halt in the middle of the floor, the pen clenched tightly in my fist. I froze.

Holy shit. Holy fucking shit.

"I have been looking forward to making your acquaintance. I sent my man to fetch you some weeks ago but received word that he received a bolt through his neck. How distressing that news was, and quite a shame. Finding a competent underling is as difficult as training a worthwhile apprentice."

The river.

He tried to have me killed.

"*You* sent the attacker," I whispered. Too frightened to look at him and too frightened to move. I stared at the open door. My legs and arms began to shake.

"Attacker? No, dear, he was there to bring you home. Perhaps he was not as competent as I assumed. He blathered for days before his departure. 'Deliver h-he-her to Burchard, de-liver un-un-to Burchard.' Goddess me, his chattering went on and on," the conjurer chuckled.

"Burchard?"

"Yes, Burchard, that is *me* dear... Have you not read your history books?" He paused, waiting for an answer that didn't come. "Well, no matter, I can smell where he handled you roughly—so *dead* is my preference for him anyhow—the æther mixed with your lifeblood makes the most becoming aroma. Almost like... hmm... freshly laundered linen stockings. There is nothing like rolling up a pair of freshly scrubbed socks."

"Æther?"

"Daughter, have you not been amply fed? Are you overly tired? I was told you were not a dim person, but I find I am—"

"Wait... Stop talking, please."

Breathe, Eira. You're here to mend this man. Wake up.

"Alright then," the king said, sitting quietly.

Be brave, Eira... strength of Nortia. Move your legs. No? Arms first? No.

Ever so slowly, I twisted my head. *Now your eyes. Look at him now!*

Fighting the fear that hindered both my body and mind, I lifted my face.

"I... I think it's rather unfair of you to expect me to be a fully functioning human, when it was you who came here unannounced and at this late hour. A proper introduction would've been appropriate."

The king sat cross-legged on the edge of the bed, his chin resting on a propped fist.

"In *my* palace, I introduce myself as I please."

Shut up, Eira. Shut your fucking mouth!

"Of course, Majesty, it-it's just you sat on my bed—you made the fucking lights come on with your... your *brain* magic, and I—"

His flaxen-eyes widened, and his mouth—Cato's mouth—turned down in a disappointed grimace. My anxiety increased twofold.

Control, Eira!

"Such vulgarities are unseemly, my dear; I would appreciate you refraining from their use while in my presence."

"You're serious?" His brow flicked up in a gesture identical to the expressions I'd seen on both his biological and adopted son's faces. "A single foul word hurts the sensibilities of a man who's made attempts on his children's lives? A man who-who traps his kin in water bubbles of doom!"

I regretted the question the moment it fell from my mouth.

What the nether is wrong with me?

The king, in a floor-length coat of short-napped fur, stood and rounded the bed. He was tall and big-boned and moved as gracefully as a seal through water.

"Please stop coming toward me," I said while placing a hand in front of me and shifting back to my knees.

"I honestly would, but we will soon have company, daughter, and I am particularly concerned with your lack of attire." He pulled the white coverlet from the bed and faced me. Squinting his eyes nearly shut, he shifted his gaze back and forth between the ceiling and the fireplace.

Kill me now. Strike me dead, Viktos. Fry my mortal body and allow me to meet grandmother Merrias.

This entire time—through this *entire* conversation—I'd been on all fours, as naked as the day I'd entered the world.

"Here little Marmot, I feel as if Ambrose would frown upon his bride-to-be cavorting around her father-in-law, displayed as you are. I would not have him think ill of you."

Ill of me? What the fuck's a marmot?

With a tentative hand, I reached out and grabbed the blanket from his outstretched arm, making sure to keep a good amount of distance between us at all times—he was a trickster. All of this could very well be a ploy.

"Thank you. Now please, Majesty, would you mind leav—whoa!"

My fingertips pulsated... like a heartbeat drumming steadily under my nail beds.

"You feel it?" he said while scratching at his bearded chin. The skin above the thick and wiry hair was mottled red and looked uncomfortably dry, flaking onto his coat.

His words transported me. Was it only a week or so ago that Cato asked me the same thing? I remembered the tingle, the little electrical charge when our fingertips touched in the back room of Verus's study. This was different. That had been a light and pleasant sensation; this was a flow—a pull from within my... my being.

I stared at the balding monarch, unsure of whether I should speak or remain guarded.

"That is our connection." He smiled with genuine delight, revealing a mouth of cracked teeth. "Such a blessing for you and me. We will change lives together."

I wrapped the cover around my torso and kicked out at its length, struggling to find my feet. My brain was rapidly becoming as tangled as my body.

"Your Majesty, I've been looking forward to meeting with you, but I don't remember the last time I slept well, and again, honestly, I'm simply not prepared." I smacked at the volume around my legs and yanked at the material, trying to free myself. "Frankly, at this point, I'd request a do-over were it possible."

I made it to my knees but gave up on standing in my makeshift dress. I closed my eyes and rubbed my temples.

I didn't have a plan.

I should've had a plan.

I'd expected a formal meeting of some sort—an introduction where I could make my case. Shit, a one-on-one with ample snacks and an ample number of guards nearby would have been ideal.

"Daughter Eira?"

"*What*?" I snapped so harshly that the king hopped backward and pulled his arms to his chest.

Derros's dick. Why am I like this?

Breathe; don't cry.

I slapped my hands over my face, feeling the bitter sting of tears.

Shitty Troth. Horrible, failed Troth.

"My, my, I see what is happening. Come sit on my lap, little one."

I dropped my hands and blinked stupidly at the Monwyn sovereign.

He sank down on the end of the bed, patted his knee, and then flicked the bottom halves of his coat off his thighs. A sharp odor filled my nostrils.

"When my sweet daughters were babes, they would get just as agitated when their minds were troubled... Papa's hugs were always a reliable cure. Come now—"

"No, I—" Like someone had poked me firmly with their finger, there was an odd pressure in the center of my lower back. "Your Majesty, are you conjuring right now? Are you *compelling* me?" I looked him squarely in the eyes but knew the tremble in my chin betrayed the ounce of bravery I'd found.

"Please, call me Father Burchard, dear... and no, what you feel is our connection... the tie. Come, child, and I will explain."

There it was again, and stronger this time—like a string had been attached behind my navel, and the king himself was tugging rhythmically on its other end.

I rose and stepped forward. I couldn't stop myself. I *wanted* to sit on that fatherly thigh. I *needed* to sit there.

Shit, shit, shit.

The deep, flowing sensation began anew, pulsating first in the toes of my extended foot, then traveling up the length of my calf, until the entirety of my limb was engulfed in a measured draw.

When my knees neared the king's legs, I met with an invisible wall. It felt like that moment when your arm falls asleep while reading in one position for too long, but it covered the front half of my entire body.

I closed the small gap between us and became fully immersed in the—whatever it was—connection or... tie. The heavy vibration-like sensation softened to a light hum as I reached for him. I became light, buoyant, and peaceful.

It felt incredible.

My shoulders dropped, and the jaw that I'd held clenched, for what felt like days, loosened. I took a full and cleansing breath and felt the air reach to the very bottom of my lungs.

"Here, now." The king patted his leg once more.

Tears sprang to my eyes. An unexpected pang of loss—the need for my father rested heavy in my heart. I lowered myself, perching upon the costly, gray, brocaded silk that covered his legs. He even smelled like a dad, like black tea and old parchment.

"There now, darling, tell me everything. What has settled so heavily upon your mind?"

I twisted and draped my legs over his side and tucked my head under his bearded chin. His arms came around me, solid and sturdy.

I was secure.

Relief poured through me, a balm of tranquility coated my skin, and my anxieties eased with each of my exhalations.

"Father Burchard... the Gaean ruler means to have me. He knows I'm different, and I-I'm terrified." Under my head, I heard the unsteady beat of the king's heart. The sound was strong, but its rhythm was unusual—two quick beats and one that seemed to hold on too long.

"Sweet girl, if the Primus-King lays so much as his pinky upon you, I will flay his wives and have their skins tanned for the binding of my books. I will grind his bones into bread flour. You need not spare him a thought."

I nodded into his chest—the strange beat a soothing song being sung to my soul.

"He wants to breed with me, or maybe use my blood, and he... might be my sire."

An age-spotted hand settled on my cheek and tenderly tilted my head upward.

"No, daughter. If he wishes any of those, he is no father. A father's love is constant and steadfast; we protect our babies." I felt another light touch on my head—smoothing my brow. "Let us speak of more pleasant things. The news from Verus is that you may be with a little one. She would be my first grandchild, you know. I do not believe Aberus, my eldest boy, has reproduced, although I am not certain. I miss my firstborn fiercely. Do you know where he resides?"

"I don't, no..." I said honestly, leaning further into the chest that felt like physical solace.

"Ah, it is probably better for *our* fledgling relationship that you are unaware of his location." I felt rather than saw his sadness. "Now, our connection. My abilities come from borrowing bits and pieces of a person's energy—that is where the æther resides. I replace it with—"

"Father, release her!"

I raised my head and blinked through the fog swirling around in my mind. Ambrose and Cato were running toward us.

My men.

The wooden door slammed shut, cutting them off from my view.

"Will you not let them in, Father Burchard?" I asked, looking up into eyes that were so lovely. They were the same pale yellow as the lichen that had clung to the tree trunks near Stormridge.

"I would, daughter, but I prefer not to give attention to mannerless outbursts."

"They do tend to rush in," I agreed, "but they're concerned for my safety. You've attempted to murder Cato, so I feel he's rightfully upset."

There was a massive boom, then a loud bang on the door, followed quickly by even louder thuds.

"They are good boys, though Catommandus can be overly serious—he gets that from me, I am afraid."

The sound grew louder, accompanied by angry shouts and muffled curses.

"You would think when they reach adulthood they would stop making messes, and yet…"

The head of Ambrose's spiked mace broke through, high up on the door. Shards went flying, and the end of a concrete column came smashing through the hole that the smaller weapon had left.

"Your Majesty, return to your apartments at once. Do *not* defy me."

My heart jumped.

Cato's voice.

He was so matter-of-fact and authoritative in his speech, and I loved every one of the precisely enunciated words that came from his mouth. I wiggled around on the king's lap and hugged my knees to my chest. I could barely contain the happiness I felt in the presence of the man I loved.

"Catommandus, must you always be so abrupt with me? So formal?" There was a distinct note of sorrow in the king's rolling voice.

"Father, return my betrothed to me at once. It is our first night in the palace, and I would see to her needs," Ambrose called out. I could hear the tension in the strain of his words.

Cato's foot came crashing through the bottom half of the door, and as suddenly as it had come through, his leg flew backward like the doorframe had physically rejected it.

My ears filled with pressure, and, for a brief moment, my vision spun in circles.

With an audible pop, my ears returned to normal, and Cato and Ambrose were sealed out of the room by an invisible barrier.

"That's impressive!" I giggled and clapped my hands.

"Your Majesty, unseal the room *now. Do it.*" Cato's voice went flat.

My heart broke at the sound. *He needs me.*

"Children, calm yourselves. I was in the middle of explaining matters of immense importance to my daughter-in-law. Oh, of course—Congratulations, Ambrose, my boy! I am thrilled by the prospect of a Joining. Now, my dear... watch."

The brothers continued yelling from the connecting room. I could hear them and the thuds of their booted feet and weapons on the entryway, but it was as if the air itself prevented them from entering.

The bathing chamber door swung open, catching my attention.

Moving like a thin line of ribbon through the air, a rope of water made its way toward us from the darkened room.

"I am sure Catommandus has told you I tried to drown him. The truth is, I simply needed him to let me have my space. He can be overbearing and downright restrictive."

I nodded my understanding; he did often make demands.

In front of us now, the water snaked and coiled around itself until it formed a clear, shimmering sphere.

"Father, do not harm her or I swear—"

"Oh, look!" I squealed.

I reached into the floating orb.

"Eira, no. Stop now!" Cato cried out.

I pulled my hand back, and with it came strands of the bright-red fiber I hadn't cleaned from the tub. Ambrose had woven them into my hair earlier in the evening before we'd made our splash in the Den.

"You should have met me three hours ago, Papa. I was radiant! So well put together, and incredibly confident in myself."

"You are adorable, all mussed as you are," Father Burchard replied, scrunching his nose sweetly. "There is no reason for you to put on airs around me; just give Ambrose some heirs at some point, hmm?" He winked.

"I see what you did there—so clever." I smiled up at his kind and weathered face.

His nicked-up finger rose, and my eyes crossed as I watched it near.

"Father, father!" Cato yelled, "I beseech you... do not hurt her."

The king tapped me lightly on the tip of the nose and then grazed my temple as he lovingly tucked a clump of loose hair behind my ear. He shifted slightly and turned his attention to the door.

"Kitty Cat, how long has it been since you recognized me as your sire, my precious boy?" The king gently rocked me in his arms. I could sense his love, and I could feel his affection like a physical presence. "I commend you for caring deeply for the well-being of your brother's mate. She is extremely important to our family. You will protect her, yes?"

"At *all* costs, Majesty," Cato breathed. He looked close to hysterics. His body strained against the transparent barrier, and a sheen of sweat showed on his forehead. His palms bled, torn by the sharp wooden particles that now lay scattered about.

"Good boy. Now, before I leave, there is something you need to be made aware of." The orb that hovered in front of us began to roll and tighten. "Had I wanted you dead, Cato... as you keep telling people..."

Becoming more compact and dense, the ball spun around and floated to a chunk of the broken column that lay on the floor. The globe spread itself evenly around the stone surface before seeping into its pores.

I watched in awe. This power, his ability, had to be divine. Surely the Goddess must have blessed someone for them to—

The explosion shook the floor.

It rocked the bed and blew my hair back over my shoulder.

I felt shockwaves deep in my chest and watched bits of concrete fly with such force that they embedded into the walls.

"You see, my dear, I love my children, even if *they* do not see it themselves." The king pinched my cheek and shared a lopsided grin before looking at the door. "From their expressions, it seems like we should finish our conversation another time. No matter, I will find you soon enough."

Nothing remained of the column—nothing but the dust floating in the air.

"You will go nowhere near her!" Cato shouted. "Ambrose, take her this instant."

The barrier ceased to exist, and Cato lunged toward his father, a blade in one hand and a set of irons in the other. Ambrose was a second behind him.

"Catommandus, stop the dramatics. I will come without the aid of shackles."

The king placed me gently on my feet and looked at his sons.

Cato's red-smeared hands went to the fur collar at his father's neck, and he hauled the taller man to his feet. "If you lay a hand on her again—on Ambrose's future wife—I will snuff you out of existence, old man, even if I must follow you to the nether to ensure you stay gone."

The king didn't react; he just looked at his child, his eyes glistening with unshed tears.

"I should have raised you to be gentler, Kitten."

Cato placed a pin in the cuff's locks and jerked the metal chain that linked them, leading his father away.

When the two men disappeared, Ambrose wrapped me in his giant's embrace and pulled me roughly against his body. He held my head against his chest, and I heard his ragged breaths as his chest rose and fell.

"Eira, what the *fuck* was that?"

Chapter 2

THIS FUNNY FEELING

He's so upset. So angry.

I'll fix this.

"Ambrose, my betrothed, I never told you how beautiful you were in the Den—so handsome and confident... Your hair was just lovely. Not a single piece got out of place, even when you were fingering—what? What's wrong?"

His mossy-green eyes narrowed.

"Come with me." He grabbed my hand, and we walked silently through the airy common room. Before I could admire its elegant furnishings or the balcony that opened off its back, I was hauled away, much like the king had been.

"I simply love Cordillaria's decor. It's all bright and dainty, yet built so solidly... much like you."

We came to a rapid halt. Ambrose grasped my chin, and moved my head from side to side, inspecting me like he was appraising a jewel.

"You insult me, Nortia. There is nothing *dainty* about me... Have your eyes gone dim?" He curled his top lip, bristling at what was supposed to be a compliment.

Oh, goodness, I'm making things worse.

He pulled me through an arched doorway, trimmed with white marble tiles, and we entered a bed chamber decorated in rich jewel tones. It was very different from the rest of the neutral palace, but not nearly as dark and domineering as Verus had been. A bed that could easily sleep four sat on a raised dais that ran the length of the back wall, and a short flight of steps curved out from the front of the platform and flared out into the room.

"Ambrose... Amby... what's wrong? You're too magnificent to be so upset. Your rosy lips are too frowny right now, and your brow has never creased so deeply." I knew I was making things worse when his hands went to his forehead, feeling for the line that marred his poreless complexion. "Here, let me smooth your fine beard—such a glorious beard you have, all shaped to perfection and full."

He leaned down, bringing his handsome face directly in front of mine. When I reached up to rub away the lines of concern he flinched and pulled back as if burned.

"Whereas I would normally encourage this level of adoration... I fear you have been possessed by the nether scourge or perhaps poisoned."

"Silly man, I'm quite fine. Now, hold my hand, almost-husband." I threaded my fingers through Ambrose's long digits and led him to a leather sofa topped with a multitude of gold pillows.

"Sit," I said sweetly.

"Nortia, you do not get to—"

"Sit!" I said again, stamping my foot to emphasize my seriousness. I could ease his tension but only if the brute would listen.

"Gammond's balls," Ambrose muttered. "Fine, here I am sitting. Will you return to your normal, moderately sane self?"

"Yes. I'm so pleased." I smiled. "Now catch me!" I skipped the few feet that separated us but stumbled over my makeshift blanket gown. "Hang on." Untucking the edge of the coverlet, I let it fall to the floor, where it pooled around my ankles. "Here I come!" I giggled, hopping the remaining two feet that separated us.

"Look here, Nortia; wait, Eira, you are not—"

I sprang off my toes and took flight, landing heavily on his oversized lap.

"*Gods*, you are not some small child. You could have injured my—"

"Ambrose," I interrupted, placing a finger on his lush lips. "You aren't normally so tense. You know we are very lucky, you and me. You fought off a troll. We didn't die. We slayed the vilest of courtiers at the Den. We're a very good team. Do you need kisses? I think you need kisses." I held his dazed face between my hands and showered his neck and ears with quick pecks.

"Eira, stop! What has happened to you?" Ambrose chided, his eyes wide and deeply concerned.

He batted at my hands and attempted to capture my arms.

"We are to be married. We'll need to share kisses when we're happy *and,* most importantly, when we're sad," I said, meaning every word. "If this fake union is to prosper, we need to be comfortable sharing and touching."

Perfectly formed fingers wrapped around my wrists and pulled at my hands. His mouth parted, and though it looked like he was confused, I knew Ambrose...

"That's perfect!" I pressed my lips against his and slid my tongue past his teeth. "Mmmm, yes, this will make us both happy—you do taste nice." I felt his member stir beneath my thigh and squirmed around until I successfully straddled his hips. "When you were handling me in the Den, I became quite wet. In truth, I didn't expect that to happen. Cato makes me the wettest—have I told you that I told him, that I love him? I do, even though I worry it's much too soon to be feeling that way. He makes me so happy, Baby Bear."

I shut my eyes and spread my legs wider so that I could wedge my vulva more securely around the stiff ridge I felt through his pants. Almost instinctually, I rocked my hips, adoring the friction of his still-growing arousal pressed tightly against my slit. I took his hands and placed them on my breasts.

"Nortia, I am not your plaything. Cease at once!"

"No."

"What do you mean, no?" He balked, jerking his head back.

"Ambrose, I *know* what you require." I sped up the motion of my hips and let my head drop back. "Plus, it feels wonderful. Will you lick my breasts? The pierced one first. Cato did it once, and it was simply decadent... and I fondly remember *your* nimble tongue."

I watched his eyes haze over, and a blush spread from his open shirt collar to the top of his neck.

"Well, uh, yes, I think that I could maybe accommodate such a *sweetly* delivered request."

He was moving too slowly. I jutted forward, popping my peaked nipple squarely into his warm mouth. I wrapped my arms around his head and leaned in.

"Can you breathe?" I asked. My breasts covered him from nose to forehead.

"Doesn't matter," he mumbled around a mouthful of areola. He swirled his tongue around my sensitive nipple, much to my delight.

The door behind us creaked open.

Ambrose attempted to pull away, but I force-hugged his head.

"Brother, I suggest you dislodge yourself before I separate your tongue from your teeth."

Ambrose flailed around until his hands found my face. He pushed so hard that I nearly lost my seat when my death grip failed.

"I am trying, Cat. Something is wrong with her... incredibly fucking wrong."

Cato!

I swiveled my head and drank in the view of the most exquisite man to grace Ærta's soil.

"Hello, my love! Mmmm, Ambrose, expose your length, please. Just seeing him makes me more amorous." I rode his clothed hardness while trying my damnedest to kiss any inch of exposed flesh I could find. "Move your hands, you goose." I swatted and evaded his attempts to push me away. "Don't deny me your affections!"

I reached between my legs and grasped his erection. His hips thrust hard into my palm.

"Unhand me, woman!" He shoved at my shoulders, looking past me. "Cato, assist me!"

"Yes, come join us, sweetlove!"

A pair of familiar hands tugged at my underarms, but I wouldn't be unseated quite yet. I tucked my feet firmly under Ambrose's thighs and let my head fall back to the point that I felt the tips of my hair tickle my backside. I looked into the face of my lover and knew the purest joy.

"Cato, Ambrose isn't willing to fuck me, but you will, won't you?" My lips quivered, fearful he'd also reject me. His nearly black eyes softened, and the thin golden rim that surrounded his pupil glowed in the half-light of the room.

"Eira, off. Get in bed," Cato said sternly while finger combing the hair from my inverted forehead. He bent his head over my face and pulled at the corner of my eyelid with one finger.

"All of us. We'll all get in the big bed. You both left me, and I was so frightened until Father Burchard showed me his magic. It's going to be tough taking care of you both, you know."

Cato flicked his eyes up to Ambrose, whose head I could feel shaking back and forth between my arms.

"We will *both* stay with you." He nodded.

"And we will have sex. You promised me we would. I waited, but you never came." I whipped my head forward and captured Ambrose's scratchy cheeks between my hands. "I don't love you, Ambrose, not like I do him." Cato chuckled softly behind me. "He makes my heart do funny things... You just make my vagina feel funny."

"*Cato,*" Ambrose pleaded with his brother.

This isn't like Ambrose. I pressed my hand to his forehead. *Not fevered.*

"We will see to your needs, Eira. Climb off... When was the last time we had a meal?" Cato's voice, and the promise of food, coaxed me into action. "Ambrose, get her a shirt or something."

"Boop!" I poked the tip of Ambrose's arousal when he stood, and then I twirled around on my toes to face Cato.

"My love, you're hard for me as well. Have I told you how much I treasure your perfect penis? You're delightfully thick and not too long, like Ambrose. With him—you know, the first time—it struck my puss like a punch to the face... until it flopped out like a flaccid fish."

"Is that so?" Cato asked with a half-smile pulling at his lips.

"Yes," I nodded. "Yours is perfect... It fits my passage all snugly, and I love the way my lips pop right over the ridge of your head when it's in my mouth." I closed my eyes and smiled while I imagined tasting him again. "You know, I'd like to mount you. I've never orgasmed while riding on top, and I think it looks—Oh, hello!"

There was a man in Monwyn-blue livery standing in the open doorway. I waved and gave him my most winning smile. The servant swept into the room carrying a gold tray topped with steaming bowls and a pile of bread I could see from twenty feet away.

The man stopped short and stared in my direction.

"You're very attractive, sir. Would you describe the length and width of your penis? Is it veiny or perhaps thicker at its base?"

I walked in the man's direction, holding my arms wide.

The servant looked a lot like Ambrose had earlier, wide-eyed and mouth agape. Despite the face he was making, he was very pretty. No surprise there; Monwyn was full of attractive men. This one looked to be somewhere in the middle of his second decade and had a wispy head of fine, honey-blonde hair and a cute button nose.

"Get out, Bem. Leave it and go," Cato said from behind me.

The servant hurried into the room and dropped the tray, which clattered loudly on the table. He lowered his eyes to the floor after off-loading his burden, turned quickly on his heel, and hurried away.

"He didn't like me?" I asked, concerned I'd done something wrong.

"I am sure he liked you a great deal," Cato replied.

"Most probably, I'm very pretty and have a good personality, yes?"

Cato laughed in his low, throaty manner.

The best sound. His laughter was more provocative than even his growls and groans.

"If you find yourself chilly on a cold Nortian morn,
You should dance with your lover as a way to stay warm.
Just know, fair daughter, in this land frozen white,
Before your husband comes home, kiss your lover good night."

I sang my song loudly and wrapped my arms around myself.

"Dance with me?" I asked Cato. He wanted to dance as well... I could tell. He'd sucked his lips tightly into his mouth, and his shoulders were shaking with clear enthusiasm.

"Of course." He took my hand and led me into a few short steps. He pulled me close and twirled me around before throwing his arm up in an expertly executed flourish.

The way his body moves...

When he fought, it was like he danced, and when he loved me...

"Can we have sex? I'm ready *right* now." I shoved my face into his coat. My head fit perfectly into the crevice that his pectoral muscles made. "You are my favorite smell—cedar and toasted cloves. Do you love me still?"

"Very much, I do."

"Oh, good." I rubbed my cheek against him and continued swaying to the beat of the song in my head.

"Eira?"

"Yes, love?"

"Release my cock."

My hand was lovingly running the length of his hardness.

How wonderful that his body shows its desire. Clever Goddess.

Cato pulled back, holding me at arm's length. *Am I so vile?*

My heart broke.

He dropped my hands... and it shattered my soul.

He walked away. The man who'd pledged his love...

That motherfucker!

"Cato, I'm tired of waiting, and I've been very kind thus far. So do lie down. I can put in the work." I reached out and took a step toward him... and he took a simultaneous step back.

"Eira, let's go and—"

"You don't want to share in my joy? How very confusing! You are responsive, you said you loved me, and I have just gone from a pleasantly wonderful arousal to one that is nearly scorching."

Cato put his hands out and slowly moved away...

"What you are experiencing, Eira, is—"

"I. Said. Lie. Down." Out of the corner of my eye, I caught sight of Ambrose inching closer to my side. I snapped my head in his direction, and he froze in place. His smile was sickly sweet.

Ambrose doesn't do sweet.

"Simmer down, Eira; cease your boil."

"Cease your mouth, Ambrose, or come and put it to good use."

Little shadows began invading my periphery. Both of these fools were trying my patience.

"I am willing to volunteer my services," said Cato.

I whipped back around and narrowed my eyes at the man who *supposedly* loved me.

"One of you better... and I don't care who. But one of you better drop your *fucking* pants before I trash this palace!" I ran the distance to the table and snatched up a tall drinking glass. With all the might I could muster, I launched it at the far wall. Its orange contents splattered across the floor before it shattered on impact.

"To your knees, Eira, this instant," Cato barked.

I dropped to the ground with not an ounce of hesitation and leaned forward until my elbows rested on the cold floor. The unmistakable sound of a belt being slid from its loops came from behind me, and elated, I bent further still, letting my breasts drag the marble below. I shimmied my rear in the air, excitedly anticipating the pleasure that was to be *all* mine.

"Give me your hands."

My Goddess-given gem pulsed with a heavy beat. Already, I was swollen with arousal.

"Take them, Cato, and then take me hard—so hard. The warrior-king Cat... I want to be covered in your release." I reached behind my back, and he threaded his solid arm beneath my elbows. "Yes! Don't ease yourself in; just take me in one go," I begged. My body shook, and my breathing turned ragged. Waiting was the cruelest of punishments.

The room went dark, and a thick leather strap cinched tightly around my wrists.

"Wh-what's happening?" I asked.

"Eira, you are compromised."

Cato's traitorous hands lifted me to my feet as my vision was obstructed by a cloth covering. My lips trembled, and there was no controlling the tears that cascaded down my cheeks.

"But... but Ambrose, even y-you don't want me?" I cried out. "You... you would sex up a boat barnacle, if it had a willing hole."

The liquid warmth of my angst rolled down my chest. I had never been treated so poorly, not in all my years. My laments turned into soft cries, which amplified into wretched sobs. "You can't leave me!" I wailed, while they pulled back my arms and secured them to some solid form. "You're leaving me, and... and my vagina weeps!" I screamed.

"Good Gammond, Cato, give her an arm back. The guards are probably on their way. Shut her up!"

"Ambrose, she has been conj—"

"She can fuck herself or use *my* fingers, but make her stop! They will assume I have pledged myself to a she-demon."

One arm broke free, but my head was still covered. Blindly, I lashed out and managed to grab a thick wrist—I didn't care who it belonged to.

"Gods, Eira," Cato hissed through clenched teeth as I forced his fingers between my legs.

"Steady, Cat, control yourself," Ambrose said.

"No, Cato, love, you needn't. Submerge yourself into my heat. I am dripping with—"

My moan echoed around the room.

I dropped my knees and let my legs fall wide as two thick fingers pushed past my entrance. I fed them to myself until his palm rested tightly against my pubic bone.

"Thank you, love, thank you, Cato, thank you—gods, I ca-can't take..."

He hooked his fingers and thrust forward, rubbing the delicious nerve endings deep inside me.

My eyes rolled to the back of my head.
And then I soared.

Chapter 3

BORKO

"**S**top shaking me, asshole."

"Nortia, it has been nearly a full day."

Fucking Ambrose. He was awake, and from the sound of it, he was full of his aggravating Ambrose energy. *Piece of shit.*

"Is your mind failing you, Scion? Has your beef brain gone rancid? Wait, of course it has, you giant fucking potato." He jabbed me in the ribs with his sausage-sized fingers, and I kicked out a blanket-covered foot intending to break his jaw. "After my *more* than stellar performance in the Den, *you* said I could sleep for three days—a sworn oath! Quit poking me, damn you. I swear to the Goddess, I'll break your bones, Ambrose."

"You have shown an aptitude for it. I feared Cato's hand mangled after you man-handled him last night, you nasty little nether-spawn."

I pulled the covers up over my eyes and sank back into their warmth.

"Eira, are you well?"

That voice irritated me a little less.

"Cato?" I asked, managing to crack open a single eye. The light of the nearest lamp seared my vision like the white-hot Solnnan sun.

"Mmhmm."

"You wake for him, but you greet me with your ungodly grunting and the appalling stench of your breath." Ambrose sat down beside me and destroyed the perfectly shaped cocoon in which I'd nestled. I twisted my head around and glared at his too-big face.

"I like him more than you, whiney heifer."

Ambrose reared back. Like lightning, his hand shot down and slapped me soundly on the backs of my cover-padded thighs. I ignored him and turned my head in Cato's direction, smiling as warmly as my grogginess would allow. My heart fluttered in my chest.

"What are—" My cover disappeared. "Ouch! Godsdammit!"

Ambrose found his mark. I scrunched up into a ball and rubbed my stinging backside.

"She is fine, Cato. She has re-entered her true harpy form."

I sat up with the intention of slugging Ambrose in his beautifully straight nose, but the back of my head pounded so badly I was barely able to maintain my upright position.

"Drink this," Cato said while stretching across the bed and pressing a mug into my hands. "It will help."

I smelled the strong brew and took a sip of the dark liquid. Its scent was heavy and fragrant, and its flavor was harsh and wholly bitter.

"Eira, how much do you remember about meeting His Majesty?" Cato asked, tilting the warm mug to my lips.

I drank deeply and thought back through the fog.

Sex Den... bath... bed.

Heat prickled across my chest, and I felt the color rising to my cheeks. I laid my head on my forearms, and the shoulder of the robe I'd been dressed in fell to my elbow.

Oh, snowballs.

"I remember it all. I was fully aware the entire time, and I'm so incredibly sorry for how I behaved. Truly, I am." I sat the mug down on the bedside table and rubbed my hands up and down my biceps, suddenly chilled. "I'm so cold."

"Cold? You don't get cold." Cato glanced at Ambrose and then back to me before crawling across the bed and climbing in behind me. He wrapped his arms securely around my shoulders, and I leaned back into his warmth, settling comfortably into his embrace.

"I... I feel fine, I think, other than needing more rest. I'm just drained," I replied.

"Eira, my betrothed, rest assured that had *I* felt threatened by your untoward advances, I would have restrained you. You aren't my match physically by any means," Ambrose interjected.

"I'm honestly surprised you didn't take advantage."

"Oh, I wanted to... I just knew Cato was coming back."

"Ambrose, I swear on Lykksun's legs you are..."

Cato swept my hair over one shoulder and nuzzled my neck with his nose.

"Are you warm now?" he whispered.

I pulled his arms more snuggly around me. He skimmed his mouth along the edge of my ear and then tilted my face up to his.

"Disgusting. You two make everything awkward. And if a servant were to appear, Cat, she is *my* wife, remember?"

Cato hovered his lips over mine, undeterred.

"Papers have yet to be signed, brother. She remains free game, and if you wish to play against me... you are certain to lose," Cato ribbed. "Unless you feel you can rival a man whose appendage has been dubbed *perfect.*"

"*Ugh!*" I pulled the heavy, teal blanket over my head and squished myself so low my head rested on Cato's stomach.

"Are you embarrassed?" Cato yanked the blanket from my hands. "Your words were both accurate and deeply romantic... You could say them again, but speak up, so Ambrose can hear." Cato tickled my sides, and I squirmed away from him and fled across the bed. "Eira... I do not take kindly to your running."

That stopped me.

He batted those seductive gold-tipped lashes in my direction. A tingling sensation swept across my chest, and my fingertips felt electric. I pushed the neckline of the too-big robe back over my shoulder, but it slipped down again.

"That scrap of silk will do nothing to ward off my advances."

My mouth went dry. Cato came up on all fours and began slowly advancing, moving a single limb at a time—a lion stalking his prey.

"Remove it... *now,*" he purred.

My hand went to the sash.

"Cato! Where the fuck are you? Wake up, brother. Our father infiltrates my bed chamber, turns her into a raging nymphomaniac, and yet you are *still* attempting to wet your prick? Come on, *Protector*, who will stop her from fucking the gardener, or, or that old woman who knits my stockings?"

A rough-textured hand settled on the middle of my chest and pushed me backward. Cato crawled over me and straddled my thighs between his muscular legs.

"I will ensure that my *very* willing, *very* perfect cock is the closest one to her at all times." His eyes locked on mine. "I wanted nothing more than to mount you, darling, but I was uneasy with your lucidity or lack thereof." Cato lowered his lips to my collarbone as he dropped down slowly, letting his weight press me into the mattress. "Did I not tell you to lose the robe?" He parted the ultra-fine fabric with his fingers.

"Cato... Ambrose is—"

"A big boy who knows when to exit." He blew a stream of warm breath under the silk I wore, and it billowed in the air. "Outstanding." He tucked his head under the fluttering fabric, and his lips circled my nipple.

I grasped his bearded cheeks and heaved up.

"No. Ambrose is right." I stared into Cato's lust-filled eyes and steeled myself against the feelings he stirred down below. "What if it were Septimus who'd been nearest to me? Cato, I would have done it. I would have fornicated with your uncle."

That worked.

The corners of Cato's mouth pulled down, and he sat back on his heels, unconcerned with the erection that pushed against his linen pants.

"Forgive me." He rubbed his hands over his face and scratched where his nascent curls were starting to coil at the bottom of his neck. "You are both correct." Cato scooted to the edge of the bed and gestured for Ambrose and me to follow.

Ambrose, fully clothed and combed to perfection, walked after his brother, and I, still not fully awake, followed at an extremely leisurely pace, struggling with the robe that was clearly made for a human three times my height.

We entered the common room that connected the husband's chamber to the wife's. It was sparsely furnished and yet somehow still homey. The large and airy room was strewn with tan-and-white carpets and tall, diamond-patterned couches lined the side walls. Inset marble arches accented every corner, each housing a different statue. The most eye-catching was a rendition of Merrias wielding her sword against a sea monster surging from a crest of waves.

A stunning balcony, off the back wall, housed pale wooden chairs, upholstered in gray-blue velvet, which were set up in an intimate cluster around a central table.

By the time I finished my investigation of the chamber, Cato was seated and tearing his way through a massive spread, stacking his plate well over two layers high. He glanced up briefly, grinning, and waved me over with a flaky loaf of bread.

Love.

Like a brilliant light it illuminated my world from the inside out.

"Come eat. Brief me on exactly what occurred right up to the point where Ambrose and I became involved with His Majesty." He kicked out the chair closest to him and sent it sliding backward, never pausing in his chews.

"Still hungry? Do you feel the effects of my blood, even now?" I asked.

"Yes… and yes. Eat. You skipped too many meals on our travels."

I didn't need to be told twice. On the road, my appetite had been squashed by constant unease, physical hardship, and even the putrid stank of troll. Just thinking about it, I could smell the decaying scent of century-old meat.

Sharp-footed pixies tiptoed down my spine, causing me to shiver. Cato eyed me suspiciously.

"Troll," I murmured while shrugging a shoulder to my ear.

He nodded, understanding, and then shifted a chunk of cheese to his other hand so he could caress my arm.

Utter romance.

I chuckled to myself. Our new relationship was *very* different from the ones I'd daydreamed of in my younger years—no slow walks in the snow or holding hands during the Whaling Festival. Nope. So far it was *have a snack, sweetheart and please don't fuck my brother when I'm in the palace.*

"You are amused, my soft-hearted assassin?"

I cringed at his choice of endearment.

"I was until you opened your mouth."

He looked down his nose and narrowed his eyes. His thumb pressed down in the middle of my palm, massaging it thoroughly.

With his other hand, Cato shoved a bunch of grapes in his mouth. His eyes rolled up under his lids, savoring their sweetness, and when he came back from the Goddess's plane, a lopsided smile spread across his face.

Assassin. Murderer. The defining memory of traveling the road from Colpass was not the lives I had ended, but fear. Fear that I would never get to share moments like this with him. Cato had been in danger, and in the moment, it was as if a powerful force had taken control of my body.

I'd do it again.

"I'd walk the nether if it meant saving you," I breathed, my chest expanding with the magnitude of my feelings.

His eyes shifted back and forth, focusing on everything but me.

"What?" I asked. "I'm pouring out my heart, and you're searching for more treats?"

He brought a fist to his mouth and stared at me while he tried unsuccessfully to stifle his laughter. "You think you saved me?"

"Of course I saved you. And I think I did a fair job of it considering I'd never held a blade or bow."

Cato leaned over his chair and wrapped his fingers around the back of my neck. He drew me forward and brought me close to his face.

"You are so fucking gorgeous." He pressed his sausage-scented lips firmly against my mouth. "Lower that brow, ma'am." He kissed me again, softly this time. "It pleases me to know you were concerned for my welfare. Aiming is difficult... for some. But, I have been shot through a half-dozen times; I had little to fear from the assailants."

My stomach growled loudly.

"Go fuck yourself, Cato. I took one bad shot. Just one." I tore a roll in half and stuffed a hunk of cheese in it before smashing it between my hands and biting the flattened sandwich.

"Did you all leave me anything to eat? Will I *always* be the uncared-for partner in our threesome?" Ambrose dropped into a chair on my other side.

I knew the tone. Weepy, dramatic Ambrose was threatening to rear his cranky head.

I snatched a plate and jumped into action.

"Ambrose, there are sausages, ham, eggs, and rolls. Would you like some soft cheese or grapes?" I asked, already spearing the choicest bits for him. He wiggled his broad shoulders and looked up through his thick lashes. His compressed lips returned to normal.

"Are you unable to serve yourself, *my prince*? Too delicate to lift your royal hands?" Cato chided.

"Eat a dick, brother," a much happier Ambrose snapped back before shoving a runny pile of brie-topped bread into his mouth.

I grabbed my second roll and coated its top in butter and honey.

"Eating for two?" Ambrose said, staring directly into Cato's eyes. "Do you feel, Eira, that it was the first or eighth time that my seed fertilized your sinfully curvaceous body?"

Oh, shit. Shit!

I dropped the roll to my plate, unable to take another bite.

"The king knew about the possible pregnancy... and I told him about the Gaeans... He threatened to murder their entire royal family, and I think maybe *eat* the Primus-King. I just let it all out. Oh, my gods." I knew I was beginning to sound hysterical, but I couldn't control the panic as the words flowed. "He wanted to know where your older brother was. I can't be trusted—never tell me where he is." I wrung my hands on a linen napkin and then twisted it into a tight knot. What else had I told him?

Ambrose paused while biting through a sausage link, but Cato continued eating unfazed.

"Oh Goddess, Cato, *he* sent the river attacker, and he smelled gross just like that man did, right up until I touched him, then it was like the best scent... like I was exactly where I belonged. Like your father was... the most wonderful person I'd ever been near—a safe harbor in a raging storm. He spoke of regicide and made it sound reasonable. Oh, and apparently, we have a connection; he didn't have time to explain before—"

I paused in my recap and glanced up at two identical expressions—eyebrows raised and drawn, mouths pinched in concern.

"He smells?" asked Ambrose, wrinkling his nose.

"He did, yes. Did you smell him, Cato? It was like vinegar mixed with death."

Cato shook his head.

"I have never smelled it, no. But I do know that you will need to learn to debrief more succinctly. That was a haphazard retelling at best."

My mouth fell open.

"Let me remind you, *Cato*, I'm not a soldier." I pointed a finger to the middle of his broad chest and poked him hard. "Don't treat me like one." We'd had this conversation before. "I'll 'debrief you' however the fuck I feel like debriefing you."

He stared at me and stewed, drumming his finger on the table in the same tempo at which he currently worked the muscle in his jaw.

"You are right," he sighed. "I am finding it difficult to separate the role of lover from Protector." He leveled his gaze in my direction. "From your ill-flowing, chopped-up chatter, it seems His Majesty was aware of your *uniqueness* before we arrived. That or he has turned a person in my employ to his cause. They will be rooted out and dispatched if so." Cato sat back in his chair and crossed his arms. He looked straight ahead, his mind already filing through the dossier I knew he must keep.

"Dispatch them?" I asked, slapping his thigh with my napkin. "You think someone should be put to death? What if the king compelled them with his conjuring? That would be no fault of their own." I didn't want to think there may be others who had already met that end.

"Innocence is not the point, Eira. Either they are willing spies or they are mindless thralls who cannot remain among the civilized."

I waved my hand in front of his face, trying to capture his attention.

"Cato, if they were coerced by the corruption, they aren't guilty of any crime. I refuse to believe you would snuff out an innocent life with such little regard." I didn't know why I'd even said it. I knew Cato well enough to know that he would do exactly what he thought must be done.

The atmosphere turned heavy.

"You would have me do what? Corral them in a barn and watch them slowly starve to death. What kind of life would that be? You have yet to see what happens when he traps them. They do not think on their own—cannot eat or bathe. They shit themselves and have no consciousness. Ending them is mercy, Eira."

The picture he painted was a grave one, but surely they could be restored.

"Cato, he mentioned training apprentices. If someone was learning from him, would they present like those mentioned, or would we even know?"

"Fucking nether... no, most likely not... and Eira, hear me now. I will seek swift vengeance upon a traitor. Do not meddle in these affairs." Lines of unease formed around his downturned mouth. "I was gone too long, or maybe I never had the control I had imagined. He should never have been able to free himself to find you. It is evident he is more powerful than I had assumed... than any of us had assumed."

Cato rubbed his eyes and slid his hands down his cheeks.

Had he slept at all since returning?

"When next I meet with him, I would like to—"

"There is *no* next time." Cato's jaw set firmly.

"Wrong." I sat up straight and prepared for battle. "There will absolutely be a next time. I'm here for this reason. *I* chose to come here. Not for you, not for Verus, but for the people who still love their monarch and deserve to have him restored." I hammered my fist down on the table and dared him to say otherwise.

Cato shook his head and took a long sip of the dark liquid in his mug.

"I am with my brother, Nortia," said Ambrose, who'd remained quiet until now. "Do not be fooled by the comfort you felt with him. It was a magi's trick."

"I'm not an imbecile, as you both well know, and like you, *Crown Prince Ambrose*, I've committed myself to a job here, and I mean to do it."

Cato scoffed indignantly, huffing out a rush of air so hard that it hit me in the face. Ambrose crossed his arms.

"Look here, you overbearing sack of turd—"

"Cato," Ambrose interrupted, "she and I have a long day ahead of us. Move this along, or don't, but we will be leaving."

"We do?"

I wanted to cry. Had they never experienced bone-crushing exhaustion?

Ambrose pulled a timepiece from the pocket of his red brocade vest.

"The court is positively bursting to meet you, Eira. I have kept them at bay for the last day. You are to Join with a prince... now act the part," Ambrose replied.

"This is *exactly* why I don't want to *Join* with you."

"And yet you begged me to rip through that maidenhead of yours quite prettily, did you not?"

He shook his head saucily, and I struck out, but my fist met air.

"Oooo! Ambrose!"

"Will you two silence yourselves?" Cato reached beside his chair and produced a leather bag. He riffled through its contents and pulled out a thick roll of parchment. "You must both sign the contracts. With the recent turn of events, we cannot put it off."

Ambrose didn't hesitate. He stood and walked around the table, took the pen Cato offered, and dipped its angled nib into the dark-blue well of ink. He expertly penned his entire name in a strikingly bold hand.

"His Royal Highness, Ambrose Burchard Berra Odel Ricard, second heir to the throne of Monwyn, does enter into this agreement sound of mind and within accordance to the wishes of His Royal Majesty Burchard Aberus Linus Francis Badulf of Basilia." I read aloud. "Do you all have such magnificent names? What about the girls? Are they called Odela or Badulfina, perhaps?"

I was trying to stall.

I knew signing my life over was my best bet for a future where I stayed alive—and could be near Cato—but frankly, I was scared.

"Ambrose, are you sure? What do you really get out of this?"

His mouth tugged into a wry smile before he answered, "A highly sought-after Troth-wife, royal deity babies, sex I don't have to continually put effort into getting... I am set up nicely."

"I find it hard to believe you've put any effort into getting sex."

"Sometimes a person wants the holes they know, *Nortia*."

Gross. Is that gross? Fucking Ambrose.

I opened my mouth to respond, but nothing came out. The only divorces in Monwyn were initiated by husbands—but I wasn't sure even that was a possibility for a royal. I was panicky; my palms were clammy, and the desire to run out the door was growing by the second. I chewed the skin next to my fingernail until it became painful.

And then there was the issue of reproducing. That was no small commitment, especially if whatever was in me was passed on to any future children. Then there was Cato to consider—

"Eira, love," Cato whispered as if he'd known exactly where my mind had gone, "...sign it. We need the protection it affords you." He moved closer to my side and brought my wrist to his nose, inhaling gently before planting a soft-lipped kiss on the sensitive skin. "If Gaea means to take you, claim you, there would be nothing I could do. Ambrose, however, would have the power." He placed the pen in my hand and wrapped his fingers around mine. "I would die for you, Eira, but I would rather *live* for you."

Breathe in, Eira, breathe. One... two... steady, my girl.

I placed the palm of my other hand over his and nodded my agreement.

With his support, I dipped the pen and scribbled in a much sloppier hand: *Eira Verras Chulainn of Nortia, Troth, Obligate of Solnna.*

My fate was sealed.

Ambrose's arm came to rest on my shoulder, and he planted a fat, ham-tainted kiss on my cheek.

"Ask Cat his name," he muttered in my ear.

"Shut up, Ambrose," Cato fired back.

I looked from one man to the other.

"Now I have to know."

Cato waved a dismissive hand in the air.

"I have a fine name—strong, like me," he said.

"Go on, tell me. I feel that given our—Cato, I don't even know what to call our relationship—but I should probably know your entire name."

He nodded and sat back, crossing a leg over his knee. "I am Catommandus Odelgaurd Borko Lefwinnis Wilkie... of Basilia. Now, respond in a manner that leaves my pride intact."

I nibbled on my lips and looked upon the Goddess's gold-streaked son. His deliciously sensual mouth drew up into a pucker.

Borko.

"Eira... Would you like to say something?" Cato challenged.

"No, I... yes." I placed my palm on his scratchy cheek. "I'm happy I'll be naming my future children after Ambrose."

"*Ouch!*"

Cato was so fast that I hadn't seen his hand coming to pinch my thigh.

Ambrose chuckled childishly while shoving my shoulder.

"Stop it, both of you." I stood quickly, skipping out of their collective reaches, rubbing my leg with both hands.

"Serves you right," Cato murmured.

I got a few steps away and a thought hit me.

"Cato, why were you called Tommand at Verus? It couldn't have been to conceal your identity, *Emissary... Protector.*"

"It was Ambrose's *brilliant* contribution—nothing strategic or nefarious. He worried that my being an emissary, Protector, *and* the child of a monarch would outshine his entrance into the world of Obligation; there are no songs written about 'Tommand.'"

Ambrose bent and placed his mouth next to Cato's ear.

"And you didn't outdo me, now did you... *Tom...* my littlest brother?"

"Are you the baby?" I asked Cato, who stared straight ahead.

"No." Ambrose interjected, "I'm the youngest, but Aberus, like myself, grew to be man-sized." He smacked Cato on the back so hard that plates clattered across the table.

Ambrose was looking for a fight.

"Your itinerary, *brother.*" Cato withdrew a folded parchment from his satchel and passed it to Ambrose before turning to me. "We will next meet at dinner. Questions? No? You are both dismissed."

I'm what?

"Eira, come along." Ambrose turned on his heel and took off, but I stood my ground and tapped my foot on the floor.

Confusion and then understanding dawned on Cato's face.

His expression softened as he rose from his seat and took my hands into his own. He brought my balled-up fingers to his mouth and kissed each of my knuckles in turn.

"Eira, you are resilient and intelligent, and you are also the most desirable human I have ever laid eyes on. Though the day ahead may be hard," he paused and wrapped his arms around my waist, "it won't be nearly as hard as my perfect penis when next it's between your Goddess-given thighs."

"Cato! That is not—"

I never finished the sentence.

His smiling mouth came down on mine, and his tongue swept in to tangle with my own. His lips were sweet from the grapes he'd eaten, and I could feel, more than hear, the low rumble that came from his chest. I melted into him. Nothing mattered when I was here—not the king, not the Gaeans... not the unknown.

He ended our connection and brushed his lips against my chin before working his way to my ear. The fine hairs on my neck and arms stood at attention, and my mind disconnected from all but him.

"As I said—you are dismissed." He winked and walked away.

Chapter 4

A Mole by Any Other Name

"My beloved, I would introduce you to Lady Allaine Lemder."

I scrambled to adjust my robe and ran my fingers through my hair while still blocked by Ambrose's big body. He had failed to mention someone else would be here when he'd led me to our bathing chamber to "make myself presentable."

Fucking nether.

"She is to be your lady's maid for the duration of your time here and will see to your needs in the mornings and escort you to functions during the day. Lady Allaine, you are to be with her at all times, until she is delivered into the hands of myself or the Protector, understood?"

"Yep. To your hands."

I poked Ambrose's rear, but he didn't budge.

"If I'm to have a nursemaid, my princely puffin, I'd like to meet her before trusting her with my person." I pushed by him, squishing myself between his mass and the doorway.

Standing in the center of the room and smiling most cheerfully was an astonishingly tall woman, holding an armful of scrubs and moisturizers. "No offense, Lady Allaine I am sure you are most adequate at your job."

"None taken." She sat the jars down on the marble-topped cabinet and wrinkled her nose at a blue jar shaped like a heart. That one she placed at the very back of the collection.

"Nortia... dearest porkchop, she is a lady's maid, not a nurse, not a sitter. The noblewomen of Monwyn never go about unescorted, especially one Joining herself to a male of my status. Now kiss me and allow Allaine to help dress and groom you. You are to be introduced to the court today—a very informal thing—and then we will share our first meal as a family; you, the Protector, and myself."

"Fine, that's fine." I began puttering around, familiarizing myself with the space again. Items that weren't here yesterday had appeared overnight, and I would have sworn I'd left the tub streaked with gobs of red hair fibers.

"Ahem."

A few bone-carved combs caught my attention; they were inlaid with gold and had schools of tiny fish carved into their handles... undoubtedly Nortian imports.

"*Ahem!*"

I glanced up into the eyes of my angry ogre.

His hands rested on his hips, and he cocked his head to the side, which put his lush braid in danger of dipping into a random cream... but I wasn't going to tell him.

"What?" I asked, genuinely confused.

He strode forward, took a frosted pink container from my hand, and sat it down with a loud thump.

"My expectation is that, when we part, you will openly show the world you adore me. A kiss... right now."

Good Goddess. With the scratch of a pen, I've committed myself to a lifetime of this.

I flicked my eyes to where the lady's maid stood, folding little squares of cloth. She carried on as if she couldn't see or hear the argument three feet away.

Hmmm.

I crooked a finger at Ambrose, and he walked lazily in my direction.

"Bend down." I placed my palms on his chest and raised my chin.

"No, I think not." His eyes danced in his ridiculous face, and he straightened his shoulders, standing even taller than he was before.

We have moved on to the petulant Ambrose stage.

I stepped onto his booted feet and reached for his neck, but he remained completely upright, not budging an inch. I tried hopping up and down on his toes, thinking he might move, but got nothing.

Welp.

I grabbed one of two stools that were stored below a counter.

"Do you expect me to climb on the furniture... in front of the courtiers?" I asked, balancing myself on the stool's cushioned top.

Ambrose snaked his hand under my robe, and his arm found its way around my waist. He hauled me against his chest.

"No, but I *will* continue devising ways to watch your tits bounce."

A raspy sound came from the corner as my gasp of shock filled the room. My maid's laugh was reminiscent of a gruff little puppy growling at her playmates. Ambrose stared sideways at the source of the peculiar chuckle while he leaned down to deliver a chaste kiss to my cheek.

"I realize you will mourn me the instant I leave, wife-to-be, but rest assured, I will think of you often."

"Oh, indeed, not a moment shall pass in which my woman's brain isn't cluttered with thoughts of your... bulk."

The snide little curl of his top lip told me my remark bore fruit. With his hand placed over his heart, he bowed deeply and left the room.

"He seems very romantic."

"He's an acquired taste."

I faced my new employee and began my investigation. "Level with me. Have you been given orders to spy on me? To whom do you deliver your intelligence?"

Allaine raised a finely tapered brow and revealed a fetchingly toothy smile.

That's right, my towering friend. I didn't almost get through Troth training to be taken in by an amateur.

She folded her last square of cloth and shuffled her feet rocking from side to side.

"The Protector officially, but I was not asked to spy so much as to keep tabs on the comings and goings of others. And let me speak plainly: I landed this position because my father and the Protector are on good terms, otherwise, it would have fallen to a *fully functioning* miss of the court." She pointed to her wrist and drew her finger down to her elbow.

"Your arm?" I nodded in the direction of the limb that was folded up to her chest. Her left hand seized in on itself, and the arm was markedly smaller than her other.

"No, my height," she said stone-faced before erupting into easy laughter.

"You *are* impressively tall."

Her growly giggles came again. Allaine took the stack of cloths she'd folded and held them against her hip before placing them in a woven basket on the countertop. I watched as she rearranged a tiny set of brushes in a wooden box.

"I was born like this, and much to my family's horror, a Monwyn husband has yet to put himself forward."

"Are you sure you wish to be in the marriage market? In my limited experience, husbands can be fairly obnoxious." I followed her across the room and continued sizing her up. I was going to spend a considerable amount of time with this person, and I was netherbent on figuring out her angle.

Allaine turned toward me and mimicked my stance.

"Let us cut to the chase, my lady."

Well, well. I nodded in her direction. She had my attention.

"Being your maid allows me to be free of my home. I am not here to screw you over—so understand that, and try not to mess this up for me, okay?"

I kept my face impassive and watched her squirm under my bland stare. She held her own for about ten seconds before glancing down to her right. She shifted her weight from foot to foot and inhaled a little too deeply.

"You may also find that you benefit from my association, Troth Eira."

A deal? Obligate fodder.

"How so?" I asked with an air of nonchalance.

"Number one: Despite my limitations, I am highly competent, and, given the amount of eye kohl that still clings to your face, it is clear you need my help. I am adept at styling and grooming. With my assistance, you will stand a chance of looking the part of a Monwyn consort."

"Truly? Do go on." I propped a fist under my chin, giving her my full attention.

"Two: Nobody ever stops or questions the infirm girl. They—meaning literally everyone—assume I am as mangled as my limb. That has allowed me certain liberties over the years. I am privy to information well above my station, and I can get myself out of any predicament by acting sad or dim. I offer these services to you. Third: In your company, I'll be viewed as a charity case, and you, a compassionate new royal-to-be. With me, you get all of the skill of a lady's maid and informant, while reaping the social rewards as if it were a sacrifice."

I sat down on the stool, momentarily relieving her of my unwavering stare.

She reminded me of Kairus—always thinking ahead—and her candor impressed me. The information she could provide would undoubtedly prove useful.

"Your price. What is it?" I asked.

There was always a cost.

Allaine lowered her head and met my eyes. Only the subtle, anxious caress of her skirt pleats betrayed her nervousness.

"Most importantly, I expect to be treated like I am sound of mind... because I am. I am intelligent and shrewd, and though I may be limited in some capacities, my intellect is not."

"That won't be a problem; you are clearly astute. What else?"

Allaine stood to her magnificently full height, which I think would have put the top of her head in line with Ambrose's nose.

"I want rooms in the palace. I want to stay here full-time, and if you leave, I go with you. If you travel, I am *not* to be left behind. If you end up in a different kingdom, I go too. Those are my terms."

I appreciated her moxie, even if she was a little green in her ability to negotiate. I mulled over the prospect of saddling myself with another human. Ambrose and Cato were already a lot to deal with, and I had a sense that our immediate future was going to get profoundly more complicated. That said, insider knowledge could prove invaluable, and I could always find a way to ditch her if she began hindering my plans. I crossed my ankles and studied the pinkened skin of my nearly healed kneecap. Having someone in my corner who I wasn't sleeping with could be a boon.

How different my mind works from only a month ago.

"If I am to accept, I will require the following—what? You thought I wouldn't have my own terms?" Allaine clutched the bottom of her elbow so tightly that her skin went white. "Negotiation is never one-sided, you have your plans and price, and I have mine." Her eyebrows shot to her forehead, and she rocked forward, sending her skirts swaying. "You'll supply me with *any* information I ask for. If you don't know the answer to what I seek, you'll find out. I will require your confidence in certain matters as well—not all, but some. I will make it clear to you what is allowed to be shared and what is not. If you breach my confidence in any way, you will be sent back home, and all benefits and privileges that come from our association will be voided. I ask you once again... who do you work for?"

Allaine ran her finger around the metal lid of a jar that contained a fine black powder.

"The Protector gets your location and associations—with your say-so. Lord Septimus, and the half-dozen other nobles who have offered gold for gossip, get whatever you tell me to tell them." She nodded once and set the jar on the counter.

"Smart woman, I agree to your terms."

My first lackey! Accomplice... spy? Work that out later.

"I agree as well. Now, you wash while I prepare my space. You smell of pork and," she sniffed in my direction, "the Protector."

Whoa.

I didn't react to her words. I simply turned my attention to an already full bath. My robe hit the ground, and with a toe, I slung it up on the stool I'd vacated.

Allaine's eyes went as round as a grapefruit.

"That is *so much* body!"

"Is that how you truly wish to begin our relationship? How did you imagine I'd look, Allaine?" I replied while stepping down into the water.

"I-I actually have no idea where to look right now. We generally wear a light chemise when we wash."

I recalled the day of the Grooming at Verus Temple. Kairus had also been uncomfortable in the room of naked bodies.

Goddess, I beg of you. Keep my friend safe, be with her now and always. It felt like both yesterday and a hundred years ago when I last saw her walking out of our room on the arm of Scion Ozius.

Allaine did her best not to catch my eyes in the mirror. She walked backward and side-stepped to avoid having to turn; she busied herself by cleaning brushes and combs; and she sorted tiny twisting pins from a leather bag on the floor. Through all of it, she never lost the deep maroon flush that splattered across her nose and chest.

"This explains how you landed Prince Ambrose. I am fairly positive that even the bawdy women never get all the way naked. You must have been a shock to his system."

Dipping down, so as not to present her with my chest full on, I scrubbed my hair into a thick lather and hid my smile. *Me? A shock to him?*

"Allaine, not to worry you further, but Prince Ambrose enjoys bathing naked as well. Will you be able to handle—"

"Nope. I will pass clear out... seriously. If you are going to continue on this way, we *must* introduce it slowly, and I am never to be in a room where he isn't wearing multiple layers."

I did laugh then.

"Throw me a towel." She just gave me the key to rendering her senseless if the need arose—I'd just have Ambrose show an ankle.

"Gladly."

The towel careened toward my head at an alarmingly high speed. I flung my arm out and snatched it from the air.

Allaine was equal parts spitfrost and prude. An interesting combination.

"So, what should I expect at this meet and greet?" I asked while drying my feet.

"No idea. Why would I know that?"

"You are *already* paying off."

She shrugged and went back to prepping her station. Why she needed four differently sized combs was beyond me, but from the way she kept herself so well-groomed, it was clear she was the wiser.

"Hurry and sit; it will take me forever to cover up your imperfections."

It was my turn for grapefruit eyes.

"I meant all the bruises and cuts you have. Your complexion is... fine."

Such a Monwyn.

I didn't like to generalize an entire population, but so far the snippy stereotype had held true. Ah, well, Kairus had been the same in the beginning.

Allaine held out a robe and covered me quickly.

"Sit, do not move or speak while I work."

Okay, admiral. I did as ordered and faced the mirror.

"Allaine, I hope you *actually* end up being useful to me at some point."

My hair came flipping over my face, obscuring my vision.

"I said no talking." She popped the top of my head with a comb.

I may love her.

Two hours later, it became clear that Allaine's grooming skills were not merely a boast. I turned my face admiring her creation—she'd applied an icy-pink powder high up on my cheeks and lined my eyes with a swath of black kohl after plucking the stray hairs under the arch of each brow. After painstakingly painting my lids with a combination of gold and nutmeg-brown, she'd darkened my lashes and coated my lips in a nearly sheer rose-colored oil. I was very happy with what I saw.

"Where'd you learn to do this?" I asked through stiff lips. After she'd admonished me twice for moving barely an inch, I dared not relax a muscle, even if she had moved on to my hair.

"I made up my own face to pass time when my siblings were being tutored. Mother taught me the basics."

"You weren't tutored?"

She scoffed so hard that my hair ruffled.

"No." She tossed a rod into a basket on the cabinet. "And not because they thought me unable to learn; they were worried my condition would worsen if I was overtaxed in the slightest."

"Do you get worse?" I asked, curious to understand how she viewed her differences.

"No, it hasn't progressed, but my symptoms are sometimes more pronounced."

Through the mirror, I watched her as she removed the curling rods with no issue at all. Allaine was statuesque, slender, but also shapely, with dark auburn hair worn in the typical Monwyn style of curls cascading down her back. Her eyes were the darkest blue, and above them, her eyebrows were markedly lighter than her hair, so I imagined that, like the other Monwyns I'd met, she added fibers to enhance her hue.

Allaine walked to an adjoining room I had yet to discover and returned moments later with an ensemble that must have arrived on the carriage from Colpass.

"His Highness chose your gown and jewelry. He has good tastes, though I am afraid the style will cause a stir."

With a snap, she flung out a cobalt, silk-taffeta garment, embellished with triads of tiny gold spangles. As she held it to her chest, the disks caught the room's light and shimmered like thousands of twinkling stars in the night sky. *Goddess me.* Ambrose undoubtedly had a hand in designing it. From the looks of it, the dress's neckline would only cover half of each breast.

Allaine hefted the gown, and I went in arms first. My head popped through the opening just fine, but it took pulling my chest through the dress's slim-cut waist one boob at a time for my torso to emerge, as no laces or closures had been added.

The front panel of the dress's voluminous skirting split from the floor to right below my navel and showed off the semi-sheer pants that flowed widely around my legs. I walked around and kicked out, watching the effect of the bold crimson silk peeking out as I moved. I drummed on the tight fabric constricting my waist.

"I'm all hips and boobs."

Allaine pursed her lips and nodded. "If that bodice busts, the citizens of Monwyn will be forced to flee."

"You aren't wrong." I agreed.

Allaine tugged and pulled at the neckline and shoulders of the gown, stuffing bits of breast in until she was satisfied with its fit.

"If you feel it coming apart, ask me how I take my tea and I will get you out."

"Solid plan... Can I do the same if trapped by creepers or boring dignitaries?"

"That depends... How big will my rooms be?" She slapped me on the back before fiddling with an escaped hair near my forehead.

"Ruthless," I whispered while narrowing my eyes at her reflection. She flounced away and returned with a small wooden box.

"Last few items. His Highness said to affix this to the lowest point of your neckline." She leaned in close and used the elbow of her seized arm to steady the opulent bear-head brooch that she pinned near my sternum. "And this," Allaine said, clasping a delicate gold necklace at my throat, "completes the look." A dainty crescent moon charm, with a star perched on its solid gold body, hung from the chain and rested in the notch between my clavicles.

"Marking his property," I muttered.

"Oh right! One more thing—I promise it is the last." Allaine riffled through the pocket of her bag and pulled out a piece of gray fabric. "Sit again... Sorry." She went to work, slicking back the hair above my left ear with a thin-toothed comb, and then came to stand in front of me. Above my head, she opened the fabric pouch and tossed the material onto my lap while she pinned a barrette in my hair. She peered at my face intently, making sure all was in order, and then nodded in satisfaction.

She moved, and I caught my reflection.

My hands went to my mouth, but my sob couldn't be stifled.

"I take back every negative thing I have *ever* said about His Highness."

My eyes blurred, and my heart felt too big for my chest. Frantically, Allaine fanned my eyes with a cloth as I looked skyward.

In my hair was the very same ruby clasp that Nan had worn the day she revealed herself as the sole emissary of Nortia.

Ambrose had gifted me a treasure.

Chapter 5

MEET, GREET, AND MINGLE

On Ambrose's arm, I proudly strolled the vast hallways of Cordillaria Palace.

Allaine stayed three steps behind us at all times, and when we stopped, she would step demurely to my side. We were headed to the great drawing room, which was situated between the dining chamber and the small drawing room on the building's sprawling first level.

"What should I expect? How should I act?" I asked Ambrose, who was looking every inch the prince in a finely woven overcoat that hit at his ankles. The long maroon garment was patterned with birds of prey and embellished with pearls. A brooch, nearly identical to mine, was fastened to his shoulder. His bear sported a large ruby hanging from a chain in it's mouth. He also wore a thin belt of white leather around his waist, which was studded with rubies housed inside gold fixtures.

"This is an informal meeting, so no crowns or coronets. I will introduce you to the nobles who are currently in fashion, and we will skip over those who are presently embroiled in scandal or drama."

"Ostracizing people, alright. What kind of scandals are we talking about?" I asked.

Ambrose tried to hide a yawn by breathing deeply through his nose. His eyes watered profusely, and I made note of the purpling crescents above his cheeks.

"The norm really—owing a debt to the crown, caught in a nefarious plot, someone slept with someone's daughter... a blood feud. Normal court stuff."

"No, I don't know—you're Joining down on the social ladder, don't forget."

The sound of Ambrose's booted heels striking the marble floor echoed through the corridor.

"And *you* should not forget who you are: Chosen Troth, Rite Breeder, Haver of... Sparkle Blood."

"Spark—" I laughed at the insinuation. *My blood looks like everyone else's, as far as I know, but I like the idea.*

"You are my wife, my woman. You will be the mother of princes. Be proud of your position... but let me do the talking."

When we finally arrived, two guards flanking a large alcove struck their spear butts against the floor, prompting the servants inside to fling the doors wide.

"So enters His Royal Highness, Ambrose Burchard Berra Odel Ricard, second heir to the throne of Monwyn, Scion born of Gammond's Moon, Commander of His Majesty's Navy," a herald boomed from across the room.

Naval commander? That's going on the question list.

Cheers and clapping followed us as we walked forward into the sea of nobles. I leaned up to Ambrose, smiled lovingly, and acted as if I were whispering an endearment in his ear.

"Do I not get an announcement?"

He paused and looked down, his eyes going soft. His hand lightly brushed down my torso and cupped my lower stomach.

"Your uterus might."

The urge to smack the innocent smile off his well-trained-Scion face consumed me until I remembered the jewel in my hair.

I reined in my fury. This was my first public encounter as both Troth and betrothed.

I scanned the room of unfamiliar faces and felt a brief pang of resentment. This was not the path I had wanted to follow, but it was the one I chose.

My eyes found Cato. *Of course they did.*

He was my strength, my heart's song.

I took a deep breath, feeling bolstered by his presence... I'd make my own self known.

"Born under the Goddess's sky, Toppler of Guards, Survivor of the Rite, Mounter of the Virile Stud of Monwyn. Born of Ulltan and Vonnie, the ice of the north flows through my veins. People of the mountain lands—snow has arrived on the summit!"

I lowered my eyes and donned a mask of serenity and meekness.

The silence that followed was deafening... until the gruff puppy giggles erupted over my shoulder.

"Holy Mother," Ambrose muttered beside me.

He turned and faced me. Gone was the normal amusement that graced his features. I'd never experienced his profound displeasure directed my way, and frankly, I never wanted to see it again. His green eyes went flat. His face turned to stone. I could easily imagine the terror his enemies felt before he struck.

"Goddess above, she is brazen as can be," tutted a highly cultured voice.

"And her bubbies are displayed for all Ærta."

Ambrose's brows drew down so severely that a shadow was cast over his face. The weight of the ruby hair comb, seemed to pierce my scalp. I was fully aware that Monwyn was a patriarchal society. I knew that I would be expected to adhere to its customs, but Goddess be damned, I wasn't built for this level of misogyny.

I watched as Ambrose struggled to bring his ragged breathing back to order. This wasn't like him at all. His hand tightened on mine, going from a comforting squeeze to a painful pressure.

"I'll owe you an extra favor this week," I whispered before turning and smiling brilliantly at the courtiers who stood watching our exchange.

"You sure as fuck will... Now keep your mouth shut." The look of longing on his face as he caressed my cheek must have appeared so incredibly genuine to those around us, but the chill in his eyes was anything but kind.

He was a brilliant Scion.

I glanced up like a besotted girl and let my gaze roam over him, worshipping him like he was my first lover... which I suppose, technically, he was.

He steered us forward.

Colorful silks and opulent fabrics turned the crowd into a rainbow of wealth. The men, both seated and standing, wore rings and bracelets of gold and a myriad of jewels on their hands and wrists, and every courtier had three or four personally liveried servants standing at their backs.

"Lord Dumail, it has been months. How fares the western coast?" Ambrose asked a man who stood nearly his height but who was built more slenderly.

"Your Highness... good to see you in the capital again. The coast teems with tradesmen and the last contingent from Nortia returned home safely. The ice will soon set in." The golden blonde, who wore his hair in the traditional way, with a long braid and the sides shorn closely, turned to me and let his penetrating eyes travel the length of my body. "The southern ports are flourishing as well, but we have an issue with pirates harrying the trade routes near the coast that borders the Sinnons—the Protector will deal with the matter, as His Majesty's naval commander remains, as always, otherwise occupied."

Wait, was that a slight?

My scalp prickled hotly.

"Does your lady lust for any unusual items, Highness? I am able to procure a variety of exotic vegetables and lighter foods, though it appears her appetite may lean more toward cakes and heavy cuts of meat."

Filing the name Dumail under "yellow snow stain."

I bit my tongue between my teeth, trying hard to adhere to Ambrose's wishes. He knew his people better than I did.

"*I* will see to my lady's needs—and how is your mate? Still breeding daughters?"

Lord Dumail's eyes went blade thin. It pissed me off that having girls would be considered an insult, but I was simultaneously pleased that Ambrose hadn't allowed himself to be degraded.

Before I could stop myself, I lifted my hand to the Lord's forearm and innocently blinked up at him.

"You know, my mother always says that a healthy dose of raw elk makes a man's seed more potent. Perhaps you can procure a portion when the freeze ends."

Ambrose's fingers cinched even harder around my elbow. I'd be bruised tomorrow.

Dumail's face went as purple as his short coat, while he stared down at me in disdain. Ambrose nodded curtly at the ruddy-faced man, and we pivoted to our right, heading toward a table where three noblemen sat.

"Is there a tried-and-true method to make you shut up, Nortia? I am the highest-ranking man in this room, and you have yet to listen to me. You. Will. Stop. Is that perfectly clear to you?"

His brusque statement made me flinch.

"I'm sorry. I'll behave," I promised.

"See that you do," Ambrose said while looking at me through the side of his eyes. "Is the elk thing true?"

"No, but when he tries it, he'll wish on his itchy asshole that he never did. That stuff will give you the shittiest shits of your life if you don't cook it."

A one-sided grin flitted briefly across Ambrose's face, momentarily erasing the strain he'd been wearing.

We approached the seated men. One, with the aid of a cane, struggled to his feet and bowed as low as he could manage.

"Lord Salee, has it been a month?"

"Not quite that long, Highness." The lord spoke, and his words whistled through the holes left by several missing teeth. "How's my boy? I was informed a few days ago that he'd had an accident but was seen by the healers at Verus."

Holy mother above.

I closed my eyes and prayed. Prayed to the Goddess, to Mossius, and to Derros.

This man was Evandr's father. If he were younger, I would've recognized him immediately.

Guilt gnawed at me—threatened to consume me whole. I should have held onto his lifeless body and refused to let go. I should have screamed until my throat ripped to shreds. I should have demanded Cato return to save him.

"Evandr is as strong as they come; he's probably up and on his way to Solnna as we speak," Ambrose informed Lord Salee while motioning for him to take his seat again.

The lord did as he was bid and fell heavily into his chair. He nodded over and over, while another older man patted him on the back.

I bit my lip until I tasted blood.

"And is this the lovely creature who will venture south with him? Or will you reside in Monwyn after your impending nuptials?"

I began to answer, but Ambrose cut in first, "Details have yet to be shored up, but with her or without, Evandr is a prized Scion and does your name great honor—the Solnnans are pleased with their Assignments."

"My boy's a good one—humble beginnings, of course, but he's seen his way up."

I bowed my head in agreement.

"He has indeed... we will speak soon. Good day."

We walked deeper into the carpeted drawing room, inclining our heads and accepting accolades and congratulations. I took mental notes on the members of the court who seemed to shrink back or failed to offer Ambrose even the courtesy of a nod, but keeping tabs on the crests their servants wore soon became overwhelming. I'd need a journal to begin my own dossier. Any enemy of Ambrose would be an enemy of mine.

"We will pass Septimus, Eira. Do not look at or speak to him."

I snapped out of my thoughts, Ambrose's voice ushering me back to the present.

My pulse sped up in anticipation—I hadn't seen his uncle since he'd made an absolute fool of himself at the Den. Whether or not it was due to the accidental consumption of my blood mattered little. He was not a kind human. "Ambrose, were you able to tell Cato about what happened that night?"

"Mmhmm, when I clear my throat, look up to your right and smile, and then run your tongue across your bottom lip."

I kept my eyes downcast and stared at the multi-hued medallion at the center of the room's carpet. It was an odd request, but I would do as asked. *Ahhh. Red Shoes.* This was Lord Ethens, whom I'd also met while being publicly fondled.

Ambrose coughed under his breath.

I looked up, batted my lashes, and swept my tongue along the bottom edge of my teeth, skimming just a little of my lower lip.

The sides of Ethens's nose flared wide, and his eyes honed in on my chin. His gaze was disconcerting and entirely unwavering.

"Lady Troth, when your voice rang out, my heart nearly ceased beating. Such an impertinent mouth."

"Ethens," Ambrose said, acknowledging the man he'd already introduced me to in a *much* different setting.

Ethens ignored him and continued to focus his attention solely on me.

"The color you've chosen to smear across your temptingly full lips is a particular favorite of mine... like a freshly oiled slab of tuna." The image of the pink mask his "pet" had worn in the Den—and the amount of slobber that fell from his mouth—floated through my mind. "Were you mine, precious girl, I'd bruise both sets of your insolent lips, and then shower you with the most tender of care... Highness, just a single evening."

I held my tongue for the second time. I couldn't believe this man, this *noble*, was speaking in a normal volume of voice with so many others in earshot.

Ambrose didn't flinch—he wasn't disturbed in the least.

"A single evening would cost you a fortune, I am afraid."

And I'd throw a godsdamned fit.

Ethens tilted his head as he leaned over my shoulder.

"Considering I am the wealthiest man in this room... name your price," he said, dropping his voice.

"Of *that*, I am certain, sir, and if I find myself in need of coin, I will be sure to call upon you."

Ethens nodded curtly.

"May I kiss her hand as a show of goodwill? A testament of our friend-ship—our bright future?"

"You may." Ambrose pressed my elbow forward, and Ethens reached out with both hands. The heavy scent of rosemary assailed my nostrils as he bent low and twisted my palm face up.

I waited for his thin lips to touch my skin, but the pressure never came. Instead, there was a warmth that quickly turned cool.

What the actual fuck? Oh my gods, oh my filthy flipping pantheon!

A string of saliva hung from Ethens's mouth and puddled in the middle of my palm.

My stomach tensed, and the back of my throat constricted. I fought the urge to squeal and shriek and shake my hand in disgust.

His tongue shot out.

He sucked a portion of the thick spittle back into his mouth and swallowed, closing his eyes and sighing low. Lord Ethens flipped my hand back over and our palms met, causing the remaining wetness to splotch and spread between us.

I remained calm and said nothing, even while, under the guise of patting my hand in a fatherly manner, he ground his fluids in, until I could feel them leaking through the crevices of my fingers.

"Magnificent."

We walked on.

"I'm taking back the extra favor," I said through clenched teeth, even as I smiled at the next set of men we greeted.

"No, that is not how that works. Once the favor is offered, it cannot be voided." Ambrose looked down at me, every bit the enraptured lover.

"Says literally who?" I nodded graciously at an older Monwyn man and his even older partner. They sat with their shoulders pressed together and their hands clasped tightly.

"The man who, by law, will control the very ground you walk upon," he snapped.

Ambrose was filled to the brim with a fine vintage of spite.

"Did you snub me on purpose, *nephew?*"

Oh, great. I shut my eyes and took a steadying breath.

We hadn't escaped him.

Septimus's voice was committed to my memory and it was just as alluring as the head it came out of—deep, smooth, and full of male arrogance. Why the Goddess wasted such a beauteous face on such an odious person, I'd never know.

Ambrose spun on his heel and practically jerked me around to face his uncle. "Yes. I did."

What a fine-looking man. I hated myself a little for thinking it, but Cato favored him so much; surely it was the reason for the little leap in my pulse and the sudden flutter at my core.

"Low-born piece of filth," Septimus said, soft enough for only us to hear. He shifted to face me and bowed at the hip. "You, however..." He offered his hand, and like the mannered lady I was, I reached for him.

"Do. *Not.*"

Cato.

I sensed him at my back—felt the heat of him permeating the silk I wore.

"Ah, the *Dissenter* has returned home as well, I see." Septimus sneered. His sky-blue eyes slowly redirected and met mine again. He had a flawless smile—perfect teeth, a shade whiter than even the near-glowing hair on his head. "I have thought of none other since you beguiled me."

"Septimus, your wife is present; at least pretend to act the decent husband," Cato gritted out. Without seeing him, I knew his face would be a stoney mask of barely contained fury.

I looked for Kairus's mother but saw no other woman in the room packed full of men.

"Or what, false prince? Will you toss me out like you did your title? Do *not* forget who outranks whom here."

Septimus's hand closed around mine, and I gasped, caught unawares.

In the same instant, an arm shot out over my shoulder. I watched as Cato's fingers sank into the flesh of his uncle's neck, clutching the man's windpipe.

"You forgot who outranks you, Uncle," Ambrose said. "Protector, show him out."

Septimus smiled, and dimples appeared on both sides of his short-cropped beard. He stood proudly and laughed into Cato's face even as his color was deepening from loss of air. Cato could have been his dark twin—their heights and mass were identical.

"Your taste still ling—"

Septimus's voice cut off.

Cato's grip tightened, and the skin of his uncle's neck reddened. He let go, pushed his uncle backward, and shoved at his shoulder while marching him to the door. It was then that I saw the woman sitting on the far side of the room. I watched her go, wishing I'd had the opportunity to tell her how special her daughter was to me.

The noise in the room picked up exponentially.

"Serves him right. Touching another man's property without consent is..." It was Ethens who spoke.

The odd alliance continued to solidify.

"Had he touched my woman, it would have come to blows," another voice chimed in from the far corner.

I tucked myself into Ambrose's side, playing the aggrieved innocent.

"Hear, hear! A man's wife is his sacred trust!"

Ambrose ran his fingertips over my arms like he was inspecting me for injury.

"My heart, shall we stroll about the gardens?"

"The fresh air would do me wonders," I said, clutching my palm to my chest.

With Allaine hovering just behind us, we made our way to the exit, not bothering to wave or say goodbye.

"Highness, it was our pleasure."

"She's a gem, Ambrose; lucky man, you are."

A chorus of compliments ushered us on our way through the doors.

"To get to the back grounds, you leave through the grand salon. I would prefer you never leave through the great hall, which will take you to the front gardens—they are a place where lechers congregate."

When the guards threw the exterior doors open wide, I felt freedom. A gentle breeze filtered through my curls and cooled the skin that had warmed under the perusal of so many new acquaintances and adversaries.

We walked along a lovely mosaic path, and I took my first look at Cordillaria Palace by day.

The sandy-colored stone building boasted at least six stories. Between the raised wings and towering center structure, stunning rows of colored-glass windows were situated at even intervals.

It was breathtaking, despite the corrosion that walked within.

"Look up." Ambrose pointed. "Our apartments are in the far-right corner, and Cato's are directly above the grand salon," he said, moving his hand to the palace's center. "You are not to enter his rooms."

"Ambrose, that seems—"

"You are *not* to enter his rooms. Do not defy me on this rule."

He was still upset, and I got it. The last few hours had been a test of his patience, but I was just about over being his whipping post.

"My sumptuous Black Bear, can we sit a spell?" I ventured. We desperately needed to have a conversation.

He nodded while he ran a hand down his long braid, pulling the tail over his shoulder. Pointing to a bench in front of a large, round fountain, we made our way to the center of a sprawling garden that was in the process of going dormant for the winter.

"Lady Allaine, fall back and face away," Ambrose ordered.

Like the ideal soldier, she stopped in her tracks and walked dutifully toward a statue of Josa, the god who gave the world the ability to create song. The figure depicted the ever-youthful man holding a dulcimer. He had a long mantle around his shoulders and a crown of laurels on his head.

I sat, and Ambrose followed. He twisted, laid his full length out on the bench, and snuggled his head into my lap.

"Ambrose, I'm concerned about you," I began, while smoothing down a portion of the beard that had frizzled up and out of place.

His chest expanded.

"Are you, though?" he said. "Were you concerned, you would have heeded my directives and not worked to actively embarrass me in front of a group of men who barely tolerate my existence as is." He turned his face into my palm, seeking my touch.

I could kill them.

People not accepting Ambrose on account of his adoption filled me with righteous anger. He may look like a man cut from granite, but he felt his emotions deeply, his normal nonchalance notwithstanding.

"I'm sorry, Ambrose. I've never been in a situation where I've been asked to act like I've ceased to exist. It's uncomfortable, and I don't like feeling inferior or lesser-than."

"You are a Troth Eira; you have the skill set to act like whomever you need to be."

"Yes, but I was only ever a mediocre Troth, and this is daunting. If we Join, I'll be expected to present myself as an empty husk for a lifetime."

"When we Join." Ambrose took my hand and chewed on the tip of my finger.

Mother Merrias, I didn't realize how scared I was until I voiced my concern. I'd been running on such high levels of fear and adrenaline that I'd been avoiding the tough subjects. There was still so much unknown.

"List your insecurities, Eira."

I tried pulling my finger back, but he wouldn't allow it and kept right on gnawing.

"Even setting aside Ozius and Gaea, I'm also worried about not being allowed near your father—he's why I chose to come here, after all. And I'm concerned about the situation between the three of us and—"

"Have you fucked yet?"

"No, when would we have had ti—"

"Can you hurry up? My body grows tense... I am incredibly frustrated. It's been..." he stopped and rolled his head to the side, "I think it has been longer than a week, and I feel like I am dying."

I smoothed the crease in his forehead with my thumb.

"You know I don't mind if you seek outside of our arrangement, Ambrose."

"But you are aware that *I* do. I mind. Political or not, this is a Joining. This is for life. You know my family's history. Infidelity ruins lives, Eira, and not always those of the people committing the offense. Imagine if you will, our daughter, accidentally walking in on her father railing her mother's best friend." He added my middle finger to his mouth and bit the tips one at a time. "I can tell you what it feels like. I could paint you the most highly detailed depiction of exactly what it looked like and what the room smelled like. I will not do that to my family, not ever. Do not suggest it again."

My first inclination was to point out that there were currently no children, and if there were, they wouldn't understand what they were seeing for a number of years... but I didn't. The pain on his face stopped any argument I might have offered. What Ambrose had witnessed had caused him lasting trauma, and I'd be a liar if I said his viewpoint didn't shift my perspective some.

"Eira, I need your assistance in this matter. It was a part of our spoken agreement, and not only that, but as my wife-to-be, whether there is or isn't love, what I need even more is for you to believe in me." He placed my palm in the middle of his chest and covered my hand with his own. He gazed up at the sky. "The minute we arrived here, my duties became so much more important."

"You're worried as well?" I asked, thankful for his openness.

"Of fucking course I am. It was easy being the second heir. I spent my days eating, getting laid, and learning Scion leadership. Now, I will be the first married male—Aberus has refused all of the women sent to him. If something were to happen to him without him having an heir, this falls on me. All of it. You are my responsibility, our children will be my responsibility, and this entire kingdom becomes my fuck—"

"—*our* responsibility, Ambrose." I interrupted. "I won't enter this union as a burden. I know you're giving up the most. We'll share the responsibility of our future, and you know Cato will support you. Ambrose... allow me one more night, and then I will see to your comfort. I promise."

I watched his jaw work, the muscles contracting as he thought.

"Fine, but you must refer to me as Black Bear more often. I liked that one."

CHAPTER 6

BEST LAID PLANS

After an evening spent mostly by myself, we arrived at the dining hall.

Allaine had insisted on adding fibers to my existing curls, and she'd removed and redone my face twice before she deemed me fit for genteel company. I could still feel the tug of a single hair that was pulled too tight, but the thought of seeing Cato eclipsed the stinging sensation. He'd been a constant in my life since Verus, and without him, I felt unmoored.

The dining hall was set for an intimate affair. It reminded me of the room in which Gotwig had taught me the valuable lesson of never trusting, well, anyone or anything. The lower half of the room's walls were the common tan stone of the palace, but the upper portions were plastered and painted, depicting vases filled with blue and green flowers. In the middle of the hall, a long table was set, and candelabras and bowls of fruit had been situated around the woven runner that ran its length.

"Troth Solnna, I will escort you to your seat."

Ambrose handed me off to the liveried servant who'd come to fetch me.

Ah, yes. The Monwyn dining experience. My first challenge in royal etiquette.

I knew we would be assigned certain seats based first on social status, and then we would *physically* sit down in the order of our precedence while the others remained standing.

There were six formal settings altogether, and the servant escorted me to the far side of the table. I stood in front of the seat that he pulled out for me and didn't budge, much to the pride of Ambrose, who watched me from the entryway. Allaine was appointed the chair to my right. The poor thing was absolutely terrified by the prospect of being here, having assumed she'd take her meal with the servants. I told her that was a load of bullshit. She'd been at my beck and call the entire day and deserved to be waited on. Currently, she was shuffling back and forth on her feet. I'd need to make her aware of her tell.

Cato's silhouette darkened the doorway.

My mind buzzed happily as I let my eyes roam over him.

While he wore a completely composed expression—unperturbed, unflappable—I needed a moment to convince my heart to slow, a minute to tamp down what could be a very dangerous smile.

He went to Ambrose and waved him near. Both men were scowling—the news was nothing good.

Striding past the servant who attempted to lead him, Cato marched into the hall and stood in front of the chair diagonal from mine. He caught my eye and bent at the waist, bowing in my direction.

My knees went weak.

And then his face fell. His eyes shifted back and forth, and his brow furrowed deeply.

"Two places have been added. Why?" Cato snapped around and questioned a now-cowering servant who'd been innocently rounding the table.

"P-pro-protector, sir, your—"

Well, fuck.

The "why" appeared in the doorway.

"The reason is, dearest nephew, that this is a family affair, and unfortunately, *our* relation cannot be denied."

Cato's lip curled, and his eyes darkened just slightly before he adopted that smug, superior-to-thou expression that sent my libido spiraling. *Why does pompous look incredible on him?*

Septimus sauntered through the entrance, leaving his wife behind. He'd changed into a long white coat whose cuffs and collar had been embroidered in threads the same blue color as his eyes. A thick chain of state rested on his wide shoulders, and the golden head of a jewel-encrusted battle axe rested in the center of his sternum.

"Wonderful. Can the candelabras be rearranged to block the bullish head of His Highness from my view?" Septimus peered in my direction. "Though it seems my lowly rank *will* put me closest to our newest family member."

He walked to the table and stepped in front of the seat the servant pulled out for him. His lady was escorted to his other side, directly across from me. I would spend the evening looking directly into eyes shaped like Kairus's. Would I wonder the whole time if she was aware of what had transpired between her husband and myself? I recalled the instant my fingers touched his tongue, how he'd sucked them in, and how he wouldn't let go.

Here sits the consequence of my actions.

Ambrose came to his seat at the head of the table. He openly glared at his uncle as he rolled the sleeves of his coat up, revealing his shapely forearms.

"Greetings family, you may all take your—"

"My dearest ones..."

Like he'd been struck across the face, Ambrose's Scion mask dropped.

"Brother Burchard, a surprise! You are looking well. I am—"

"Thank you, Ahdmundus." The king entered the room and pulled his younger brother into an embrace. "I miss our chats. Perhaps now that Catommandus has returned, he can be persuaded to arrange them again."

"Bow to your king!" Cato bellowed.

A multitude of stunned servants snapped out of their shock and bent low, dipping their heads. By the way they reacted, I concluded that His Majesty's presence wasn't a common sight. While doubled over, waiters and groomsmen began pulling their sleeves straight and adjusting the pale-gold kerchiefs they wore about their necks.

Cato moved quickly to his father's side, and I glanced up through my lashes and watched him whisper in his ear. His hand squeezed the king's elbow, and his eyes bounced between him and his uncle.

Ambrose left the table to join them.

To my side, Allaine looked near bursting; she was wide-eyed and holding her breath. Septimus's wife stared at her hands, entirely unaffected.

"You're okay," I whispered through the side of my mouth. "Breathe."

Allaine pressed her hand to her stomach.

"Fetch an additional setting; we are honored to have His Majesty dining with us this eve," Ambrose said loudly to all those present.

At the speed of a fox chasing its prey, the servants snapped into motion, moving dishes, glasses, and flatware and weaving in and out of the guests who stood still in their spots.

They'd not covered this predicament in Troth etiquette training.

You could feel the excitement coursing through the crowd. The maids chattered and giggled under their hands, and the manservants, standing along the wall, puffed out their chests.

"I have to sit next to him, Eira. It will be me. The lowest in precedence sits next to the king to show the importance of all Monwyn citizens. I will pass out. I will eat the floor! Goddess, preserve me."

I turned to Allaine, who was almost vibrating.

"Breathe in through your nose. Hold your breath... One, two, three, four. Now slowly out through your mouth." I watched her chest rise and then fall. Her eyes went glassy. "You will be fine; you know the expectations." Ambrose bowed before her and offered his hand. *Shit.* Allaine wobbled unsteadily, but he placed a steadying palm on the small of her back, and she made it unscathed to her new destination.

The seat-swapping commenced.

With our addition, Ambrose was placed where his uncle had been, at one head of the table, and his uncle sat in the seat I vacated. The poor head servant looked to be dancing a jig. He whipped around the table, animatedly directing the new arrangement with both hands—all the while the front of his shirt was coming untucked, revealing his little potbelly inch by chubby inch.

What a mess.

My stomach grumbled loudly, which drew Cato's attention. I shrugged my shoulders.

Septimus's wife took Allaine's old seat.

The flustered head servant came to me, took my elbow, and then paused as if stricken. He looked at Ambrose with eyes the size of saucers, and he choked out something unintelligible.

"Permission granted."

Tears sprang into the head servant's eyes. At least if they fell, they'd blend in well with the sweat coursing down his temples.

He escorted me to the other side of the table, as my stomach prayed loudly that the exchanges would soon end.

A regally dressed sommelier walked out of the kitchen. With two humongous bottles in his hands, he glided out with the reverence of a priestess, and moved forward, holding the libations straight out in his arms. Halfway to the table, he glanced up from his holy path, saw His Majesty, and without missing a beat, turned and made a slow circle right back to the kitchen.

And that's when the gruff giggles began.

There is no way they interviewed Allaine before hiring her.

Cato, who was now to my right, looked to where Allaine stood across the table. She slapped her hand over her mouth, and her cheeks puffed out like an overzealous chipmunk in a pile of acorns.

My shoulders began to shake.

Oh, no. No, no, no.

The growly little laughs amplified when she caught my eye.

And then a servant tripped over his feet.

He went down hard on his face but managed to continue holding two glasses above his head. I tried to convince myself that the flexibility it must have required to have one's ass in the air and cheeks on the ground was impressive and not hysterical, but I wasn't having it and neither was Allaine.

To her obvious shame, airy little toots began squelching out from behind her hand.

I slapped both hands over my own mouth, but they hardly muted the high-pitched whistles that mingled with the pops of her hand farts.

Kill me now.

Tears streaked down my face and out of the corner of my blurry eyes, I made out Ambrose shaking his head. Another weight added to the thin ice I was perpetually standing on.

It was all just too absurd.

Here we were, Monwyn's most renowned, most elite family, dashing around a table like we were playing an uproarious game of Orca, Orca, Cod.

His Majesty stood in front of his chair and flipped out the robes he wore.

"I, for one, am pleased that our prettiest guests can still enjoy a laugh." A wide smile splashed across his face. "Why do we do this anyway? We could have been eating ages ago. Sit."

He sat, and then Ambrose, then Septimus, then Septimus's wife, then myself, then Cato, then Allaine, took our seats. "I am profoundly happy to find myself surrounded by family."

The second my rear touched the padded chair, I grabbed a linen, fearful that eye black was running down the sides of my nose.

The tie between us ebbed.

The moment my fingers neared his, the magnetic pull snapped into place.

I couldn't resist the calm.

He's just to my left. I can just reach out and...

I stopped and snatched my hand back, remembering what had occurred the last time.

My sudden movement drew his attention.

"Fa-father Burchard, may I introduce my new maid, Lady Allaine?" I motioned across the table to the young woman, whose skin was sheening with a thin dew of nervous sweat.

"Majesty!" she squeaked before nodding politely in his direction.

"What a vision for these old eyes to behold. Your family name is?"

"Lemder, Majesty," she whispered in the meekest of tones.

Lemder? There had been a Lemder at the Den. All I saw of the man was his boots.

"I know the name, good family. You are the girl, then. And your brothers, big lads?"

"The biggest I would wager. Thank you, Majesty." Though she was still an alarming shade of red, she answered most respectably.

The king turned his head back to me and leaned forward.

I watched my hand reach across the table, knowing very well that I didn't want to pull it back.

"Now, my new daugh—"

"A prayer!" Ambrose shouted from down the table.

I recoiled, startled by the sudden noise. *A prayer, Ambrose?*

The king nodded and placed hands on his brows.

"If you will." Ambrose closed his eyes and covered them with both palms. "Divine Mother, Life's Creator..."

I felt a soft scraping on the bottom of my chair and found myself sliding slowly in Cato's direction.

"... show mercy on your most humble servants and nourish their bodies with the food they consume. Look favorably upon the people of Monwyn, and we shall ever look for your divinity in the mountains."

The prayer came to an end.

"Thank you, son. Keeping the divine at the forefront of our minds will ensure a life of prosperity."

I glanced around. No one seemed to notice that I was now sitting almost a foot closer to Cato.

As dinner was served, Allaine chatted bashfully with the monarch, who seemed well at ease speaking to someone of lower social standing. Cato and Ambrose watched their interactions like a couple of hawks on the hunt, while Septimus's lady continued looking at her lap. Her husband stared at me. And I... I examined the silverware like I'd never encountered cutlery before.

The first course came out—thank goodness—carried by a flurry of servants. Two were assigned to each diner—one to hold the dish, the other to serve. I was thankful for the arrival of the food to help mitigate both my rumbling belly and the continued awkwardness of our first family meal. This course featured scallops in a light broth, flavored with garlic and herbs. Fat chunks of crispy lardon were sprinkled over the fare, and it was served piping hot. The soup was delicious, and though the scallops were light in flavor, there was enough brininess in the dish that I experienced my first real bout of homesickness.

I missed the chill, the tastes, and most of all, the comfort of my family—my real family.

"Let us speak of the Joining. I have looked forward to the family growing for years, and though I know my daughters have married well, they have born me no grands... nor have they visited. My dear daughter, you will of course be making your home here, and we will see to your every need."

The king dabbed at the corner of his mouth and then tucked the napkin into the collar of his woolen coat.

"That will depend largely upon Verus, Father. The Mantle will no doubt have opinions regarding our future placements. I was Assigned to Nortia and Eira to Solnna," said Ambrose, who had barely touched his meal.

"Cato, tomorrow we will write the Mantle. He is second in the line of succession. Unless Aberus has a wife or child tucked away somewhere, I am uneasy with Ambrose being a long distance from his home. My boy was taken from me once on account of his birth, and he has just now come back to the fold." Storm clouds rolled across His Majesty's peculiar yellow eyes. "And am I not the king? Do I hold no sway on this continent?"

"It was *you* who left me..."

Silence.

I peered down the length of the long table, unsure of what I thought I'd heard.

"What was that? Speak up, my boy," said the king, who leaned around a wide candelabra to better see his son.

Ambrose blinked slowly and twisted a spoon in his broth before meeting his father's eyes.

"I said. It was *you* who left me... and my mother. She lives estranged in another city, hours away from her children... because of *you*."

Gammond protect us.

I stiffened, preparing for the table to explode or for the water to become sharp projectiles. But the king's expression softened.

"Ambrose. There were many factors at play... and you were but a child. To that end, have you and your betrothed discussed how you will rear your children in the future? It is a conversation best had early on. Your sweet mother, Goddess keep her well, wished to raise you all from breast to empty nest, but I was of the mind that tradition mandated wet nurses and nannies. It drove a massive wedge between us."

Ambrose stayed silent and stared at the table. A servant took his untouched soup and replaced it with a salad of multicolored beets, tossed with goat's cheese and lemon juice. A fine filet and a mushy green pile accompanied a bowl of bright root vegetables.

"And here I thought it was due to her waistline rivaling that of your prize swine, brother," Septimus said.

The fuck? The actual audacity.

I glanced at Ambrose. If the comment had set *my* teeth on edge, I couldn't imagine where he was right now. I flicked my eyes in Cato's direction.

"And you are familiar with happy unions, uncle?" Cato said, looking pointedly at his aunt, who continued eating as if she wasn't a bit concerned that the men might soon come to blows.

Think, think, think.

"Lady Septimus, at Verus, I was placed in the same living quarters as your daughter Kairus. You must be very proud of her accomplishments and Assignment," I interjected quickly, hoping to diffuse the escalating situation.

"My daughter is a whore, just like her mother used to be," Septimus said before the first word came from his wife's mouth. "I am pleased, however, to know that her manipulative tendencies finally gained our family renown."

I let my serene smile fade.

Troth or not, Ambrose or not, he was insulting the wrong fucking Obligate. How a man who cavorted in a sex den and asked unknown women for tastes of their secretions had the nerve to call anyone a whore was beyond me. I'd shove this spoon down his gorgeous godsdamned throat.

The king tapped his glass with a knife and silenced the conversation.

"Hush, all of you, this is important. Now, my dear, sexuality *is* another area you and Ambrose will need to discuss. Imella was an adventurous lovemaker, and I was more inclined to a good old fashion man-on-top mounting." The king chuckled and patted the tabletop.

Oh, I'm not immune to shock, imagine that.

Allaine's eyes rolled back into her head momentarily. I worried she would end up face down in her filet, but she managed to rally.

"Majesty, please to the nether, silence yourself," begged Cato. The tension radiating from him was almost palpable.

Septimus twisted his face up in disgust, and Ambrose... Ambrose continued looking at the table as if he no longer existed. My whole heart went out to him. He was the innocent in his parent's dramatic tale.

"Boys, you are men of almost thirty years, and this, my loves, is an essential conversation." The king took a bite of green mush and continued on, "Here is one thing I should have done better, but it only occurred to me when it was too late. Partners need individual pursuits. Your mother and I were so obsessed with each other in our beginnings that when our libidos simmered, we didn't know what to do with ourselves."

"Was that when you started fucking the others?" Ambrose said, knocking beets around on his plate.

Allaine choked on her wine and smacked at her chest while the servants who'd been refreshing drinks beat a hasty retreat.

The king ran his fingers through his long gray beard.

"I was not a good father toward the end, and I was a worse husband. Daughter, what interests do you have? Non-Troth ones. I find the Obligates tend to be dully focused on economic or political minutia."

My head spun. *Fill the conversation, Eira. Say something. Interests. Non-Troth interests that aren't sex with Cato.*

"Well, I can't ice fish here, so..." I thought for a moment while spooning in some of the green mush that turned out to be incredibly delicious. "I'd like to learn botany and tend plants, I think."

"Plants? Rather mundane, but you should pursue it." Father Burchard smiled and reached in my direction. I could feel just the tiniest tingle.

"Botany? Truly? Herbalism is a profession for men," said Septimus.

"But why?" The king asked, turning to his brother.

"You made it that way," Septimus answered, his brow furrowing in confusion. "As I recall, when Imella was dabbling in the healing arts, she became grievously ill after incorrectly mixing a concoction."

"Oh... oh, yes." The king glanced down at his upturned hand, and his brows knit closely together.

I felt compelled to comfort him.

I leaned in his direction and slid my hand across the table. Immediately, it began to pulse.

Like he knew I shared the weight of his sadness, a slow, thankful smile appeared on his lips, and he placed his hand on mine. The moment they touched, the connection's energy encapsulated them. The blood in my body pulsated in the rhythm I knew would match his unique heartbeat. *I hope you feel the same comfort you give me.*

"Thank you, daughter. I appreciate it."

I wove my fingers through his age-spotted hand.

"Eira," Ambrose barked from the table's end. The harshness in his voice frightened me. "Do *not* touch another man—family or otherwise—and certainly not one so undeserving."

"Well done, nephew, take command."

I shot a look at the smooth-voiced Septimus and pulled my hand back to my lap.

"My apologies, cub, I did not mean to—"

"Do not, call me that," Ambrose growled.

"Ambrose, I understand the rage that jealousy can incite; I meant no harm, and I apologize. Now, as to the Joining—"

"After tomorrow's council, the ceremony will take place the following day," Cato interjected.

"It most certainly WILL NOT!" The king brought his fist down, shattering his plate and sending a bowl flying to the floor.

Cato bolted from his seat and stood, facing his father. As he moved, he spun my chair so that the tall back was a barrier between me and the perceived threat of danger.

The tie collapsed.

"My dear, I am so sorry to have alarmed you." I heard the legs of a chair scrape and the king's voice draw nearer.

"Go no further," Cato whispered. His voice was hushed, but it held a deadly edge.

"Fine. But hear me well, the nuptials will take place when *I* say. We will host dignitaries, foreign nobles, and people of the cloth, and we will showcase the riches of our kingdom. Do not cross me on this, children—you are nowhere *near* prepared to defy me. Besides, I had announcements sent throughout the continent the moment I learned you were coming home. I am sure guests will begin arriving sooner rather than later."

Cato pivoted, shielding me from his sire as he made to leave.

"Daughter, Lady Allaine... your company was most refreshing, and I cannot wait to deepen our acquaintance. As for the rest of you, your presence has upset my constitution."

Cato escorted his father from the room, and Ambrose appeared at my side. He snapped his fingers at Allaine, who jumped out of her chair.

"Take her immediately to our quarters—I will arrange an escort to take you home."

I grabbed his forearm with both hands.

"Ambrose, I do wish she could stay close. She was the greatest help today... Are there any free rooms she could occupy while employed?"

He glanced down his nose and swallowed hard, reigning in the anger I knew was boiling just below the surface. I figured now may actually be the best time to broach the subject—not enough time for him to ponder—and I knew he'd see straight through me were he not waylaid by his own emotions. I certainly wasn't ready to explain that I took my first... henchwoman? Minion? *Nope, not right either.*

"You lot," Ambrose pointed to a group of servants who huddled near the corner, "there is a vacant nanny's chamber one door from my own apartments. See it aired and readied for Lady Allaine."

The servants rushed to do his bidding, and Allaine took my elbow and led me to the door.

"Just a moment," I said.

I ran the short distance back to the table and pulled out the chair closest to Ambrose. *Goddess, let this be the right course of action.*

My husband-to-be glowered at me so furiously that I almost lost my nerve... but I'd come this far. I stepped onto the seat of the chair, straightened and steadied myself, and then I flung my arms wide.

"Ambrose... Black Bear—"

I never finished the sentence.

His hand came to the back of my head, and his mouth crushed down on mine. I opened my lips to receive his searching tongue and found that, though it wasn't like the fire I experienced when kissing Cato, it wasn't unpleasant by any stretch of the imagination.

Ambrose ran his hand over my backside and urged me to wrap my legs around his waist.

When my back hit the table, dishes scattered wildly, and the cold water from an overturned vase flowed into my hair and absorbed into my silken dress.

Ambrose moaned into my mouth and ground his hips between my spread legs.

Little sparks of a delectably warm fire flickered to life in my womb, and I found myself slickening.

He wrenched his head back and ended the kiss suddenly, but he didn't move from the cradle of my thighs.

"What a good girl you are," he said while cupping my chin in his big hand. "So beautifully obedient."

"Don't keep me waiting, my heart."

"Do not toy with me, Eira."

His hand tightened, and I winced at the seriousness of his tone. His green eyes flashed menacingly, and his lips set into a tight line. This wasn't Ambrose the Scion, nor Ambrose the prince. This was Ambrose *the man*.

I swallowed hard and reached down to palm the magnificent erection that pressed heavily against his layers of clothing.

"*Don't* keep me waiting, Ambrose."

Chapter 7

UNPLANNED DEPOSITS

When we made it back to our apartments, I asked Allaine to light the tapers next to Ambrose's big bed and to turn the lamps low. If he required a physical release to bring him back to the easy-going, playful man I knew, then he would have one. Scary Ambrose was... *scary*.

Sure, I imagined a scenario where tonight, Cato and I would come together and make passionate love until dawn. But that had been wishful thinking on both our parts. His duties kept him away, and right now, *my* duty was to my betrothed.

Cato would have to wait.

I would have to wait.

After towel drying the back of my hair and laying my—probably ruined—dress over a chaise, I tested a few lotions between my fingers, wondering which scent and sensation he'd prefer. One was sweeter and more oily, and another absorbed into my skin more quickly and smelled like berries.

Our previous intimacies had been short-lived or faked, and I, in truth, had little idea of what pleased Ambrose. I assumed it was anything and everyone, but even expert-level sex connoisseurs were sure to have preferences. In the long run, knowing what made him spill the swill would save me time and would be an excellent card to play in our future negotiations.

I rifled through my closet, thinking that I should dress in something seductive, but as quickly as the notion came, I shoved it away.

He was in no mood.

When he walked in, I wanted him to realize, without fail, that I hadn't played him false. I wanted there to be no doubt that I meant exactly what I'd said at dinner's end. I quickly dragged a comb through my curls and then removed every single stitch of clothing I wore.

He'd get the message.

I placed the lotions on the bedside table and fluffed up the pillows. Maybe I could start with a massage, or maybe he'd like—

Ambrose burst through the door with such force that it rattled on its hinges.

"Had you been lying, I would have beaten you. I would have turned you over my knee and whipped you until you sobbed."

I'd never feared him before, but the look on his face gave me pause—he rivaled Cato at his worst. His nose was bloody and his hair was a mess, and I could clearly see where a knot would rise on his cheek come morning. His eyes glittered not in mirth—they glinted with a sharp and sinister warning.

Ambrose looked me up and down and then nodded.

"Cato or Septimus?" I asked, wondering who I should expect to look equally rough.

"Does it matter?" He shrugged off his coat and let it hit the floor. His hands went to his belt buckle. He whipped the leather out from his loops in a fluid motion and let it clatter on the marble tiles. "The answer is, 'no, Black Bear, it does not.'" His tunic came over his head and joined the rest of his cast-off items. Dressed only in his low-slung pants, he paused and placed his fists on his hips while appreciating my body with a steadfast gaze.

As always, I was struck by his flawlessness. There was no doubt I'd aligned myself with one of the Goddess's masterworks. Broad shoulders tapered to a thin torso, which ended in the most delectable *V* shaped indentation that traveled below his belt line. Like Cato, the dark hair that covered his chest highlighted his masculine shape and reminded me of the beautiful differences between us.

"Come to me." He pointed to a spot in front of him.

I did as commanded.

"Remove my boots."

I dropped to my knees and began tugging at the stiff leather. He stared straight ahead, making no move to assist me, either by lifting a foot or starting the process himself. Task completed, I stood and waited for the next order to be issued. When none came, my hands went to the laces of his small clothes.

With a little more effort, we stood together naked.

I stared at him, wondering what the next step was in our contractual liaison... but then I remembered what it was like when Cato reached for me—the feeling of being wanted, protected, and cared for at the same time.

Ambrose remained unmoving until I wrapped my hands around his waist and laid my head against his sternum. I held him closely, enjoying the sensation of his soft skin, so warm against my own. I closed my eyes and breathed in his sweet and spicy scent. His arms dropped heavily around my shoulders and his chin came to rest on the top of my head. We stood this way, swaying in a slow, smooth rhythm, while the minutes ticked by.

"Come on." I broke our embrace and went to turn down the blankets. The second I pulled them back, Ambrose dropped stiffly onto the mattress. His face was a mask of tension, and his muscles were corded as tight as a bowstring.

"Lie back and turn over." I pushed his arm and jostled him back and forth, but he didn't budge.

"My dick is on the front, Nortia."

Fucking Ambrose.

"I am well aware. Please comply."

He grunted and grumbled, like he wanted nothing more than to throttle me, but eventually crawled onto the mattress and laid on his stomach.

I grabbed the lotion nearest me and knee-walked to the middle of the bed. I reached out and touched the smooth skin of his back, and then ran a single fingertip across his shoulder blade. His flesh reacted quickly, dotting a path of goosebumps in my wake.

"Eira, what are you playing at? You have never once been shy. Had I wanted a prude, I would have offered for that... Lulu Troth... no wait, Fara? Fuck, I don't remember, the one that looked like a fragile little mouse," he grumbled.

Farai. Sweet and sex-terrified Farai.

"Ambrose, relax. I'm not being shy. I thought you might need something more to—"

"You want me to relax? Drop your cunt on my dick and watch it happen. Bend over and let me try out that ass... I'll unwind instantly. Do you want me to use your skull? Fine, I can fu—"

Fuck it.

I brought my knee up and over his waist and let my legs spread wide. I straddled him, settling myself in front of his rear, and wiggled around until I felt stable.

"Mmmm... I can feel your heat, almost-wife."

Ope, now I'm shy.

Blood rose to my cheeks as he sighed softly. He needed pleasure in his life; he required touch, and it was my job to provide it. I dipped my hand into the jar of honey-scented cream and warmed it between my fingers before pressing my slick palms deep into the muscles of his back.

His low and guttural groan pleased my ears.

"You may actually be worth the trouble one day," he said, rolling his shoulder backward. I traced along his spine with the meaty part of my thumb, eliciting another sigh. "Where did you learn this?"

"From a Scion."

Ambrose twisted his head as far as it could go and looked at me from the side of his eyes. Before he could say another word, I pushed his face down into the mattress. I kneaded the heavy muscles of his biceps and then moved down and tackled his lower back. Even the muscles that covered his ribcage were knotted.

"Ambrose, I told Cato I loved him."

I stilled my hands and let the words stand between us.

"He told me. Go lower, do my ass."

I moved further down, bestriding his thighs, and dug my thumbs into his toned backside.

Of course he did. They still hadn't learned that maybe oversharing wasn't the best way to stay sane.

Ambrose purred contentedly and flexed his cheeks when I rubbed my hands over his lightly hairy rear, working in the lotion.

"It's just that... this makes me feel like I'm being unfaithful to him, and I worry about how he'll cope." *And maybe how I'll cope.* My body wasn't immune to Ambrose, no matter how I felt about Cato. Already, I was *very* aware of the burgeoning pressure in my lower half. "Wait! What are you—"

Ambrose shifted abruptly, nearly knocking me from my perch as he rotated underneath me. I lifted up on my knees as high as I could and allowed him to turn. The moment he settled, his hands found my hips, and he drew me back down, splaying me wide atop his stomach.

"Cato has a clear understanding of what we have agreed to. He knows the costs. He is aware of the consequences."

"This conversation was easier with the back of your head."

Ambrose pressed his lips and arched a single black brow.

"Eira, your discomfort means that for once in his life, *he* gets what *he* wants. Without the benefit of our contract, he would have nothing, and neither would you." Ambrose trailed his hands up and down my thighs. "I was just with him. He trusts me, and he trusts you. This may be a unique arrangement, but a deal is a deal. And I've had my dick in your mouth, for shit's sake, ease up on the dramatics."

"If I *want* to feel timid, I will feel timid. And if I *want* to be dramatic, Ambrose, I'll be so fucking dramatic your—"

"You weren't nervous handling me after dinner." He let his hand wander across my hip and ran his fingertips through the dark curls at my apex. "You certainly weren't bashful in the Den, or when I took your maidenhead." His voice dropped and his lids lowered.

"You made my first time *quite* memorable... nigh unforgettable." I grinned, remembering how frantically we tried to will his dead penis to life that night.

A slow smile crept across his mouth when I leaned forward and went to work on his thick pectorals. His hand drifted lower and he nestled the pad of his thumb at the top of my slit, grazing my tightening nerves with a featherweight caress.

"How will you satisfy me this evening?" he asked, blinking slowly.

I looked down at his chest, avoiding his lust-darkened eyes. How could the fan of someone's lashes stoke that warm flame inside?

"What would you prefer?" My voice turned thin, lacking its normal confidence.

I scooted back so I could better access his chest and free myself from his absurd magnetism. He followed me with those tempting fingers and bit his bottom lip as my eyes went wide. His arousal settled against my rear, hard as stone, despite having had no stimulation. He flexed his hips and ran himself along the cleft of my backside.

My breath quickened.

I loved riding the swell of arousal, the building tidal wave, and the pleasure that crashed upon the shore the moment completion was upon you—but I was conflicted about my readiness to share such a vulnerable expression with him.

"Hmmm, I was going to let you make the choice, but since you asked so nicely... your mouth has gotten you into trouble the *entire* fucking day. Or you *could* take my cock between your tits, I suppose. They are an exceptional set."

"Ambrose—please." I could barely look him in the eye.

"No—there will be none of that. I told you once your body was—"

"You were actively trying to seduce me for nefarious means then," I interrupted.

"And? There was no lie. I love bodies. Small ones and plump ones like yours. Kol was by far larger than you, and she was a top-level fuck. Goddess, she was good. Evandr was as well, so adorably short and built like a man-cube. He was always so self-conscious about his height, no matter what I told him."

"You and Evandr?" I questioned, unable to imagine the Scion's together.

"Mmhmm, he was the closest thing to a long-term relationship I have ever had."

"Did you love him?"

"No, not love… but we got along well. When we ended the physical nature of our liaison, we remained good friends, and… Nortia, are you stalling?"

"Yes. Yes, I am." I nodded.

"Allow me inside."

Ambrose slipped a long finger between my profoundly wet labia and asked me, not with words but with his eyes, if he should continue.

I tilted my hips in response, granting him access.

Have I ever had self discipline?

"I am likely to bust on your back if you keep edging away."

"Mmmm," I said, trying to stop myself from riding his finger. "Right. Yes. Okay." I rolled off to his side and began mulling over the techniques I'd learned while in class with the Vaughns.

"Ambrose, on your knees."

He popped up and positioned himself as requested.

I laid down on my back and slid my head between his legs.

Reaching behind him, I raked my nails lightly up his inner thighs until I reached his heavy testicles. His erection bobbed as I stroked and lifted them. "Tell me if you don't like this."

Arching my neck, I cupped his sac and licked at the skin between it and his tightened flesh.

"I like this," he grunted.

"Stroke yourself," I ordered.

"Gladly, but I require assistance." He leaned down and reached between my legs.

"Gods, Ambrose." Two fingers slipped into my passage, hooking gently upward. "I…" My hips rolled in the rhythm of his skillful fingers as they pressed in and out of my slick warmth.

"Had to borrow this." He wrapped his palm around his base and, with his thumb and two fingers, slid up his length.

It was my undoing—it was *always* my undoing. My skin prickled as a wave of arousal flooded me.

I drew an oval into my mouth and sucked and tongued it until I heard his first low groan. I could feel his motions as he pleasured himself and felt the continued stir of my own body. I'd seen both him and Cato handle themselves before, and even Ozius briefly. I found it heightened my arousal to a fever pitch. The bunching of their muscles, how firmly they commanded themselves—it turned my warm pulsing into a molten throb.

"Do it harder," he moaned.

I doubled down and nibbled and pulled his skin and testicles until his hips jerked above me.

"*Shit*, Nortia, how I have missed this."

I shimmied out from under him and pressed him back to the bed. Ambrose watched in rapt attention when I dipped my fingers into the honied cream and wrapped my palm around his erection. I lowered my head, and while working him with one hand, put my mouth around his tip.

"This is as delightful as the view," he rasped.

I traced his divot with my tongue and outlined the ridge that separated his head from his shaft. Then I ever so slowly ran my mouth down half his solid length, licking in circles all the while.

"I look forward to mounting you. I recall your depths being quite satisfactory."

I pumped my fist faster.

"I will take you with my mouth next time and prepare you well for taking *all* of me. You will feel every inch of what you didn't experience our first time."

I tightened my grip and tasted his salty response, unable to hush the moan that escaped my lips.

"When you are my wife, I will spill myself into you—in that tight slit or between your lips. Your body will *always* take from me."

Stop talking. Oh, my Goddess. Trying not to want this.

"Harder, I want to hear your noises... yes... drink me down, wife. Drink me."

I palmed him as vigorously as I could and sucked and tongued until he was writhing beneath me, bucking his hips steadily. My passage thickened and filled with a mouthwateringly wonderful pulse. I pressed my thighs together in an effort to rein myself in.

He would take me if I asked.

"Fuck yes, my skilled harpy, I will make good use of you."

Fingers tangled through my hair and pulled my head backward. Ambrose pushed me off and went to his knees again.

"Open," he ground out. I obeyed, and he plunged his length between my lips, holding my face steady as he fucked my mouth.

I was on fire—a raging flame in the inferno of his unbridled passion.

On all fours, I imagined him at my back, satisfying that ache within. I purred out loud and felt him grow harder.

"Fuck, yes." With a sharp cry, he released himself in strong, warm waves that hit the back of my tongue and mouth. I drank down his potent essence.

"Thank you, Eira... for Gammond's sake, thank you." He held my neck tightly and continued pumping his hips until he spent himself completely.

I sat up and wiped the side of my mouth, relieved to see a smile on his face as he flopped down and settled into the bed.

"Did... did you swallow it?" he asked.

"Yes." I eyeballed the shit-eating grin on his face and watched as his sable-lashed eyes dance wickedly. "It's literally what you told me to do."

For a full half-minute, Ambrose stared at me like I'd lost my mind. Then he erupted into that wonderfully loud laugh of his and giggled the most manly of giggles.

"I tell you to keep your mouth shut multiple times a day, and you simply cannot comply, but I speak in the language of seduction, just once, and you gobble me down in the most perfect act of submission. Where *are* your priorities?" He reached for me. "Come here, naughty Troth."

I smacked his hand and scurried across the bed.

"No. I refuse."

"Too bad. I cuddle after coming." He sat up, captured me by the ankle, and pulled me back between his legs. My side pressed against his chest, and his arms encompassed me. He held me firmly in place. "Shall I satisfy you, Eira? You must be disgustingly stimulated—being in the presence of my unbound glory tends to have that effect."

He wasn't wrong, vain as all nether, but not wrong.

"No, I'm tired," I said, shoving at his arms.

"Saving your screams for Cato? I will only allow that for a short while." Ambrose nuzzled my neck with his bearded cheek and tightened his embrace.

"You think *you* control them? That's pretty fucking presumptuous."

He let go and grabbed the covers, dragging them over us both.

"Oh, no, you misunderstand. *You* will have no control when I take you."

"That confident?" I smirked.

Ambrose turned us over and tucked me securely into his body. Immediately, I felt sheltered... safe. I'd become accustomed to sleeping next to him or Cato, and after the incident with their father, I was a little afraid to close my eyes without one of them nearby.

"Wife, we will kiss each other on the cheeks every night before bed."

"Really? Why?" I turned and faced him, and he tucked his arm under my neck and guided my head to his chest.

"It seems like something a healthy couple would do."

My sweet, deeply scarred husband-to-be.

My heart expanded.

"It seems reasonable enough." I nodded while absentmindedly swirling my finger in his chest hair. "Ambrose, how did your uncle react to you humping me at the family function?" I chuckled, much calmer now that our first contractual encounter was out of the way.

"Oh my Goddess, Eira, it was fucking hilarious. You left, and he challenged me for your hand. The servants were so undone by the shouting that one pissed his pants, and then a maid was so appalled by the soiling that she dropped a caramel pudding, splattering that fine white suit Septimus wore—it looked like he made an unplanned poo-deposit in his pants." Ambrose chuckled with an abundance of glee while squishing my belly roll gently between his fingers.

"And your aunt? What was her reaction?"

"She just sat there."

"Sat there? I couldn't imagine the level of embarrassment I'd feel if my partner made such a scene." *Gods, I had made such a scene.*

"Ambrose, what's her name?"

He shrugged and rubbed his cheek against my head.

Nameless. Absolutely criminal.

"Good night, almost-wife."

"Good night, shit-loaf."

Chapter 8

Does the Nose Know?

I opened my eyes and stared at Cato's perfection. I still couldn't fathom that he was a part of my reality. The rise and fall of his chest drew my eyes, and I watched contentedly, wondering about the little tics and movements that took place on his face while he slept. Was he thinking of me when the corner of his mouth hitched up? When the lines appeared next to his eye, was he fighting the wraiths in his head?

He wore the same clothes he had on yesterday, and along his cheekbone, his skin was puffed and bruised. There was a nearly healed cut under his eye, pink against his warm complexion. They must have had quite the brawl last night.

I hadn't heard Cato come in, but must have sensed him. I was wrapped up and entwined in his limbs, clinging like he was my anchor in a raging storm.

There was no way he could be comfortable.

My elbow stuck into his ribcage, and my knee was shoved up high between his legs. His only pillow was his hand, and the angle of his neck looked anything but conducive to a good night's sleep.

I moved away as slowly as I could.

His eyes popped open.

A slow, irresistible smile curved his lush mouth, and I melted.

Cato blew back an errant hair from my forehead as his mouth descended, pressing ever so lightly on my own—like a feather drawn across my lips. His hand rested against the curve of my jaw and wandered back to wrap around the column of my neck.

"I knew this charade would be difficult... but the intensity of what I experienced seeing you on his arm—watching you surrounded by the covetous filth of the court. I would end them all if you asked me to do so."

"Cato, don't allow yourself to—"

"And watching you herald yourself into that room," he placed the tip of his nose to mine. "I swear to Mossius, I was this close to flipping your skirts and showing them how *I* venerate my goddess."

I breathed in, allowing the scents of cedar, dirt, and blood to permeate my lungs.

"I have no idea to what you are referring, Protector. I do understand that there was an incident yesterday where an entirely crass woman made a spectacle of herself. *I* would never." I turned innocent eyes on him.

"Oh, you are not she? Forgive me," he whispered. "Then I will seek out the mystery woman who hardened me to the point of needing to hide my lower half behind the sizable head of a snoozing Count Minred."

"Goodness me. What will you do when you find her?" I asked while tracing the edge of his lower lip with the tip of my finger.

"Fuck her, I suppose. I see no other options to assuage my desire."

"And if she refuses you?" My hands went to the buttons of his shirt. With each that opened, my mouth became drier.

"Then I will find another to slake my lusts. I prefer dark-haired, large-chested women, preferably with Troth training—they understand discretion."

My mouth fell open, and he mimicked my expression.

I knew he was teasing—and I was literally sleeping with his brother be-sides—but somehow I found myself jealous of a mythical liaison with a woman who was... me.

"Is something wrong, love?"

He knew exactly what was wrong.

He smirked at me, his eyes searching mine, as he slid his hand down to the small of my back.

"Cato, I know it seems silly considering our circumstances but..."

"Shhh," he silenced me with a kiss. "I like you envious. Knowing you want me makes me... violently cheerful." He dropped his hand lower and squeezed my backside.

The last button of his shirt released, and I spread my hands over his chest, finally having unearthed my favorite buried treasure.

"Per our contract, I believe the *only* woman you are allowed to know, physically, is she who lies before you... legally speaking."

"Yes, of course, that must be why your sharp little claws are sinking their way into my flesh—your concern for my legal standing."

My hands drifted up to wrap around his neck, revealing the crescent-shaped indentations that peppered his clavicles. I pressed my mouth to each one in turn.

"There, there, jealous love, *this* belongs to you—mark me as you see fit."

I trailed my fingers down his stomach and dipped them below his waistband.

"May I make a request upon this body?" I asked, enjoying the sensual surge between my legs.

I draped my knee over his hips.

Cato's face lit up with a silly grin.

"I see where your *priorities* are, ma'am."

Ooooh, fucking Scion! I pulled back and glared.

"I can't believe you'd bring that up. Look, he shoved his dick into my mouth and *told* me to swallow it. He literally said 'drink—'"

Cato's face fell like he'd been told a friend was mortally wounded.

"Oh, dammit all—he didn't tell you?" I covered my face with my hands. "How is this ever going to work? I'm so sorry. What even are the boundaries in all of this?"

"It will work," he said sternly, pulling my hand down and replacing it on his chest. "There is no limit to what I am willing to endure, Eira." He rolled over me, pressing me into the mattress. His belt dug painfully into my pubic bone, but I couldn't care less. The heaviness between my legs—the feeling of intense infatuation—drowned out all else. "And had I more time, love, I would remind you of exactly to whom you belong... alas, you are due in the ladies' solarium in an hour's time."

"An hour!" I screeched. "It took us twice that time to comb my hair yesterday. Move away."

He rained kisses on my shoulders and cheeks, laughing at my feeble attempts to remove him.

"Where's Ambrose?"

"Off being a prince. I will escort you this morning. Go on." He rolled over, and immediately, a piece of me was missing.

On quick feet, I wrapped myself in my too-big robe and made my way through the common room.

My bedchamber door had been repaired.

The room had been cleaned and made right again. No remnants from the blasted column could be seen, and the bed had been remade and was now covered by a thin red blanket with large blue tassels hanging from its corners. There was still no lock on the door, but clearly that wouldn't stop His Majesty from entering, or Cato, or Ambrose, for that matter. When the king chose to find me, I doubted anyone's ability to stop him, given what I had witnessed.

I ran through the bathing room door and encountered a space filled with flowers and heavily scented herbs.

"What in the—"

They were all nestled into beautiful clay pots, all of them differing in color and design. Plants were scattered everywhere, some on the floor, others on the countertop, reflecting in the mirror, making their numbers appear even greater.

"Oh..." My eyes misted over as I ran my fingertips along the soft petals of a bloom that was both purple and yellow.

"You can eat that one; it's called pansy," Cato said, his voice soft.

I plucked a petal and placed it in my mouth. To my delight, it was a tad spicy and tasted very green.

"And this is why you smell of dirt." I glanced over my shoulder and watched a warm blush filter across the tops of his cheeks. "Are you aware of how ridiculous Nortians become when given flowers?"

"I am not," he said, shaking his head. "Enlighten me."

I turned my attention from the long dancing fronds of a purple and green plant and looked to where he stood, leaning against the doorframe with his ankles crossed. He rubbed the fabric of his sleeve between his fingers.

"Some say it's the most reliable way to entice a lover to the altar."

"Are Nortians so fickle?"

I dropped a shoulder and let the neckline of my robe fall to my elbow.

"Come, show me how much you appreciate my gift, woman."

I closed the distance quickly, fully expecting him to open his arms and embrace me, but he just stood there.

"No kisses?" I pouted.

"Uh-uh, no, not sufficient—do you know how long it took to gather these?"

"I'm guessing a delightfully long hug wouldn't be adequate compensation either?" I shook my head, feigning concern.

He waved an arcing arm across the room.

"Do you not see the vast wealth of vegetation that sits before you?" He scowled down at me while making a show of surveying the bounty. "I think not."

I twisted around on the balls of my feet and ran my fingers through my hair, shaking it out as I walked toward the bath.

"I believe I only have a single item of greater worth." I stopped, loosened the belt of my robe, and let the garment fall in a silken puddle. Continuing to the chaise that sat near the side of the bath, I crawled onto its cushioned seat. On all fours, I presented him with my backside, spreading my legs as far as they could go on the narrow piece of furniture. "You will find me more than ready if you feel it's an adequate return on your investment."

I looked over my shoulder. Cato had already freed his arousal and was sliding his fist down its length.

"*This* is a fitting compensation," he ground out. His eyes went dark as he crossed the floor. The razor-thin circle of gold surrounding his pupils expanded as his eyes dilated.

He took my rear in his hands, squeezed, and ran his fingers over each mound.

"Then take your earnings, sir—and take them fast."

He slid the tip of himself up and down in my wetness, riding over my sensitive clitoris.

"Flowers are not a suitable apology for my leaving you unsatisfied for so long," he said. Cato swirled his head around my entrance, teasing the sensitive flesh. I dropped to my elbows, ready for the whole of him. There was nothing like the feeling of him pressing me open, spreading my walls, and filling me entirely.

He slid his thick crown into my passage. My skin warmed and flushed—my breasts tightened.

"Sink into me, Cat, *please*." I was desperate, panting so hard that I was close to hyperventilating.

"With pleasure." He bent over me and—

"Eira, are you okay? Stomach upset?" Allaine sang out her chipper song from the other room.

Cato took off running, heading toward the closet.

I flipped onto my rear, crossed my legs, and pretended to study a leafy stem that smelled heavily of citrus.

"Whoa! His Highness took notes..." Allaine entered the bathing chamber, pausing every other step to assess the new additions—doing her absolute best not to look at me.

I reached down and turned on the water with my foot.

"I don't suppose you know what occurs in the ladies' solarium, do you?" I asked, trying desperately to act casual.

"Nope. Sure, do not," she said while stretching her seized arm. She pressed her palm forward, slowly bending the limb at the elbow, and then took her time pulling each finger back.

"Is it painful?"

"It can be, but the level of discomfort changes."

"And the healers?" I asked honestly, wanting to know more.

"Have done what they can. Hurry up, or your hair will never dry."

I nodded and dutifully hopped into the tub and hastily scrubbed with a spicy-smelling soap—nutmeg and a hint of vanilla.

"That one smells like the Protector, too."

I watched Allaine sniff the air, moving closer to the closet with each inhalation.

"He stayed in the adjoining chamber when Ambrose was last here," I lied smoothly. "I imagine these were brought in for him." I gestured to the array of soaps and scrubs.

"That makes sense; the brothers seem close." She turned around and began moving plants to the back edge of the counter space, bringing each pot to her nose first. "My brothers are similarly adjoined."

I bet not.

"How much do you know about flower care?" she asked.

"Nothing. I'm from the deep freeze. We don't have them there."

I hurriedly climbed out of the bath and wrapped up in a plush towel.

Allaine headed toward the closet again, chatting as she went, "I'll fetch your ensemble for the day. His Highness—"

"No! I will pick out my clothing," I yelled. "I'm an Obligate. *We* choose what we wear. Obligates have a choice!"

Allaine stopped in her tracks and held up a hand in supplication.

Too much, Eira. Bring it down.

"Okay, alright, but if he comes for my job, I'm tossing *you* under the cart." She went to pull pins and combs from her bag.

On my toes, I scurried toward the closet, shot around the wall that hid it, and ran straight into Cato's outstretched arms.

He was beaming.

That smile, those dimples... the alluring little valley in the middle of his top lip. *Ugh. So delicious.* I looped my arms around his neck and grinned back, shoving him deeper into the forest of dresses and coats that hung from the ceiling.

"Do you need my assistance?" Allaine called out.

"No, I'm fine, just eyeing the options."

I clutched a handful of his shirt.

"Why did you button this again?" I whispered.

With nimble fingers, I began unfastening but became frustrated with the time it was costing me. Cato sensed my aggravation, and yanked the sides apart, which sent buttons flying around the small room.

I was on him in an instant.

Emboldened, I leaned in and swirled my tongue around his nipple, sucking and biting the flesh until it peaked.

"Fuck, yes." He closed his eyes and raised his arms, grabbing the bar above us. I let my towel drop and rubbed my breasts against him. The feeling of his hard body touching the softness of my own was intoxicating. It was like pure energy swirled inside of me, spurring me on.

"I refuse to send you to the solar in the guise of a wet dog. Hurry up!" Allaine yelled.

I took a deep breath and pulled away.

"I'm coming, Allaine. What I wear is *incredibly* important, vital even, to the impression I wish to impart."

I snatched three random garments from around me, not paying a bit of attention to what came away in my hands.

Demanding lips settled on mine.

"I want you." He palmed my breasts, thumbing the gold bar that pierced my nipple and squeezing them with his rough textured hands.

"I'll stay in this closet forever. Fuck the solar."

Cato was the one who pulled back this time, but his hands lingered.

"I love you," he mouthed soundlessly.

"I love you," I whispered back. My fingertips tingled, and the air seemed to twist around in my lungs. I felt our union in my soul.

"WHAT?" Allaine hollered from the other room.

"I *said*, what about blue?" I rolled my eyes, thinking on the fly.

"Are you dim? Always blue, it's Monwyn!"

I ran out of the closet, not trusting myself to look back.

Allaine was standing next to the chair, tapping a comb loudly on the table.

"So you went with red? And orange. A statement for sure—not a good one but..."

I glanced down at my hands and straightened my spine. The orange chest support with embroidered dogs would look excellent poking out over the red overdress, and, oh, I would be pairing them both with screamingly fuchsia silk pants.

I donned the outfit and sat for Allaine, who did her best to address my hair and cosmetics.

"You will have to wear it straight and long. There's barely a curl or wave to be found, and we don't have time to make it happen."

"That's fine. I'll just braid it back." I began finger-combing the semi-dry tresses.

"Absolutely not; I can explain away the outfit but not the hairstyle."

"What in the nether is wrong with a braid?" I stared at her reflection in the mirror.

"That is a man's style. Not happening. I am keeping this job."

I dropped my hands as she angled my face to better apply my cosmetics.

"That's ridiculous."

"Like your outfit," she quipped.

I looked at my reflection. She wasn't wrong.

I did stand out. I didn't blend in well with the regal aesthetic of the palace or the soft look of their womenfolk. The silk overdress was so shiny it was nearly reflective, and its neckline scooped almost below my bosom, showing off the most comical undergarment in existence. Its leaping dogs were embroidered in all manner of hues, with clever knots and loops making some have shaggy fur and others spots. I loved the damn thing, but Monwyn, I doubt, would appreciate it.

"You ready?" I asked Allaine.

"Of course, but we are to stay put until the Protector arrives."

Shit!

"Allaine, fetch my lotions from Ambrose's room. I was told to clean up our mess and wouldn't wish to anger him. Grab them quickly."

"You failed to pick up your crap and now—"

"What does the 'maid' in 'lady's maid' stand for?" I faked an incredulous expression and looked down my nose. Honestly, I thought her unabashed opposition was hilarious. I would have dismissed her on day one had I actually taken offense.

"Let's not make this a habit."

The instant she walked out, a lusciously disheveled Cato ran out of the closet. His beard was a scraggly mess—the sides of his shirt trailed behind him, and he held his boots tucked under his elbow.

"Stealthy kiss." He pecked my lips and flew by.

Chapter 9

UNDER THE INFLUENCE

"Y̲ou look... healthy, Lady Obligate. A proverbial rainbow of... of fashionable uniqueness."

Cato offered me his elbow, settling his scowl first on Allaine and then me. Though his face was set in stern lines, amusement flickered in his eyes.

"Thank you, Protector, I'm feeling most vibrant."

He'd managed to change his clothing in the scant quarter of an hour he had between running off and arriving at the apartment doors. Water droplets still clung to his beard, and his golden-brown hair had yet to fully dry. Today, he was dressed like "Tommand," in a well-fitted but subtle blue long coat, a crisp linen shirt of muted gray, and tall black boots. He wore no adornments other than the signet ring that marked him as Protector.

"Does your betrothed share in your tastes?" he asked.

"Ambrose? Indeed. We are in discussion of multi-hued, matching garments for our Joining. He is adamant about appearing more brilliant than the palace's rainbow windows."

"Hideous," Cato murmured.

Grumbly laughter sounded at my back.

"Ignore him." I shot a look at Allaine, whose face was scrunched up in amusement.

Our triad walked through the vast halls of Cordillaria, passing the dining hall and grand drawing room. We turned left into another endless corridor.

"This is the king's personal library. The courtier's library can be found in the opposite wing on the first level. When Joined to His Highness, you will have permission to enter this study, but until then, keep to the public one."

I nodded as we continued our journey, pleased to learn that tidbit. Reading for the sake of pleasure sounded novel.

"Here we are. I believe the solarium to be the most enchanting chamber in the palace." Cato opened the door and propelled me forward. "Enjoy your day."

I snapped my spine straight, recommitting myself to the purpose of saving Monwyn... and then I saw his uncle's wife sitting primly in the distance.

My stomach lurched.

What must she think of me after our first family gathering?

"Protector," I spun around and dropped my voice to a whisper, "your aunt's name is?"

Cato furrowed his brow like he was attempting to solve the most complicated of equations. A soft line appeared on his forehead, and his eyes went distant.

"Mallie-something or another, I cannot quite remember. Do ask her."

Troth face, Eira. Troth face.

I managed not to spit on his shoes, but didn't conceal the indignant flare of my nostrils or my unladylike huff.

Disappointing.

"Hmmm." I looked him up and down before twirling the loose fabric of my pants dramatically and sashaying into the room, knowing very well that his eyes were still upon me.

As Cato claimed, the solarium was truly marvelous.

The ceiling vaulted three stories high, and nearly the entire exterior wall of the sun-drenched chamber was made up of a massive window that reached from floor to ceiling. No shutters shielded the glass from the elements, but thousands of prisms hung down from its cornice, at various lengths, forming a dazzling curtain.

Multicolored beams of light bent across the walls and floors, some the length of my pinky, others dozens of feet long. Rainbows twisted and swayed gently, fading in and out with the movements of the clouds.

I headed toward the diminutive blonde, who sat alone.

"Good morning. May we join you?" I asked in a most pleasant tone.

A quick glance and a soft nod was all the response we received.

"I will fetch refreshments," said Allaine, who sped off to a stocked sideboard.

I claimed the seat to Lady Septimus's left and placed my hands demurely in my lap.

"Have you been enjoying your stay at the palace? Have you been here long?" I inquired.

"No, Obligate Solnna, thank you for asking."

No, it had been awful, or no, it hadn't been long?

She turned back to the window, and I took a moment to survey the rest of the room. In the far corner, several music stands sat in a group, and behind them, on the wall, hung lutes of varying sizes, wooden flutes, and a psaltery. Opposite the musical section was the sideboard where Allaine was plating an assortment of treats, and around her, there were several small tables, some directly in the glass-filtered sunlight, others behind shade panels.

I turned back to my tablemate and stared at the back of her head.

Talk to me, auntie. Just a few words.

I squinted my eyes, bidding her to speak with the silent force of my will.

Companionable silence then, alright.

Like the other Monwyn women I knew, she wore her hair in fat ringlets to her waist—hers were a cool, ashen blonde, much darker than her husband's silver-white locks, the ones so like Kairus's. Her sweet pink dress added to the air of femininity that she embodied, as did the delicate jewels around her neck and in her earlobes. Diamonds and aquamarines had been set in her multi-tiered neck-lace—the bottommost strand lay at the edge of her finely embroidered neckline. The tiny, white chain stitch must have taken someone months to create.

Allaine returned with a pile of snacks skillfully balanced on a plate held under her chin. Looped in her fingers, she carried three glasses of a thick brown-green liquid mottled with gray flecks.

"Here we go." She held the delicate cup to her nose and sniffed. "Let's see, lemon, parsley, apple, and something else." She took a little sip and screwed her face up thoughtfully. "I am unable to place it. You?" she asked, holding the cup under my bottom lip.

I took a swig and held the sweet, but slimy, liquid in my mouth. It was definitely herbaceous, but I shook my head, unable to identify the flavor.

"It is cucumber," said Lady Septimus in a hushed voice.

Both Allaine and I turned in her direction, but she continued staring at the blustery scene of the outside world. The branches of ornamental trees and fat browning shrubs danced in the wind and tapped against the panes of glass.

"Of course. Such a light aroma, but very distinctive all the same," Allaine added, taking another sip.

Small talk. I don't like it.

I helped myself to a lettuce and bean spread sandwich and munched on the raw sticks of celery and carrots that had been provided. I'd thought the little pasties were perhaps filled with spiced fruit or honied cream as they had been at Verus, but when I bit it in half, unsalted leafy greens and onions were its only stuffing. It wasn't bad, but yesterday's breakfast had been a feast, comparatively.

"Is this the normal morning meal?" I asked.

"It is," came the quiet reply.

"Huh." I could just imagine Ambrose's face when he bit into these. I'd seen him eat a chunk of cheese the size of his hand with great gusto, and maybe this was why.

"Aunt," I said, hoping she wouldn't take offense at my familiarity, "before the day gets away from us, what are you called? I'm ashamed my betrothed didn't properly introduce us... but his head is so very full of matters of state."

She turned her fair head, and for a moment, I stared at Kairus—bright rounded eyes of blue, a dazzling heart-shaped face.

"I am called Lady Septimus, Joined to Lord Septimus, seventh son of the late king; may Merrias guide him."

An invisible wall of formality wedged itself between us. But I didn't want to give up.

"If we are to be family, should I not call you by your first name? Especially in such an informal setting," I questioned while gesturing to the empty room.

She placed her bejeweled hand on the table and turned herself to face me squarely. She smelled of—

"Honeysuckle, what a lovely scent. Do you make it yourself?" Allaine asked, inhaling deeply.

"No, it is a Gaean import." She straightened the bracelet at her wrist. "Lady Troth, my given name is Lilium, but I am hesitant for it to be used publicly."

Lilium? What the fuck had Cato said? Malla... Mellie? Clueless ass.

"May I ask why?"

I noticed how fine and dainty her slim neck was as she gracefully batted her lashes.

"My husband prefers Septimus; it conveys the importance of the lineage."

"Well, Lilium, I'll remember that when he's around, if that's okay with you. Now, who else are we expecting? I'd thought the ladies' solar would be bustling with liveliness and... ladies."

Lilium's expressions were so subtle they were almost unperceivable. Just the barest movement of the corner of her eye and the slightest pucker of her lips indicated she'd heard me at all.

"Lady Colvine is at court, I believe, but she normally stays in her husband's apartments when he visits the stateroom. You might meet her when they take their afternoon promenade."

"That's it? Nobody else?" I asked.

"Perhaps a few, but none that I am in contact with, no."

"That's a load of polar bear poop, if you ask me."

"I didn't."

I grimaced and shoved another dinky sandwich in my face and then looked to where Allaine sat munching contentedly on a stalk of celery.

My mood began to worsen by the second.

"Lady Troth, you mentioned my daughter, Kairus, at dinner. If it presents no trouble to you, would you inform me of how she fares?"

The request elevated my dwindling spirits.

"Of course. Before I left, she'd just been Assigned and was the picture of confidence." I reached out and placed my palm over her hand. "She received the most prestigious of placements and was clothed like the most regal of queens. She bore the colors of every kingdom on her collar and was excited to begin her new adventure."

Lilium gently pulled her hand back and tucked it under the table.

"There is no other Troth like her... She is quite literally the best of us."

She nodded and cast her eyes downward, but not before I saw the emotion there—pride followed quickly by concern.

"Thank you for saying so."

We sat in another lull of awkward silence before Allaine—bless her soul—chimed in.

"I'll play a tune."

She was up and out of her seat, as eager as I was to avoid another round of random chatter.

I followed her fleeing form and watched as she chose a lyre from the wall. She stretched her fingers and arm out methodically before putting the instrument into her affected hand and pushing it slowly, using her heightened muscle tone to secure it against her knees. With a skillfulness I would not have expected, she launched into a lively song. I made a mental note to stop doubting her abilities. She played as well as any young woman might.

"Troth Solnna."

Yes!

I schooled my excitement and remained the picture of decorum.

"Yes, Lilium?"

She visibly shrank back from the use of her own name.

"I have been tasked with befriending you."

I sighed and nodded slowly, understanding her immediately.

"What does he want from me?" I whispered, matching the volume of her voice.

"I am never privy to that information, but his desires tend to point back to producing an heir or furthering the royal renown."

I inhaled deeply, regretting immensely that I'd egged on Septimus's sexual appetites in the Den.

"He is rather preoccupied with you—becomes aroused when he speaks of you and—"

"I... please know... I have no intentions when it comes to your husband, truly. I don't want any sort of relationship with him other than that which is strictly familial, and maybe not even that."

The barest hint of a smile appeared on her lips and then disappeared as fast as it came.

"I welcome anyone who turns his attention away from myself."

Goddess, is he that awful? Does he abuse her? The thought made my stomach sour.

I'd find out.

"Lilium, how about we become the fastest of friends then, just as he wishes?"

She straightened the dishes on the table, moving so precisely there were no scrapes or clatters as she set the cups on top of the saucers.

"His intentions will not be decent—they never are—and playing his games usually proves unwise for his adversaries."

"Has he ever played them with a Troth before?" I asked, trying to gain an understanding of his reach.

"Not that I am aware of... and while I appreciate your effort in befriending me, I must decline. It is safer for you and myself that way... for many reasons."

She lowered her lashes and turned, fully committing herself to the role of Silent Lady at the Window.

The door opened and caught my attention.

A middle-aged gentleman entered the room. He had a noticeably slumped posture and a protruding belly that stuck out from his slight frame, like an olive on a toothpick. He looked directly at me—his sunburnt cheeks were mottled with the remnants of red acne scars.

Allaine's song ended right as the man reached my side. He stood there, just a foot away, awkwardly glancing between the floor and my face.

"Greetings, may I be of assistance?" I asked.

The man scratched at his neck. His receding hairline made his forehead stand out prominently, even more so because the stringy straw-colored remainder was pulled back into a severely tight tail. He looked vaguely familiar, but I couldn't recall if we'd been introduced or not.

Allaine made it back to my side and stood next to my chair.

"I got told tah take y'all to the library."

His dialect reminded me of Demma's Gems and the kingdomless people who lived in the mountains.

"Lady Septimus, would you like to join us in the library? Our escort…" I turned to inquire about the manservant's name.

"Bem."

"Bem?"

Bem!

The same Bem I tried to magically manipulate into amorous congress? No fucking way.

Viktos, strike me dead! The Bem I remembered had been a strapping, virile man—not a paunchy, round-shouldered, slump. This fellow had seen at least five decades. *Shit, no wonder he's uncomfortable.*

"Thank you, but I will remain here until I am retrieved." I hardly heard Lilium speak over the roar of my own perplexity.

"Lady Eira?" Allaine bent down closely and looked deeply into my eyes. She inspected my countenance and laid the back of her hand on my forehead.

"I'm good. Spry even. Shall we?" I bounced up from the chair, more than ready to leave the room.

Bem hurried ahead to open the door. Our group turned right outside of the solarium, and eventually, we came to yet another narrow corridor that spanned the length of the palace. As we traversed it, I paused at each of the paintings that hung in the space. Many of the past Monwyn royals wore crowns. Others were decorated with military distinctions. Some of the portraits were so old they looked two-dimensional—no use of shading or perspective—but as we traveled further in, others were so brilliantly captured that it was as if the subjects were alive and standing before us.

"That's His Majesty," Bem said.

Hello, Daddy...

I went all warm and tingly.

And then I wanted to smack myself repeatedly.

Burchard was the sun-kissed Cato. His sandy hair was worn in the long, braided style that was so popular here, but his mouth was a replica of his son's. I rubbed the tips of my fingers together, itching to reach out and run my hands down the masterpiece.

The king, who I was ogling like a besotted girl, had hazel eyes in his younger years—the corruption, I assumed, had turned them into the color they were now. He had thick lashes like Cato and a deep dimple, though only on one side. Septimus, Cato, and his father all seemed to share a strong family resemblance. I wondered if Aberus, the eldest brother, did as well. I hoped not, given the prickles of sweat I felt beading between my bosoms.

Bem's voice brought me back, "If ya need something, ask the Scholar. His sight ain't good, but his mind's fine." He pointed to an arching double-doored entrance a few feet away. A mountainscape was carved across both panels of the light wood, and in its foreground were subtly stained flowers of green and gold. A guard stationed at the side of the archway pounded the butt of his spear against the floor before admitting us.

"Our thanks, Bem. I imagine we will be here for quite some time."

He turned abruptly and walked away.

CHAPTER 10

ENOUGH

The smell of old books and fresh parchment enveloped me, sending my spirits soaring to the roof. A calm washed over me, and the tension in my neck and jaws lessened. I was ready for a bit of solitude, to lose myself in something other than life's complications or my body's complicated desires.

"Greetings, Troth Solnna." A severely stooped old man shuffled his way over and adjusted the spectacles that slipped down to the tip of his nose. "I was informed by the Protector that you would be perusing the stacks this afternoon."

"Good day. Would you be the wise Scholar I've heard about?"

When he smiled, his saggy jowls lifted, and the loose folds of skin under his neck wobbled.

Gods, I love grandpas. Little old men were simply adorable.

His blue and brown robes swallowed him whole and hung heavily to the floor—as if he had never altered their size as age inevitably changed his stature.

He pushed those wayward glasses back up again and squinted at me with the sweetest eyes.

"Flattery? Didn't work for the last Obligate—won't work with you."

Oh.

Okay.

"Listen well to the rules of my domain—are you listening, girl?"

"Indeed, I am." I took a small step back as he took one forward.

"One," he held a crooked finger so close to my face I could smell his cheese breakfast. "No food or drink is permitted. I would toss out even the king himself for endangering these volumes on account of thirst—do not do it."

I held up my hands and bumped Allaine's leg with my hip. She held up her hand as well. The Scholar inspected us closely, narrowing his beady brown eyes to the point where they all but disappeared.

"We've got nothing on us."

"Two." His second finger did touch my nose this time, but despite my flinch, he continued laying out the law. I'd give him the benefit of the doubt, though—maybe it was his limited vision. "The back portion of the library is restricted to healers and men of science. Are you a healer or a man of science?"

"No, sir, but I—"

"Then stay out. You are not permitted—I don't care if you are the king himself."

"Noted," I said flatly.

"Three." He flicked the tip of my nose cruelly. "Unless His Highness Ambrose comes to sign them out, you are not to remove a single volume from this room. I will not have them lost amongst your frippery."

"That's a load of horseshit."

"Four." He slapped my hand hard. "Vulgar language is not permitted in this chamber—who raised you, girl?"

Does Ambrose even read? I'm ready to burn this bridge.

"If you have an issue abiding... you will be escorted out. I don't care if you are the king himself!"

I wrapped my arms around my back and squeezed my palms together.

Allaine's long-fingered hand settled on my waist.

Nod and smile.

"It won't be an issue, good Scholar. Are there any other regulations I should be aware of?"

"I would have informed you if there were, ignorant girl. You may enter."

Head held high, I entered the library. My nose still smarted from his mean-spirited flick, but I decided to ignore the insult and instead immerse myself in my surroundings.

I walked slowly, inspecting a title here and pulling a tome there.

This was one benefit of Joining up.

"Do not remove it unless you intend to read it!" The Scholar yelled from across the stacks.

I ducked into an aisle and led us deep into the rows of shelves that nearly reached the ceiling.

This was no Verus study, but it was certainly a vast collection.

"Did you see him flick me? Have I been transported to an alternate plane where mean little goblins rule the land?"

Allaine cringed.

"I did. I am so sorr—"

"Don't apologize for his actions," I hissed. "Does a primer exist on these shelves that will spell out what I am and am not allowed to do in Monwyn? *The Vagina Bearer's Guide to the Mountain Lands*, perhaps?"

Allaine dropped her brows low and looked at me thoughtfully.

"Well, no but—"

"Right now, I'd like to smack his nose with each of his precious volumes. Maybe punch his... his old man's kneecaps with," I grabbed the nearest book, "*Progminiture and Genealogy in the Storied Courts of Hain.*"

Allaine's eyes sparkled above her smile.

"Gracious, Lady Troth, are you often given to such... brutality?"

"Well." I thought for a moment. Was I overreacting? I wasn't usually this bad, unless... "Oh, praise Derros."

"Well?" she questioned, raising one impeccably manicured brow.

"My courses must be starting. Now, given his assault on my person, I believe I'd still feel the same way... but my bleed seems to amplify everything I feel twofold. I'm bloated up like a tubby seal and could barely breathe in yesterday's dress. Goddess, I've never been so excited to have my womb purge itself." I patted my stomach and did a little shuffle.

My companion's face crumpled. Utter horror etched itself across Allaine's lovely features. Her dark blue eyes welled, and lines appeared around her tensed mouth.

"You were not hoping to bring forth a child... one conceived of the Rite?"

I held her gaze.

"I would have been honored to have borne His Highness's child... But you see, Allaine, that child would have been taken from us. That would have crushed my spirit." The lies slipped out with such ease.

I was beyond relieved, but not because of Verus.

"I cannot imagine how difficult that would have been." She squeezed my shoulder and looked at me with a pity-filled stare.

"I need you to locate fresh pads and the medicine that will stave off cramping."

"Yes, that is no issue. We can have everything sent to your rooms."

"Thank you, I'll need to place an order for a tincture to keep me infertile for a little while as well. My... my heart needs to heal, and I don't think I have enough for another dose after my flow—"

"Stop speaking!" She flung her hand out and covered my mouth.

"Whap va mever errr ewe dnnnng!" I jerked back, but her hand clamped tighter to my face.

"Eira, I am all for harmless civil disobedience, but that talk will get you punished."

"What?" I spat back in a tone louder than intended.

"This conversation, the one we are having right now—it's illegal." Allaine waved her hand across her face frantically.

"If Verus can teach us about the herbs and tell us to *use* them on others, then I should absolutely be allowed to order them. And are you telling me that even Ambrose, second-in-line-to-the-throne, wouldn't be able to procure them?"

"He would, I imagine, but—"

"But nothing. That's a fucking bag of bear turds."

"VULGARITY is not permitted in my domain! Remove yourself at once!"

The Scholar. Clearly, his ears were not as aged as his eyes.

Come kick me out, old man.

I reached up and tugged Allaine's shoulder, bringing her face down to my level.

"Remember, you and I... we have an agreement."

I turned sharply and sped down another row, snatching up several of the smaller volumes I thought might interest me.

"Troth, return to this spot immediately!" The Scholar's voice came from the side of the shelf we'd just vacated. The nasty mite gave chase!

"Put these down your dress, Allaine. You have more room than I do," I hissed.

"You cannot be serious."

"As an iceberg. You want to come with me when I leave?"

The silent stare-off lasted only a second before Allaine began stashing books into the chemise she wore under her thick gown.

"If I am caught, I swear—"

"I'll take the blame. Come on." I sprinted down the aisle, passing up books on dancing, cooking, and courtship, and finally, my hand landed on two smaller tomes on the subject of botanicals.

Allaine tucked the thin, leather-bound books into her neckline and shimmied until they dropped to her natural waist. Both disappeared under the flare of her bosom.

"Act natural—neutral face, brows at ease, drop your shoulders, don't press your lips like that." I thumped my fist on her back until she let her shoulder sag, just in time for the geezer and his lackey to turn the corner.

"Scholar, is that you? I can't seem to find my way out of this maze." I looked around, acting for all the world like a lost soul standing upon the blade.

"Stay put, unholy Troth—dirty-mouthed and dull-witted. You are banished until you learn a lady's etiquette!"

He ambled forward with his arms stretched out, trying to maintain his wobbly balance. Behind him was the guard who'd been stationed outside.

"Check her. Pat her down thoroughly before she leaves," the Scholar ordered.

"Sir knight, I would think well before laying a hand on me."

The man's eyes flickered beneath his klappvisor helm, as he weighed his options.

The Scholar spun to face his defender.

"This is not *His Highness's* jurisdiction. It is mine!" he screeched.

The Scholar turned again, dug his arthritic fingers into the top of my chest, and tore at my orange support.

I batted his hands away, frankly shocked by the liberties he took. I didn't care how old he was. He jerked me forward and reached down my dress. His hands slid over my breasts and pinched and poked until I began to see red.

"You're right, Scholar, this *is* your domain. Just a moment, and I'll make your task easier."

I began to unbutton the short length of my overdress's gold closures.

He shoved his glasses up on his nose and moved closer, eyeballing my fingers.

"Woman!" He blanched so hard that his saggy jowls flew back. "Do not dare expose your arms in this sanctuary, y-you lady of the night!"

"Hold this." I looked back at Allaine and tossed her my dress. The extra fabric would conceal the books better, and it was time to lay the elder low.

"I insist on proving my innocence, *Scholar*. I have never stolen someone else's property, and though it may shame me before the Goddess and all who bear witness, I feel for the sake of my husband's honor, I must erase the stain you have thrown upon my person." My hands went to the laces of my support, and with agile fingers, I unknotted the ladder lacing and pulled it free in one swift motion.

The old ass spun and fell into the guard's arms.

"Daughter of the nether! Spawn of demon seed! Harpy sent to devour humanity!"

I opened the sides of my support and held it wide. My breasts dropped and shook freely, unrestrained and wobbling.

"Do you see any books, good soldier? Please inform the Scholar of your findings, sir."

The guard waited until the Scholar took a breath between his curses.

"Slut of Ærta! Prince's whore!"

"Scholar, there are no books on her person."

"Shall I heft my mounds? Remove my pants so you may examine my slit? I daresay I could fit one, perhaps two, in my whore's cunt. It's a divinely stretchy organ." I reached for the closure of my pants.

The armored man tried to right the ancient fiend in his arms, but the Scholar flopped back and went boneless in the soldier's hands.

"Leave at once! You are not welcome here and are banished! You have desecrated this temple of wisdom with your foulness."

"Was it my arms or tits that caused the desecration?" I questioned. "At what point did it become tainted?"

I drew the support around my front and went about lacing it.

"LEAVE, WITCH," he cried, inching his way toward me again.

"We will do just that. Good day to you, Scholar—and if you ever touch me without my permission again, I will snap your old thumbs." I nodded to the soldier, who stood stock still, and then twirled about and ushered Allaine quickly to the exit.

"Where is the Protector's office? I should like to see him immediately."

I took a random right turn and headed down the hall.

"Eira, slow down. We need to wait for Bem, and for Goddess's sake, we need to get you dressed."

"No. I'm not putting it back on. I've got anger-sweat dripping down my back. How my arms caused such a reaction is beyond reason. It's not rational. It's absolutely absurd! At Verus, the Monwyns had half their breasts showing." I wagged and waved my hands above my head while Allaine did her damnedest to shield me with her tall self.

"Yes, but they were not betrothed, Eira, *you* are. You have been claimed; you are off the marriage market. Surely you are aware that demurity is prized in a wife and will be expected."

I stopped short, and Allaine continued surging forward.

"Truly, is that truly a law here?"

Realizing I was no longer behind her, she whipped back around.

"Not a law, no, but the upper echelon certainly adheres to the custom."

"And women are okay with it? And their husbands? They're all fine with the strictures? Ambrose loves my boobs, and so do I."

I squeezed past her attempt to block me and took a left at the end of the hallway.

"I... I have no idea how the others feel. Now, stop. Think for a second. If I lose you, I get sacked."

The entrance to the grand salon was up ahead, which meant the steps leading to my apartments were as well. I ignored the grimaces and stares of the men filtering out of the dining hall and stomped my way up the steps.

I took a sharp left at the top of the flight.

"Our rooms are this way," said Allaine from a step or two behind.

"I know. But as I told you, I wish to speak to—what's that?"

My ears perked up, catching a sound that didn't seem to belong near the quiet of the royal chambers.

"What?"

"Shhh, listen, do you hear it?"

"Yes, but I—"

The familiar sound took me north, back home, but not in a pleasant way. I rushed down the second-level hallway. The faint smell of alcohol and medicinals clung to the air, and as we came to the corridor's halfway point, the sound took up again. It was the full-bodied groan I had come to associate with a birth going wrong.

"We cannot be in the healer's quarters, Eira."

"Turn around and leave or don't. Unlike the rest of this kingdom, I'll give you a choice."

There it was again.

Gods, that sound—I'd hoped, many times over, to never hear it again.

Silence.

I put my ear to the door nearest me and heard nothing within, so I hurried to the next.

A raw-throated, hopeless moan, sent frozen shards shooting through my soul.

I tried the handle, but the door had been secured. Putting a fist to the wood, I pounded on the entrance.

"Finally. Morroe, give me the—Madam, remove yourself from these premises," said the man whose hands and front were coated in sticky streaks of fresh blood and rusty brown remnants of that shed some time ago.

As if possessed, I pushed past the man, not caring that my support and stomach drug across his soiled apron in our brief contact.

"Stop this instant!"

I ignored him but listened as Allaine did her best to calm him by offering some sort of "had the wrong room" explanation.

I made a quick assessment. The air was humid and hot because of a large pot of water boiling on a hook above the fireplace. It was letting off an aroma I was not familiar with—burnt-smelling, and heavy with an alcohol-based scent.

A young woman with heavily swollen feet was laid out on a bed, her bent legs hanging limply to her sides. As evident by the clots on the rumpled towels near her rear, she'd lost an incredible amount of blood... blood that I could see was still hemorrhaging from her passage.

"Healer, what have you attempted to staunch the flow?" I asked, leafing through my memories.

How did Momma handle this?

"It is of no concern to you what procedures I have performed. The babe was not born living and soon the mother will follow. It is as Mossius wills. Remove yourself from my facility."

"Where is m-my baby..."

A small bundle lay wrapped on the end of the bed, and its mother, near delirious, slowly rocked her head back and forth on the pillowless mattress.

I examined the room again.

"Where is the afterbirth? Has it come?"

"You have no authority to ask—"

"WHERE IS IT?" I bellowed at the healer, who still stood in the doorway.

Darkness closed in on my peripheral vision.

Not now, Mother Merrias, not now.

Knowing the chaos I could cause if the shadows continued, I took a steadying breath and felt for the beat of my heart—begging it to slow its pace.

"Allaine, help me, please."

I didn't wait for her answer.

I approached the mother's bedside and began rummaging through the sheets and towels that were scattered around the bed.

"Guards! GUARDS!" The healer shouted from the hall.

My companion came to my side.

"What are we looking for?"

"It will be about this big, most likely oblong, with a cord attached to it." I held my hands up, showing her what shape to look for.

Allaine went to the other side of the bed and fell to her knees, where she began searching through the towels that had fallen onto the sheet-protected floor.

Mossius, lend me your wisdom.

"Here it is... I think this is it." Allaine breathed heavily.

I ran to her side, nearly losing my step as I rounded the end of the bed.

"Don't stand yet." I knew the look on her face. Many a husband had passed out as their wives did the bloody work of birthing. I was afraid that, from her height, if she hit the marble floor, she'd be gravely injured. "Scoot back and remain seated."

With some difficulty, she inched back, taking the floor covering with her. Her back hit the nearest wall, and she tilted her chin up and shut her eyes.

On my knees, I held the placenta and turned it about, inspecting it from every angle. When I was young, my mother insisted I learn this skill for instances where the weather kept her apprentice from attending a birth. She'd drilled into my head what the structure should look like and what to look for when—there it was—a portion of the afterbirth was missing.

"She's retained, healer."

"Drop the refuse as I have ordered."

A red-smeared hand bit into my shoulder and yanked me backward.

My hip took the brunt of the impact as I hit the tiled floor. A sharp pain stunned me to stillness as it radiated throughout my lower back.

"Healer, please... she's retained a portion of her placenta. It must be removed. It must, or she won't make it."

The mother began to weep softly between her heart-wrenching wails.

I rolled over onto my knees and made to stand, but the back of the healer's hand found my cheek, and I staggered once more.

"Unbelievable," he hollered. He pushed a hand through his long salt and pepper hair, which turned the graying portions pink.

"Healer, please... please listen," I cried.

"Silence yourself—Protector, there you are, this woman—"

Only the whites of the healer's eyes showed as he sank to his knees.

Cato was by my side before the man collapsed into a pile on the floor.

"Cato... Pro-protector, please let me go to her."

Cato looked between me and the mother, who'd gone an alarming shade of pale purple... Except for the scarlet that stained her cheeks, it burned brightly against her skin.

"Troth Solnna, I—"

"*Please*," I begged. His understanding eyes reflected dark cinnamon in the glaringly bright lamplight.

He stood, took two steps backward, and nodded his head.

I scrambled to my feet and leapt into action.

"You come here." I pointed to the healer's apprentice, who had just materialized with a fresh stack of towels.

He moved toward his prone master, but Cato grabbed the man by his collar, twisting the garment around his fist. He held the young man mere inches from his face.

"You have but a single chance to obey me—do what she asks."

The apprentice dropped his light load on the floor and, without further comment, came to my side.

"This is the Goddess's domain now," he said in a hushed tone.

"It is, and through her, knowledge comes to us all. Rub her stomach, rub deeply, like this." I looked at the distended belly before me and took his hands into my own, modeling the right depth and intensity. "Yes, that's perfect." He did as was asked and performed the technique well. "She may scream out or become unconscious." I wrapped a towel around one hand and pressed it down against her pubic bone. "Mother, stay with me. Mother, I need you," I chanted, speaking simultaneously to my patient, my own mother-mentor, and the Goddess herself.

With my thumb pressed against my pointer and middle fingers, I entered her passage as gently as I could, but without wasting a moment. I'd seen my mother do this procedure at least three times but had never carried it out.

I closed my eyes and allowed my fingers to be my vision. I wasn't sure what I was feeling for but knew that if anything felt attached or didn't give way easily, I had to stop or risk causing more damage. I swept my hand around, thoroughly searching the cavity, until the tips of my fingers came into contact with a small blockage situated just beyond the cervix.

"Great Healer, born of She Who is Without Limit, be with me now. Mossius, guide my hands. Deliver this mother from her suffering," I prayed.

Palpating the uterine opening, the remnant of tissue came away and into my palm. I matched the dark mass to the missing portion of the placenta. It was now complete—how bewildering to think that such a small thing could cause such catastrophe.

Thank you, Mossius... Thank you, Momma.

"Continue rubbing—this is a basic step when a mother hemorrhages. Always check the placenta before burying it." The downward tug of the apprentice's mouth told me exactly what value he placed on my advice. "Retrieve the towels."

Over the next few minutes, the flow of blood lessened substantially.

"She may die yet," the apprentice muttered while placing the stack of linens in my hands.

"Quit saying such things in front of your very much alive, patient," I whispered. The mother, whose glassy eyes stared at the tiny bundle on the bed, was slowly regaining her presence of mind. But the most difficult part of her journey had yet to come.

I cleaned the mother's thighs and changed out the heap of blood-soaked towels below her. She turned her head and her exhausted gaze found mine.

"Give me my baby," she breathed raggedly.

I caught a movement in my periphery.

"No. Protector, this is where I draw the line." The healer woke but remained sitting on the floor, rubbing his neck. "There is no life in the child, seeing it would only harm her mental capacities."

"I want my baby," she pleaded.

I couldn't take my eyes from hers. The red-ringed pools of her desperation would live with me now. How horrific to lose something you worked so hard to create.

My heart shattered. I remembered this part too. It hadn't happened often, but when it did, the devastation was like no other.

I crawled over the birthing bed and took the bundle in my arms. Hot tears rolled down my cheeks and flowed down my chest.

But I couldn't.

I didn't have the strength to pull the thin covering from its little face, even if it was the mother's wish.

"How do I help you?" Cato stood behind me.

I crooked my finger, and he brought his ear to my mouth.

"I... I can't look. My heart can't take it."

When he nodded, the soft hair that curled around his ear ran across my lips.

With a tenderness one would not expect of a man in his profession, Cato lifted the babe from my arms. His heavily scarred hands unwrapped the child's coverings, and he rocked the little one gently as he walked the infant to its mother and placed the babe on her chest.

Cato sat down next to her and listened as she spoke to him in weak whispers.

"My boy is beautiful." The mother trailed a loving finger down the perfectly formed profile of her babe.

Cato nodded and hummed his agreement.

I squeezed my eyes shut, trying in vain to stop the tears that seemed to flow in infinite supply.

"Padrig will be so upset. It should have been me—not our precious boy."

"He will be relieved that you are well, and that he has not suffered two losses this day," Cato assured her as he swept back the sweat-soaked brown hair that hung limply in front of her eyes.

She kissed the little one and brushed his cheek lightly with her own.

"He will want him entombed in the state yard, but I would like him placed next to his sister, near the apple tree on our estate—I could visit them both there."

My eyes snapped open, and the tears ceased.

The blackness closed in. Would they dare keep a mother from her children?

My skin tingled—fiery prickles ran across my shoulders, and my stomach roiled, threatening to spill its contents.

I'd had enough of this fucking place for a lifetime.

"C-cat-Protector. I'm ill." Cato's head flew up. "My vision swims."

He was on his feet in an instant.

"Healer, see to the mother and child." He glared up at the man, who was a head taller than himself. "You struck His Highness's betrothed—prepare for an audience with the Council."

Were I not on the brink of throwing up, I would have taken enjoyment in watching the healer recoil like he'd been scalded.

"Come." Cato helped me to my feet and escorted Allaine and me to my apartments. On the way, he paused and waited every time I was overcome by dry heaving, not leaving my side until we were ensconced in the safety of my chamber. By then, I was back in control of the shadows that lurked behind my eyes.

"See her bathed, Lady Allaine."

Cato bowed at the hip and left without another word.

Chapter 11

Never Go to Sleep Angry

Unless You're Smashing the Patriarchy

"You should join me, Allaine. Today was—"

"Eira." I opened one eye and watched my tall companion as she offloaded the books hidden around her person. "We need to talk boundaries."

I sank further into the almost painfully hot water, letting it work its wonders on my battered body. My hip ached and my shoulder burned, but it was the malaise in my mind that felt the rawest. By the dull tone of her voice, I knew Allaine was feeling similarly.

"I'm sorry for putting you into the situations I did today, especially without preparing you for what you might witness. My mother always prepped me if she knew the birth would be a tough one. I've not been so considerate." I splashed the hot water over my chest and watched my skin turn red.

Like I was wont to do, I rushed in headlong. I'd not given thought to anything other than getting into that room.

"No, not that. Stealing books is nothing. I've lifted a host of more valuable items... Nobody searches the broken girl, Eira. And the birth, you saved her."

I spared Allaine a look. I still didn't have a solid read on her.

"What then?" I asked. I needed to get to the crux of the issue quickly, as my mental capacity for dealing with others was dwindling.

"It's the nudity. Eira, I have seen *my own* boobs less than I have seen yours."

I shook my head and saturated my hair while searching her face.

She was serious. Absolutely, actually, serious.

"Theft gets a go-ahead, but breasts are plain out? What bothers you about them?"

"Goddess alive, I hate myself for what I am about to say," she replied.

"I'd rather you be a truthful prude than a lying one."

I kicked out and made a little splash, but she still didn't look me in the eye. This really was an issue.

"Out with it," I said, becoming more irritated by the second.

"Breasts are a spouse's domain," she said, clipping off each of her words.

"Archaic Monwyn bullshit," I muttered under my breath.

Allaine came to my side and laid her long body out on the chaise. She stared up at the ceiling while she chewed on her lip and pressed her thumb deeply into her shoulder socket.

"Well, old-fashioned Monwyn or not, Eira, I am fine committing felonies by your side, but that does not mean I will eschew our cultural practices. If anyone ever does choose me, I want to have saved *all* of me for them."

Allaine kicked off her leather shoes and let her leg fall beside her. Her long and thin foot skimmed the surface of the water.

Though it rankled me, I had to acknowledge that her opinion was just as valid as my own.

"Allaine, if you prefer keeping your tits pure, then that's the right decision for you. Just promise me you'll choose a partner you like—one who won't treat you like a possession or flick your nose when he, she, or they're aggrieved." I turned my body on the submerged bench and laid my head against the side of the tub.

"I will need suitors before I can promise to reject them." She laughed her gruff little laugh, and I smiled to myself.

We passed the time in silence, her rhythmic kicking lulling me into a sense of tranquility.

"I was terrified."

I didn't have to ask what she was referring to.

"Same," I admitted. I closed my eyes and sent a silent prayer to Mossius, asking that the mother survive. The reality was, the apprentice had been right; she might not.

"It was actually the most horrific thing I have ever seen. Is blood normal?"

I nodded my head.

"Not that much, typically, but yes, it is."

I couldn't recall the first birth I'd attended or even the first where there were complications, but a few of them stuck with me, even years later. How strong women were when they brought life into the world—and when they saw it pass beyond this realm.

"We don't attend births here like they do in other kingdoms. It's between the experts and the mother."

I nodded absentmindedly. I'd learned of the Monwyn birthing practices while attending Matters of Unity at Verus and still found them shocking.

"Back home, when a woman nears her time, all of the town's matriarchs visit her. If there's a loss, like the one today, they let the mother mourn and take turns caring for her home until she's more stable. I plan to speak to Ambrose on the matter. The attending healer should have known how to handle the situation. It's rare, but not so uncommon that it wouldn't have been written down in some text or passed along by his mentor."

Allaine did turn then, seemingly unbothered by my chest bobbing above the waterline. I crossed my arms anyway and sank further down.

"You think His Highness will change one hundred years of Monwyn tradition?"

I shrugged and then turned my attention to digging the gore out from under my nails.

"People call Nortia backward. If that's the case, this place is positively primitive. I'll put speaking to him on the top of my list."

"You have a list?"

"I will when you procure a stack of parchment for me."

Allaine's mouth fell open and then turned into her brilliantly toothy smile.

"I'll have Bem fetch some while you wash. Please ensure you are *covered* when I return."

"Yes, my lady." I sharked my hand through the water and then flourished my wrist like a practiced courtier.

"We may not survive your period if you are this much of an asshole the whole time."

She left, and for the first time in a while, I was completely alone.

The cathartic flow of tears could finally come.

How many women had lost their lives here? How many had lain bleeding while the healers did nothing more than mop up the blood?

I dunked my head under the water and scrubbed violently at my hair and body. The scrape of my nails helped me feel something other than anguish.

As I toweled my hair, I rifled through the nightgowns that had been placed in my closet. The winters here better be frigid, or I'd have to go back to sleeping naked. Then Allaine really would lose her mind.

I chose the gown made from the lightest material. It was long and blue and had frilly layers of ruffles at its hem. I padded over to the toilet to relieve myself and put the gown over my head while seated. Sure enough, when I wiped, spots of pink showed on the linen scrap. After tossing the soiled wipe into the bucket of water and ammonia, I folded a handful of fresh ones and layered them into my underwear. That would have to do.

"I need a plan," I said to a dark green plant crowned with little yellow flowers. I grabbed the books Allaine had stacked on the counter and brought them with me to the bed.

We'd managed to abscond with six volumes.

One was a mythology book I wanted the moment my eyes fell upon the title. *Mountain Myths and the Creatures of Old*. Cato hadn't had time to fill me in on trolls or the like, and if I ran into some other supernatural something, I wanted to know what I was dealing with. Two of the tomes were about gardening and botanicals. *Ærtan Rainbow: Propagation and Planting for the Mountain Climes* looked like a brightly colored children's book with lots of images and step-by-step guides, and the other, *Horticultural Study for the Advanced Botanist: Plant Theory and Progression*, may as well have been written in another language.

The remaining three, I had to admit, were the random grabs of a woman caught up in an anger-filled adrenaline high. One was a cookbook, another a devotional, and lastly, one was called *The Model Conduct of a Man in Harness*.

The last title made me miss my own soldier.

I'd hoped, rather foolishly, that our budding romance would involve wrapping up in each other's bodies every night and setting the sheets aflame with our lovemaking, but alas, so far that hadn't panned out. This morning's antics had just whetted my appetite for him even more... and now I wasn't sure *when* I'd see him next.

Allaine entered the main room, humming the same tune she had plucked out in the solarium.

"A nightgown? You are due at dinner in an hour," she said.

"I'm begging off. Can my dinner be sent here?"

Allaine tossed a leather-bound booklet of parchment on the bed and flung a pen atop it.

"Can you... I don't know... think of everything you need at once, and then send me on your errands?"

I crawled into the bed and grabbed my supplies.

"You know, I think being a lady's maid is your true life's calling. You're so selfless, so patient, and so caring."

She rolled her eyes so hard I thought they'd get stuck and then strutted back out the door.

Okay, list making.

I need one for identifying and caring for plants, and another for fixing the king. That one needs to be written in code. Allaine could help me sort through the plants over the next few days, and I'd need to gauge the brothers' levels of "freaking out" before broaching the issue of their father again.

I turned to a page in the middle of the journal and at the top wrote, "Assisting the Chef." I didn't know if conjuring functioned like following a recipe, but I had a cookbook amongst the others here and needed plausible deniability if someone meddled with my journal.

I began scribbling the outline of my plan.

Assisting the Chef

Step 1: Find out where the kitchens are located so you can get to know the chef better.

Step 2: Discuss the ingredients needed for making a delicious meal.

Step 3: Make a list of the people the chef has created special courses for and determine which foods have tantalized their taste buds and which have not.

I could only think of three steps at the moment—find out where the king did his dirty deeds, figure out how magic worked, and determine who he was conjuring upon and observe them for a period of time. *Oh, one more.*

Step 4: Find out what's in the chef's special cakes that makes me so happy.

Determining why being near him made me feel so calm and content was a priority, and only the chef/king could answer that.

I laid my journal down and rubbed my lightly cramping stomach before perusing my plant-based books and compiling a list of items I'd need. There was so much more to gardening than putting stems in the dirt.

The doors of the common room opened and then slammed shut.

Ambrose and Cato were arguing back and forth about something, and both came bursting loudly into my haven. Allaine followed a few paces behind—her panic filled eyes shifting frantically from side to side over the top of Cato's head.

My men were home. *Goddess help me.*

"What have you eaten today? Have you consumed anything not delivered by Bem or Allaine? Any medicines taken?" Cato launched into a series of questions while laying the back of his hand against my forehead.

"No, I—"

"No fever." He looked at Ambrose before snatching a pillow from behind my head and pushing my back to the mattress. He laid his ear on my chest and held a finger in the air, effectively shushing the others.

"The beating of her heart is steady," he assured his brother.

"Will you all stop? I'm fine." I smacked the top of his head twice.

"So, you are lying then?" Cato hefted me back up by the arm and caught my chin in his hand.

"No, prickface—Protector. My courses have begun, and I have cramps and no access to the necessities I require," I ground out through clenched teeth.

From the corner of my eye, I saw Ambrose's face crumple. He sank down and sat on the edge of the bed, facing away. His chest visibly deflated and his shoulders sagged low.

"Allaine, you are dismissed for the evening. Thank you for your help today." She bobbed her head and all but ran from the room. I pushed away the hand, still monitoring my pulse, and crawled my way to Ambrose.

I got up on my knees and wrapped my arms around his neck from behind.

"My protective and strong, Black Bear," I said, placing a kiss on his temple. "The chances were less than slim, but I know you were taking the role of becoming a father very seriously. I'm so sorry you're hurting."

He tilted his head back and rested it heavily on my shoulder. His lower lip trembled and I held him closer.

"Ultimately, I know you are right. I think not knowing my own parentage made the idea of having a child more meaningful, though. My own life was more important all of a sudden."

I kissed his fuzzy cheek and rocked him gently. I hurt for him, even if *I* felt relief.

"You know what? I bet we'll have lots of fun trying in the future—yes? When we decide the time is right, it will take a lot more than once a week to conceive, and I know there are many interesting positions that the healers recommend—from the back, ass in the air. Super deep penetration to send your semen soaring. All the fun for the best odds of fertilization..."

A loud sputtering cough came from beside us. *Poor Cato.*

"Calm down, Cat, she rightfully won a year and a half before I get a babe on her."

"Two years," I said, remembering differently.

"Don't press your luck. This prime specimen of manhood will reproduce with unmatched swiftness. I imagine we will conceive within a week's time."

"I'm sure we will. Now—because you all enjoy living in fucking antiquity—there are a few things I need you to do."

"I believe I have an engagement, state matter and all." Ambrose sighed and tried to rise, but I held him in place.

"Fine." He nestled his nose against my neck, content to be there for the moment. "What do you want?"

"First, you need to figure out a way to make it look like you checked these books out. If you can't, your Scholar is likely to call for my arrest... and if you haven't heard yet, after attempting to shove his hands down my dress—"

Ambrose bolted to his feet, knocking me backward onto the bed.

He and Cato collided at the door, each vying to be the first one out.

"She is *my* wife, Cat, move or be moved."

"And she is my—"

"Get back here!" I hollered at them both, "Right now, turn around."

Cato's chest was heaving, and Ambrose wore the same expression he had when he'd clubbed the troll to death—bitter and deadly.

"What? Are you going to kill the nonagenarian? Sit down." I pointed to the end of the bed, and both came back into the room, but neither sat.

"Look, he wouldn't stop calling me names and hurling accusations, so I gave him what he wanted"—I crossed my arms and looked between the brothers—"and took my clothes off."

"You did WHAT?" Ambrose bellowed while slapping his hands against his thighs.

"The books were down Allaine's dress, and he wasn't going to stop until I proved myself innocent, which leads me to the bigger issue here."

"What the fuck, Eira?" Ambrose clenched his hands into fists, squeezing and releasing them over and over. Cato, on the other hand, was having trouble keeping his expression neutral; the corner of his lip kept twitching, and he cleared his throat repeatedly. "You have *got* to keep those milk monsters contained. My wife's tits—"

"—Belong to your wife," I interjected. "And I'll show them to whomever I want."

Cato took a step forward and then sat down next to me. He reached over my thighs and pulled me onto his lap.

"You can show them to me anytime the mood strikes."

He crooked his finger and motioned for me to come nearer. I brought my lips a scant half-inch from his. I could smell his alluring scent, and I could see his chest hair just above the collar of his shirt. How his body hair could drive me wild, I couldn't fathom, but just that little teasing flash whetted my appetite.

Brief pulses of excitement fluttered through me.

"Do you want to see them now?" I let my voice drop low and watched his pupils enlarge. I twisted my finger around the dark-gold hair near his temple.

"Yes," he breathed. His calloused fingertips traced my high neckline. "This gown is hideous." He grabbed a fistful of the ruffles at my neck.

Surging to his feet, Cato dumped me onto Ambrose's lap.

"Godsdamn!" I screeched, ringing my arms around his neck to stay steady.

A few seconds later, a servant appeared at the entrance bearing a tray. I hadn't heard him enter at all.

"Troth Solnna's meal, Highness, as ordered."

"You may enter." Cato, standing as rigid as a Verus soldier, nodded in my direction.

The servant, dressed in formal livery of blue and gold, walked in and sat the platter on the end of the bed. Celery and carrots, a clear broth, and a small mound of shredded chicken made up the contents of the meal.

"You may take it back now... please," I said in a polite tone.

The servant, still bent in a low bow, flicked his eyes up at Ambrose, clearly confused.

"I'm not ill. I don't need to be fed as though I were convalescent."

Still hunched over, the servant's eyes sought out Cato.

"Th-this is standard fair, ma'am, T-troth Solnna."

"Ambrose, my seductive snow-goose, on what did you dine this evening?" I slowly looked up into his face.

"Ahh, it was a fine roast; you could not imagine how tender it was. It was served with a medley of tubers fried in tallow and..."

My blood ran hot. Molten level hot.

I couldn't be sure I hadn't levitated off Ambrose's lap, but I *could* see with certainty that the brothers knew they were in for a storm.

I cocked my head to the side, staring Ambrose down first.

"This..." I balled my fists. "This brings me to my next point of discussion." I swiveled my head to address the servant. "Take this tray and kindly get out. Protector, tip the man for his trouble."

Moving as fast as Cato in a tussle, the servant snatched the tray up and turned on his heel, shaking his head the whole time.

Cato moved nearer Ambrose, and I leveled my gaze at the brothers.

"Things will change around here, or I *will* be taking my chances with the Gaeans."

Ambrose had the audacity to cross his eyes, and Cato furrowed his brows so severely that I wondered if he'd mistaken me for an opponent. "So far, just today, I have learned that your healers are morons, that you purposefully keep women stupid, and that you restrict their diets, which is, I'm guessing, another garbage preference your men have. That, and I can't even access my own birth control without your permission." My body shook, and my voice trembled with righteous indignation.

"Cato, you are the one who loves her. Weigh in, brother." Ambrose peered down his nose and stifled a yawn. He then pulled his timepiece from his pocket and glanced at the time.

"Listen to me well, Ambrose." I walked up to the seated giant and brought my face nearly to the tip of his perfectly straight nose. I batted the watch from his hand and sent it flying across the room. "I will *not*, do you hear me, *not*, give birth in a place that will sit by while I hemorrhage to death, and I will burn this palace to ash before I allow our daughters to be spoken of like your uncle did your own mother."

You could have cut the tension in the room like a knife through candied fruit cake.

"Now *you* listen, Eira," Ambrose growled.

I ripped at the ridiculously frilly hem of my gown and dropped to my knees.

"As you command, almost-husband, lord and master, please tell me how to live. Guide me with your manly, man-brain, for it certainly knows how I think and feel."

"*Goddess alive!*" he hollered. "Cat, will this creature venture forth every time it menstruates? How often does it happen? Twice per year, every other month?"

I whacked at Ambrose's stupid knees, smacking them both until my palms stung.

Cato smiled at his brother and chuckled.

Wrong move, my love. Wrong. Fucking. Move.

"Are you entertained, Cato?" I turned on him, and from the way his lips angled downward and one brow shot up, he was fully aware that he'd fucked up. "I suppose this might be funny to the very man who has upheld these laws and benefited from these customs for years. Tell me, while making plans to kidnap a woman from Verus, did you keep a tally of the women who died in childbed? YOU ARE NO INNOCENT!" I shouted, stumbling over my gown while trying to rise. Cato crossed his arms over his chest and looked at me blandly while the muscle in his jaw ticked rapidly. "I want nothing more than to punch that cheek back to stillness right now."

Bolts fired. Target hit.

"There are things that cannot be changed, Eira, and Monwyn traditions run deep." Cato closed the distance between us and took my hands in his. "And we have bigger issues right now—keeping you safe outweighs all."

"You're wrong. I will never be safe in a place where I have no value. And don't you dare say I'm different, or have goddess blood... or it's because you love me." He lowered his face, tilted my chin up with his rough hand, and looked into my eyes. "Love them too, Cato."

"I would venture to say that those things make you a great deal more important."

Not getting it.

"You would *venture*? Okay. Well, until you learn your aunt's given name, see her and acknowledge her existence, I refuse any *venture* with you—oh, if your narrow mind doesn't comprehend what I'm saying, it means we're not fucking until you fix it." I glared over my shoulder at Ambrose, who was picking fluff from his ridiculously ostentatious, silver-embroidered cuff. "And until one of you procures the herbs I need, you're both cut off, contract or not."

Cato rolled his shoulders backward, which made his neck crack and pop. His nose flared at the corners, and there was an edge to his voice. "You would not deny me."

"I *am* denying you. And I'll scream until every guard comes running if you so much as brush a fingertip against my arm. How would that look, Cato? Caught with your brother's betrothed. Oh, wait. Silly me, it's probably fine. I imagine the Monwyn consequence for rape is also nonexistent."

Cato's hand shot out, and his fingers sank into my bicep.

"Do not *ever* use my name in conjunction with that word, not ever." He shook my arm, emphasizing his words. "It is time you calmed yourself, Eira. If you wish to speak constructively about the issues you have brought forth, we will do so appropriately."

I shrugged his hand off and took a step backward.

"Excellent, ink me in for the soonest appointment you have, Protector." I moved across the room and stood next to the door. "Gross. That title seems so off-putting, now that I know it extends to only half your citizens. Both of you, get out."

Ambrose came to stand before me.

"You *will* come to my bed. We have an agreement."

I breathed in deeply, attempting to repress the desire to shove my fist into his crotch and mash his testes like butter in a bowl of boiled turnips.

"Of course, betrothed mine, *if* you are able to secure my medication... but do remember how sharp my teeth can be. Also, I need menstrual supplies, something for my pain and—"

"Something to render you unconscious?"

"No, I need a sharp blade, some alcohol, and a shovel."

Ambrose paled, and his gaze shifted to his brother.

They were looking over my head, no doubt communicating, as they did, with no words. Ambrose's fingers found mine. He patted my hand and blinked at me like I only had one oar in the water.

"Eira, you will never be strong enough to physically restrain—"

Merrias's fucking blade.

"For my plants! I'm not ready to bury you yet, but you better believe if I was... Cato, get me some real food."

"Will it stop you from shrieking like a godsdamned wraith?" he asked, rubbing his temples with his hands.

A chill, colder than an unexpected snow squall, blew down my spine.

"Do wraiths exist?" I whispered, suddenly less concerned with smashing the patriarchy and more concerned with a nefarious, nether-born entity fusing themselves to my soul.

He nodded, his expression serious.

"Ambrose, you sleep. I will procure the items she needs—Bem is at the door."

Ambrose hurried to leave, but I swung my arm out to stop him. His distrusting eyes narrowed to slits.

I pointed to his jaw, and then snapped my finger back toward my mouth.

"Good night." I popped a kiss on one of his fuzzy cheeks and then the other.

"Good night, wife."

He pecked my cheek and tapped my nose with his pointer finger.

"Well, I hate *the fuck* out of that," Cato grumbled. He stormed out of the room with a cackling Ambrose on his tail.

CHAPTER 12

IT'S ALL FUN AND NAMES

A few hours passed, and my eyelids grew heavy.

I'd need a dictionary to decipher the more advanced botany book; words like rhizome and cultivar didn't exist in my current vocabulary. Recruiting another agent to retrieve the tomes I required would take time, and I couldn't stomach the thought of having to apologize to the Scholar and beg for readmission. The rainbow book proved to be much more my speed, with its hand-drawn pictures and more simplistic descriptions. I was already able to identify some of the plants I'd been given. I knew I had an aloe vera, and remembered that it was a component used to calm my skin after the painful ordeal of the Grooming. It would need to be placed in sandy soil in order for it to thrive. Another flower I was fairly certain I recognized was a compass plant. It was tall and had yellow flowers, and according to the book, it liked to grow along lake borders. I'd need to get it out of the bathing chamber quickly to keep it alive—it needed way more sun than it was currently receiving.

"Am I allowed admittance?"

I flung my head up.

Cato had entered the room without making a sound, or I was so entirely engrossed in the topic of fish guts as fertilizer that I hadn't paid attention. He walked through the threshold with his hands full of items and his leather satchel hanging heavily from his shoulder. He began unloading his burden. Two canvas bags were placed on the bed's end, and from a third, he pulled out three items covered in checkered linen towels. I could smell the delectably savory goodness that was hidden from my eyes.

Silently, he arranged the offerings, lining up each item in a perfect row.

I'd been so hateful to him earlier and knew well that there were far superior methods of communicating. Even though I still stood by my proclamations, ranting and yelling rarely yielded results. I was just so overwhelmed. From my studies, I'd known that Monwyn would be different, culturally. But I had assumed their deeper issues would be displayed more subtly. The indignities heaped on me in a single day proved that notion incorrect.

Cato turned and walked toward the door.

"I... I really miss you," I said as he made to leave.

A smile tugged at one corner of his mouth and then the other.

Just like that, the frostiness of my earlier anger all but melted away.

"I wasn't going anywhere." He pulled the door closed. "I have arranged the night off—and after cleaning up yet another of His Majesty's grotesque messes—I could not wait to view something as beautiful as you."

I tossed back the covers and drew the cumbersome gown up over my knees.

"Get in here. Take your clothes off first," I commanded. I couldn't wait to have him under me, above me—his lips on mine.

"You first."

I could already see the crotch of his pants becoming snug. I jerked my ruffled hem, pulled it over my head, and kneeled before him in nothing but my underwear.

Like a beacon in the night, his eyes went immediately to my piercing.

"Now you," I breathed, already anticipating the view. His hands settled on the back of his neck, and he pushed his torso forward in a deep stretch. "Not fast enough." I crawled to the end of the bed, pulled his shirttails from his pants, and splayed my hands across his stomach before letting them drift up to comb through the dark hair on his chest. He pulled the still buttoned shirt over his shoulders, and I laid my head in the center of his sternum—cradled between his dense muscles.

My near-constant trepidation was silenced. The anxiety, the fear... gone.

I swallowed hard and sniffled, attempting to stop my tears of relief. I didn't want our first night to be ruined by my rapidly oscillating emotions.

"Eira?" Cato said while trailing his fingers down my spine. "Talk to me. Share your burdens." He grabbed his discarded shirt and worked it over my head without ever fully breaking contact with my body. "Everything else can wait."

Welp.

Tears flowed. His gesture caught me off guard and punched me in the emotional gut. I'd been forced to leave everything I owned at Verus, and if I could have grabbed a single item before running, it would have been my father's old, oversized linen shirt. I used my gown to wipe my eyes before climbing to the far side of the bed.

Cato walked to the hearth, built up the fire, and turned down the room's glowing lamps. He stopped at the end of the bed and held up the first canvas bag.

"Garden stuff in this one," he lifted the other, "personal stuff in this one."

"Th-thank you," I choked out, still caught up in my emotions. I hugged his shirt around me and inhaled its familiar scent.

He lowered the bags to the floor, and after wrestling with his boots, he unlaced his pants, folded them neatly, and laid them over the footboard.

"Talk." He slid in next to me and scooted himself over until my side pressed fully against him.

I had so much to say, and yet, I didn't know where to start.

"Cato, do you trust me?"

Silence.

Like my anxiety, his chest rose steadily.

"I trust you," he said in a serious tone. "There are times when I question your choices or feel as if your decisions are not as sound as they could be. But the results of your actions tend to be surprisingly inclined toward the positive." He placed his lips on my forehead. "And you should see how provocative your furious little self can be."

"You know, I find your ability to insult and then reel me back in to be equally as profound." I chuckled aloud, feeling calmer by the second. "Okay, so I want to show you something, but I need you to really trust me, Cato. Really, really." His body stiffened just ever so slightly, but he nodded. I squirmed out of his arms and grabbed my journal. "Read this."

Cato scanned the open pages and sighed. He ran a hand over his jaw and then worked the flesh of his temple in small circles with his fingertips.

"You thought to hide your plans by turning the king into a kitchen servant?"

"No, Cato, I knew *you* would see through it—but your father has appeared twice now without your knowledge, and we need a strategy."

Silence again.

I didn't have to look to know he was scowling. I could feel his gaze burning the back of my head.

"He has presented me with new challenges, yes."

"Which is why we need to change tactics." I twisted, raising myself on my knees, and straddled his legs. I needed him to look me in the eyes and understand how serious I was.

"And you mean to sway me to your cause by riding me until thinking is nigh impossible?"

I inched closer to his chest and slid my arms around his neck.

"Would that work?"

"Most assuredly." Cato put his hands on my behind and massaged the flesh there. He kneaded and rubbed my cheeks, pressing my pubic bone against his burgeoning erection. I laid my forehead against his and he shifted a hand to his underclothes, easing himself into a more comfortable position.

"I must be allowed to have contact with your father."

"No." With both hands on my shoulders, he pushed me backward until I was sitting up straight.

"No? Cato, this is what I'm here for. It's my choice. It's *my* path. What reason have you to deny me? This was your original plan."

He searched my eyes, his thin golden aura contracting as his pupils expanded.

"Eira, the thought of you with him... He has killed, abused, and tainted so much of what I once held dear. As you know, I purposefully swore off attachments so that I could tend to him and the kingdom. I thought I could keep him from taking more from me if I had nothing... but then you stepped into my path."

I didn't yell, didn't rage, just listened as he continued.

"If he harmed you, I would spend the rest of my life in shackles. I would smile to the crowd before my body swung."

I traced the scar on his shoulder with my fingertip. His death was not something I would allow myself to contemplate. But still, I needed him to hear me.

"Cato, smell my wrist."

He arched a thick brow at the odd request, but when I raised my arm to his nose, his lids closed and his waning arousal swelled again.

"Do you think that's a normal reaction?"

He laced his fingers through my own and nipped and licked just below the thickest part of my palm. A little jolt, a tiny but pleasurable tingle, took me back to the first day I met him.

"Do you often smell a woman and become so aroused your penis could punch through ice?" His length was a pillar between my legs. Hard and proud. "Your uncle reacted this way as well." Darkness moved across his face. "Your father can smell it too, though he doesn't react like you or Septimus—praise the Goddess. This spot is where his lackey—the one who was meant to take me from the river—dug his nails into me and cut my flesh. It's the combination of my blood and the æther used to compel him. You see, Cato, I *must* speak with him again. He's the only person we know who may have knowledge about who or what I am."

Cato ground his teeth—I could hear them scraping together.

"And how do I quiet the mind that screams for me to deny you?"

I leaned forward and ran my nose against his smooth lips.

"Trust me. That's the only way. I don't think he means to harm me, Cato, and if he does, it's a risk I'm willing to take to give you back your father—to give Monwyn back *their* father, and to stop the spread of what once nearly destroyed Ærta."

Warm hands skimmed down my waist and rested on the outsides of my thighs.

"I will concede only if I am present when you meet. If I feel you are in danger, you are not to question my actions or commands."

Against my forearm, I could feel the pulse in Cato's wrist quicken.

"I agree. When next you see him, please set up a meeting. I'd like it to be located in the place he conjures so that I may—"

"Absolutely not."

I leaned back and looked skyward.

Womanly wiles it is.

"I'm awfully hot." I unbuttoned the top of my shirt and displayed an ample amount of cleavage.

"I am not some pubescent boy, Nortia."

With a little shimmy, I let the shirt drift down my shoulders and pressed my arms together, which lifted my breasts closer to his face.

His tongue dipped out to moisten his lips. *Mmhmm.* In answer, I rocked forward and let my shirt fall from where it caught on the hard tips of my nipples.

"What about now?" I traced my tongue along the edge of his ear. "Hmmm?"

"Not a chance in the nether." His face remained impassive, and he sat as still as a statue.

I pushed back and stood up on the bed, using his shoulders to steady myself.

"Spread your legs."

He obeyed, and I stepped between them.

"Would you like to taste me, Cato? I recall you saying—the first time your head was between my thighs—that I was your new addiction."

His fingers wrapped around my ankles.

"If *you* relent, Eira, I will ensure you glimpse the afterlife. You deserve a thorough tongue-lashing." He smoothed his palms up my legs, lightly raking my skin with his nails.

Damn. There was a counter effect to my game of seduction. I was horny. And I could think of no better way to be sent to Merrias.

"Nope." I shrugged. I needed to up the ante in my gamble. "My current fantasies revolve around you spilling your hot streams into my tight little passage. The thought makes me uncontrollably aroused." *No lie detected.*

Cato snatched at the ties of his small clothes and pulled his cock free. He was thick and stood boldly at attention—his color deep and his veins engorged.

"Mount me, directly."

My resolve melted like a snowshower in the sun.

"Let's blame this failed coercion on my recent brush with conjuration."

I pulled at my laces but stopped short.

"The blood, it will be such a mess and—"

"I give no fucks, not a single one." His penis bobbed, and I swear to the goddess it was waving to me, beckoning me to its cause. "The thought of your blood mingling with the taste of you, gods have mercy on my soul."

I jerked the remaining lace at my hip and dropped the bloodied mess to the side of the bed. Thankfully, it landed soiled side up.

"Now, that is *my* woman." He looked up at me and ran his hand down his length. The muscles in his arm shifted and tensed, and his breathing hitched when his hand glided back over his tip. "You actually smacked your lips, hungry goddess." He laughed and held himself straight for my descent. "Wrap me in your heat, love."

I dropped to my knees and felt his thick crown poised at my entrance.

"Ohhh..." I lowered myself an inch. "I could come right—what are you do-ing?"

He slid his fist up his shaft, halting my ability to continue taking him in.

"There is a promise you have yet to make me." His eyes glittered wickedly. "Do you not recall it? No matter, allow me to remind you..."

Asshole. Fucking sexy, vile asshole. I was keenly aware of what he referred to.

"... The night you *thought* you saved me. Perhaps you have attempted to block the deceit from your mind... Recall if you will the injuries to your person and the lies you told me." He swept the back of his fingers across my clavicle. "I still see the faint bruise on your shoulder and the skin healing on your thumb. I will have your word now that you will never withhold information from me again... or we can stop here."

My mind screamed for me to promise him anything—my lusty vagina seconded the notion.

"I would have lied to you and met your father behind your back, you know... had you not trusted me."

"I expected nothing less. You are nothing if not determined."

Arousal coiled low in my stomach and snaked through my passage. I writhed against his fist, but he held firm.

"I don't want to lie to you, Cato. I don't want to hide things. But you must make me a promise in return. We will settle our differences together—until we are both satisfied with the outcome—you can't just make decisions for me."

He let his fist drop—just an inch—but what a divine inch it was.

His eyes crinkled at their corners as he watched my reactions.

"I can promise that, yes."

"Then we have an accord. No more fibbing."

Another inch.

"Fuck me until you can no longer breathe," he growled. "Then will I flip you over and take my fill."

He moved his hand and I—

Oh right.

I braced my knees, halting my descent.

"Your aunt's name?"

"Do not do this, Eira. Please, to fucking Derros, tell me you are joking."

Be strong. No unequal partnership, Eira. Don't give in to the dick.

I sat up and let his glorious fucking appendage fall from its home.

"No. Cato, I'm not. You can't expect me to give in to your requests and then also dismiss the issues that are important to me."

"Dellia?" His hands went to his head. "Mell-Melli something?"

"No, I'm afraid not."

I could have wept.

"Gods-fucking-dammit, Eira." Cato dumped me over and hit the ground running. "Don't you dare fall asleep... nether fucking—Lucila?"

I shook my head and shrugged my shoulders while watching him practically jump into his pants.

He ran out of the room at full speed.

"Ambrose," he hollered, "a shirt at once!"

With him gone, I located my discarded underwear and the bag of items he'd brought me. I changed into a soft, thick pad and took a little sniff of the painkiller. My cramps were light now, but tomorrow they'd be unbearable if they were like my normal, non-manipulated cycle. The medication smelled familiar, but I'd start with a small dose just to make sure I reacted well to its contents. Plus, if the healer had mixed it himself, I wanted to proceed with caution.

I scrunched Cato's shirt to my nose before pulling it back over my head.

I love him. I lust him too.

The door slammed loudly in the other room.

"Eira!" Cato shouted.

"Hang on." I looked at my reflection in the mirror, made my hair more presentable, and dabbed a little vanilla perfume behind my ears. *Goddess above, your daughter begs you... Let him know her name.*

When I passed through the door, he was shirtless again and was working his pants down. His coppery skin glowed warmly in the firelight, the shadows emphasizing the planes of his wide chest.

"They left the palace yesterday. I ran the distance to their residence. They were gone. I ran to the king's library." He hopped on one foot, pulling the other free from a pant leg. "The original lineage book is still in the scriptorium, and the copy was, of course, sent with Ambrose to Verus. I threatened the Scholar, but he was unable to recall the name on account of a 'great scare' this afternoon... and then I found Septimus's manservant, who was leaving the palace."

"And you've returned successful." I clapped my hands in excitement. I was still ready for him. My energy renewed itself and bound through me like a beaming light.

"Come to me, love." He wrapped me in his arms, and I circled his waist with my own. He gazed down at me, desire smoldering in his dark eyes. His lips parted.

"It's Rose."

"Cato!" I wailed. "No, it's not Rose! You didn't find out?" I shook in frustration. "I'm stupidly aroused, ridiculously turned on."

"Violet?" He walked our bodies back to the bed, kissing every inch of my face and neck. "He told me she was named after a flower, but he had never addressed her by a given name."

"No, damn you, not Violet." I dug my heels into the thick carpet.

"Verbena? Dahlia? Daisy? Fucking CONEFLOWER?" he hollered.

"No, no, no, and NO!"

He twisted my body and shoved my back, which brought my thighs to the bed's edge.

"Give in, Eira. Give up and I will find out come sunrise. I will hold the palace hostage until I am told... I will beat Septimus within an inch of his pitiful shit life. I will reintroduce myself appropriately as her kith and kin." Cato's knee pressed between my legs, and he pushed my back until my stomach was flush with the mattress. "I have never begged for flesh, but Eira, I am burning for you. Ambrose may call you his, but you are the *only* wife my body will know."

Wife.

Our future painted itself before my eyes—the gray hair, our wrinkles, and our laugh lines.

Cato thrust his hands under the back of my shirt and ran his calloused palms alongside my waist.

"Your curves—you were formed to fit me. I am convinced of this." Cato groaned behind me and pushed his hips into my backside. "Allow me to enter you, love."

He cupped my breasts from underneath and skimmed my taut nipples. I was unable to draw a cleansing breath. My man wanted me, and I craved him like a mug of warmed chocolate in an icebound Nortian winter. I lifted a knee to the mattress to open for—

Fuck.

Fuuuuck!

"C-Cato... no."

He stepped away from me and dropped to his knees. His ragged breaths filled the otherwise silent room. I turned around, uncomfortably aware of the aching throb of my arousal.

"This is too important, Cato." I kneeled by his side and took his face between my palms. His eyes were closed, and he gripped his thighs tightly. He was struggling to center himself.

"Then..." his words were strained, "then it is important to me as well."

Could feelings grow deeper in an instant?

"Oh, Cato," I said, pressing myself against him. I brought my mouth to his and kissed him softly... almost shyly. "I don't have words adequate enough to tell you how meaningful that is to me."

"Your lips around my cock would be sufficient," he murmured.

He was visibly frustrated—all tight muscles and still *very* hard.

Think, think, think.

"Ahem," I cleared my throat loudly. "Prepare yourself for an evening of contests!"

I thumped him on both shoulders and stood, placing my fists on my hips.

"Evandr?" he asked.

"Evandr." I nodded. The memory of being tossed about while holding onto the Scion's naked back flashed through my mind.

I took Cato's hands, placed the tips of his fingers on my brow, and prayed for us both.

Goddess, heal Evandr fully. Let him know life.

"Contest number one," I proclaimed, "A feat of constitution!" I let my eyes go round and swung my hand wildly around the chamber until it pointed to the still-wrapped foodstuffs. "Though I do not know the contents of the fare you have procured, dear sir, I challenge you!" I stabbed my finger at his stomach. "Whoever can eat the contents of their package first will be the victor. What's the prize you ask?" I cupped my hand around my ear and looked at Cato, who remained silent. "Eh, eh?"

Cato looked at me blandly. "What's the prize, Eira?" He asked in a monotone voice.

"The prize, *you ask?* Well, it's a..."

His bottom lip quivered in amusement. "Wait, no, let me choose. I want sex prizes. I demand nasty, filthy prizes, yes?" He perked up.

Goddess. Steering him away from the physical would be tough.

"A hand-drawn picture, you say? Yes, indeed! That is exactly the spoils the winner of this bout is to receive."

Cato puffed out his chest and inclined his head.

"I accept, but madam, since the moment you forced your delectable blood upon my person, I have been insatiable. I will eat you under the table... or on top of it if you prefer."

I ignored the fire in his eyes and went to grab the loosely wrapped bundles. The fat, flaky pastries had lost their warmth, but I could still smell the freshness of their crusts.

My stomach growled louder than three aggrieved Ambroses.

Cato crawled across the floor and dug into the pants he'd not bothered to fold. He located his timepiece.

"Ready... and..." As fast as a hare on the run, he stuffed the bready goodness in his mouth. "... Gwoo!"

"You cheater!" I yelled while I shoved the moon-shaped pie in my face.

Cato wagged his eyebrows suggestively and tossed in another chunk.

We chomped and chewed and made silly faces, hoping to throw each other off our game. In the end, he swallowed his last bite a mere second before I did.

"You unethical, ignoble Protector! I would have beat you had you played fair."

"Fair was not mentioned in the agreed upon terms... I play to win. Consequently, I demand my prize."

I leaned forward and flicked a flaky crumb from his beard. He caught my hand in his and pressed my fingertip to his lips. My stomach clenched as my heart took flight.

"Just a moment..." I hopped up and grabbed my pen and parchment, and doodled a quick scene. "... aaaand finished."

My rendering was breathtaking.

Reaching over the foot of the bed, I handed Cato his hard-earned winnings.

"Oh, oh gracious. These sticks are supposed to be..."

Looking down my nose at him, I adopted the haughtiest expression I could manage.

"It's you and me when we first met at Verus. You're the angry one, if you couldn't tell."

"Yes... yes." He twisted the paper upside down. "I see it now, I think. Those uneven slashes are my brows and the, uh, minuscule tombstone is my—"

"It's your scowly mouth all turned down..."

He blinked rapidly, continuing to survey my masterwork.

"So it is... I will cherish the work of such a talented artisan..." He paused. "Is this my perfect penis?"

I bent over and glanced at where he pointed.

"That's my leg, Cat, my whole ass leg."

He stared at me, and his gaze softened. A tender smile lit up his face.

"What?" I asked, looking around the room. He rose and joined me on the bed, lying on his side.

"Come here."

I knee-walked toward him and lay down, mirroring his position. "Eira, I am not sure why the Goddess gifted us each other, but every night and every single morning, when I am granted a new day, I thank her." He brushed his hand through my hair and moved closer, his solid stomach pressing against my soft one. Our chests met, and he reached behind my thigh and pulled my leg over his hip. "Some men run from this... some swear it off, never satisfied in the embrace of a single human. But how can they stray from the very eyes through which they see the world's beauty?" He tilted my chin and slid his knuckles along my jawline. "Do not look away, sweetling, never shy away from me."

I glanced back up and found myself caught in the sincerity that reflected in his expression. *He* was the conjurer, pulling me further into the spell he cast.

"I never considered a future where I'd become enamored with someone like you, Cato."

"Like me? What am I like?" He asked while drawing circles on the dip of my waist.

"Battle-hardened," I chuckled, "a man of means. I was looking forward to having my bodily itches scratched by a partner here or there. I had no plans to bind myself to anyone. Least of all someone so beautiful."

"Compared to Ambrose, Eira, I am quite average in looks."

"You are a god walking the mortal plane." I smiled softly at the copper blush that crept across his cheekbones. "A person who cares for their family, who is devoted to their kingdom. And I have never felt so wholly desired, Cato. It's wonderful and disconcerting, and..."

"... and I am happier in this moment than any other I have experienced in my life. But I am also more fearful," he finished my sentence.

I tucked my head under his chin and nestled into the crook of his neck. I blew lightly into the hair on his chest and watched the dark fluff dance.

"How can I ease your fears?"

"Will you give up on meeting with my father?"

"No."

"Perhaps you will consider *not* fighting for the salvation of Monwyn's womenfolk then? I can already see a storm brewing with you at its center."

My silence was answer enough.

"I suppose, then, I should prepare to spend the next decade dousing fires and putting down civil wars."

"Most likely. I already have a few ideas. For example, would it be possible to offer a food *choice* to the ladies at the palace? They could choose between their normal rabbit fare or something heartier—how many ladies reside here currently?"

"Right now? Seventy-five, not including their maids."

"Seventy-five! Cato, I was expecting you to say six or something. Where are they? Why don't they come to the solarium? Why haven't I seen them?"

He pulled his lips into his mouth and let them go with a *pop*. I knew I wouldn't like his answer.

"You will not like my answer."

I threw him a sidelong glance. "That's okay, because Ambrose and I are throwing a party, and only the women of the palace are invited," I said.

Cato raked a hand through his hair.

"You are? You have discussed this with His Highness?"

I turned my big blameless eyes on him.

"Mmhmm. Sure have."

He pinched the bridge of his slightly crooked nose between two fingers.

"Gorgeous little liar, I will need to call up an extra battalion when that occurs. Keep me abreast of your soirée plans."

"Will do. Now, can you please do one more thing for me?"

"You... you need something more than being permitted to actively dismantle what my family has built over their long, and might I say historied, tenure?"

He laid his forehead against mine and ran a hand up the middle of my back.

"I do. And this is even more crucial, Cato."

"Name it," he said, looking at me seriously.

I placed my hand against his cheek and locked my gaze on his.

"Discover your aunt's name. If I'm forced to spend another night without your perfect self lodged between my legs, the safety of your citizens will be the least of your worries."

CHAPTER 13

MOUNTAIN MOUSE

Every time I stirred in the night, Cato woke and kissed my cheeks, chin, or nose. We'd stayed up late discussing my thoughts on how husbands could still feel protective of their wives and daughters while at the same time allowing them more freedom.

I made him aware of how Allaine was both over-sheltered *and* cast aside as a woman with a challenge, and though he was initially concerned that her limitations would compromise her ability to serve me, I assured him that her intellect was a much sharper weapon than any she could hold in two hands. He understood how the Monwyn emphasis on bodily perfection kept her from certain opportunities, no matter how bright her mind was.

"Eira, I dreamed of that mother last night. I would not survive the loss of our child, or one born of you and my brother."

"You would, Cato, like the mothers and fathers who have suffered likewise since the beginning of time. Trust that the little one lies protected in the arms of Merrias."

He nodded, and his lashes fluttered shut once more.

In the morning, before he left, Cato carried me to the bathing chamber, where I spent an hour doubled over from the pain of my monthly flow.

For the next two days, I remained ensconced in my bedroom, begging out of my commitments in favor of nestling in my bed and reading my books.

On the third day, Bem informed me that a location had been arranged for the flora currently taking up space in the bathing chamber. As my flow was much lighter now, I decided to venture out and meet the lead gardener.

"Praise Josa, I am at the end of my rope with all that *dirt* in my space. Eira, the weather is turning. You may want to wear more than a light layer," Allaine called out from the main room.

Today, she'd painted me in hues of peach and pink and insisted on adding in a few light brown locks to create even more volume in my hair. When full enough for her satisfaction, she pulled back small sections on the left side of my head and secured them with a triad of golden barrettes. The flower-shaped fasteners, gifted to me by none other than Lord Ethens, were painstakingly enameled by hand. Ambrose had sent them to me two days ago with a note insisting I wear them when I felt "more like myself and less like a leaking shew."

I opted to wear a simple woolen gown of amethyst today, and per Allaine's suggestion, grabbed one of the new creations that the Millanderers had sent over. A servant had come with this particular gem yesterday morning. The teal coat's hem hit my knees—Monwyns seemed to prefer floor length. Instead of sleeves that buttoned tightly from elbow to wrist, these belled out over the first knuckle of my hand, and when I folded them back, brilliant red stars and tiny little moons were embroidered on their golden undersides.

"One last touch... this one is sent from..." Allaine poked her head around the bathing chamber entrance and glanced at the tag on the wooden box she held. "The Honorable Lord Tom? I don't think I know a—"

I ran the distance and startled Allaine, who reflexively jerked the box to her chest.

"Tom was a good friend of Ambrose's—from Verus."

She nodded and lifted out a glittering brooch.

I wasn't a woman who dreamt of jewels or finery, but I decided then and there that receiving the occasional prize would be just fine.

Tom.

I smiled fondly at the name Cato had hated so much.

Allaine held the creation up to the light. Three whales, whose bodies were made of gold, studded with chips of onyx and diamond, stared back at me. The pod circled a square cut sapphire the size of my thumbnail, and fixed strands of seed pearls made it look like the orcas were surrounded by bubbles.

The inclination to run through the halls and leap into Cato's arms overwhelmed me, but instead, I nodded and smiled politely.

"It's a lovely bauble, Eira."

Bauble my ass. Relinquish my treasure or I'll maul you as I snatch it up for my dragon's hoard!

"Tom was well off then? Do you know where he stood on giant-sized ladies?"

I'll stand over your giant-sized grave, if you don't step the fuck back.

I shook my head politely and flicked my eyes to my maid's.

"Allaine, you are the perfect height. You are jaw-droppingly statuesque. And he works in government. Last I heard, he had taken up with one of the instructors at Verus—a skinny fellow with intense eyes, poisoned us all at an Obligate luncheon. I'll be sure to inquire about height preferences among Ambrose's *other* eligible pals."

"Not holding my breath."

Oh, Allaine.

She pinned the brooch to one of the lapels that flared out across my chest.

"That's where you'd be wrong. If Verus taught me anything, it's that people are attracted to all varieties. Despite Ambrose being a flawless specimen, the Obligates came in all shapes and sizes, with an abundance of differences that made them unique. Some had blemished skin, and one had flesh that was both brown and cream... He was gorgeous. Others were more heavyset, one had gapped teeth, and another had the most beautiful eyes you've ever encountered. One had breasts larger than your head, and one was honestly devoid of any color at all. When it came to who got close to each other or who paired off sexually, it was never who you might suspect, especially after people started sharing intense experiences."

Allaine looked unconvinced.

"Look, lady-giant, all I'm saying is, don't sell yourself short." Allaine pursed her pretty lips. "Wrong choice of words, but I don't give a shit how people here have made you feel—no, that's a lie—I give a major shit about that. What I'm trying to say is, if you want a husband or a lover who is worthy of you, your height, your arm—none of that will matter to them—or rather it will, but because it's just another thing that makes you, you. You can't take yourself off the market because you assume people won't like the product. You at least have to give them a chance to check out the goods."

Allaine squinted a single blue eye and tapped her light-pink polished fingernail against her teeth.

"That is the most Trothy advice I have ever been given. In what other ways can you relate my life to a commodity?"

"Aggravating woman," I muttered while raising my arms high, helping her shrug into her gray woolen cloak. "Also... I could probably relate all aspects of your life to an economic function. Continue ribbing me, and I'll make it my top priority."

Bem coughed, announcing his presence at the door.

"Come on, y'all." He turned on his heels and walked away.

We followed our escort through the halls and emerged on the backside of the palace into a gray and blustery day. My hair whipped around and stuck in the glossy oil applied to my lips. Bem, who appeared to be in a constant state of disheveledness, pulled a soft, blue knitted cap from his pocket and shoved it down on his head.

In the distance, the mountain ranges that surrounded Cordillaria loomed. To the north, toward home, their summits were covered in white, and to our east, where Verus was nestled, the Sinnons were cloaked in the shadows of the overcast sky.

There were fields between the hills and the palace. They didn't look at all like the manicured plots of the gardens in which Ambrose and I had strolled. They were dry and yellowed, and much of the once green foliage had snapped in half under the force of the wind that always seemed to blow here.

Two people stood in the center of the closest rectangle of land, and both were waving us over.

Allaine and I hiked up our skirts and tip-toed our way to the middle of the field. Little spikes of plant matter stuck to my coat, despite my efforts to shake the bits off.

"Hi."

"Hello." I smiled down at a little girl who wore a straw hat and a bright checkered dress. She had a delightful smile and her features reminded me of a little one born in Nortia last year—smaller ears and mouth, the most perfect button nose. She grinned back and resumed her work, collecting little pods from the brown stems that shot out from all over the ground.

"Greetings, Troth Solnna." The man, also wearing a wide-brimmed hat, inclined his head to me and then to Allaine. "His Highness Ambrose indicated that you have an interest in growing. He has arranged a location for you to pursue your hobby."

"Papa, here go." The child pressed two handfuls of pods into the basket, and her little upturned eyes crinkled happily at her father.

"Me more?"

"Yes, tot, find more. We want to fill this to the top." The gardener drew his finger around the inside rim of the basket, indicating the right level. "I am Maihon, and this is my girl, Mae. These beans will yield us next year's harvest."

He cracked open the dried vegetation and withdrew three tiny rounds, which he held out and dropped into my open palm. "This is the truest indicator of wealth."

I examined the white-colored bits and handed them off to Allaine, who observed them closely.

Maihon sat his basket on the ground and rubbed his lower back as he rose again. He started walking and flipped his fingers in the air, motioning for us to follow.

"These plots will be left fallow. We let everything grow as nature intended, and when the soil is worked again in another year, its nutrients will be restored. These smaller parcels of land are the king's private acres, where we grow his favorites, all within the city limits."

Mae ran up and grabbed her father's hand. The wind knocked off her hat, revealing stick-straight, strawberry-blonde hair pulled back into a short tail.

"Mae day?" she asked while tapping her hand against her chest.

"Mae will celebrate her tenth year in four days' time. She is quite excited, as I am allowing her to have her ears pierced."

"Pretty ears... ears... ears." She smiled and tugged gently at her earlobes.

"You are the prettiest girl in Ærta with or without them, my bitty one, but how can a papa say no?"

I scooped up the hat and carried it as we continued on.

"To the left, come late spring, we will fill this area with tomatoes and cucumbers. To the right, small, rounded squash and more beans. Up front, we will plant flowers to attract the pollinators."

"Pollinators. Bees, right?" Bees sounded dreadful. I'd read about them in my book. They were bugs with built-in blades.

"Bees, yes, and butterflies. The wind as well."

Maihon removed his hat and the little linen cap tied under his chin. He used his sleeve to wipe the sweat from his bald head before tucking the covering into his pocket.

"The little shed ahead. That's yours, and don't fret if you lose many plants initially. It's not as simple as baking a pie." Maihon patted his belly while he looked around for Mae.

"I've never baked a pie but will take you on your word."

Half of my new-to-me space was made of wooden slats. The other was a wooden frame whose walls and ceiling were made of semi-transparent glass.

"Here is your key. I have another, as does the Protector."

Well done, Cato. Well done.

"What's the larger building behind this one?" I asked, noticing an exact copy of my shed but on a much larger scale.

"That is the healer's shed. It is fully off-limits. Only I tend to the life within. It prevents mix-ups. You would hate to reach for the ashwagandha when you meant to grab the turmeric." Maihon chuckled at the joke, which only he understood. "Her Majesty, Imella, used to tend her pots here. She spent hours in there pruning and propagating. I do believe she penned a volume on the plant's uses. You could find that in the library."

Beside me, Allaine sputtered and then covered her growly laughs with fake coughs.

"Oh, yes, I'll be sure to look into it."

Mae, who was running in a large circle, shot past us and ran into the shed. The smell of vegetation and dirt and something foreign infiltrated my nose.

"Cat!"

"Where?" I swung my head around the door and beamed up at... nothing.

"Cat, cat, CAT!"

A plump tabby lay on the ground, happily receiving belly rubs from the high-spirited girl.

"Pet him gently, Mae. There you go." Maihon gestured to the animal. "This is Duke McFluffins, the true King of Monwyn. He keeps the vermin out of the garden and little Mae as happy as a ladybug. Well, that's a poor comparison. Ladybugs are nature's assassins, but they sure are pretty."

"Ladybugs?" I pictured a mite with curling hair down its back and a set of stylish eyebrows.

"Bright red with black spots," Allaine supplied. "Never kill them—it brings you bad luck."

"I don't plan on killing anything." I nodded confidently.

"I'd wager my boots you kill every one of your wee shrubs within the next month," said Maihon, slapping his thigh good-naturedly.

"Well damn, thank you for the note of faith, Lord Gardener."

Maihon's laugh boomed loudly in the small room.

He reminded me of Mariad.

My stomach lurched, tightening with a sudden and intense jolt of anxiety.

How could I be thinking about a hobby when the trajectory of my life's path was so incredibly unstable? When I was already the source of so much discord.

"Some die, as all things do… but, as you grow, they'll grow too." Maihon scratched the reddish beard that he kept short, like Cato's, and then replaced his head covering and hat. "I've arranged for the servants to bring your plants here. I'll be getting back to my work now, ma'am."

I shut the door and turned my key in the lock.

Allaine and I fought to keep our skirts down in the gusts and began our jaunt back toward the palace.

"What else is planned for the day?" I asked, hoping to have enough free time to plan out my ladies-only soirée.

"You have a formal dinner with Lord Ethens immediately following prayers."

"Ethens? Really? That's going to be a nether of a meal. Now, lead me to the library, soldier." I shot my fist into the air with an overabundance of confidence.

"Are you serious? There is a sliver of skin showing at your wrists—that will put the Scholar at risk for apoplexy. Where would the kingdom be then, Lady Troth?"

I dusted off the sleeves of my coat and shook out the sticks and brambles that had adhered to the wool.

"Allaine. I'm *incredibly* charming. Don't you look at me like that. I can't pretend to make amends while standing out here. And I do recall someone saying, 'I go where you go'."

She stopped abruptly, and I sped past her.

"I agreed to that *before* discovering you cause calamity in every room you enter… I was waiting for the shed to burn down, or, or for you to toss out a tit in exchange for seeds."

I looked up at her with the most incredulous expression I could and stared her down.

"You aren't wrong!" I doubled over and laughed so hard I snorted. "Allaine, here's your second economics lesson of the day. Always—*snort*—read the terms—*snort*—before you commit to the contract."

"Yeah, yeah." She performed a low curtsy before we set off again. "I bow down to your Trothy wisdom."

I was still giggling intermittently when we entered the grand salon. Like normal, no one was really about—just a few servants shifting furniture and a group polishing the floor.

"Eira," Allaine whispered.

The tightness in her voice made me turn.

Sweat beaded on her forehead, and she'd gone all sour about the mouth, puckering her lips and swallowing over and over.

"Are you alright?"

She clutched her stomach.

"I need the chamber pot. Do you see Bem?" She looked around, frantically surveying the room.

"No, but Allaine, you can go. I'll be—"

"—Just fine," said a familiar voice. Allaine attempted a curtsy, and I spun around. "Her dear father-in-law will be guard enough. Would you not agree?"

"Your Majesty." Her head lurched forward, and her neck worked up and down as she fought to stay in control of her bodily functions.

"Run along, dear. There is no place safer for my daughter than in my care."

"Yes, Majesty, I will return quickly."

I watched Allaine make a hasty retreat, shrugging off her heavy cloak as she went.

"What have you done?" I asked, keeping my distance. "Have you poisoned her?"

He shook his head and waved a hand.

"I simply sped up the functioning of her bowels. Once she eliminates, she will be the picture of health."

"With magic?"

"With milk of magnesia."

He took a step forward, and I took one back.

"Are you afeared of me, child?" His expression of concern looked genuine. Wisps of his scraggly brows hung down over his eyes, and his wrinkles sagged sadly.

Am I scared of him? I thought for a moment as I assessed his stance and expression.

"No. No, you… I don't fear you. But I would like to keep my wits about me. I acted all manner of awkward shortly after our last encounter."

He swept his arm wide, and the silk of his tunic danced in the draft that blew through the door behind us.

"That should ease with time. It did for me. Our connection is the strongest I have ever personally felt, but I am not sure how long it will take to settle. Shall we?"

I kept my distance but followed him. I might not fear him, but the thought of being without an escort *did* give me pause. I would do myself no favors by forgetting I was a woman wanted.

We traveled the hallway until we came to the dining room.

"Majesty." An armored guard held open the door, and the king and I entered. We didn't stop to sit at the table, as I assumed we would.

We entered the kitchens, where dinner preparations were underway. Not a single servant bowed, or looked askance when the sovereign of their kingdom passed through the bustling room that smelled of yeast and baked goods.

"Just through here, it is the only place I can find solitude anymore. Catommandus keeps the reins taut." His Majesty opened a large larder door and ushered me inside—still following my wish for him to maintain his distance.

The scent of butter and raw meat was strong in the small room, and the temperature was much cooler than in the kitchen itself.

"You conjure in the meat closet?" I asked, confused as to why we were standing among the beef.

"No, not usually. But soon the halls will teem with the individuals tasked with seeing to my security."

"*Your* security? Haven't you been the one causing the issues?"

The king blinked down at his folded hands.

"I am tasked with a great burden in life, whether or not you've chosen to believe it so. I have accepted my fate as it is, but I must continue studying and learning that which will ensure the safety of Ærta's people. The lives of a few dozen goats are a small cost, no harm done."

Goaticide?

I leaned back against an empty shelf and studied him.

"The herder who raised them for milk and cheese might see the harm," I said, "and did the Protector have to deal with cleaning your indiscriminate slaughter, or do you tidy up after you massacre?"

"We must all make sacrifices, my dear... all of us. Animals are killed to feed the palace daily. The herder was financially compensated—my son can tend toward the melodramatic, but messes come with his job." He cocked his head to the side and turned toward the door. "Come."

We strode through the kitchen again, and the king nabbed a few raw buns from a flour-dusted tabletop. The maid rolling the blobs of dough between her palms stopped and confusedly began counting her goods.

We hurried through the dining room and headed to the exit. His Majesty looked both ways and together we sprinted toward his personal library.

The lock turned without either of us laying a hand on the mechanism.

"They always check here second." He nudged the door with his toe and bumped it open with his hip. "We should be undisturbed for a solid twenty minutes."

I followed him through the threshold, and behind me, the door shut with a click.

"Ambrose is going to be furious when he learns of our meeting. He's agreed that we can meet in the future, but only when he or the Protector is present," I lied... sort of.

Sad eyes met mine. The hurt in them looked fresh... raw. He sighed and appeared more fragile than he had even at that catastrophe of a dinner.

"I do not understand why my children think I would harm you, daughter. I above all understand your importance in this world."

The fireplace roared to life, unaided, and the king placed the uncooked dough into a thick-walled vessel that he covered and placed near the flames.

"What did you do to the goats, Majesty?" I fought but lost the battle with my curiosity. Cato had said it was grotesque. *Goatesque, even*. I chuckled to myself. *Gods, Eira, what's wrong with you.* My mission here was to find out how he worked—to glean any information I could from the source of corruption himself. *Keep that in the forefront of your mind.*

I watched as he shoved the rounded oven backward with a poker and used a small shovel to pile embers on top of its lid.

"I accidentally siphoned the entirety of their æther. I was attempting to separate the varying components of their blood. Rats proved much more simplistic, but I am disappointed to say I did not have the strength to manage the more complex creatures. Have a seat, Marmot." He pointed behind himself to an overstuffed leather chair.

"Marmot? You've called me that before. Is it a magical term?"

"It's a fluffy rodent, my dear. An adorable little creature, they live all over the ranges."

A rodent.

I went to the chair he indicated and sank into its softness. The king's library wasn't large, and for that matter, the room didn't contain many books—perhaps twenty, maybe less. Like Ambrose's rooms, this one was all bold colors and heavy, dark furniture. A massive tapestry hung above the large desk that sat at the room's center. The scene woven into its fibers depicted a man, robed in blue, with several golden necklaces. He balanced a snow-capped mountain atop his shoulders.

I swiveled in my chair and studied the rest of the chamber. My eyes stalled on a painting of the royal family. The king, looking so much like Cato, stared back at me.

"Aberus was eight months or so when it was commissioned. I imagine Catommandus was probably already tucked safely in Imella's womb by then." He chuckled.

Imella looked so happy—her beautiful bronze skin glowed, her dark hair fell past her shoulders, and she was proudly holding her eldest in her arms. "After all of our boys came along, my precious girls arrived. Never let anyone tell you boys are easier to rear. My little ladies were my purest joy."

"That's surprising," I muttered under my breath.

"Is it?" The king pulled the cookware off the fire, catching the bowl's wire handle with the curved end of the poker.

"Considering I've not laid eyes on more than three women since I've been here, yes. Where do you think the others are? Locked up, perhaps?"

The king's mouth moved silently as he pondered my question.

"Now, dear, we are adamant about keeping our gentlewomen safe. Can you imagine a life with no strong men? What would happen then?"

"If there were no men, who would be attempting to harm us?"

His eyes widened, and he tilted his head while he weighed my words.

"I see what you have done there, daughter. I see."

The king juggled the piping-hot buns in the air as he made his way behind the desk.

A light pulsing took up in the center of my chest. I could barely discern it from the beating of my heart. But it was there, and it was different.

"*Ohh!*" I blanched hard and hopped back in my seat. "There it is again, the connection." The same sensation I had experienced on my first night here. I felt it pulling at my navel.

The king placed the steaming rolls in front of him and then scooted himself backward.

"Is that better?"

I nodded, breathing more briskly from the excitement the pull had caused. Again, it was like a rush of happiness, and... and something akin to that moment when someone you loved hugged you close.

"Before my boys so callously interrupted our last conversation, I was preparing to speak to you of the tie you feel. It is something I can experience with most living things, though not at the same intensity as I do with you."

He slid a bun in my direction and sat back.

The roll's warmth seeped into my hands.

"The tie is what gives me the ability to conjure. It's the fuel, if you will. When I run out of that fuel, so do my abilities wane."

"So you *were* siphoning me... like you did the goats? The goats who are now empty, bloodless husks?"

The king tittered and spoke with a full mouth, "Yes, I suppose so. But unlike the animals—the whole herd of which would sustain me for a few hours—you, daughter, allowed me to be at my peak without a bit of indication that it weakened you."

I raised the roll to my mouth but never managed to take a bite.

"Close your mouth, dear. You'll catch flies."

My mouth snapped shut.

"Majesty, next time, you should *ask* if I want my æther, or whatever, sucked out of me. Did you ask Evandr, or Cato, for that matter? I'm guessing that's why they've both lost their coloring... not just from being around you as they assume."

"That's correct. It occurs when I pull from someone over an extended period."

"Did... did the goats turn colors before they died?" I asked, managing a morsel.

"No, I pulled from them as quickly as I could—you know, your æther allowed me to get out undetected *and* call the herd to me with just a thought. Everyone thinks conjuring is all hand flourishes and intonations, and maybe it is at the beginning, but after twenty years or so, it just becomes a part of you. Finish your roll. Dinner is a long way off."

I bit a chunk of bread, trying to figure out what came next.

"How long have you been conjuring?" I asked.

"Since I was six years of age, daughter. It was your ancestor—a grandmother, I imagine—who revealed my ability to me."

"My Gram!" I nearly choked on the gummy ball in my mouth. I couldn't imagine my diminutive, white-haired Gram involved in anything other than sipping diluted wine and discussing the weather.

"No, not your Gram in Nortia. I believe that woman to be the mother of your potential father—not the Gaean one, but that odd little fellow who teaches at the temple."

My mind spun, and my vision rotated momentarily. I gripped the chair's arm to steady myself.

Gotwig's mother was my Gram? Maybe? File it away and move on, Eira. Gather info and go.

"Majesty, please explain it all. From the beginning, if you don't mind."

"As you wish, but we will need to move again in... approximately eight minutes."

I waved my hand, gesturing for him to hurry.

The king leaned back and crossed his leg over his knee. His eyes looked beyond the room as he went back into his past.

"When I was a boy, I often found myself at odds with life. I was a dutiful child: every night I prayed, I excelled in my studies, and my parents doted on me lavishly. But I wished for the life of another. Nothing here fulfilled my dreams. As an Obligate, I suppose you might relate to being born into your future."

"Mmhmm, I can."

"Being in the line of succession affords one few freedoms. People assume it is about indulging in every whim—really, it is four meetings a day and worrying over whether the color of your coat makes the right impression. You are unable to leave the grounds without escort. Eating what you want is right out; Goddess forbid you consume a heap of onions and then breathe upon a Solnnan dignitary. And are you aware that, as a child, when I became ill with even the most common of agues, my siblings were sent off for months at a time? I wished to become a jeweler—wanted to polish gems until they gleamed and create all manner of trinkets."

"And... and my ancestor?" I prodded; if this was what I was like during a debrief, perhaps I did need practice.

"Daughter, let's not make a habit of interrupting," he chided.

I schooled my face and threaded my fingers tightly together. *Don't punch the king, don't glare at the king.*

"Now, where was I? Oh, yes, one evening I had been praying with all the might of my child's heart. I asked the Goddess to allow me to explore the kingdom and beyond. I wished to see the fire mountain and travel to the ruins of Taleer. I have always been fascinated by the tales of the desert communities. Ahhh, anyhow...

The very next morning, I was called upon by my uncle, the then Protector. He was such a proud fellow, built big like my Aberus, and had the same shining hair as Ahdmundus. Half his nose was missing from a duel, but it never seemed to affect his confidence."

The king went silent, and I watched as his face hardened. His eyes clouded over, and his mouth drew down on both sides. He walked his fingers along the fabric-covered arm of his chair and bounced his leg rhythmically.

"From my lips to the Goddess's ear, my prayers were answered that day. I was to join him so that I could accustom myself to surveying the fiefs and borders. I can still recall dressing in my hunting leathers for the first time and how proud I was to show them off to my servants before leaving. We rode out of Colpass—which used to be our capital—and headed south. My uncle, Magnus, was regaling me with information on which farmers would soon retire and whose sons would let their family farms fail, when all of a sudden, out of a clear blue sky, a bolt of lightning struck the very tip of his outstretched finger. He and his mount were felled in an instant. The first time one smells a fresh carcass burning, it is enough to turn even the strongest man's tummy."

The blood drained from my face. The idea of lightning striking outside of a storm made my stomach sink to the very bottom of my torso.

"Oh dear, don't tremble. He was an odious man, given to abusing children and inclined toward a perverseness with animals. Had I been older and stronger, I would have put a blade to his neck well before that day."

I pressed my lips and gave him my most accusatory side-eye.

"You judgmental Marmot! I do *not* harm animals for pleasure, and I have *never* laid a hand on a child. Now, do you wish me to finish, or do you plan to continue weighing my sins like an Ærtan-bound Merrias?" The king wagged his finger at me like my own father had done countless times.

"No, no, pray continue—the filthy uncle had just been fried by mystery lightning."

The king leaned forward and propped his chin on the palm of his hand.

"Naturally, my horse spooked and ran us deep into the woods before I could bring her back to head. That's when she appeared—your ancestor. You do favor her some, around the nose, but she was light brown of hair, not dark like yours, and her eyes were the color of celery... or a green gladiola."

"My mother's eyes are green," I said.

"She was much too old to be your mother, my dear. Do keep up."

Monwyn male: an intensely aggravating species whose most prominent feature is a head as dense as the stone they mine.

"Most likely, she was a great-great matriarch. Well, to sum it all up, she explained that it was *she* who caused the lightning. She had been waiting for an opportunity to speak with me, and ridding the world of Protector Magnus was her way of announcing herself."

Oh shit.

"Our time is dwindling." His Majesty glanced at the door. "So, in a nutshell, she offered me the ability to conjure if I promised to fulfill two requests. One, I had to find the writings of the Magis—which my Kitty Cat did inadvertently while out training with Septimus—and two, I would locate and protect her deity-blessed, Obligate descendant, who would be born in the North. Funnily enough, Catommandus helped with that as well, now did he not? Such a good boy, though I suppose the real credit goes to my cub for capturing your heart." He chuckled and steepled his fingertips.

"That was a big fucking nutshell." My mind was at full capacity, and I was having trouble compartmentalizing it all.

"Daughter." He looked genuinely offended at my word choice—eyes wide, forehead wrinkled. I chose to ignore him. He could deal.

"Majesty, many Obligates have been born in the North. How did you determine I was the right one?"

He combed his joint-swollen fingers through his thick beard and compressed his lips briefly.

"Do you recall a woman by the name of Olena?"

Hot prickles skated across my skin.

I nodded, terrified of what he'd say next. Had he tortured her into revealing information? Had he intercepted my beloved childhood tutor as she'd left Nortia for her own home?

"Clever woman, in my father's employ for decades..."

Deceitful hag!

"She was always loyal to the mountain kingdom, even though she took her commitment to Verus seriously. She was able to confirm your existence by swiping a bit of blood and having it sent here. It was easy to keep up with you after that. I tried to nab you up as a child, but that Primus up there thwarted my every attempt."

I was at a loss for words. On one hand, I was oddly comforted by the notion that Olena had been an actual tutor and not simply a double-crosser. On the other hand, she was sure to have supported my kidnapping. And how did this man sit here and admit to such a horrid offense?

Goddess, I implore you... Set extra blessings in your stars this night and send them to Primus Adrielle.

Even though it hadn't happened, the thought that it could have made me—

"Why the attacker then? Why did you send him to the river that day? I was on my way to Verus, so...?"

"Not 'attacker'—I wish to reiterate that he was given no such orders. However, your disappearance would have been much easier to cover up. Wild animals, a kidnapping, you running off with a lover—all of those things would have been simpler to explain away than trying to alter your Assignment. My reach is not without limit. Had I known that my boy would win you over, the time and resources I could have saved would have been considerable. It truly was divine fate that brought you and he together."

I slapped my cheeks vigorously between my palms trying to come to grips with it all.

"We must leave. Rise up." The king popped up out of his chair and made his way to the door. "Come, daughter, I will take you to Ambrose. Please inform him that I, too, am saddened that you were not with child. It will happen in time."

The king moved through the halls quickly, and I trailed behind him, barely able to keep up. For a balding and wrinkled elder, he was still swift.

"MAJESTY, HOLD!" someone yelled at our front.

I passed through the invisible tie that sent electric tingles down my arms and legs... and face-planted into the king's back.

The connection snapped into place.

"Sleep, Levaunt."

I watched the guard in front of us hit the floor.

"Step over him, dear. He will wake in a few hours." The king bent low, securing Levaunt by the underarms. "Grab his feet."

I complied happily, already æther drunk. I assisted in dragging the sleeping man's body into a room whose door swung open with an unvoiced command.

"Thank you, Marmot."

He took my arm and led me forward. I smiled up into his gentle face. His round cheeks and wrinkly eyes reminded me of the delightful, bearded seals from back home.

"You're welcome, Father Burchard."

CHAPTER 14

SUGAR, SPICE AND AMBROSE LOOKS NICE

BUT WHEN DOESN'T HE?

My men.

"Ohhhhhh! I missed you!" I squealed while flinging my arms wide.

Together, Cato and Ambrose sat behind a massive table in the center of the rather plain room. They looked so sweet with their heads together in deep conversation. Ambrose flipped the tail of his braid between his fingers while concentrating on a missive in his hands. Cato busily scribbled away on a parchment.

"What the fuck?" Ambrose leapt to his feet, knocking his chair over with the momentum. He charged around the table, which took him some time, as the thing was enormous, taking up almost the entirety of the chamber. Its shiny, marbled top reflected the light of the many-armed chandelier above it, and baskets of bread and bottles of wine sat around it at various intervals. I couldn't imagine how the slab had gotten transported into this room or how heavy the piece was, but it made sense that the monstrosity rested atop what looked like a short wooden wall.

"How in Gammond's—Step away from her Majesty. Do it now," Cato demanded.

So upset. Always so worried.

"I am here to deliver her into Ambrose's capable hands. Her lady's maid took ill. Would you rather she roamed the halls unescorted?"

Ambrose looked like a bull, his head down and his eyes flashing dangerously as he came quickly toward us.

"Oh, love puffin, I'm fine, let me hold you until you're happy once more."

Ambrose grabbed my hand and jerked, pulling me against his side. I forgave him the harsh treatment, as I very much enjoyed being pressed into his warmth. I squished my head into his underarm and flung my arms around his waist.

"You smell like cake... spicy cake." I sniffed him like a curious puppy—a series of short inhales and a long and refreshing exhale. Yep, a yummy, spicy cake. He palmed my head and twisted me about; two heavy arms came to rest around my shoulders, locking me into place. "I enjoy your hugs too, almost-husband. Perhaps when we retire this evening, you will allow me to hug your lengthy appendage with my woolybu—"

His big hand smacked over my mouth.

"Father, why does she do this?" Ambrose hissed.

"It affects everyone differently, cub, but I imagine it to be one of two things."

"What does? What things?" he shouted.

"The connection we share—you are aware she is different, yes? The Marmot contains a powerful energy—"

"Marmot? You will cease insulting my wife at once. A filthy, disease-ridden nuisance—I think not."

Father Burchard continued only when Ambrose ended his rant, "... and when we are tethered, it heightens her emotions. Currently, she senses you are upset so feels the need to comfort you. If you make her sad or reject her, she could become inconsolable or injure herself in her effort to make you better again. Anger her, and she will fight you tooth and nail. So calm down and allow her to care for you. Keep yourself in check and let it play out. She will learn to control it in time."

I became entranced by the motion of Ambrose's chest, while listening to the beat of his strong and steady heart. The timbre of his voice was a comforting hum in my ears.

"Now, alternatively, son, if it is not the connection, the possibility of a Mating or Fate Bond is possible. Did she become indecently sexual after our last encounter?" Father Burchard waited for Ambrose to reply.

"Oh, I did, Father. I tried soliciting Be—"

Ambrose slapped his hand across my face again, covering me from nose to chin.

"I will take that as a yes. Bonds exist between two people who have a chance at reproducing and bearing offspring born with the ability. Many claim to fall in love at first sight... Bond, nine times out of ten."

"Ambrose—get her out of here. She cannot be in this chamber," Cato interrupted from across the hall.

I pushed against the delightful pillow of Ambrose's torso, seeking Cato.

"What do you mean, Kitty Cat? Why can't I stay with my men?" I asked, hurt that he would request my removal in such a rage-filled tone.

"Oh, oh dear, does she consider me more than just a doting father? Oh, no, no, that simply will not—"

"No, vulgar old man. She does not!" Ambrose bellowed. His hand moved up to my forehead, and he pulled my upper half back to his body.

"Thank the Goddess for small mercies. Now, boys, I have only experienced a Bond once and can tell you, I would have done any number of unspeakable acts to get to her." The king's shoulders rolled forward, and his eyes flicked back and forth like he didn't know where to look. "I... I... did do unspeakable acts... and we all know how poorly it ended."

Cato's body appeared in front of me, blocking my view.

"Please stop, please don't fight, I can't take—"

"No, daughter, we will not fight." Over Cato's shoulder, the king's face blurred as my eyes filled with tears. "And, Marmot, you should be thrilled to feel a Bond with Ambrose, it is such a blessing, but if it is a Mating Bo—"

"Eira, listen to me... You have to listen, alright?" Cato dropped his face to mine.

I nodded as much as I could with Ambrose's hand locking me into place.

"Are you upset with me, Ca-Cato? Please don't be, I don't know how to change me."

"Listen to me, Eira... We need you to leave."

Parted.

Rejected.

Never to see him again.

I struggled against my captor.

I fought Ambrose, stomping his feet and clawing his hands. I wouldn't leave Cato. I couldn't even if Mossius demanded it.

He tightened his embrace and lifted me off the floor, high enough that only my toes touched the carpet.

A knot twisted painfully in the pit of my stomach.

"You... you don't want me anymore? But we mated. You said you loved me. You said we—"

"Eira, stop divulging *our* business," Ambrose demanded.

My low keening turned into a deep and painful wail.

"But, Ambro—"

"Eira. Women are not permitted at state functions. Do you understand? It is not you; it is—"

"Of fucking course…"

Cato's eyes jumped between his father and Ambrose.

Your mistake love.

I kicked and caught Cato right above his groin, knocking him back a step. I cracked my heel against Ambrose's shin and shoved my elbow into his stomach the moment his arms loosened.

"Unhand me!" I bit the fingers that bound me and took off the second they unfurled. "I. Hate. This. Fucking. Kingdom!"

"Daughter, your language! Goddess, forgive her she—"

I stopped in my tracks, pivoted as hard as I could, and shoved a finger into Father Burchard's chest. I was ready to wage my war. Ambrose captured my other arm and twisted it behind my back.

As quickly as it came, the connection doused my fury. It swam and swirled its way through the middle of my chest.

My eyes drifted shut.

"I'm sorry Papa, it's just that… you murder a host of goats and suck them dry… but my one little word upsets you. That doesn't seem quite right. And why can't I be in this room?"

The king's eyes softened as he reached out and straightened the lapel of my coat.

"I am sorry about the goats, dear. They were innocent, yes? And that upsets you? And this," he looked around the room, "this is because I never wanted Imella to learn of the tragedies that existed in our world. Perhaps another of my failed attempts to protect her."

"Oh, Papa," I reached for him but Ambrose held firm, "you love her still."

"There was never a time I did not," he said with a weak smile.

"The Honorable Lord Septimus approaches!" a herald bellowed from the hall.

"Gods balls," Cato muttered, "bring her."

Ambrose pulled me along at a jog and shoved me under the table the moment we neared the seat he'd originally occupied.

"Remember, be nice to her. You have to be nice. Calm," Father Burchard said.

I heard Ambrose's muffled curse above me.

Cato's head appeared under the marble slab.

"Eira, if you don't make a sound until this meeting ends, we will bring you—make you—give you—anything your heart desires, understand? No noise." He smiled broadly and nodded his head up and down.

"It will be sex! And maybe a cake! Probably at the same time!" I whispered excitedly. This was a great bargain.

Ambrose's head appeared next to Cato's.

"I will fuck you on top of a cake while you eat cake. I will rub it all over those beautiful tits and lick off the cream. I will coat myself in sugar and let you have your way with me for the next *week* if you manage to stay silent."

"Yes, yes! Cato, can you top that?" I asked, backing myself further under the table on my hands and knees.

He pinched the bridge of his nose between his fingertips.

"Majesty, brother! It has been too long since your name was recorded at the Council. I welcome you back to your rightful seat."

"Thank you, Septimus. With the auspicious events taking place in my kingdom, I felt it appropriate."

I watched from under the table as both men sat down and shifted in their seats. The king sat at the table's head, and Septimus took the chair next to him.

"The Honorable Lord Ethens joins the Council, followed by the Most Reverend Father Townell!" exclaimed the herald.

Toenail? Gross name.

"Lord Dumail, Keeper of the West!" The herald continued. "Master Healer Santerson and His Most Renowned Royal Scholar enter!"

I covered my mouth with both hands.

Sex and cake! Sex on cake!

"Thank you, gentlemen, for gathering on such short notice—" I heard Cato say.

"Before you begin, *Protector*," a voice interrupted. I pulled my skirt out from under my knees and crawled my way closer to the new speaker. "His Majesty sits before us, and you see fit to lead as if you had not forsworn your heritage."

Septimus. I clamped my teeth together and crawled back toward Cato, whose knuckles were turning white where they dug into the arm of his chair.

"Brother mine, *I* placed that burden upon my child, and I have come to the conclusion that..."

Father Burchard's voice faded away.

My heart hurt. How long had Cato endured such hatred from his kin? I moved forward cautiously and placed light kisses on each of his scarred knuckles. His palm opened, and he slid a finger down the bridge of my nose.

I'm here, love.

"Perhaps Ambrose, then? Perhaps *he* should lead…"

The men above me continued squabbling, but my concern still centered firmly around Cato.

He was my Ærta—my world.

I rubbed my cheek against his scarred hand, reveling in his caresses. His touch brought me to life.

His finger traced my bottom lip, and I caught its tip between my teeth.

Cato pulled back and shook his finger in a *no-no* gesture.

Not kisses then?

Oh, he wants something else.

My hands went to his laces, and his flew above the table.

"I… uh, I agree," Cato said above me. "Ambrose, brother, please open the meeting. Before we hear the grievances, read the letter that has arrived from Verus—here you are."

Cato leaned toward Ambrose, and I snatched the single remaining lace of his underclothes, which parted, freeing something much better than a finger.

I love penis. So much like a mole rat when flaccid, but the Goddess knew what she was about when she made them expandable.

"Are you positive, Protector? I have no issue with your—"

I kissed the tip of his halt-erect member.

"Yes. Yes, I am positive… Begin. Read it now. Immediately." Cato pounded his fist on the table.

His arousal filled thickly, and I drew him into my hungry mouth. I missed the taste of him, salty and bold… and the profound knowledge that he wanted me above all others. I twisted my tongue around the ridge of his head and sealed my lips over the bead of essence at his tip. *Mmmm.*

"This Council is in session." Ambrose's strong voice rang out. "The following is written by the hand of Their Holiness the High Mantle. 'Greetings to those who walk in the light of the Goddess's embrace. We are most joyful to hear of the union between your son, Scion Ambrose, and Our Troth, Eira of Solnna. May theirs be a fruitful and blessed union. We await the announcement of their nuptials and will pray that Mossius keeps them both in good health.'"

Well, that was lovely. I happily rocked my head back and forth while settling my hand around the base of Cato's perfection. I held him upright so I could trace the prominent vein on the side of his erection with the tip of my tongue. My arousal settled heavily between my legs—that rich, full, and wet pulsing.

"'You will be glad to hear that Scion Evandr opened his eyes today, and though there will be a lengthy recovery ahead, he is expected to regain his health.'"

I dropped Cato's cock and hugged my arms around my shoulders. Tears burned my eyes—for once, their cause was happiness.

Cato's hand caught my jaw.

He guided my mouth back to rigidness and worked his hand into my hair, where he pressed and pulled, urging me to take him deeply.

I obliged with all the passion I could summon. I took him in until he bottomed out at the back of my throat and then relaxed my muscles and took him further still. I'd take him to the Goddess plane.

"I am pleased… to hear of his recovery… and will make a-a note to his… his father," Cato said. His hands left my head, and I could hear him scribbling above me.

With his length held in my mouth, I unbuttoned my overcoat and carefully sat it to the side. I was too turned on and too joyful to be trapped in its layers.

Evandr lives.

My hands skimmed up my dress, and my nipples, which were already sensitive from my courses, puckered up. I dipped my head down, licking his cock while massaging my hardened peaks with my palms.

"Expect your Obligates to report to Monwyn in short order. Greggen and Zotikos are excellent candidates for interkingdom relations, and Richelle and Cinden are masters at solving social complications and securing beneficial relationships."

Eeeeek! I pulled back and danced the quietest dance under the table. There'd been a part of me that assumed I'd never see any of them again, but now the full realization that I was soon to be reunited with my brother and sisters had me soaring above the clouds.

Cato snapped his fingers.

He pointed to his glistening erection and… it wasn't enough.

I was overcome by the need to share the Goddess's gift with him.

I wanted him buried to the hilt in my slit.

My breathing became labored.

I wonder.

I hiked my skirts and spun around under the table. I pressed my slickened opening against his legs and rubbed myself against the padding in my underwear. He parted his knees and my rear pressed against the seat of the chair.

Not enough friction. Reaching back, I fumbled with my ties.

I squatted and then lifted until I was above his knees and my back was flush with the table. The tip of him struck the wrong entrance, and I tilted and struggled, trying to lift myself just another inch. *So close!*

"We look forward to receiving our new Obligates. Protector, are you prepared for their coming?"

"Coming. I am close to come-coming up with, and finalizing a plan—Your Highness." Cato pinched my rear and pushed against my backside.

I was on fire. Literally burning. My fingertips felt so near to scorching that I'd swear I could smell smoke.

Ambrose.

Longer.

Always horny.

I fought my layers and crawled my way over to his legs. *I love these thick-thighed Monwyns. Surely Lord Gammond is built similarly.* I could see the outline of his penis through the absurdly tight pants he preferred.

My mouth watered. *Cake and sex. Sex and cake.*

I placed both hands on his knees and inched his legs apart. I ran my fingers up his already hardening length and began undoing his laces.

"*Oh!* Dearest brother, Catommandus, there is more. Please read the rest of the missive, I am left speechless by the, um, riveting news."

Ambrose shifted toward Cato and with one hand, pulled himself free. He let himself hang over his underclothes.

Level: expert.

I was on him like a horse to a sugar cube. I sucked him hard and nipped his tip as I drug my teeth lightly up his length. I tightened my lips around him and took him as deeply as I could.

I needed it hard.

Cato launched in, "Some unfortunate news from Verus. It seems that Scion Castor met his end while escorting Scion Ozius to his homeland, where he was to make provisions for his Assignment in Boldorva. They are still searching for Obligate Ozius and are doing all they can to locate him after such tragedy. Please pass on to her family that Troth Kairus is willing and ready to head across the seas on her own, and we have the utmost faith in her abilities."

That was the cover-up they'd gone with. Fine by me.

Ambrose was fully erect, throbbing and colored like the tantalizing flesh of a plum. I made my move. *Please, Goddess, let my aim be true.* My lust was blinding. I could no longer see.

I turned and raised up, sliding backward as far as I could go. Ambrose, bless him, grabbed his cock and angled it downward. It wasn't much... but it was enough. He pushed past my entrance, flexed his fingers around my thigh, and slowly towed me onto his length.

Delicious fucking torture. Inch by blessed inch he filled me.

"And my abilities," Ambrose crooned out above me, "*never* doubt my ability to perform... my duties to this kingdom."

Never. Never will I doubt... holy fucking gods above and below me. In and out. In and out. How could he still remain inside of me when he'd pulled out at least six inches?

"'Postscriptum: Emissary Nanetta of Nortia, asks that you pass along the following: she will make a trip to Monwyn to discuss the arrangements for Scion Ambrose's relocation to Nortia. We leave the matter in her hands and trust her judgment implicitly.'"

My Nan! I wiggled and bounced and reared back hard. *Ouch!* Too hard.

"*Godsdammit!* Godsdammit, I say! Yes, indeed. That's FINE news, Eira is—will be elated!" Ambrose smacked the table once and then again.

I bucked again and Ambrose dislodged, his semen leaking down my legs.

"Thank you for sharing the information, my sons. Now, what is this I hear about grievances?" the king asked loudly.

"Master Healer, your complaint," Cato said.

I backed up to Ambrose's knees, ready to receive *my* prize. I felt a tap on my rear. When I looked over my shoulder, he tucked his completely spent biscuit dough back into his pants, leaving me in an unfulfilled state of near ecstasy. He shooed me away with a dismissive flick of his fingers.

Fucking Ambrose.

I anger-crawled toward the head of the table in an attempt to hear the king better.

"Thank you, Protector. Esteemed members of the Council, my complaint is against the foreigner in our midst. The very woman with whom your *adopted* son plans to Join is a danger to all those in this palace... this entire city, I would venture. The woman in question clearly feels her station outranks our own and I accuse her of trespassing. She entered a birthing chamber and manipulated her way into taking over my duties."

I sure as fuck did.

"What of the mother and child? Why were you unable to perform your duties?" I heard the king ask.

"The babe—a boy my liege—was born with his cord wrapped about his neck and did not survive. The mother had complications, but in the end lived. I happened to be accidentally incapacitated."

"When you found yourself incapacitated, I am assuming it was my daughter—Eira is her name, by the way—who tended your patient?"

"It was, sire, however, in accordance with—"

"Was she successful? I was unaware she was a woman of science," the king cut off the healer.

"We-well, that is just it! She is not."

"But... she was able to deal with the issue?"

"She... she was."

"And what had you done beforehand to save the mother?" Ambrose asked from the other side of the table.

Silence.

"Prayers were made to Mossius, Highness—again, in accordance with proper practice," said the master healer.

"Son, where did Troth Eira receive her education?"

"From her mother. She was the village midwife."

"We are lucky then, that she was near when you were unable to perform your duties. I would have hated to lose a citizen of child-bearing age. It is unfortunate you were not able to witness her methodology."

"But, majesty, women are forbidden from entering the chamber. It was your father's law and..."

I lost the healer's words, so I inched closer to the table's edge. The connection tingled in my stomach.

Stupidest law I've ever heard. It's exactly where women belong.

"It would seem that my future daughter feels that women are exactly the ones who should be present..."

Women know vaginas.

"Because they understand... the... anatomical functions on a personal level. I do see the sense in that. Cato, form a committee. Research why the mandate was created in the first place. It was not something I ever questioned. You may sit, master healer."

Thank you, Father. I lay flat on my back and brushed my fingertips into the invisible tie in front of my stomach. Closing my eyes, I let my head rest against the table's carved base.

"... at that time... th-th-the woman removed her gown." I fought through my grogginess, recognizing the stuttering voice. "She bared her demon teats in my presence, and we cannot forget the shock our guard suffered. He's barely a man of twenty years. I was in megrim for hours after the incident. The jolt to my system, the utter disgrace done to my sanctuary, was abominable."

I poked my finger in and out of the tie until a movement caught my attention. Septimus uncrossed his ankles and leaned forward.

I bet his penis is a replica of Cato's. Mmmm, the dark version and the light version. I sat up at once and pinched the skin of my cheeks until it hurt. *Oh fuck, Eira, stop.*

"Scholar, you have surrounded yourself with books for too long. She's magnificent, heavy, and pierced like the most obedient of Monwyn ladies." A cacophony of chuckles came from above. Septimus moved his hand to his crotch and adjusted his hefty bulge.

Runs in the family.

"As I understand it, you accused my betrothed of theft and demanded the guard search her person," Ambrose stated. "Had he laid so much as a finger upon her, I would have removed his testicles, Scholar."

"You place her above the laws of this kingdom. I for—"

I lost his voice. He must have turned to address another. I stretched my neck out as far as it could go without fully immersing myself in the tie.

"... if she's so incredible, Septimus, why not marry her to Aberus! Make her a Queen, allow her to run the entirety!"

"Silence yourself this instant." Ambrose shoved backward in his chair and got to his feet.

"Brother—Majesty. Breeding her within your bloodline is a plan worth considering. Catommandus, the dissenter that he is, would prove a better option if, for some unimaginable reason, you found her unworthy of your firstborn."

Ambrose stepped toward his uncle, but Cato lunged at him, and held him back.

"Ahdmundus, do not speak of my children with such unabashed disrespect. It has not escaped me how you leer at my daughter. I expect you to comport yourself appropriately when in her presence."

"Do you, Burchard? You and I both know your history proves that fidel—"

"Septimus—my remaining sibling—stop yourself."

I held my breath and grew uneasy. The connection between the king and I started to physically cool, turning my warm skin icy.

Septimus sat back, and Ambrose regained his seat.

"Dumail. Ethens. State your business."

I caught the word *pirate* from the discussion above but found myself too engrossed by the tie's change to really listen. Holding my stomach, I applied pressure and rubbed my hand in a circular motion, attempting to thaw the freeze.

"Ambrose, the funding is simply not there. Campaigns are costly. You do not control the purse strings, prince or otherwise. Dumail, we will discuss our strategy soon—I have you on the books. Ethens?"

Mumbles came from above.

"That is most considerate of you, Ethens. We will talk perimeters at this evening's dinner," Ambrose effused. "If there are no other items of business, this Council is adjourned."

The king rose first, followed by Septimus, who went quickly to his side.

I poked my head out, ensuring everyone had left before I allowed myself to breathe comfortably again.

There was a scuffle above me—quick shuffles followed by a grunt and a loud thud.

"Ambrose, did you?" Cato shouted.

"Fuck her? Just a little."

CHAPTER 15

THE COUNCIL

A crash rang out from above, like metal smacking against stone.

"Get out! Find His Majesty and stay with him. Put Bem at the door."

"Cat, you cannot blame me for—"

"Out," Cato growled.

He was livid.

I tracked Ambrose as he made his way to the door and snapped my head back quickly to avoid being stepped on.

"*Oh!*"

Fingers wrapped around my ankle and yanked. I dropped onto my stomach as the hand dragged me backward, my dress rolling up around my hips as it caught on the carpet.

"We have unfinished business, *Troth*," Cato spat out the last word.

I twisted my upper body in an attempt to see him.

"Cato, it was—I was under the tie when—"

"I don't give a fuck. The only thing Ambrose has done is make you slicker for me. Remove your clothing."

I didn't hesitate.

I grabbed the scrunched up gown, yanked it over my head, and immediately started unlacing my chest support.

"Shoes? Stockings?" I asked, entranced by the view; his shirt was gone, and his pants were in the process of coming off.

"You heard me. Nothing between us."

Cato lifted my foot and began inching the silk off of my toes. When uncovered, he placed my ankle on his shoulder.

"Just look at you, flushed and panting... so perfect." Two fingers nudged at my entrance and slipped slowly inside. He steadily eased his way in and cupped the palm of his hand, placing it snug against my pulsing gem. I dropped my knee to the side, inviting him to take more. "How you swell around me. You are such a pleasure to use." He moaned while crooking his fingers upward.

"C-Cato," I choked, moving in unison with the rhythm he set, "I think I'm... magical."

"Do you doubt the fact? With a look, you turned me prisoner." Cato bent low and swept his broad tongue across one nipple and then the other. Under his weight, my elevated leg pressed backward into my chest, allowing his fingers to sink deeper into my passage.

"N-no... *actually* magical," I moaned.

I ground my clit into the meaty part of his hand while his fingers picked up speed, gliding smoothly in and out of my wetness.

"We will discuss it later." He held my breast in his hand and ran the rough pad of his thumb around my areola until my nipple stiffened and stood out.

"But, Cato I—"

"Your pleasure is my art—I am the composer..." His tongue flicked against my gold bar, and he swept it into his mouth, "...your cries are my symphony." Pain and pleasure mixed as he lifted my breast using only the piercing. He released it without warning and stared, transfixed, while it wobbled and trembled. "Exquisite."

I reached out blindly, searching for something to hold on to. My nails scratched at the carpet in vain.

"I think your uncle—Oh my Goddess, Cat—ha-has a Mating Bond... like you." I arched my hips into his hand as his movements became less genteel. With every fourth stroke, he pulled his fingers free, smearing my moisture around my clitoris. The lubrication and the heat of my arousal turned his calloused fingers to the softest silk.

"I have found idle amusement imagining Septimus's face staring up from his coffin. Knowing *you* are his desire, while *I* possess you... it makes me feel like I am a prince after all." He slowed his pace but stroked me with more authority, rolling his fingers, commanding my response. "Would you allow me to slide my cock between your lips as he watched? I would brand those breasts he obsesses over with my essence, look him in the eye, and tell him, '*This* belongs to *me*.'"

I ran my hands through the hair on his chest, finding his nipples and sliding them between my fingers, pinching lightly.

"I met with your father, Cato. It was accidental... sort of—"

"Eira, shut the fuck up." A strained half-smile appeared on his face.

Cato rose up on his knees, and his head struck the tabletop.

"Make me?" I rolled up and slipped the tip of him into my mouth.

His rough fingers wrapped under my chin and tilted my head back as far as it would go. The thin aura of gold glittered wildly in the dark pools of his eyes.

"Lilium," he breathed.

Done.

I was done.

"Get out," I commanded.

He quirked a brow.

"Out, now," I repeated, pointing to the chair in front of us. "I'm going to ride you until I scream."

Cato sank down into the chair his uncle had vacated, and I straddled him; the chair was *just* wide enough to accommodate us both. He placed his hands between the chair's arms where they pressed tightly into my thighs, but I moved them to my rear.

"I'll wear tomorrow's bruises as badges of honor," I whispered.

"My woman. You are *my* woman. Never forget it, Eira... they do not crave you like I do—their infatuations will never transcend my obsession."

"In your arms, I am a goddess." I reached between my legs and guided his girth to my entrance. "Let me reward my disciple."

I slid down him slowly, savoring the pressure of his unyielding erection as it stretched my walls. I sank until I could feel the press of his sac against my wide spread cheeks.

"I live for that sigh. I breathe it in—it gives purpose to my existence." He looked me in the eyes and took both of my breasts into his hands. "I understand now why the bards say to seek your eternal reward not in the afterlife... but between your lover's thighs."

"Touch me," I begged, reaching between us, parting my lips, and exposing my bud of nerves.

"I'd rather watch." Cato took my fingers into his mouth and then guided the wet digits to my clit. He slipped his hands under my rear and lifted, while I rocked against him and fingered my hood.

I tilted my pelvis and entered that space between reality and dream. My consciousness floated. I was lost in the sounds and sensations. The scent of cloves and cedar surrounded me, mingling with the earthy aroma of our bodies. I would never tire of this.

"Will you breed me one day?"

Cato's hips jerked, and he pumped harder beneath me.

"Godsdamn woman, are you so ready for me to cross the finish line?" He chuckled.

His laughter was my everything. I brushed his golden-brown curls off his forehead and stared into his eyes. I softened the churning of my hips and set a slower pace while planting kisses on his close-cropped beard.

And then my mouth met his. He parted his lips, and our tongues touched, wet and desperate. The sound of his hips smacking my thighs made my moisture flow. His heavy grunts, mixed with my desperate cries, sent me over the edge.

My walls began to spasm. Little flashes and pricks of pleasure glimmered in my womb.

I tore my mouth from his, gasping. Warmth spread over my body, and I was shaking, on the verge of climax.

"I can't slow, Cato. I can't wait... I tried, but..."

"Take what you need, love."

I captured his mouth again, my tongue stroking hard against his. I rode him madly, grinding and twisting my hips with no inhibitions, impaling myself onto him in the rhythm my body demanded. My eyes rolled back. The delicious pressure mounted within me, and I gripped his chest so viciously that I feared puncturing his flesh.

His deep and throaty growl was bliss to my ears.

At once, everything and nothing mattered.

"I'm going to come, Cato." My toes curled, and I squeezed my passage tightly, overtaken by the power of my body's response. "Oh, Goddess. Oh, my Goddess!" Through the slits of my eyes, I saw him watching me, and then...

"Cat, fill me... fill me, please." I was still coming when he stood, dropped my back to the table and began thrusting his hips upward while yanking me down onto his length. "Don't stop! Do. Not. St—"

Cato bit down on the top of my breast as his body went rigid.

I opened my mouth to scream, but no sound came forth.

I froze in the ecstasy of pleasure-pain.

I was pure energy, pure life.

Cato's eyes closed.

He groaned low—a rich and long-held rumble that I felt to my toes.

"Nothing better," he breathed, "there is nothing that compares to this... to you."

His body stilled, but he didn't pull out—just remained joined to me while spreading light kisses over the bite mark that now showed red on my chest. "Nothing."

Chapter 16

I'LL HAVE WHAT HE'S HAVING

"Greggen openly loathes me, and he happens to be from Baldorva… or have you forgotten?"

"No, I haven't forgotten—but he is a weak representation of a people purported to be bloodthirsty slavers. He is nothing more than a ridiculously tall child." Cato's palm came to my cheek. "I would have broken his legs, you know. You took that pleasure away from me. You and those dangerously sharp teeth."

"I left my mark, and it was enough," I chided.

I watched Cato's curls dance in the breeze of our balcony refuge.

"So you did. And speaking of, you will start training again with Ambrose in the mornings. So far, we have taught you what amounts to nothing. We will need to work in your apartments as the training rooms are for—"

"Don't finish your sentence if it will spoil the first lovely afternoon I've had in over a month."

Cato smacked his hand playfully over his mouth, and in the same instant, the door flew open, admitting a sweat-soaked Ambrose.

"Why do you two interrupt me? What could be so incredibly important that you would disrupt my regimen?"

He strode in, and the foul smell pouring off of him assaulted me like a thick and funky blanket tossed over my head. He wore the tight and tall underwear that he'd worn once to a Maneuvering at Verus. He'd sworn it was the secret to keeping up his appearance.

"Gods, you smell horrendous. Does your regimen consist of rolling in cow patties and pig slop?" I asked while fanning my hand in front of my face.

"You insult *me*, my soft-bellied bride? This is the musk of vitality. Man-stank."

Ambrose stopped directly in front of me, legs spread and fists at his hips. A yeasty aroma issued from his crotch, mixing with the animal stock smell.

How something so pretty could produce such a—

"Kiss me. I command you." He bent at the hips and tossed his head, which flung his sweat-soaked braid over his shoulder. Droplets of stinking wetness peppered my dress and arms.

"I will not! Don't you dare come closer." I kicked out to keep him at bay, but he swiped at my heel, smacking my foot down. An onslaught of stink permeated the air.

"It is unacceptable how my physique diminished while lazing about at Verus temple. When I walk the aisle at our nuptials, I will paint the masses green—see them simply disgusted in their envy. It is *my* day, you know. I have been looking forward to it since I paraded into Mama's garden cloaked in her wedding mantle. I daresay these shoulders filled out the garment even then."

"We have a confirmed date, then? And will you be wearing her dress to our ceremony?"

His eyes turned to daggers as he walked around the table.

"We do; I was making plans with Cato before some idiotic drunk and a conjurer interrupted." He blasted me with a pointed look. "We are to Join in less than a weeks time. It turns out my manipulative father sent not just announcements but *invitations* to every corner of the continent. Scouts are saying guests will arrive imminently. Do not fret, though. Traveling through the mountains is risky this time of year—it would be foolish for all but the Solnnans to make the trek.

"Less than a week. Okay. I can do this. I can Join with a man who smells of a decaying cow's ass."

Cato's hand came to rest on the base of my neck, its warm weight a comfort to my sudden panic.

"Ambrose, you were called here because Eira has information that you will benefit from hearing."

"Then why not brief me like normal, Cato? Oh right, you are ensnared in the tangled briars of her pussy patch."

A cold wind blew through the tall, white columns that formed a semi-circle around us, thankfully muting Ambrose's stench. I snuggled deeper into the blanket Cato had wrapped around our shoulders and looked out over the balcony's edge. I wasn't cold, of course, I was as cozy as could be, burrowed up with the man for whom my heart beat.

The balcony, which was right off the apartment's common room, was a marbled haven. Two glass doors were its only entrance, and the half-wall that surrounded its perimeter was tall enough to afford us some privacy, situated as we were on the second floor.

The times when Cato and I could exist beyond formalities and pretenses were rare, and I relished each second, happily soaking up every touch, every breath, and every feeling.

"Pour me a drink, wife. Earn your keep."

Ambrose propped his feet in the chair across from him and leaned his head back, eyes closed.

Oh, I'll get you a drink.

I threw off the wool coverlet and set a glass right in front of the giant. Fetching the pitcher of warm spiced wine, I poured the fragrant beverage until the liquid formed a dome over the vessels rim. One of Ambrose's mossy-green eyes opened, watching my every move. I smiled my most winning smile.

"Nasty, spiteful, hag."

He dropped his boot-clad feet to the floor and noisily slurped the wine until he could pick the glass up without the threat of spilling.

"Cato, has your father tried killing you since we arrived?" I resumed my comfy spot and leaned my head against his shoulder. He took my hand, pressed his lips to my inner wrist and inhaled steadily. His gold-tipped lashes closed.

"Just once," Cato replied between pressing kisses to my wrist and palm. "I forced him to stop eviscerating a herd of goats—he attempted to slice off my hands."

"You interrupted his practice," I said matter-of-factly.

"And is that suddenly okay, Eira?" Ambrose interrupted. "Is he your pal now? Are you selecting fabrics for your apprentice's robes?" He dragged a hand over his mouth and scrubbed at his beard.

"Before this devolves into one of your childish squabbles—my love, succinct and to the point, *please*," Cato interjected.

I snatched my hand from his, but with a quick flash of his arm, he recaptured it and placed it back at his lips. Amused dark eyes stared back at me in challenge.

"Your father sucks out people's æther. It's like energy, soul juice, or something. That's what fuels his abilities. It's also what makes people's hair and eyes lighten—not their proximity to him. He's *leeching* from you. There are also Bonds that draw together those who could potentially produce children with the ability to conjure. I feel like Cato and I have a Bond. I believe Septimus and I also share a—"

With a jerk, the chest that was my pillow disappeared, and I found myself face-to-face with a furious Cato.

"You wish to lie with him? Septimus?"

"I don't want to *lie* with him, no... but my, well, my vagina might... just a smidge."

A light pulsing took up in my core. *Not healthy, Eira, no good.*

"Touch him, and you forfeit your every freedom," Ambrose gritted out between clenched teeth. "A magical attraction does *not* negate the terms of our contract, and if you are found with any but us, your life will change, Eira, for the worse, much worse."

"Is that understood?" Cato added.

"Ughhh." I sighed loudly and looked at each in turn.

"Oh, and I think he read my mind. That's important; you need to know that." I offered, ignoring them both.

"Septimus?" asked Ambrose.

"No, your father, and he can suck me for unlimited energy power and it doesn't deplete me like it did you or Evandr."

"His Majesty *sucked* on you?" Cato's expression turned feral. His dilated pupils went to pinpricks, and his brow set low casting a shadow over his features.

Slowly, he rose to his feet.

"No? Yes? I don't know how it works, which is why we must meet with him. Settle down—it was *you* who gave him what he needed to learn it anyhow."

"I did what?"

"You found and gave him the Magi's writings. That's what he said."

Confusion flickered in Cato's eyes.

"I have no recollection of such a thing."

Ambrose shifted in his seat and reached for the pitcher again while I tugged at Cato's arm, pulling him back into my embrace. I settled his head on my breasts and rubbed the knots from his tense neck. With the lightest touch, I ran my fingertip down yet another scar that ran vertically behind his ear—I thought I'd already found them all.

"Cat, arrange a meeting with our father tonight. I am told he barely sleeps. I need a better understanding of what is happening to my wife."

"My *mate*," Cato said, turning his gaze to his brother. I nuzzled his neck with my lips, hoping to calm the anger I sensed stirring within him.

Ambrose tilted his head to the side.

"Catommandus, you are losing control. Do you not see it? Are you able to perform your duties as Protector, or are you faltering?"

Under my hands the muscles of Cato's shoulders strained to cording.

"Ambrose, I suggest you and Eira make your preparations for dinner."

Ambrose drummed his fingers on his knee and then flicked his head towards the double doors.

"Come on, chubby Marmot."

"Ambrose!"

"What? I love your curves."

I found myself ensconced in a carriage flying down the streets of Cordillaria. My stomach churned with every sway and bump as the wooden wheels rumbled across the paved streets. I'd never been trapped in a vehicle traveling at such a speed. Stone structures and multi-level homes flew by as I looked out the window. Things here were so different from my homeland. Everything here felt so sturdy, so permanent.

It was interesting to me how geography had such a profound impact on where and how people lived. We used wood, thin metal, and ice up north. Massive stones wouldn't make it that far without sinking into the snow.

"You do see that Cato has changed, yes?" said Ambrose, who rode in the seat across from me. He looked beautiful tonight; he wore his hair down, except for two delicate braids at his temples. Those were pulled back and secured with a gold clip, fashioned in the shape of a sword.

I remained silent, pondering his words.

"Since he took my blood. He's been—"

"Less careful, taking risks, quick to rile."

I nodded and pulled the coach's curtain closed, hoping to calm my nausea.

"Come snuggle." Ambrose leaned forward, reached across the distance, and guided me to the cushioned seat beside him. He placed his arm around my shoulder, and I clung to him, taking solace in his stable presence. "I am hoping we can guide him back to normalcy. Though *he* may be pushing it from his mind, the Gaeans are still a threat even here, and there is also Solnna to consider. We will need to placate them after the loss of their prized Obligate. You would think, as prince, I would have unlimited funds, but that is not how the title works."

I couldn't suppress the shudder that ran down my spine. At the mention of Gaea, my mood darkened.

"It makes me wish the Joining were sooner, in all honesty."

"I agree. All of Monwyn will be at your service then." Ambrose leaned down and kissed my forehead, "Though I may not be the one you love, I will protect my property unto my own death... and that will include you very soon."

My heart skipped a beat and for moment I couldn't breathe.

"I remember the day of the First Maneuvering, do you? As I recall, you were the only one even close to taking Cato down."

Ambrose let out a high-pitched, raspy laugh. It was so opposite of his hyper-masculine Monwyn persona.

"I was spectacular, wasn't I?"

"You were. You are." I smiled into the side of his chest, remembering just how spectacular I had found him, and his body, those first few days at Verus. "I know you'll keep me safe." He took my hand into his much larger one and inspected my nails. "How should I act at dinner? Submissive? Like I was at the Den? Head down, eyes lowered?"

"No—as much as it pains me to say it—be yourself... Ethens seems to like it."

I shot my fist into his stomach where it landed with a soft thud against the violet silk vest he wore.

"We should resume your training at once. Your muscles lack—"

"Fuck off."

He pulled me tighter, nearly cutting off my air supply.

"Your ladies' soiree will occur in three days, by the way. The husbands have petitioned for the right to be present."

"Three days! You couldn't have consulted me? Three days to plan and... husbands? The point was to be free of them."

Two quick raps sounded from above, and the carriage slowed.

"We have arrived. You look lovely, by the way—red suits you."

"Highness." The door opened, and Ambrose climbed out, blocking my view. He turned to take my hand, and I ducked down, still getting used to the weight and height of the curls atop my head. Allaine had fashioned the style by adding multiple hues of brown fibers to my crown and sweeping the ringlets up as tall as she could. The jeweled barrettes that Ethens had gifted me showed prominently at the front of the mass.

When I looked up, I was surprised and perhaps a little disheartened by the quaint two-story home in front of me. For all I'd heard of his wealth, I expected to be dining in the most opulent home in the capital… not a modest, gray cottage. The two-story home had rose-colored shutters and a host of pots containing spent herbs. I could still detect the fragrance of rosemary and thyme as we ventured up the walkway. There was a cluster of chairs on the terracotta-colored porch, and I could see lacy, white curtains in the low light that shone through the windows.

The front door opened as we approached, and a middle-aged butler bade us forward.

"Cloaks," he said while snapping his fingers in the air.

Two servants rushed forward, relieving us of our outerwear.

"This way." He snapped again, and the two younger men scurried off from the dimly lit foyer. We followed the man, who was dressed in a basic gray short coat. We passed through a sitting room, done up in shades of green and inundated with floral prints. The couches were floral, the pillows flower-shaped. The artwork depicted fields of pink, red, and gold. And the lace didn't end at the windows. Practically every surface barring the fireplace's mantel was covered in frilly tatted cloth.

As we continued, it dawned on me that there were no modern lamps on the walls at all. Instead, the light came from tapers and old-style lamps like my gram used to use—with wicks embedded in cork, floating in globes of oil.

The dining room was much the same. There was a wide stone hearth, whose flames were stoked high, and surrounding it were bundles of roses strung upside down and hung from the ceiling. A table, set for three, was positioned near the fire. Plain copper stemware and plates were laid out, and there were only spoons on the table. I saw no other cutlery.

An intimate affair then.

Ambrose was led to his seat and immediately took his ease, and I stood and waited for our high-ranking guest as custom dictated.

"Precious Troth of Verus… you should have been seated before this boorish man. Surely, he agrees that your countenance is the most regal he has ever laid his eyes on?"

Lord Ethens had arrived.

Slight of build, with a face as plain as they come, the basic coat of brown that he wore belied the man I had met before. The man in the Den had been clad in a shocking ensemble of fuchsia and red.

"Oh, I doubt that, Lord Ethens. He's quite fond of his own countenance."

The side of his thin-lipped mouth hitched slightly as he swept his brown braid over his shoulder. Like Ambrose, the sides of his head were shaved down, with the middle length left to grow long.

"I have no such deficiency. If you find yourself tempted by coin or precious stone, I would gladly make you a worthwhile offer," our host said.

I let my eyes drift around, taking in the decades-old decor, and settled my gaze, questioningly, back on our host.

"While other men spend their fortunes on worthless manors that suck them dry, or waste their funds on the newest fashions and frippery, my assets increase daily. There are many who crow loudly, pretending to have wealth. I use my wealth to pretend they don't exist."

Hmm... Good sense and confidence.

"In another realm, perhaps. But you see, Ambrose has captured my full attention with his *more* than satisfactory assets."

A smile stretched wide across Ethens's mouth, the first I had seen from him. It transformed his plainness. Despite being well into his fourth decade, his sugary-sweet grin lent him a kind of boyish charm. Where they were mediocre before, now his hazel eyes crinkled endearingly at the corners.

"Your impertinence is delectable," he said while coming to stand in front of his chair.

"Are you surprised that His Highness's *slave* girl has a mind of her own?" Ethens's mouth parted slightly, and he leaned forward, placing his palms flat on the table in front of him. "Did you think I would forget the way you referred to me in the Den?"

"Ambrose." He twisted his head and studied the Monwyn prince. Ambrose sat with his ankle propped on his knee, one perfect brow arched. "What would you have from me? Name it."

"I am too jealous by far, Ethens—between her rosy petals lies the key that unlocked my every desire."

"Yes... they are spectacular, Highness. Full and lush, pouty when riled."

"No, Ethens... not those lips," Ambrose purred.

The lord's Adam's apple bobbed as he swallowed loudly.

"Lykksun's mercy, I must sit before I make a spectacle of myself." He dropped into the floral chair, and I followed suit, straightening my spine and lowering my eyes. "Let us enjoy a meal while we get down to the reason for our rendezvous."

The butler snapped, and the same two servants who had taken our cloaks dashed into the room with laden arms.

"I despise waiting for courses. I wish to have all of my delights at once."

The servants set several wooden platters before us and revealed a tantalizing spread.

"Lady Troth," the butler began, "before you, we have cabbage steaks, heavily peppered and roasted in oil from the rift valley, each smothered in a sauce of cream and aged cheese. To the left, flat beans with onion, and to the right, carrots marinated in vinegar and mustard seed. In the large bowl is a savory oat dish, flavored with garlic and topped with mushrooms and soft poached eggs."

I drummed my fingers excitedly against the table, ready to dig in, but paused when I realized both men were staring. Ambrose rolled his eyes, and Ethens's shoulders trembled ever so slightly.

"Highness, does she often dance about when presented with her meal?"

"She does," Ambrose sighed, "every time."

Ethens's eyelids fluttered shut.

"Gammond delivered the ultimate package right to your royal lap. I hope you are worthy of his gift."

"You question my worth?" Ambrose sat up and leaned forward, his top lip curling.

Oh, nether.

I dipped into the bowl of oats and dug out a spoonful, slapping the fare on my plate with a plop. If they wanted to fight, I'd be happy to eat in the corner.

"I question everything, Highness."

I tucked in while listening to the back and forth. After a few minutes of escalation, I hailed a servant. The man ran quickly to my side and bowed low.

"My apologies for their bickering. This dish is superb. I don't recall ever having oats prepared in this manner, and I am simply in love. Are you able to deliver a message to your master for me?"

The servant flicked his eyes to the argument embroiled Ethens and back to me.

"I do realize I could do it myself, but my husband-to-be is *so* suspicious."

The servant nodded, and I whispered to him between bites.

"Eira, what do you need?" Ambrose said in a gruff tone.

"I was making inquiries about the dish; wouldn't it be outstanding to serve it to our guests after our Joining?"

He huffed exaggeratedly and turned back to Ethens. "Now answer my question. Why are we here?"

I awkwardly spoon-lifted a round of cabbage, careful not to let a single smidge of sauce fall from its toasted layers.

"Because of that very thing." Ethens nodded in my direction. "Joinings are expensive, Highness, and so too are reputations."

The complex, buttery, and smoky flavors hit my tongue all at once. He may live like a pauper, but Ethens ate like a king. *Mmm, this is a close second to fucking.*

Two heads whipped around, one set of eyes wide and round, the other sharp and focused.

"Was that not in my head?" I asked, smiling weakly while I swiped at the errant glob that had settled on my chin.

"She drenches at the mention of cake." Ambrose took a heaping scoop of beans and a steak of cabbage from the platters.

"Ambrose, I do not!"

I scooped up another mouthful of oats. Another bit of yolk dripped from the corner of my lips. Ethens shot to his feet and reached across the table.

Ambrose launched himself forward, catching the lord's hand an inch from my nose.

"If you touch her... I will ruin you."

Ambrose brought my yolk-covered fingers to his mouth and sucked my sticky digits clean.

Like a man entranced, Ethens watched, unblinking, until his servant refilled his cup and then bent to his ear.

My stomach tightened, and a tingling thrill swept through me.

Ethens nodded to his help and slowly reclaimed his seat, but not before granting me a look at the not-so-mediocre part of him. I'd all but forgotten the wine-cask-sized appendage he wielded between his legs. Like a baguette sticking out of a basket—a bun served with an arm-sized sausage—it was visible even under the heavy wool pants he wore. Goddess me, I couldn't comprehend the mechanics of living with such a thing.

"When did you become so averse to sharing, Highness? So boring... but I digress. Partly on account of your heritage, you are not popular amongst the court. I am willing to ensure you and yours are seen in the best light, which will no doubt prove a costly endeavor. Being an Obligate and Joining with another will help, but if you've read your history books, the unpopular, even those *born* of royal loins, have toppled—rather gruesomely in some cases."

Ambrose remained silent, but I could see his mind working. He let his lashes drift low and propped his chin under his fist. I knew his adoption was a sore spot for him, and I myself had heard many outright nasty comments from those of lesser status.

"Lord Ethens, your kindness is appreciated," I said. I reached out to Ambrose, and he took my hand in kind. "What is it you want in return?"

"What are you willing to offer in return?" he asked.

Never let anyone name their price open-ended. Devotee Mariad's advice floated through my mind.

"Be done with the charade; you invited us here for a specific reason. What need do you have of us?"

"Not *us*, Lady Troth... just you."

I inclined my head and kept my expression neutral.

"Go on."

Ethens fiddled around in his seat, no doubt adjusting his horse-sized man part.

"I seek a wife."

"A noble one with an impeccable lineage? A wealthy one? One who will not mind your... hobbies?"

Ambrose dug into his meal while Ethens chewed on a mouthful of beans and carrots.

"I want a companion. I need an heir as soon as possible, and she *must* be respectable. I don't care what she looks like; enough makeup and the right outfit and I will rise to the occasion."

"Mmhmm, there's more. *Spit it* out, Ethens."

A sputtering cough came from my side. I jumped up and pounded a choking Ambrose in the middle of his wide back.

"I'm fine... fine," he wheezed, wiping at the corners of his mouth.

I took his face between my hands and placed a little kiss on his brow before squirming my way onto his lap. Ethens needed to know we came as a team.

Ethens sat back and slunk low in his chair. He took a long drink of wine and studied me over his glass.

"I want a ranking woman. A Nortian baroness, an Obligate, perhaps a Gaean princess. Any of those would be acceptable."

There it is. He wanted the renown of royalty or religion. He didn't need the dowry of a Monwyn heiress.

"Did you purchase your title, Lord Ethens, or was it granted? You don't come across as old blood."

Ambrose went rigid under me. *Not a dinner friendly topic I suppose.*

"Shrewd *and* astute." Ethens chewed thoughtfully and took another helping of oats. "My people originally came from the islands, the Kingdom of Inglis, before the war. We were nothing there, and even less after its fall. My family was bestowed the title for services rendered during the battle."

"And a woman of status will..."

"... shine brighter than any Monwyn miss could."

The Nortian baronesses are near the end of their child-bearing years, but their daughters could be considered. Cinden or Richelle. The idea of either of them calling this cottage home seems absurd. Gaea I'm sure has lots of princesses, but negotiations would mean communicating with the Primus-King.

Ambrose swept his hand around the curls at my back and brought them to rest over my shoulder. The action pulled my head gently to the side.

"Were I to negotiate such a contract, we would be paid in...?"

"Lands, shares in trade endeavors, temples built with you named their patron."

"All of those things sound quite nice, but there will be an upfront cost for the work of securing a contract like the one you wish—and of course, as Obligates and royalty, the right to choose will be theirs or their father's. No matter how loudly your coin speaks, they may refuse you."

Ethens sipped his wine while he thought.

"Your fee would be what?"

"You will arrange a shipment of whalebone products. They will be distributed to the poor of Monwyn in Ambrose's name for the duration of three years. I will require a Solnnan servant who is comfortable making the journey between our kingdoms, and you will pay his yearly fee. In addition, you will foot the cost of our Joining garments. They will be quite pricey—the Millanderers know the worth of their craft."

Ethens eyes darkened over the rim of his drink.

"All of that for an arrangement that might never come to fruition? I think no—"

"Did you think I wouldn't sweeten the deal? How dare you, my lord... you didn't let me finish."

He sighed loudly and circled a finger in the air, motioning for me to continue.

"I thought you might enjoy a spot at the bedding, which will occur following our Joining. I recently won a bet where Ambrose promised to—I don't remember the exact words—fuck me on cake, with cake, while eating cake... Something to that effect."

"Draw up the contracts." Ethens dropped his head into his palms and grunted loudly. "And I'm buying the cake."

CHAPTER 17

IS THIS HEALTHY?

"What do you know about Ethens, Allaine?"

In my closet, I changed out of the red dress patterned with large, gold medallions and wrapped Ambrose's robe around me.

I weighed the fat purse of coins that Ethens's servant had slipped into my coat as we left and hid it in the lining of a fur-lined gown that I would never be able to wear without bursting into flame. Ambrose and Cato may think themselves in control, but I'd be damned if I left my fate solely in their hands. This entire plot could tank for any number of reasons and it wasn't like having one more person watch our consummation would make it any more embarrassing.

"My father holds him in high regard. He seems to be a man of strong faith and morals. He attends temple and has his hands in a ton of philanthropic endeavors."

I wondered, briefly, if it was her father or one of her brothers who I'd "met" in the Den? I remembered the boots but never saw the man's face.

"Ethens and I danced at a fair once. I was hiding behind a sweets vendor after having snuck out, and I think he felt bad for me. He wasn't light on his feet at all, but he was a good conversationalist. And he didn't gawk at my arm. He did, however, rat me out to my father, who I think lost his mind over his baby being alone. I didn't glimpse the sun for a month afterward."

I made my way into the bathing room and saw my companion stifle a yawn.

"Are you feeling better? I was worried about you this afternoon."

"I am. The illness passed quickly but has left me—Your Highness!"

"Head to your rooms, Lady Allaine. I am most capable of undressing my lover." Ambrose sauntered into the chamber in nothing but a pair of long, gray pants.

His hair was fully unbound, flowing down his shoulders and ending mid-back. He was eating a sausage.

Allaine went pale, and bright fever splotches raced across her cheeks. She stared at the comb-filled basket in her hands like it was the only thing tethering her to this realm.

"Allaine, thank you for running the bath. Please retire," I said, keeping an eye on her balance. *Poor thing.*

She bobbed her head over and over and dashed to the door, nearly taking out a stack of towels in her flight.

"Ambrose, how are you eating again? I'm so bloated on cabbage and beans I might float away."

"The man had no meat. Did you notice that? No chicken, no beef, no sausage." Ambrose scowled and shoved the remainder of the length into his mouth.

"Probably because it gets stuck in your teeth? I bet he hates that," I joked.

"Meat makes muscles. I need two pounds daily to keep in top form." Ambrose whipped off his pants in a smooth motion and strolled toward the tub.

"Are you taking my bath?"

"This is *my* bath, selfish. Do not forget who affords you this lavish lifestyle," he grumbled while lowering himself into the *T* shaped tub. "Wash my hair. I'm tired, and we still have to meet with my father."

"Alright." I enjoyed fussing over his hair. In the past, it had put me into an almost meditative state. I gathered my hem above my knees and made my way behind the tub, nudging bottles and jars of soap out of my path.

Ambrose needed touch, and I didn't mind the chore.

He dipped his hair into the hot water while I sat and dangled my legs over the edge and into the bath. Sure enough, long bruises had begun appearing on my thighs from my earlier excursion with Cato. Just the sight of them rekindled a flicker in my core. Sex with Cato was—

Ambrose flopped his mass of hair in my lap, slinging water over my thighs and soaking the tile under my butt. *And I am committing a lifetime to this.*

"Which cleanser do you want?"

"The red jar."

I intentionally dipped my hand into an orange container and slapped a blob into the middle of his head.

"What's this scent, Amby-bear? I like it." I sniffed the very un-Ambrose-smelling air.

"Neroli, you oppositional little shrew. It is Mama's favorite."

I scrubbed the suds through his scalp and massaged his head with my fingertips.

"Your mother is Taleery, correct?"

"Mmhmm. She was the last of her line. Her people remained in the desert kingdom after the war and continued trying to rebuild. Her betrothal to my father was a last attempt to connect to the trade routes. It was not a successful endeavor."

"And what remains of the kingdom, anything?"

"Ruins," Cato answered.

He slipped through the doorway and stood, leaning on the doorframe with one ankle crossed over the other. "I have traveled through all three of the former kingdoms. Spirits are their only residents now."

My eyes roamed from his feet up to his face—rumpled pants, torn at the knee, his collar splattered with blood and sleeves heavily grass-stained.

"Cato, are you unwell?"

A deep furrow creased his forehead.

"Tell me how your evening went. We will speak of me in a moment."

He walked into the room and turned a chaise around to face the tub before reclining on its surface. His fingers went to his temples, pressing and kneading the tension there.

"Cato, let me—"

I tried to stand, but his raised voice halted me. "No, love, stay where you are."

The words stung, despite the endearment.

Ambrose tilted his head back, his eyes connecting with mine. He shook his head gently and patted my knee.

"As it turns out, Cat, Eira paid attention in some of her Troth courses. Ethens was eating from her palm. We have secured garments, charitable donations, and... and cake of all things."

"Don't forget my Solnnan manservant."

"There is no way in the nether you—"

"And he wants?" Cato interrupted.

"A wife with a lineage. Princess, Obligate, the Queen of Solnna perhaps," I said not hiding my smile.

Cato pressed his lips together, as his color deepened. "He and Troth Cinden would fight like feral cats in a dominance match... Richelle would giggle him into a fit of lunacy. He would have to look less like a big toe to capture a queen."

I nodded in agreement. He wasn't wrong. Cinden would take one look at the lacy curtains and laugh. Richelle, she would... well, she'd be adorable surrounded by the floral prints. A lesser-queen's daughter *might* be persuaded by his coin.

"I could honestly imagine Richelle clapping her way through the Den. 'Look at that splendid outfit, Ethens, outstanding! So very pink, it matches her areolas perfectly!'" Ambrose's chuckling sent little waves of warm water up and down my calves.

"My plan is to present his offer, send it out, and then whatever happens, happens. Nowhere will the contract say a Joining *must* take place. Also, please invite him to the bedding ceremony, Protector."

"Are you fucking serious?" Cato rubbed his eyes and leaned back against the rounded head of the chaise.

"Cat. Please tell us what's wrong." It tore me to pieces seeing, almost feeling, how upset he was—how utterly drained he looked.

He sat up and twisted, settling his boots on the ground.

"The 'us' you speak of is exactly what's wrong." He paused briefly and looked beyond where I sat. "My every minute is consumed with thinking about or planning the next time I see you, Eira. I look at my brother and think of hurting him while at the same time knowing that I love him." Cato hung his head. "Ambrose is correct; the safety of this kingdom has become infinitely less important than my need for *you*."

"Cato, I—"

"Brother, we could stay in Colpass for a time and give you room to clear your mind."

Cato's head snapped up.

"If you make to remove her, I will hunt you down and bury you while you still breathe, Ambrose."

"Cato! You'll do no such thing. You've stared down true evil: trolls, wraiths, and assassins. Ambrose is none of those, and you know it."

"I do know it, which makes this all the more damning."

"How do we help you? You know we'll do anything to—"

"Would you, though?" Cato shook his head back and forth, and his eyes began to glisten.

"O-of course we would. Cato, we—"

"Eira, when Septimus trained me, he taught me that pushing my limits led to the control I needed to fulfill my role. If I am to have power over this, power over myself… I must push the boundaries and expose myself to the trauma causing my weakness."

I thought for a moment, pondering his words.

"I understand the theory behind exposing yourself, Cato, but it also seems like a path to further harm. I don't understand what you need. Should we abstain for a period of time? It could be—"

"No, Goddess, no. The thought sends me into a rage."

"Then what?" I asked, concerned to the point of tears.

"You and Ambrose will perform while I maintain my distance and overcome my emotional reaction."

"You're joking." I grabbed a towel to dry my hands. "This is asinine. You need to rest, to take care of yourself."

"Fuck off, brother. What you are asking for is cruel. I revel in the art of exhibition, but you are not made as I am."

Cato balled his fists against his forehead.

"I no longer flinch at the reeking stench of troll or the sight of a man cleaved in two. I can bludgeon a woman until only her viscera remains and eat dinner an hour later. It was exposure that allowed me to master the trials I have faced."

I scooted backward, aiming to put distance between Ambrose and myself, but he caught my foot and held tight. I kicked out, but he didn't let go.

"What you are asking for sounds like a recipe for destroying your mind—and the relationships we have built between us."

"It is what I know. It is what has worked," Cato said.

Ambrose nodded once, stood, and turned. He slid his hand past my knee and reached under the side of my robe.

"Ambrose, don't entertain this."

He pushed the wet silk up, exposing my thighs and the curls at my apex.

"He knows his mind, Eira. We do not. I would do anything for my brother, *anything*."

I searched Cato's face. The muscles in his jaw clenched and released, and his respirations were uneven. The dark eyes that held mine were obsidian—I could no longer make out even a trace of the golden edge that normally surrounded their center.

"And I know nothing?" I asked, bracing my hands against Ambrose's chest. Water trailed down his torso, and his erection nodded above the surface of the water.

He reached a hand out and cupped my vulva. I closed my eyes and shook my head from side to side.

"Eira, if I feel like he's a threat to you, I will snap. I must reconcile this fight in my head. Please, love, if you are able, if you can, enjoy his touch."

This wasn't real life.

This was backward.

Is this how Monwyn men are made?

Ambrose drew his finger up and down my cleft.

"Yes or no," he whispered so softly that I didn't think even Cato could hear it. His green gaze captured mine, and I saw the concern written plainly on his face.

Could I do this to Cato?

For Cato.

I closed my eyes and sat in the solitude of my mind. I couldn't think of an alternate solution.

Stiffly, I nodded my consent.

"S-say it, Eira." Cato's voice wavered.

I squared my shoulders.

"You may touch me," I said in the clearest tone I was capable of.

Ambrose shifted to the side, giving Cato a direct view of us, which meant I had a direct view of him. *Strange and thoughtful, Ambrose...* Though his hand hadn't stirred my passions, I think he knew that seeing Cato might.

Ambrose guided a finger past my entrance and into my passage.

"More," Cato gritted out in a lifeless and flat voice. "Please her or I will bust your face wide open."

Ambrose knelt on the tubs floor, bent low and spread my thighs. His mouth found my entrance and he began dipping his tongue into my passage rythmically. I clawed the marble floor, caught in sensations of both pleasure and shame. I shifted my eyes back and forth, going between Cato's reactions and the expert tongue flicking over my sensitive skin. Being with Ambrose had never been as intense as making love to Cato, but he knew his craft well.

I could feel the warmth spreading across my chest—my body reacting even while my mind was in turmoil. A soft moan slipped from my lips when Ambrose joined a finger to the ministrations of his mouth. He applied light pressure to the top wall of my passage and rubbed me until a jolt of deliciousness ran clear to my stomach.

"More." Cato's fists shook, but he didn't look away.

Ambrose placed his hand in the center of my chest and pushed my back to the floor. He wrapped his palms around my thighs, and he pulled me forward, sliding me over the water-slicked tiles and onto his erection.

I closed my eyes as he worked his long length into my body in a series of short strokes.

His breathing hitched in his throat. He withdrew and entered me over and over until he was slick with my moisture.

I dug my fingertips into his shoulders and held fast. He was beautiful to watch, even under these circumstances. His mouth slackened and tendrils of his hair fell over his passion-hazed eyes.

Ambrose increased his pace, thrusting until he was moaning low in his throat. Water sloshed over the bathtub's rim and ran into my hair.

"Cato." I looked to where he sat. "This isn't healthy."

Goddess, no.

Droplets of Cato's blood fell from the fists he clenched, and crimson splatters dotted the white floor.

Ambrose licked and kissed my sternum and breasts, and he placed his hand under my rear, tilting me up to receive him. Reflexively, my legs circled his waist, and my hips bucked, urging him on.

"Brother, please stop... please." Cato was bereft. I'd never heard him sound so pained.

Immediately, Ambrose pulled away from me and took a step back while throwing his hands into the air. He spun and faced his brother.

"Take her, Cat. Relieve yourself."

Cato surged to his feet.

"I cannot." A violent shudder wracked his body. He shook like an addicted man in the throes of withdrawal. "We meet with the king at first light."

He turned on his heels and disappeared through the door.

I sat on the edge of the bath, stuck somewhere between bewilderment and mortification.

"That was horrific." Ambrose was the first to speak. "I do not derive nearly as intense a pleasure from being pressured to fornicate."

"*You* were pressured?" I snapped out of my stupor and slid into the tub. "You jumped right in."

"Of course. I took the orders I was given. Am I not allowed to experience feelings at the same time? Now, help me."

I finished washing and glanced up.

Ambrose looked ill. He stood slightly hunched over, and his brows nearly met in the middle.

"This has never happened. I am in considerable pain."

He weighed his arousal in his hand.

"You could take care of it yourself."

"And you could, for the second time in your life, do something nice for me. I will take anything."

There were lines around his mouth, and he'd gone back to looking like a massive ball of stress and strain.

I nodded. I didn't like to see Cato in pain, and, it turns out, it hurt me to see Ambrose that way as well. I stepped up on the bench seat and bent over the edge of the tub, lying my belly against the cold tile floor.

"Can you reach if I'm... ohhh..."

Yes, he could.

"Still wet. Your nasty slit must be deity-blessed as well." Ambrose held my hips as he penetrated me from behind.

Guilt and arousal coursed through me.

"Nasty? There is nothing about me that is na—"

"Mmhmm, your moisture tells me you want it all, and I will teach you the nastiest things I know. Remember the first time we bathed together?"

Of course I did. I went from wanting to kill him for trespassing to trying to fuck him in a three-second loop of temporary insanity. I bit down on my lip and let my eyes drift shut.

"In the future, Eira, we will kiss intimately. You only ever kiss me when you're faking it, and I am not satisfied. We will have heat between us, wife. We will share our passion and longing. I will probe you with a host of interesting items, and you will return the favor. I want you to use me. Tie me up and take your pleasure. Force me to my knees and fuck me until I scream your name."

The friction of my nipples sliding against the marble floor sent twists of excitement spiraling through my stomach. Ambrose's words gripped me like the fingers caressing my sides. But I wasn't ready to let go—to share my release with him. It felt too intimate, too personal still. I wanted that part of me to belong to Cato, but he was certainly testing my resolve.

I needed this to go faster.

Recalling a piece of advice from my course at Verus, I crossed my ankles and clenched down on my pelvic muscles before backing myself onto him roughly.

"Mmmm, there's a good girl." His fingers dug into my hip bones. Instead of thrusting, he rolled his pelvis against my rear, and his testicles hit against my overstimulated clitoris.

"Ahhh... there we are. I love butting up against your cervix. Knowing I am as deep as possible—ramming the very entrance to your womb."

Holy fuck.

He grunted in my ear, and I felt him pulse inside me.

"Ouch!" A big, wet palm landed hard on my rear.

"Thanks, hun. I owe you one." He leaned low and whispered.

"You owe me two, *hun.*" I stepped off the platform and grabbed a jar of soap. "There is something seriously wrong with you, you know?"

"Really? Why would that be? You did not seem to think there was something seriously wrong with me a moment ago. And before you answer, I was blessedly aware of every squeeze and contraction you made. I keep track."

"Pardon me?"

"Keep track. I write down what works for you and what doesn't. How else do you tailor an experience?"

Ambrose climbed out of the tub and toweled himself off.

"I... I just lie back or... or hop on?"

Ambrose's mouth fell open.

"Eira, you are so crass. Just entirely insensitive to the needs of others."

I ignored the man-child and washed his mess from my vagina.

Clean and dressed for the night, we made our way to the bedroom.

I climbed into bed and held the covers up.

"Ambrose, what are we to do?"

He stretched his long body beside mine and patted his shoulder. I curled up closely and sighed into his chest.

"Whatever he needs, it is all we can do."

Chapter 18

MONWYN'S AND THEIR MINES. QUARRIES?

Pardon me... it's a cavity.

"I expected first light to include light."

Cato tightened his hold around my waist and leaned in closely.

"To meet someone at first light, you must be up well before." He pressed his cheek to mine, and his lips settled under my earlobe.

"Did you plan this dark excursion so you could hold me so closely, Protector?" I asked while trying to twist around to face him. Our mount was keeping up the solid pace he'd set but wasn't going fast enough to prohibit conversation.

"It did not cross my mind even once." He chuckled. "Though it certainly is a perk." I leaned back into him, seeking closeness, but the hidden armor he'd donned pressed hard against my spine. "Your safety is currently more concerning than my obsessive need to touch you."

Images of last night floated through my head, cooling my love-warmed mind.

"Cato, what of your safety? I'm sure your hands still hurt, and I cannot abide the fact that I took part in causing you pain. Will you be asking me to... perform for you again?"

There was a long pause.

"When I picture it, Eira, my immediate reaction is still one of a violent nature. When I am able to cope with the image in my head, I will reassess the magnitude of my response and make a determination as to my needs. Was it so awful?"

"Cato, loosen your grip." He relaxed the arm that had begun to bind my waist tightly.

"Apologies, love," he whispered.

"The act itself, no. Ambrose is... He's fine. Hurting you? That was horrendous."

The horse turned sharply, and we left the paved path and headed into a field of tall grass.

"I will not ask it of you again unless it is entirely necessary."

"Are you sure we shouldn't *all* slow down on the physical intimacy? Would that not help you to acclimate, taking it slow?"

"Frankly, the more I fuck you, the better I feel about someone else getting to fuck you."

"I'm not sure that makes sense." I was a little lost in his rationale. "But by all means, fuck me as often as you can."

"I intend to," he stated matter-of-factly.

I laughed out loud and turned my face up, catching his wicked half-smile. There was a promise in his eyes, one I couldn't wait for him to fulfill.

On the other side of the field now, Cato slowed our mount and took us over a tall hill. We followed its gentle slope back down.

"While you're in charge of my safety this fine morning, who is guarding the king?"

"Bem."

"*Bem?*"

"Bem," he repeated.

"Poor-postured, pot-bellied, doesn't-say-much Bem? The Bem I tried to—"

"Yes, Eira, judgmental brat, that Bem." I held tightly to his leather-cased arms as we rode down a sharp decline. "Much to my embarrassment, it has been two years, maybe more, since I have been his equal in our sparring matches."

"Look me in the eyes, Protector. I think you're lying to me. I think that—"

"Who do you think has protected *me* all these years? Do you think I could ever shut my eyes if there was no one to thwart my enemies? If there was no one better than me, when would I take a shit? Ask yourself that. And fucking would be right out. No time for my hobbies."

"Shitting and fucking, huh?" I laughed. I was trying to imagine any scenario where the fleshy Bem would be victorious over Cato or even Ambrose. "Are those your favorite hobbies?"

"No, I also work with string—look over there." He pointed a finger into the distance.

A tiny sliver of sun appeared over the top of a mountain range and cast a gentle morning glow on the world in front of us. I squinted my eyes, attempting to bring into focus what my mind couldn't understand. There appeared to be a massive hole in the ground, one large enough that most of Verus temple could have rested in its depths.

"Is that a mine?" I asked, knowing how important the rock and mineral trade was to the kingdom.

"It is a quarry, or more specifically, it is a basalt cavity. The dark and lighter striping you see is from the scoring of our chisels and pickaxes. We use what is pulled from this location to pave our streets. Basalt is durable and plain, but it often contains the geodes that give us amethysts. I have seen all shades of purple quartz pulled from this location—lilac to deep violet, reddish to plum."

"So you like rocks?"

"I'm Monwyn." The side of his mouth quirked.

So adorable.

"My favorite mineral is zincite, and my favorite gemstone is orange sapphire, but you will not find either here..."

Cato continued, expounding on the history of certain minerals and the cultural significance of some stones over others. I listened to him, happy and content to hear him speak of something he enjoyed, while I relaxed in his arms.

As we neared the quarry's edge, I looked down into the yawning chasm. I gripped the sides of Cato's thighs as a short-lived wave of vertigo hit me.

"I don't like this. We're too high up. Why isn't there railing?" I squeezed my eyes closed and leaned in the direction of safety. "Take us back that way, please. "

"The meeting will take place in the middle of it."

"In the middle of this canyon?" I ventured another peek, and my stomach flipped and flopped. "No sir. I don't like it-it's vastness."

"Is the ocean not vast, Nortia? And you have peered over the balconies of Verus—stared off Mount Gammond and into the wilds."

"And?"

"And I will guide you down. The ladder is perfectly sound and—"

"Okay, fine. But never choose this location again. Never." My palms began sweating, and my heart felt as if it were beating a million thumps per minute.

"I chose the location based on the intel *you* provided. The walls should contain the king—unless he can fly, Goddess forbid. The location is remote enough that if there is a need to subdue him, permanently or otherwise, there would be none to bear witness, and most importantly, he is unable to pull his magic fuel from the stone that will surround us."

"Though he could certainly make it explode," I offered.

"Eira, shut up."

"Eira, shut up," I mocked in my deepest voice.

His laugh rumbled through the air.

The ladder wasn't as horrific as I expected. It was more of a scaffolding with wide rungs, not narrow wooden slats, as I'd feared. We successfully descended and began our hike into the quarry's center—now maintaining a proper and very formal distance between one another.

"They are right up ahead," Cato said, pointing to the right of a little canvas-topped lean-to. I could see several more of the white tents dotted near a massive divot on the far side of the cavern.

Ambrose was standing alongside Bem, and the king sat between them, on a short, cross-legged folding chair. Another seat lay about a horse's length away from him.

Bem was bundled up in all brown, not his usual blue livery. Ambrose was ensconced in a coat of muted gray, which matched the garment the king wore. Both of them blended in well with the basalt backdrop. Without their patterned silks and brocades, they looked much more like commoners, not two of the highest-ranking men in the land. As we neared, I could see that standing out of earshot, two additional guards had come along. One of them was Levaunt, the man I'd recently helped His Majesty stash into a closet.

"Eira, my dove," Ambrose greeted me. "I assume the Protector was able to deliver you to us with little issue?"

The king smiled kindly and waved me over to the empty seat.

"No trouble at all. Thank you, darling." I curtsied and walked between two mounds of rubble before sitting. "Your Majesty."

"Daughter, might I offer you my coat? The air is brisk, and my boys mannerless."

I kept my face serene, despite Ambrose looking like he'd just swallowed something sour.

"No, Majesty, the cold doesn't bother me, but thank you."

Cato stepped forward momentarily, cutting off my view of the others.

"Bem, perimeter."

Without reply, the Protector's protector walked away, and Cato filled in his empty spot, standing over his father's left shoulder. He turned in a circle surveying the entire area and nodded to each of the guards before crossing his arms over his wide chest.

"Ambrose, begin. I would like to return before the palace wakes."

Ambrose's wide-skirted coat billowed around his legs as he moved. He still stood close to the king but now looked him in the eyes.

"Father, Eira asked me to arrange this meeting as she feels it necessary to discuss her concerns about your highly illegal activities—the likes of which you seem netherbent on including her in."

The king's pale eyes crinkled, and his bushy mustache hitched, revealing his cracked-tooth smile.

"Of course I am delighted to spend time with her, but we could have easily held our conflab in the warmth of our home." He lifted his arms, and his heavy sleeves fell back, revealing shackles.

"Protector, are those truly necessary?" I asked. Seeing the older man in the confine of his bindings hurt my heart. His liver-spotted skin was thin, and the metal would rub it raw.

"Do not question my measures," a stern-faced Cato said.

I arched my brow in his direction but gave no reply.

Cato turned, began rummaging around in the leather satchel he frequently carried, and pulled out two leather-bound books.

"And yes, they are necessary." He took a couple of steps in my direction, then reached out and handed me the tomes.

The volumes were small and very well-used. The texture of the leather was worn smooth where a reader's fingers would have held the book open as they leafed through the pages.

Ambrose squatted low and circled his arms around his knees. He balanced his nearly seven-foot frame impressively well on just his toes.

"Eira would like to understand the Bond you feel we share. She seeks knowledge of how it will impact our lives as we prepare to Join."

"Mmhmm, mmhmm." The king nodded his head up and down. "First, I will say, Fated *or* Mating Bonds are possible, and I am not sure which you may sh—"

"Majesty, my apologies for interrupting you, but would it be problematic for you to address me when answering the questions *I* have? I don't mean to be contrary. It just seems appropriate."

Ambrose and the king cocked their heads to the side and simultaneously raised their chins. *Infuriating and charming.*

"Right, yes, of course, daughter. That seems reasonable." He shimmied atop his chair and turned to face me directly. "Now then." He smacked his knees soundly with his shackled hands. "When I was navigating the ties of my own Bond—the one that tethered me to... to..."

"Your whore," Ambrose supplied.

The king's face fell, and his chest rose. He held his breath for several seconds until he released it all at once in a long sigh.

"The book you hold, the smallest—the green one," he pointed to the tome in my left hand, "classifies the various naturally occurring Bonds. Open it toward the middle and look for a thickly lined chart."

I flipped through the pages until I found what he described. The handwriting was incredibly light and fine, and the words were so tightly squeezed into the available space that it was difficult to make out the contents.

"You will see the most basic of Bonds first. This connection is *forced* by a conjurer—Oh! Like Crimlow, for example."

"Crimlow?" I questioned.

"Oh, dear, yes, you met him just the once."

I'd never wanted to know his name. Suddenly, the twisted attacker who'd haunted my dreams took on a more human face.

"That level of binding gives the conjurer," he pointed to himself, "the superior role and the bindee, the subordinate."

"Pri-mer-pri—" I struggled to make out the tightly sandwiched letters.

"Primitive, sweetheart. Primitive Bond. It's the simplest."

"And next is the Mating Bond?" I traced my fingertip below the sentence.

"Yes, that one is not forced; it is innate. Perhaps we are born with it? You will find much is not explained."

"It says 'animalistic sexual appetites. Chasing, hunting, with a focus on breeding.' This is what you experienced with your... your lover?"

He nodded.

"May I ask what happened? Are you still bonded? Is it as intense as it is between...?" I let my voice fade away.

The king looked at Ambrose, who was rubbing a chunk of rock between his fingers. He stared at a pile of rubble, seeing something the rest of us couldn't.

"My cub, can you bear it?" asked the king.

Ambrose balked at the endearment but inclined his head.

"Very well. A new Obligate arrived here some twenty-two years ago—maybe longer or less—it all runs together now." He stopped and placed his bearded chin between his hands. "I had never dealt with Chosen Ones. They have the propensity to think they know better than a seasoned monarch, but I digress. Imella, unlike myself, was effervescent—she loved to meet new people from differing kingdoms and befriended our newest Troth almost immediately. It was a year or so after the Obligate had arrived that Imella insisted I meet her bosom friend, and I agreed. Our connection was instant. I could scent her, feel her on my fingertips even when standing away from her. She felt it too." Again, His Majesty paused. His eyes misted over, and his throat worked up and down. "I couldn't control myself in front of my wife... or my children... and had no regard for any other than she."

Tears gathered in the corners of his yellow eyes and then fell, running crookedly along the deep folds of his aging cheeks.

"If it's too painful, please don't—"

"He deserves the pain." Ambrose's voice was flat and his eyes hard. "Continue."

His father nodded faintly.

"I removed Imella from our Joining bed and replaced her with another. I sat Soolie beside me at family dinners, danced only with her at balls, showered her with a monarch's wealth... and then... she fell pregnant with our child."

Ambrose sneered openly, but Cato remained impassive. A stepsibling, a woman replacing their mother. No wonder the wounds ran so deep. I reached toward Ambrose, but he brushed my fingers away.

"The tale does not end happily, I am afraid, but could it ever have? Our Bond changed just a few weeks before her courses stopped. If you continue reading, you will see that the Mating Bond breaks when successful procreation occurs."

Like taking a shot to the chest, I recoiled and slammed the book shut.

This is how it ends.

"Try not to worry, dear. It is very much the case that you could still find yourself compatible with each other afterward, though the unnatural lust subsides."

"Do the two of you still—"

"She took her life, daughter. She was an unmarried child of Gaea. Her shame for her actions... *our* actions... was more than she could bear. I regret to this day not reaching out and trying to do more for her."

My eyes blurred.

Will you breed me one day?

"Imella, rightfully, distanced herself, and... here we are."

The king sagged into himself.

My inhalations became tight and short, which caused my vision to see-saw. How could I bear it ending? Never hearing his laughter, his whispers. Never seeing the dimple on his cheek or holding him in my arms.

"Daughter, wait now, your tears break an old man's heart. There is a real chance you share a Fate Bond with Ambrose. It presents the same, physically, but the souls are tied permanently—open the book again, read it aloud."

I wiped the tears from my face with the sleeve of my thin overcoat and riffled through the pages once more.

"Wh-whereas Mating Bonds *may* pass the ability to their offspring, the issue of Fated Mates will *always* carry the capability to conjure. Fateds are bound until the time that one meets Merrias."

The thought of Cato in the afterlife without me by his side made bile rise in my throat.

"But, Majesty, how will we know? What of one's heart—of love and the life we build together?"

"Like everything, Marmot, you take the chance and pray for the best outcome."

I tried my best to refocus, to rein in the emotions that were screaming to burst forth—to remember what I was here for.

I couldn't look at Cato. I'd blow our cover.

"Can you share a Mating Bond with multiple people? Or a Fate Bond and Mating Bond at the same time?" My reeling mind went to Septimus—Gammond save me if we actually shared either. There was something there, but it wasn't like what Cato and I experienced.

"I am sure that is within the realm of possibilities, but I feel it would be incredibly rare. I admit to having no evidence, but the æther works as it wants."

The four of us sat in the odd silence—no sounds of nature could be heard this far into the massive rock cavern.

Ambrose stood and kicked at a dusty mound of pebbles.

"I need you to answer one more question."

"Go on." His Majesty's eyes refocused on me.

"Your story about how you came upon your ability. I have shared a similar experience, though I do not believe there was lightning involved."

"She exploded," Cato said.

Ambrose laid his hand on his father's shoulder and squatted once more, putting himself at the king's eye level before he spoke, "There was no sound, everything was thrown back, not even the grass remained around her."

The king's eyes flashed knowingly.

"I cannot even *begin* to imagine the ramifications for this world if you are both deity-blessed *and* house the ability. You must attempt to draw the æther, daughter."

"Absolutely not!" Ambrose shouted.

Cato's face darkened. "You would risk the life of my brother's wife-to-be. Think of the damage you have already caused."

"Catommandus, she will come to no harm. She will either be able to pull or she will not. If she has the ability and cannot learn to control it—that is where the potential for great destruction lies. I can guide her through the thick of it, and she cannot use the æther to conjure unless she is taught to do so."

"Without my consent, you will do no such thing, Father; hear me well." Ambrose shot to his feet and came to my side. His heavy hand fell on my shoulder, and he pulled me tightly against his thigh.

"Ambrose, I know this scares you. You were hurt so badly." I stood and took his hands into my own, warming his chilled skin in my palms. "But what of our future? I can't explode around our children. What if I hurt our loved ones because I never learn dominion over myself?"

"If you end up like him, you will hurt them anyway."

"I am *not* your father, Ambrose. We were born of different circumstances. And... and if you and I share a... a... Bond, we must prepare ourselves for the eventuality of how it may end. I've run away from so much already, and you have protected me like the most noble of men, but this we must face head-on. Together."

"I simply cannot let—"

"Brother mine," Cato stepped toward us, "trust your woman."

Ambrose blinked his eyes and stared at Cato while adjusting the collar of his coat. In turn, Cato dropped his left shoulder barely an inch and placed his right foot to the side. I'd seen them do this before when encountering trouble on the road from Colpass, and before that, when the Gaeans had attacked at Verus—they communicated without words.

"My sons, listen to me. While under my roof, no harm will come to my daughter. I was charged with her protection well before you were placed in your mother's womb—or hands in your case, little cub."

"And what, pray tell, are you protecting her from if not yourself, old man?" Steel flared in the king's eyes.

"Watch yourself, boy. I am here to ensure she thrives and will eliminate *any* who dare abuse her. That includes those who do not have her best interests in mind." His eyes bore into those of his adopted son.

"But why, father? What horror lurks in our world that is more odious than yourself?" Ambrose stepped forward, shoving me halfway around his back.

There was fury on the monarch's face. His eyes took on an inner glow, and his lips drew back, showing gritted teeth, and then, as quickly as it came, it disappeared. His hands trembled slightly, and a tic appeared in the muscle under his eye.

"Ambrose, sweetest of my boys..." He shook his head, and his chest visibly deflated. "I do not know what the danger is. I know no specifics beyond what Eira has, no doubt, told you. But I agree with Kitty Cat. Allow her to explore what the Goddess has planned for her."

Ambrose turned back to me. He bent at the hip and brought his face to mine.

"Do you want this? You are aware of the consequences of a conjurer discovered? You will be put to death, Eira. Verus and the High Council will demand it. My title, his title," he flung his hand toward his father, "will not stop them."

I heard the king scoff but kept my eyes focused. I knew how serious this decision was... the severity of the consequences that might follow.

Was anyone truly ready to face their demise?

Was this why my mother ran?

I thought of her strength and the chances she took to keep me from the maltreatment she'd known in Gaea.

"I would try." I brushed my thumb across his dark beard and ran my fingertips from his cheek to chin. The gesture wasn't false on my part, not done to further our ruse. It was *our* future at stake here—mine and Ambrose's.

"So be it." Ambrose hung his head.

"Cato, uncuff me." The king held his wrists out to his son.

"No, and do not ask again."

The king rolled his eyes skyward and made to stand. Cato shoved him back down.

"Catommandus, quit that. I will need to be near her while she attempts the pull. Ambrose, given your Bond, I believe she would feel most comfortable taking from you."

"No. She will take from me," Cato said. "Ambrose has never been pulled on and it appears I have. And from the looks of him, you nearly sucked Evandr dry."

"Evandr is a good boy, my favorite captor by far. Ambrose, do you agree with this?"

"Do I have a choice, Protector?"

"You do not."

"Then we begin," the king declared. "Cato, to your knees, right here." He pointed to the open space in front of him. "Eira, do the same. If it works, you may be wobbly the first time."

Cato dropped and sat back on his heels, and as I approached, he offered me his hand. Immediately, I felt that static surge of energy between us. He guided me down gently, and I arranged the folds of my dress, tucking them under my knees—pillowing them from the rocky floor.

"Listen closely, dear. As a potential novice, you will need to make contact with his flesh. The hands are not an easy place to draw from on account of the thicker skin. The neck is an option, but I would suggest the eyelids. Now, when you place your hands upon him—do you know how you can still see the light and shapes and colors against the darkness of your shuttered eyes?"

"Mmhmm, I do."

"You will follow those lights, explore them. Let them take you. It will be important to keep your eyes closed the first few times, or you will be transported out of the... the... I do not have a word for it—the siphon. You will feel it pull in your middle."

"Oh, through my belly button—where you pull from me?"

The king's smile was genuine.

"Yes, sweet one. Your... let us not call him victim... let us say, your snack. Your snack will not feel it, but because of how green you are, you might in this instance. Alright, let us try. Place your fingertips on his eyelids like you teach a child to pray."

One... two... three... breathe, Eira.

I was afraid. So very afraid.

Cato's eyes softened, and he reached out and took my hands in his. He placed my palms against his face.

He knew. Of course he did.

"Very good. Now, Eira, close your eyes."

I followed his directions and looked at the patterns of light that danced on the back of my lids. How was I supposed to follow it? Stare directly at it? Chase it as it twisted like the colorful kaleidoscope my grandmother loved so dearly?

I tried to keep my focus, but everything kept changing. Little flashes moved in and out like clouds moving in front of the sun. Dots and blobs swirled and peppered my vision haphazardly.

"Eira, stop. Do not try looking in a single space. See it all and clear your head. No thoughts, no imagery. Just follow."

I breathed in deeply and tried again.

I looked at the little starburst to my right and the dark spots to the front, concentrating as hard as I could. *Don't follow a single entity, Eira. See it all.*

Time passed, and my knees throbbed.

I stayed like this for what felt like an hour, my eyes still jumping between light and movement.

"Nothing, Your Majesty, there is nothing."

I opened my eyes and jerked my head backward, surprised by the trancelike state I found myself in.

"Perhaps then you do not carry the—"

"No wait, something was different when I woke. Cato—Protector. May I try again?"

"Yes," he said without hesitation.

I placed my fingertips on his eyes. I dropped my shoulders and willed myself to breathe softly, naturally, through the anxiety that welled inside me.

The light.

I allowed myself to take in the entire scene as it moved. As the lights flickered and streaked—it felt like my eyes were being pulled in two. *One, two, three, no, Eira, don't count.* I cleared my mind as best I could and tried my damnedest not to think about thinking.

Move away from it. Go.

Silence.

Shadows.

I *knew* the shadows—I'd met them twice before.

I followed the darkness as it closed in on my periphery. As if it had taken me by the hand, it led me behind my eyes.

The pull.

The siphon.

The light didn't beckon me. It was what lay in between instead.

There we were in the distance, Cato and I. So beautiful, so peaceful. I had no doubt we were Bonded. Just look at the way I touched my lover. The connection moved between us, a diffused glow of soft orange and red.

I heard him sigh contentedly and saw his middle arching toward me.

I felt it too, like the gentle tug of a string.

Yes, love, I'll take you inside me. Look how lovely we are, the way my chest rises and yours falls.

Cato slumped forward.

His body knocked mine to the ground.

"Too much, Eira. Pull back." I heard a voice somewhere in the distance.

Then came a blinding light.

Blinking against the sun's rays, I came to, my eyes burning and blurred. Cato lie heavily upon me. I could feel his breath on my cheek, and when my eyes focused, I watched a light smile appear on his lips.

"Hand me the books, my cub."

What?

I tapped Cato's back, and when he didn't move, I began shoving at his shoulders. His body rolled to the side, and he lay there, absolutely still.

"Yes, right there, Ambrose."

My head swiveled drunkenly on my neck.

The king was no longer shackled.

"Ambrose, stop!" I yelled.

He gave no indication that he'd heard me, and the Magi's books were in his hands.

"GUARDS!" I screamed, still trapped under Cato's armored legs. I heard the clank and scrape of metal drawing near. *Thank Goddess.* I tugged and pulled my skirts, desperately trying to free up my legs. The hem ripped, and I staggered heavily before righting myself enough to stand.

"No!"

I stared in horror. The king gripped the guard's face. Around his fingers, the man's skin bloated and began bursting. His fingers sank deeper, and blood began oozing out of the cracking wounds.

"Stop him! Please!" the guard shrieked. "Goddess save me."

Saliva flooded my mouth.

The guard crumpled onto a pile of rubble and wailed while blindly flailing his arms. The king turned to Ambrose and raised his hand.

"Give me my books, child."

I shoved off the balls of my feet and surged forward. With all the strength in my body, I threw myself at the king. My outstretched hands seized the column of his neck, grasping the tendons and sinking in my clawed fingers.

I drew deeply, pulling his æther through the cord that tethered him to my stomach. I consumed his strength and made it my own.

I was invincible. Strong and solid. I could feel the fibrous tissue of my muscles expand and æther swell within my chest.

The world went white.

Chapter 19

BONDS AND TIES AND CHAINS

Oh, my!

"Eira, wake!" The rough hand on my chin shook my head back and forth. "Live, damn you, wake!"

My eyes fluttered open and then squinted against the sun's rays. A high-pitched whistle ebbed in my ears.

"Cato?"

"I'm here, love." He ran his hands over my body, feeling for broken bones. He lifted my skirts to check my legs for injury. "Can you sit?"

"I think so." He inserted his arm between my shoulder and the ground and aided me until I remained upright on my own.

"My gods, Cato."

I surveyed the damage.

Ambrose and Levaunt lay ten feet away, and both were covered in a fine powder of obliterated rock. They were in the process of helping each other up, thank Goddess, so I knew they were safe. I could see that the sleeve of Ambrose's coat had torn, and blood was blooming through the fabric.

With Cato supporting me, I made it to my feet, and together we walked through a large, cleared circle, about the size of my room at the palace. The area looked like it had been recently swept clean and polished to gleam like a fine gray marble.

Bem subdued the king, and from the looks of it, it took little effort. The monarch was lying on his side, covered in a pile of dust that Bem was attempting to sweep from his shoulders.

"Eira, to me," Ambrose said, not in a stern tone, but one tinged with relief. Cato pushed me gently in his direction. Ambrose wrapped me in his embrace, rocked me gently, and spoke soft words into my ear, "Simply amazing, my strong harpy—my powerful, magnificent woman."

Behind me, I heard the king groan and turned to see Bem helping him to his feet. Cato assessed the fallen guard.

"Boys, I would wager my finest steed that she is in fact... a conjurer."

I broke from Ambrose's arms and stomped my way to the king, nearly slipping on the shiny surface of the blast's epicenter.

Cato stepped into my path.

"Back up, Protector. He can barely raise his head."

Cato held his palms up in supplication and stepped back as I rushed past him.

"Father Burchard!" He flinched as I pointed my finger at his face. *Goddess, his face.* I cupped his once furry cheeks in my hands. Most of his beard had been singed off. "Derros's dick. Your eyes!"

Cato and Ambrose crowded me while their father slumped against Bem.

"How will we explain this?" Ambrose asked.

"I have no idea, brother."

The king grinned and took my hands into his. He tossed his head back and burst into loud laughter.

"Sweetling, it appears your papa is no longer the most dangerous thing in these mountains."

I stared at my reflection in his now snow-white irises.

The world spun.

Ambrose caught my arm before I went down and steadied me against his side.

"I-I need to sit." Ambrose and Cato looked around; there were no longer chairs, no longer any jutting rocks. Ambrose tucked his arm under my knees and lifted me into the air before bending low and placing me gently on my backside. "Cato, what of the other guard?"

"He no longer suffers." He touched the pommel of the knife at his hip.

Merrias guide him home.

I squeezed my eyes shut.

"Father, how dare you use me? How dare you endanger my future wife?" Ambrose approached his father so swiftly that the king swayed on his feet.

"Now, Ambrose, I did not pull from you. I merely—"

"There is no merely, Your Majesty. You take from others and bend them to your will. You kill, you force, and you endanger, which is *why* we must keep you sealed away."

"Perhaps, if you had given me your trust in the first place, I would not have needed to continue my studies on whomever I could draw near. Have you thought of that, my boy?"

"Trust you, father? Like our mother trusted you?" Cato said.

"Do not speak of trust, *brother*. At least you have it—you *both* have worked to coddle me, keeping me from growing into my role as prince."

"Is this about... Ambrose, you are a dithering man-child, and as I told you at the Council you cannot campaign without..."

The voices raged around me. Back and forth, they shouted.

And here I sit alone in the knowledge that I am exactly what I've been taught to fear.

I was an Obligate, chosen to keep the world safe from the corruption, and yet it was clear... I *was* the corruption.

I turned on my knees and crawled away. The sick and heavy feeling of bitterness flooded me. I tilted my head to the sky and squeezed my tear-filled eyes as tightly as I could.

I didn't ask for this. Why would you do this to your faithful daughter? Will I never get to live the life I choose?

I followed the rules, Mother.

I need you, Momma.

Why? Why was this the—

High on my cheek, I felt a shock—a prickle that quickly dissipated. It was followed quickly by another.

I cracked my eyes open.

Flurries fell around me, glittering like glass beads in the sunlight.

Thank you, Momma. I miss you so, and—

"I said what I said, Cato! Have you lost the ability to hear words that aren't your own?"

For shit's sake...

"Fuck off, Ambrose, you know naught but leisure."

"Boys, my children, stop this at once!"

I twisted around on my knees and stood—my half-second of tranquility ruined.

The buffoons were nearing blows.

Cato snatched Ambrose by the front of his coat and squared up—Ambrose met him toe to toe. He towered over his brother.

"Children... children!" Father Burchard did his best but was too weak to intervene. Bem stood there, looking bored.

"And you know *naught* but a short dick!" Ambrose balled up his fist, slamming it into the side of Cato's head.

Cato took the hit—not fazed in the least—and bent low, gripping Ambrose around his torso. He shoved his knee into the flesh above his brother's groin.

"Call me that again, thin-pricked slut."

Bunch of fucking children, all of them.

Cato lashed out at Ambrose and punched him squarely in the throat.

That was enough.

"Stop! I didn't sign up to be your mother, and I certainly won't be my husband's babysitter. And you, Father Burchard, this is a learned behavior." Out of the corner of my eye, I saw Ambrose rear his fist and swing. "JUST FREEZE, ALL OF YOU!"

Bem fell to the ground and the king to his knees.

Cato stood frozen, except for—Holy Goddess in the Cradle! His lips stood out from his teeth, his cheek a wave on the side of his face where Ambrose's fist had impacted his jaw. The skin on the back of Ambrose's knuckles rippled like a puddle after a pebble disturbed its surface.

"Holy fuck."

Bem's arm was bent at the elbow, and his body was dead-man stiff. His legs were so straight that, even lying on his back, his heels didn't touch the ground.

"Cato?"

Nothing.

"Ambrose?" My throat tightened. His eyes flicked a scant millimeter.

He was still in there.

"Oh, Derros, Derros, Derros." I twisted around, looking for the books. I'd done something horrible, and I had no clue how to undo it. I ran around madly, scrambling to turn over rocks and scattering piles of dust. Goddess forbid they'd turned to ash like the king's hair.

The lean-to that had been beside us no longer stood, but I saw its canvas top settled on the ground yards away. Nearly out of breath, I ran and pulled at the folds of the tarp, praying all the while. In the jumbled pile, I found one of the tiny volumes and a torn half of the other. I found the missing portion scattered around the tent—the pages tossed about by the wind. I jogged back as quickly as I could while leafing through the parchments.

Render, no. Decimate, surely not. Embolden. Purge. Reanimate! I slowed just enough to better see the wispy handwriting. *If the blood of a cross-born is ingested near the time of expiration, the subject will awaken reanimated. The resulting creations are highly susceptible to Primitive Bonding.*

The Awakening.

I'd thought the tale of the rising dead was meant to keep children in line. Evandr? Gotwig? Were they...?

"Daughter," I heard the king's frail voice as I reached the group again.

"Papa, help me fix this! Please!" The quivering of Cato's hand caught my attention.

"You must calm down, daughter. You cannot reverse when agitated."

"Calm? Tell me how to be calm after what I've done—after what *you've* done!"

"Your inability to control yourself will lead to another incident—filled with æther as you are."

I took a shuddering breath and nodded.

One... two... three... Steady your heart. Slow your breathing.

"Play what happened backward in your mind and whatever command you gave, say the opposite. You must counteract the—"

"Move for me!"

I turned and looked at my men.

They remained still.

"Fuck! Fuck! FUCK!" I slammed my hands against my thighs and at once the arms of Cato, Ambrose, and Bem mimicked the motion.

"Father! What have I done?" I cried.

"If you do not calm, and watch your foul mouth, you will not be able to undo your binding. Now, turn around. Chin up. Have a bit of confidence in yourself."

I brushed away my tears. Three pairs of hands echoed the movement.

"Listen to me. You told them to freeze, and the opposite of freeze is not move. You cannot let your emotions trigger a cognitive barrier as you counter. Think it through. What is the opposite of move?"

"Stop... rest?"

"Don't use 'stop'; you could *stop* them from functioning altogether. Do you understand? Try 'rest' out on Bem first. He's the least important. Now, do not be sentimental. This is the only way to learn control."

I crawled over to Bem and bent low so I could whisper into *his* ear alone.

Shame on you, Eira.

I took a breath and reversed the imagery in my mind.

"Rest," I whispered. Nothing seemed to happen.

"Test it out, dear."

I threw my arms up in the air, and when Bem made no movement I internally rejoiced. Though he still lay on the ground as if encapsulated in ice.

"Now the others."

I hopped up on my feet and twisted, just in time to see Cato and Ambrose spin around and face the opposite direction.

"Rest."

I flung my arms over my head but closed my eyes, too terrified to look. "Did it work, Papa?"

It did sweetheart—you may stop now.

I turned to the king and nodded before taking on the next hurdle.

You can do this, daughter mine.

"I can. I can do this."

I focused all of my energy on where Cato and Ambrose stood close together.

"I shouldn't think 'melt.' That could result in catastrophe."

Correct.

"And 'thaw'? Would they... would they perspire?"

I am not sure, dear. You need to think a little differently but also on your terms. Think of something that will solve the problem in relation to the word itself, something that would have no detrimental effects. When you were at your most cold, sweetheart, what made you return to a more comfortable state?

I thought back. The most frozen I had ever been was undoubtedly the day our priestess had prayed over Kan Keagan's lifeless body. I'd stood my ground and watched as she anointed him, even as a snow squall raged around us. The others sought refuge, but I refused to leave. I recalled the priestesses's red robes flying around her in the wind, and the beautifully brown face of my beloved mentor contrasting with the snowscape. When it came time for the intercession to Merrias, where the mourners lift a list of the deceased's virtues to the Goddess's ear, I knew only love. I whispered to the Goddess of the good he had done for a little Nortian Obligate—of the joy he had brought to her life.

There it was.

I closed my eyes.

"Fièrena."

And what does it mean, dear?

"In Solnnan it means 'to keep warm.' It's what I would say to my mentor before he'd leave for the night. He was always so cold."

My eyes snapped open when I heard two thuds and a pitiful groan.

I ran the distance to where Cato lay, rubbing his shoulder, and threw my arms around him, toppling him backward. My mouth was on his before I knew what I'd done. Cato stared up at me, his eyes wide. I shimmied off of him and launched myself toward Ambrose.

"Darling, I was so worried!" To outdo the greeting I gave Cato, I jumped onto Ambrose's prone form and proceeded to inspect every inch of his face before hitting him with the most sultry, sexy kiss I could manage. I groaned and moaned, and his firm arms came around me.

"And Bem! Oh, Bem, I'm so sorry." I hopped up and out of Ambrose's embrace and hustled my way over to the fleshy man. I was going to sell this charade.

I flung my arms wide. Bem caught me around the waist, slid his palm up my back, dipped me low, and sealed his lips to mine.

Oh my!

I tossed my head back in a full-bellied cackle. It was barely daybreak, and yet, it had been the most absurd couple of hours in my highly absurd life.

"Eira, my lovely wife-to-be. It is only that the Protector values Bem's existence that I have yet to run him through. Do stop yourself."

Bem winked and let me go.

I spotted Levaunt sitting behind a large rock and prepared to give him his lip-lock. He shook his head and held his hand up.

"Boys, help your father to his feet."

I swung around.

"Not yet. Stop where you are, both of you." With my fists on my hips, I faced the king. "Father Burchard, you used your son to benefit your greed, which resulted in the loss of an innocent life."

With the books in my possession again, I could continue advancing my skill sets. I must achieve the highest level of magical ability possible to ensure I can protect you when the time comes.

"That is no excuse for selfishness. Have you ever thought to—I don't know—tell your sons everything, work to repair your relationships, and prove yourself worthy in their eyes?"

I am the villain in our story. They will never see me as I am, and I have come to accept that fact.

"If they didn't love you, they would've ended you long ago. They wouldn't have tried to save you from yourself. I think you're just as stubborn as they are. *That's* what I think."

I felt a looming presence behind me, but I didn't acknowledge the brothers.

"Eira, you aren't well. We need to get you back." Ambrose's palm found my forehead, and Cato took my wrist in his hand, checking the pulse there.

I shook them off.

"Look, if you can't take the heat of this conversation, that's fine, but he must atone for his sins, like any other human."

"Mmhmm, and you need rest, and perhaps food, and a healer to look you over, so let us go," Cato said, speaking to me like you would a child. "You probably cannot understand right now, but you are hallucinating—having a very intense one-sided conversation."

"That's bullshit, Protector, utter bullshit."

They cannot tell that you have cemented an Infinite Bond with me. I can speak through your mind, and if you tried, you could answer through yours.

"Bullshit!" I jabbed my finger at the king. "A polar-bear-sized bag o' bullshit!"

You no longer feel the connection as intensely, correct? It is because we are now linked. You are quite close to me right now and are wholly unaffected.

"Wait, say something else."

I dropped to my knees and put the tip of my nose against the king's.

"No more of this. Ambrose, grab her."

Perhaps it will be our secret.

His lips never moved. There was no outward indication that he spoke.

No. I won't lie to them, father.

Very well, daughter.

I allowed Ambrose to assist me to my feet, then squared my shoulders and faced both my men.

Ambrose, Cato, I have managed to create an Infinite Bond with your father. He's in my head. Is that clear?

"Daughter of mine, precious child. You do not have an Infinite Bond with *them.*"

I puffed my chest out and tried again.

"Ambrose, Cato, I have managed to create an Infinite Bond with your father. He's in my head. Is that clear?" I propped my hands back on my hips and waited for them to respond.

"About as clear as mud," Ambrose said, reaching out to check my temperature again.

"We must leave. Father, you will ride with Ambrose. Bem, call the healer immediately and have him looked over. Levaunt, you will ride ahead and tell Lady Allaine to prepare herself for Eira's arrival. If she needs an assistant, have her call someone from the kitchens."

"Why would Allaine need assistance? Don't discount her—I won't have it, Protector. She is capable and—"

Ambrose came forward, sighed deeply, and dropped down to one knee. He took my hand.

"Know that my feelings have not altered, and I still wish to move forward with our Joining."

I tried to take a step back, but he wouldn't drop my hands.

"Allaine may need help, sweet dove, because, like my father, your glorious mane is singed, nearly to your scalp."

"What?" I glanced at Cato, who nodded curtly, confirming his brother's words.

Gingerly, I slid my hands out of Ambrose's.

With trepidation, I touched the crown of my head and felt the rough, burnt tips of what remained. It was akin to petting a wire-haired donkey who'd not been brushed in a month.

I picked at the coarse little tufts and watched the soot fall to the ground.

"Listen well. Troth Eira pulled the king from a fire caused by improperly stored mining explosives. His eyes have suffered damage, and the healer, in consultation with those at Verus, will be working on a solution to restore him. Majesty, do not leave your chambers for the next few days. Eira, focus. Retrieve the books and come with me. Am I understood?"

Immediately, everyone moved in a different direction. Levaunt shot off at a run while Ambrose and Bem began kicking and throwing handfuls of dust on the polished parts of the ground.

Cato came to me and took my elbow.

Silent tears rolled down my cheeks until we reached Cato's mount.

I hugged the big horse's face—he and I had a history after all—and stroked his lovely black mane.

And then I lost it.

My body shook, and I didn't stifle my need to wail as loud and forlornly as an arctic wolf in the night. I leaned into Horse Ambrose and let myself slip down his sinewy leg until I dropped in a pile beside him.

"Eira, love," Cato whispered between my blubbering. "For what it's worth, I would have no qualm's about fucking you here on the ground, even snot covered as you are."

My fingers curled around a rock, and I launched it at the asshole, missing him by just an inch.

"If only your conjuring skills were as poor as your aim."

Chapter 20

THE THRONE ROOM

"Lady Allaine, your references led me to believe you were a competent practitioner in the art of coiffure. The current configuration simply shall not do."

For the fourth time, Allaine's dark blue eyes clouded with tears.

"Apologies, Highness." She hiccupped loudly in an attempt to hold back her sobs. "But there is no hair left to... to coif! She is nothing more than a dog with the mange." Fat tears rolled down her red, mottled cheeks.

"You are being too kind—she looks like one of those birds of paradise when they molt, all bald spots and scraggles, and the skin of her head is so alarmingly pale compared to the rest of her." Ambrose ran his finger over a particularly bright area of my scalp.

The right side of my head had frizzled to nothing more than tufts, and the left hung in patchy layers of various sizes. The middle of my head retained some length, and an awkward tail hung down my back, matching the half-sizzled forelock in the front.

I shouldn't be upset.

This was nothing in the grand scheme. The guard who died—he would never comb his hair again. My hair would grow back. And if, Goddess forbid, Ambrose or Cato had been hurt or worse... My vanity was shameful at this point, and yet, I was still crushed.

I sat up straight and peered at my reflection.

I am more than my hair.

I am more than this face or body.

I am more.

"Shave it off."

Allaine swayed on her feet.

"Snap out of it. Fetch your shears. Do it now."

"I do not own shears, and I cannot abide cutting off what remains of your crowning glory." She wept openly this time. "Will I remain employed? A plucked goose cannot be re-feathered."

"Ambrose, off your ass and fetch your blades."

In the mirror's reflection, I saw him visibly recoil and then toss both hands over his mouth.

"Eira, a scarf... a long veil would—"

"Allaine will add to what's left on top; you will shave the sides." His eyebrows shot to his forehead. "Ambrose, you fuck men—I'm sure the style will suit your needs. Now, move."

I dove off my stool and threw out my arms, but Allaine, Goddess bless her, had already hit the floor in a dead faint.

"Gammond's balls! Get her up."

With little effort, Ambrose scooped Allaine from the floor and swept her out of the room.

I laid my cheek on the countertop. I was entirely overwhelmed by what had occurred at the quarry. I was a conjurer, a Chosen Woman, and deity-touched. I'd agreed to be none of those things. I wasn't asked. I wasn't given an option. I wanted to wallow in self-pity and be left the fuck alone by both the celestial and earth-bound.

"Let us begin before I lose my nerve." Ambrose returned with a massive wooden chest in his arms. He sat the box down and pulled open two stair-step compartments. He had more combs than Allaine could have dreamt of, a removable section of cosmetics and paints, and another devoted to hair care.

Ambrose.

My heart swelled in my chest, and the tears threatened again.

Like me, he wasn't given the option to choose either. Not the circumstances of his birth, not his status as a Chosen Man, or even to whom he would be Joining.

He deserved so much more.

"Wait just a moment." I ran quickly to the closet and reemerged as fast as I could. He stood examining a long razor, checking it for nicks and dullness. Two additional blades and a set of shears on a towel sat next to a bowl of thick cream.

"Ambrose, I want you to take this. It's an engagement gift."

"Ooo!" His face lit up when I placed the heavy bag in his hand.

"It is high time you recognized the gravity of aligning yourself to my person." He eyed the coarse brown bag suspiciously. "What is it? Your wrapping is... a little mundane."

"Open it."

Ambrose scoffed as he picked at the fraying cord with two fingers.

"Eira." He paused and looked up at me. "Eira, my Goddess. Where did this... how... this is a small fortune. I do not understand."

"It's for the campaign you've been going on about. I want you to go on it, or fund it, or run it, you fucking ingrate. Whatever it is, Ambrose... I want you to have it."

I expected a retort, some quippy comeback.

The wetness in his eyes, however, was the only thank you I needed.

"Ambrose, I want our children to have a say in their lives. I want..."

"... to make me fall for you. Is that your plan?"

Wait, what?

Ambrose moved toward me, and I took a step back.

"No, no, Eira, never back away... Playing cat and mouse is a favorite pastime, though I usually prefer the role of the rodent."

My heart sped up as he continued walking forward.

"I'll have my kiss now—one like lovers share."

My back hit the wall. Warmth flooded me as he bent low.

"Eira, I have had to fight, tooth and nail, for every scrap of respect and authority I have gained. My mother is the only person in my life who has never used me to advance their schemes. And now you... Is this what it's like to be trusted—to feel cared for?"

The fine hairs raised on the back of my neck.

I did care for him. I cared deeply.

The most gentle lips settled on mine.

Holy mother. It felt as if I was seeing him truly naked for the first time.

"Thank you, wife," he whispered.

"Silly shrew! The ambassadors take precedence over your ridiculous little lady's soirée, so just forget it. It's cancelled." Ambrose paced back and forth in the antechamber that led to the throne room. "You are Joining to a *royal* family, and the kingdom should be your foremost priority."

Fucking moody bitch.

"You... you think my priorities are to Monwyn? I'm the Troth of *Solnna*, my mother is missing, I am being chased by my maybe-daddy-king, and I can *fucking* explode. But, absolutely, my number one priority is looking pretty for a bunch of people who, I guarantee, are nothing more than bootlicking flatterers."

"Keep your voice down," he gritted out. "Bem, there you are. You will escort Troth Eira. How do I look?"

"Like you've got a few more miles before you hit mediocre," I spat.

Ambrose curled his lip and peered down his perfect nose. I couldn't help the jibe. He was just *so* uncharacteristically flustered.

"Why are you so nervous?" I asked while straightening out his silken collar, "You do prince stuff regularly. Where's my unflappable Scion?"

He shivered like he was standing in the midst of a blizzard.

"I have never sat the throne. Father or Aberus have always taken the lead."

"Ambrose, you were raised for this and—"

"And I am the child of a slut, a street walker, a lady of the night—that is what they see."

He looked away while pressing his fingertips against his closed eyes.

"Look at me." I grasped his hand between my palms. "You will cease referring to your bearer as such. You were born of a woman who wanted you to exist. She didn't have to carry you, but she did. She bore you in battle, just as any queen would have."

Ambrose placed his forehead against mine and breathed deeply. His mouth worked up and down and sweat collected at his temples.

"ENTER PRINCE AMBROSE'S BETHROTHED." The herald's voice belted out so loudly that I could easily hear him through the sealed doors.

The doors parted, and the beat of the guard's spearbutts echoed around the vast chamber.

My throat constricted. Perhaps Ambrose had the right of it after all.

I had never seen a crowd so large. Not at the ball during the Third Maneuvering, not when the Obligates received our hallowed Assignments. This was a proverbial ocean of courtiers sitting in ornately carved chairs. It was an endless display of opulence. From the looks of it, they had managed to heap on every scrap of fur or piece of gold they owned.

"Walk, Lady," Bem muttered.

"Right."

I put a foot forward and commanded the other to follow.

If the solarium was Cordillaria's rainbow-bending diamond, then the throne room was surely its crown. Thick columns of white ran along the perimeter of the room, and at their tops stood statues of the old gods. Their outstretched wings were gilded to a gleaming gold, and their faces looked down upon the masses in judgment.

Breathe, Eira. You are Troth. You are Chosen. Play the part.

I dropped and tilted my head ever so slightly so that I could look up from under my lashes and meet the eyes of the mightiest nobles in the land. I would present to them first with femininity and softness, and then let them glimpse my strength. I wanted them to fall in love with me—revere me. I would ensnare them wholly, and without their knowledge, integrate Ambrose into every aspect of their lives. I'd weave my web so tightly around them that they'd not find their way out.

I can be their perfect woman.

I folded my hands and made a show of inhaling deeply and expanding my chest. My breasts pushed up over the neckline of my gown. *Let them think me fearful. Let them think me nervous. Let them think me pure and small.*

The whispers began.

"... almost a catastrophe."

"She pulled his body from the flames."

"The poor dear... but what bravery, she..."

"Lady, you'll stand on the other side of that there crowd. I'll be between you and them," Bem whispered.

I looked up briefly to see the spot he referred to and let my eyes take in the majesty of Monwyn's highest seat.

The dais was the focal point of the massive hall. Swaths of dark indigo velvet hung from a pearl-encrusted oval that was attached to the vaulted ceiling and draped down to the floors. Twinkling garnets and soft-orange stones were configured on the back wall, creating a mosaic sun that looked like it was rising up over the crowd.

The twisting bodies of two leviathans had been painstakingly chiseled into the magnificent chunk of granite that was the throne of Monwyn. Their eyes were set with sapphire slivers, and their sharp fangs had been fashioned from the iridescent shells of abalone.

Bem released my elbow, and I walked to my spot on the right side of the room and stood between the throne and court. Murmurs swelled around me.

"Not the usual look to her."

"No longer a beauty..."

"Now enters His Royal Highness Ambrose Burchard Berra Odel Ricard, second heir to the throne of Monwyn!"

The doors opened once more.

The gathered assembly stood—barring two or three I made note of—and bowed as Ambrose entered.

He was a vision.

Somewhere, he'd managed to find his confidence once more.

His head rose above almost all in attendance, and he held himself poleaxe-straight. He'd chosen a coat of blue that was so dark it appeared black. Even his glossy raven tresses seemed to disappear into the fabric. The golden bear brooch was pinned to his shoulder. Hanging from its mouth was a chain whose end was a silver and diamond crown. He insisted that I wear the matching one today.

Ambrose flicked his eyes to mine as he passed by, and I let a sweet smile play on my lips. A smile meant only for my husband.

And then Cato appeared.

Catommandus.

The prince of my body and the king of my soul walked the aisle—his brother's protector.

When he dressed in formal silks, he devastated my senses. When unclothed, I could weep at the sight of his rugged beauty. Seeing *Sir* Catommandus, in a full harness of leather and plate... it took all of my strength not to drop to my knees in worship.

A flame ignited within my chest, and I now recognized the tightening sensation of æther as it mingled with my body's responses. My core pulsed deliciously, and my passage thickened. I squeezed my thighs tightly and fought back a groan. My nipples tightened and pushed against the silk of the crimson gown I wore. My fingertips tingled. I ached to touch him.

He could command me as he saw fit.

I would obey.

His hard obsidian eyes, ringed in autumn gold, looked out from a helm of blackened steel lined in finely detailed brass work. The spaulders at his shoulders and the greaves covering him from knee to ankle matched the opulent helmet. The chest piece he wore, a black coat of plates, had been riveted in such a way that his torso was a sunburst of gold. A sword was strapped to one of his hips and a mace to his other. Both had chains connecting their handles to the lions' heads that were mounted where his shoulders connected to his chest.

My warrior-god walked among mere mortals.

The dangerous set to Cato's eyes reminded me of the night he'd chased me as I fled through the trees—how he'd stalked me, pursued me like a predator, and then mounted me like an animal from behind. He'd fucked me for his own pleasure that night, under the darkened sky in which Maressa, the hawk-born goddess, stood watch over her forest.

Sweat trickled between my breasts.

Cato's eyes found mine, and the corners of that magnificent nose flared.

If he demanded that I lay upon this floor right now... I would spread my legs and let all those gathered bear witness.

He passed me by and marched to his position behind the throne.

"Esteemed nobles of the court, you may be seated," a man robed in faded yellow said in a scratchy voice.

The highest-ranking men sat. The lesser nobles and well-to-do merchants remained standing like me.

"Lords of Monwyn! The economy thriv—"

"Primus Thierry," Ambrose interrupted. "You may continue with the address in just a moment." Amongst the crowd, heads whipped back and forth, and what started as whispers turned into a swell of boisterous concern. "Silence. Silence!" Ambrose's voice thundered above the crowd.

You could have heard the drop of a veil pin on the ground.

"Before the rumor mill spreads its vitriol, *I* would address you." Ambrose raised his hand.

Cato rounded the throne, and Ambrose bent to speak into his ear. Cato shook his helmed head, but Ambrose dismissed his brother with a wave.

Cato clipped a bow, turned, and came toward me.

"You are summoned," he murmured before proffering a gauntlet-clad hand. He was livid. I recognized the angry waver in his voice as he gritted out the words.

Cato escorted me to the front of the dais and left me standing in its middle to face the crowd.

Ambrose stood.

"As no doubt you are aware, His Majesty found himself the victim of an incident in the basalt quarry. Improperly stored explosives ignited, and as we carried out the monthly survey, the king found himself amid the flames. Though the healer assures us that he is healthy and hale, it will be some time before he is ready to walk amongst the populace. Rest assured, we have sent missives to Verus and Cult Mossius, and the most knowledgeable of practitioners are being consulted. The Protector is carrying out an investigation into who is responsible for leaving such dangerous equipment unsecured. The culprit will be found and hanged unto death."

"And rightfully so!" an older gentleman yelled from the front row.

An upsurge of agreement followed.

"History has shown us the danger of carelessness!"

Ambrose walked back and lowered himself onto the throne.

"Before you stands my woman. Come to me, Eira."

I stepped up on the dais, and Ambrose reached out. He led me around to the side of the high seat and held my hand in his, resting them both on the throne's arm.

"My woman threw herself into the flames and pulled him to safety. His own stalwart guard had perished from asphyxiation, and yet this fragile soul threw her own body into the furnace to save him. Troth Eira will bear the next sons of Monwyn. She will be honored as a heroine. Gentlemen, look upon her. Though she finds herself maimed and disfigured, she deserves to be cherished and guarded for the selfless act she committed this day."

Goddess Ambrose, disfigured?

I looked shyly at the ground.

Ambrose slid his hand behind me and settled his palm on my backside.

The crowd erupted.

Cheers and shrill whistles pierced the air, and shouted accolades erupted from the second-floor gallery, where the gentry, the countrymen, had an allocated space.

"Her divine purpose has been served!"

"Chosen to deliver us from evil!"

"Mother of Monwyn..."

A fucking good liar.

I bowed my head and tucked in closer to Ambrose's side. *Yes, boys, listen to your mother. I'll raise you better—I'll drag you kicking and screaming from your decades of antiquated nonsense.*

"Primus Thierry, begin again."

The robed Primus blinked from behind his spectacles, which made his eyes look as round as saucers, and I noticed that one of his pupils was markedly larger than the other.

"I-is she to remain on th-the dais, Highness?" The elder gentleman croaked out.

"Yes. Does her location present an issue?"

"I... well... I... the area is reserved for ranking members of the royal family."

"Quite so. Just a moment."

Ambrose shifted his hand to my back and applied pressure. I was hesitant to move, but he was insistent. He dragged me front and center and then smoothed his hands down my sides before yanking me backward. I fell into his lap so hard that my chest bounced up and down, and my skirts swung about, giving the crowd a glimpse of my ankles.

"*Now* she is not touching the dais." His muscled arm came around me and he rested his other hand between my thighs.

There was laughter from the crowd, and some man was bold enough to whistle.

Ambrose ate it up.

He hiked my skirts up further, revealing just a hint of my tied garters. Satisfied grunts added to the already ridiculous ruckus.

I heard a deep growl from behind the throne.

"Settle down, settle down, and wait for the bedding ceremony, fellas," Ambrose exclaimed in a congenial tone.

The roar swelled again and then finally died down.

How is it possible that all of these men are disgusting?

"Thierry... Thierry, come back, deliver your report," Ambrose said loudly.

Sure enough, the Primus had ventured to the side of the dais and currently looked to be embroiled in a conversation with a statue of a manticore.

"Right, right." Thierry ambled back to the front of the crowd. "*Ahem.* The Obligates assigned to Monwyn—two males and two females—will arrive late tomorrow or early the next morning."

Eeeek!

A single sentence lifted my spirits sky high.

I had thought it would be another week before they arrived. Preparations must have been underway even before they'd sent the last missive. And of course, I hadn't thought about how slow communication could be in the mountains. In Nortia, sleds carried news quickly.

"We w-will make them welcome and place them in their new positions upon arrival. His Majesty does warn, however, that he has concern for a particular S-Scion who will be placed in our midst. In an effort to link the two hemispheres, Verus has Assigned to us a man hailing from Baldorva to act as—"

"Unacceptable!"

"Slavers and animals!"

A wash of incensed shouts and curses drowned out the stuttering Primus.

"Verus would not dare!"

"M-men of Monwyn, calm yourselves—settle! His Majesty has charged our Protector with k-keeping a close watch over the foreigner, and we are all asked to be wary."

Another low growl came from behind the throne, as well as the telltale sound of metal scraping against metal.

Cato hated Greggen. Not only had he *not* followed the guidelines of the Third Maneuvering, but he had placed his hands upon me and convinced me that my Nan was in dire trouble.

Greggen can rot.

I raised a hand to my dry eye and feigned wiping a tear from my cheek.

The courtiers pressed forward as if my feminine weakness compelled them.

Cato stepped from behind the throne and stood at Ambrose's other side.

"Run him through, Protector!"

"Save our children!"

"SILENCE! CALM, I SAY!" Thierry screamed above the crowd, which finally simmered to a more manageable volume. "Um, l-let me see here..." He pulled a little fold of parchment from his pocket and adjusted his eyewear. "Oh, right. The Scholar died in his sleep. That's all. Thanks for coming."

The Primus sauntered down the aisle, saluting the men he passed.

Derros's dangling dong... I killed the Scholar with my tits.

He'd gone belly up from boob-induced heart failure.

Ambrose sensed my unease and patted my back like he was consoling a child.

"We will pray that Merrias guides him well into the afterlife. A monument will be erected in the courtyard to honor his long-time service." He placed his fingertips on his forehead, and the mass mimicked his actions.

Ambrose signaled, and the massive iron-bound doors at the front of the hall opened.

"We invite into our presence the Ambassadors of Solnna!" The herald cried from the back of the room. Three representatives, two clad in purple gowns and one cloaked in a blush coat, came to stand before the throne. Behind them, two men followed, carrying a large chest between them.

"We understand your Queen sends tidings," Ambrose said.

"Her Sol-Blessed Majesty sends her most heartfelt greetings. Though she will be unable to leave her kingdom to attend the union of *our* Obligate, Troth Eira, to the son of Monwyn, she sends gifts and wishes you well. Her Majesty expects that—if we are to lose one so precious to us—reparations will be made. It is suggested that twenty thousand pounds of white marble, fourteen pounds of malachite, two wagons of copper, and two ships of basalt would be fair compensation."

A lazy, lopsided smile spread across Ambrose's face.

"We will see the request doubled. She is worth far more."

The ambassador bowed deeply at the waist and then motioned his men forward. The chest was laid before us.

"For Your Highness, golden arm cuffs, set with diamonds and sapphires. The stones were pried from the very belt worn by the Monwyn general, Catom, after his body was recovered in the aftermath of the Awakening."

The cuffs glowed resplendently as they caught the light of the multi-tiered lamps that fell from the ceiling. The ambassador handed the treasure to the woman at his left.

"Obligate Solnna, by aligning our kingdom to such an esteemed royal family, you do us great honor. To you, we gift the Diadem of Taleer."

With gloved hands, the ambassador lifted the diadem above his head. "Before the kingdom fell, the jewel was smuggled into the lands of Solnna for safekeeping."

Ambrose's breath caught in his throat, and my hand went to my chest.

The tall, arch-shaped headpiece was covered in a shining corona of amethysts and diamonds, set in fixtures of gold and silver. Strands of the same stones fell from the wonder's sides; they would cascade from the wearer's temples to their shoulders.

I broke my silence.

"I am not worthy to have such magnificence bestowed upon me."

"Our queen—*your* queen—disagrees. The desert matriarchs were held in the same high regard that we hold you."

The ambassadors each bowed in turn and then made to leave.

"Wait, please, just a moment," I said in the Solnnan tongue.

A genuine smile lit up the face of the blush-coated man. He inclined his head and then laid his hand over his heart and bowed.

"Please tell our Queen that I am humbled to receive this treasure and that I have not, nor will I, forget my duty to Solnna."

He walked forward and reached out. I turned back to Ambrose and dipped my head in question. He nodded his assent.

I stood and took the ambassador's hands in my own, and like the Solnnans were wont to do, he pulled me into his embrace.

"Mariad sends his greetings, little one; the diadem bears a missive."

"Thank you, kind sir." I dropped into a formal curtsy and then returned to Ambrose's lap.

The ambassadors left while a group of Monwyn guards collected the chest and spirited it away through a side door.

"Monwyn welcomes the worthy Kingdom of Gaea and calls them into our presence!" shouted the herald.

My palms began to sweat.

Gaea.

I'd managed to feel safe enough in my new mountain home that they'd become a lesser worry, a distant second to my conjuring father-in-law-to-be. But now, here they were, walking into my haven.

They represented a criminal—a man who had stolen my mother's youth and tried to have me forcibly Assigned to his kingdom. When his guile failed, he had resorted to open, murderous violence.

Ambrose bunched the back of my dress in his fist.

"Open for me."

"What?"

He descended. He slid his tongue into my mouth, ensuring those closest to us would see it reaching in to mingle with mine. He pushed against the back of my head, deepening his reach. His other hand slid down my stomach and cupped my most intimate part.

This kiss was possession.

This kiss was a message.

Ambrose thrust his tongue in and out of my warmth, and I moaned deeply, announcing to those before us that I submitted to him completely. Which was a load... but I'd play the game that kept me safe.

A throat cleared.

Ambrose ignored it and tugged at my bottom lip.

He hummed low in the back of his throat and made a show of adjusting the bulge in his pants. After what must have been another half minute, he pulled away and swiped the pad of his thumb across my mouth.

A tad flustered, I looked up into the very serious faces of three Gaeans—two very young, and one in his sixth decade or so.

"I find it difficult to leave our bed chamber for any length of time... Proceed." Ambrose sank his hand further between my thighs.

"Ma'am, Highness. The Primus-King sends heartfelt regards to the mountain people and prays for your health and continued wellness." The older ambassador's voice was low and melodious, and his face was entirely serene. "It is my pleasure to announce that he will be making the journey to attend your Joining and looks forward to breaking bread with family."

With family. Goddess, protect me.

Ice tumbled down my neck and spine. Ambrose tightened his arm like he'd anticipated the shudder that wracked me.

"We look forward to hosting such a distinguished guest and showering him with hospitality."

Three heads nodded appreciatively. The main ambassador, who was cloaked in green and brown, motioned the two youths forward. One of the younglings had the red locks of a Scion; the other was so gangly that I thought he might tip over if he moved too fast.

"As a gesture of goodwill, the kingdom has arranged a gift for your betrothal." The Gaean turned and pointed to the malachite studded box held in the young Scion's arms.

He came forward and knelt on one knee.

The other two followed suit.

"A gift fit for a Head Queen, ma'am."

The ambassador flipped open a copper latch and lifted the box lid, revealing a red velvet liner.

I leaned forward.

Red ropes? Fibers from a prized herd, perhaps?

I squinted my eyes and craned my neck.

The rancid smell of decay doubled me over.

"No," I whispered. "No."

Lifeless amber eyes stared out from a rotting head.

Ozius.

"Close it. Now," Ambrose said quietly.

The lid slammed shut.

"We recognize this gift as worthy and send our thanks to your Primus-King."

"Am-Ambrose... Cato," I breathed.

"To the Kingdoms of Solnna and Gaea, salute!" Cato hollered. His voice carried throughout the hall, echoing off the walls.

"SALUTE!" The crowd yelled back in a chorus of voices.

Ambrose stood and took my hand amid thundering applause.

Once again, a group of guards ushered the "gift" away, and the ambassadors took their leave.

Tears stung my eyes—my hope was that the onlookers would misconstrue them as overwhelming gratefulness and not disgust.

"There is one last piece of business." Ambrose drew me to his side and tucked me against his body. "Though there are only days before I Join with our heroine," his fingernails ran along the column of my neck. "This evening, I leave with Captain Dumail. Together, we will right the wrongs done to our western coast by the pirates who think they can profit from us without reprisal. I will return victorious, or I will perish in my father's name. Pray for my success and watch over my woman whilst I am gone. Gentlemen, I leave her under *your* protection."

Pirates?

Battle cries erupted around the hall. Swords and knives caught the light as their owners brandished them in the air. Ambrose could no longer calm the crowd bent on vengeance. The stationed guards closed in on the masses that were caught up in their fervor, yelling as if they were demon-possessed.

Cato stepped into my field of vision and raised a hand.

He snapped his fist closed.

Like a well-trained army, every last man came to heel.

CHAPTER 21

ANXIETY

A FEELING OF FEAR, DREAD OR UNEASINESS.

"Eira, were you fucking thinking at all? Can you explain how you arrived at the notion that you should aid Ambrose in leaping into a wet and salty godsdamned nether?" Cato unbuckled the helm from his head and launched it across the room. It struck the leg of the bedside table and sent a set of jars crashing to the ground. Shards of glass flew onto the bed and floor. "And Ambrose, if you think I will allow—"

"I do not seek your permission, brother." Ambrose stood up to his full height but spoke calmly. "I am doing what I should have done long ago."

Cato flung himself into a chair and hung his head between his hands. He combed his fingers through his shaggy flips of hair and then clenched them tightly.

"Who will protect *her* when you are gone and my duties take me elsewhere? Did you spare a thought for your betrothed's safety? My *mate's* safety?" Cato hammered his metal-clad foot on the floor. "Who will protect you, brother? Who will have your back? You have never before been on campaign. The savagery you will face... Ambrose, you are not a killer." Cato stood and kicked out at the low table in front of him. His sabatons struck with such force that the wicker crumpled in on itself. "I cannot lose you."

"Cato." I went to his side and placed my hand on his forearm. He twisted from my touch and marched across the room. "Cato, I didn't know. I didn't do this to cross you, but I'm not sure I would have changed my decision anyhow. Ambrose deserves the chance to grow into the leader he wants to be. My existence shouldn't keep him from fulfilling his ambitions."

"And what of *my* existence? Do you think the Primus-King is no longer a threat? Gaea is here. They are within these walls. Do you think that stinking corpse was an apology? What you saw was an act of strength, one of power—he removes the head of a Scion, Eira, a Chosen One, and delivers it publicly, expecting no reprisal."

Too much.

It was all too much.

I sat on the edge of the bed and closed my eyes, but Ozius's face—the face of the living man, Cinden's lover—painted itself on the backs of my eyelids. *Murdered by the man he'd revered above all.*

He'd haunted me since leaving Verus. I knew he'd done wrong, but to desecrate his body and wrap it in the trappings of a gift—the Primus-King was more repulsive and more disturbed than I'd feared.

Tears stung the backs of my eyes. I laid back, pulled the blankets around me, and curled up into a ball. If I blotted out the light, would the bad memories disappear as well?

Cato paced back and forth. I tracked his location by the clang of armor which he was carelessly flinging about.

"Cato, frankly, you are not giving Eira enough credit for *her* abilities, and neither are you seeing mine. If a Gaean so much as laid a finger on her, she could detonate his fucking brains from his skull. *We* certainly cannot teach her anything more useful. And I did think about her; I commanded every man in this kingdom to safeguard her."

"Right. You did that. The last thing I need is a battalion of out-of-practice, out-of-shape, hotheaded mountain men, swinging around their dicks and swords."

I pulled the covers tighter and used a fistful to plug my ears and drown out the feuding brothers, to no avail.

"I wish you believed in me like she does, Cato. Not once did you, or Aberus, or Father *ever* think I was anything more than a shiny bauble bound for Verus. I am more than that, Cat. *I am more.*"

"That's fucking nonsense, and you know it!"

The thud of a fist forced my eyes open.

Cato's nose was streaming blood, and though Ambrose's aim had been true, his brother felled him with a well-placed arm across the chest and foot behind his knee.

I bolted from the bed, anger quickly replacing my malaise.

"Cato! Leave now. Until you calm down, you are not welcome in this room." I wanted them separated before they said or did anything that couldn't be repaired. "Get out."

Cato's mouth dropped open, and he narrowed his eyes.

"Don't look at me like that. I killed the Scholar, I killed Ozius, and *now* I'm sending Ambrose to his death." He stood stock-still in his padded arming clothes, his sun-kissed brown locks disheveled. "You heard me. Out!" I pointed to the door.

Cato ripped at the ties of his gambeson.

"Eira, I will go this once, but do not ever ask it of me again." He turned and left the room, slamming the door behind him.

I burst into tears—the fat, free-rolling tears of a scolded toddler.

"Come here." Ambrose stretched his arms wide. "All will be well." I blubber-walked into his strong embrace and pressed my face into his chest. He rocked me in his big arms, all the while cooing words of comfort softly into my ear. "Saddest, little harpy."

My head was pounding from the waterfall of tears and seemingly never-ending supply of mucus I could create, and I was exhausted. I reached around Ambrose and pulled his braid over his shoulder. I ran my finger tips over the bumpy length. He was once again my place of refuge.

"The Scholar was an old man when I was a child. Ozius's mind was as rotten as his head, and he got what he deserved." I nodded against his chest but didn't move from his arms. He tried to dislodge me, but I held on tighter. "Help me pack."

Fear gripped me. My palms began to sweat and my panic swelled. There was every possibility he wouldn't return.

"Wifeling, I should look my best when apprehending the corsairs. I imagine if I favor maroon, the bloodstains will blend in and not ruin my finer silks." He laughed into the top of my head, his breath sending little tendrils flying down over my eyes.

I reached up and ran my fingers through his beard. How could he make light of—

"Ambrose, fetch a knife."

"It is normal for partners to squabble from time to time, but Eira—"

"Ambrose, you ass—come to my room."

I locked my fingers to his and pulled his disinclined bulk behind me. He held on to the threshold of my chamber door halting us both.

"I have no time for plundering your goods. I need to save my semen. A mighty load makes men meaner, you know."

Ambrose wrestled with my arm but I held firm, pulling him with both hands. I braced my foot against the door frame and heaved.

"Give up!"

"Fine, but release your talons before you crumple my cuffs." He acquiesced and followed me into the bathing chamber. "You did get my play on words, yes? Semen, seamen? I need to save my sea-men... because of the pirates."

"Both the first and second times."

I bounced around the room, sucking in the air that didn't quite seem to quench my need for oxygen. My stomach felt like a heavy ball of metal.

"Eira, what are you about?"

I searched through a grouping of baskets until I found an assortment of medicines. I poured out my pain medication and emptied the fertility-suppressing tincture into my mouth.

"Two vials, maybe three will be enough. Stab me." I procured the thick-gauged needle that Allaine used to mend my woven garments.

"Not into it." He crossed his arms over his chest.

"I swear to the Goddess, Ambrose." I put the pin in his hand and held my arm out. "You're taking my blood. I can't stand the thought of you being hurt. Cato was right. You could die and—"

"—I would go to Merrias in glory," he said in a serious tone. "Simply being alive doesn't mean you are living, Eira,"

A wave of nausea doubled me over. The æther pooled in my guts, simmering and popping haphazardly.

"No, you will not. Promise me. You promise me right now. You will use this if you are injured. Please, gods. Promise me, Ambrose."

Cool tears slid down my panic-heated cheeks.

I snatched the needle from between his fingers and stabbed its tip into my thumb. When my blood clotted too quickly, I plunged it into the thicker blue vein on the side of my wrist and dug it around until two of the glass containers filled. I was too upset to be bothered by the pain.

"Eira, I am not without means. I have been trained. I am a Scion if you recall."

I milked my wrist, squeezing until the droplets filled the last and smallest bottle.

"Take these two and give the other to Cato." I shoved the vials into the leather pouch he wore on his belt.

My hysteria peaked. I had no control and my body knew it. I wanted to run, wanted to get away.

I bent over the basin and splashed my fevered face with cold water.

"If you are done with the dramatics—brown or black boots for boarding a vessel? I am inclined to choose the brown… It complements a gang plank."

Chapter 22

CONSEQUENCES OF MY ACTIONS

Ambrose left. He was gone and there was no concrete timeline for his return.

I stood alone on the palace steps and watched him pass through the vaulted gate on the far side of the front gardens. The strong scent of lavender wafted on the wind, mingling with the aroma of horse dung and leather. The commoners had gathered beyond the iron gates to see their brave soldiers off and were tossing dried sprigs of the herb under the horse hooves.

There was no need for me to feign worry—no need to play-act the anxious wife. *How many widows of the Great War funded their own husband's demise?*

Ambrose was surrounded by a small contingent of soldiers, and a scowling Dumail openly glaring at him as he sat atop his mount—I regretted taunting the courtier about his virility.

Actions have consequences, Eira. If Dumail so much as endangers a single hair on Ambrose's chin, I'll wipe his name from the history books.

Before he'd mounted his horse, Ambrose had shared with me that the first and only other time that he'd worn the uniform of a naval commander had been over seven years ago when he received the distinction. He had looked so proud. If it was to be my last image of him, it would be a fine one to have. Ocean blue suit, plain cut, with a woven sash of white around his hips. He wore it well; the men and women of Monwyn would look upon him as he rode by and wish to be him—or to bed him. He was handsome, strong, and had the eager confidence of the untested.

By the time I found the courage to turn away, I could no longer see the contingent, but I caught sight of Cato riding back into the courtyard after having escorted the group past the outer gates.

Though his face had been impassive when Ambrose saluted him, fist to shoulder, I knew he was an absolute wreck. He'd not bathed after removing his armor earlier, and the curls of his hair were weighed down with sweat and grime. Deep purple splotches under his eyes stood out on his coppery skin, and he clenched his jaw so tight that I was afraid his teeth would crack.

Cato rode past me without bothering to acknowledge my presence.

Bem escorted me back to my apartments.

I paced between Ambrose's room and mine, until finally settling on passing my time on the balcony.

I opened the door, and the chill hit my face, cooling the warmth in my cheeks but doing little to calm the storm swirling in my mind. Gammond's moon was high in the sky tonight. I prayed it would illuminate Ambrose's path. It was a half-day ride to the coast, and the party had planned to arrive shortly after sunrise if all went well on their journey.

I sank down onto a wicker couch, and a tiny spider scurried down my arm. It was the first one I had ever encountered—they didn't exist in Nortia. They were odd little creatures, all legs, and barely any body. I laid my head back and looked at the stars.

Momma, are you there?

I squeezed my eyes shut and listened, hoping for a sign.

Of course, there was no response, but as I breathed in the night air, her voice was clear in my mind. "Pick your head up, Eira, keep moving forward, even if your tears outnumber your footsteps." She never saw sadness as a weakness—she never hid her tears or chastised others for theirs.

"Have you tried solving your problem, Eira?" I asked the stars.

"No, Momma, I obviously prefer causing them," I replied to myself.

I longed for the piping-hot bowl of bean soup she'd have pushed on me. I would have told her about Cato and Ambrose and our "arrangement," and she would have tapped the tip of her finger to her nose and said something like, "Whatever keeps your boat afloat, but ensure you can navigate the storms."

I wish I knew more about you, Momma.

I should have asked her when I had the chance.

The spider, who was now running down my chest, dodged the flat gold beads that dotted the deep purple silk of my dress.

Did you have a childhood? Did you have a choice in bearing me so young?

Yet another life I may have ruined.

I pulled my knees in close and then transferred my spider friend to the couch cushion. I buried my head in my arms and let myself feel.

Daughter?

My head snapped up.

I do not mean to be intrusive, but perhaps a papa can be of assistance. It is a rare thing, you know, that a parent would regret a child. Even the worst of us seem to have an unending attachment to our young.

The Infinite Bond.

I dried my tears on my sleeve and then pushed back the little spikes of hair I felt escaping their confines. *How long have you been listening, Papa Burchard?*

Just briefly, dear. I decided a stroll was in order and have just left Levaunt napping. I felt, or rather, heard, your distress.

I nodded to the nothingness that surrounded me and straightened my cramped legs.

Marmot, I am positive your mother shares in your heartbreak. Though my boy is only hours gone, already I worry for my cub.

The prickling discomfort of my guilt flared again. I glanced down at my bare feet. They were speckled with bruises, and I couldn't help but feel like I deserved more of them.

Shall we practice, my dear?

Conjuring? No. Absolutely not, Papa.

After the mayhem of this morning, I wasn't sure how he could suggest I ever use the æther again.

A scratching sound came from the far side of the balcony, and two ladder legs appeared over the wall. The king's shiny bald head rose between two columns, and, moving cautiously, he managed to hoist himself over the marble half-wall.

"Catommandus was hot on my tail, but I managed to throw him off in the garden. By the by, the larder is now *off* the list—our hiding spot was the first place they checked." He waved me over. "Help an old man."

Reluctantly, I went to his aid and assisted him in sliding off the wall.

I felt the barest hint of our connection at my navel. Had I not already been familiar with the sensation, I would have mistaken it for an itch.

Together, we tugged the heavy ladder, foot by foot, until it cleared the wall and clattered to the floor.

"Are you well enough to be instigating nighttime capers, Majesty?"

The king breathed rapidly, and his egg-shaped head glistened with a light sheen of perspiration. His pearl-colored eyes stood out starkly, even in the near-dark of evening.

"I am well enough." He sat heavily and then patted the seat of the over-sized chair that Cato and I had previously shared. "Sit close. I think we should attempt turning on the lamps. It was the easiest bit to learn when I was starting out."

I sat as far from him as possible and folded my hands in my lap. I wouldn't let the tie compel me to closeness, no matter how comforting his presence had previously been.

"Will I eventually take lives with no remorse, slaughter animals, and ostracize my loved ones?"

The awkwardly bent fingers of an arthritic hand settled on my knee.

"Daughter, I was capable of atrocity long before becoming adept with the æther. The path to monarchy colored my experiences and fueled my choices much more so than my ability."

I placed my hand on his aged one and tried to rub the warmth back into his fingers. His skin was papery thin and parched.

"Wait, here." I ran to my room, procured my thickest lotion and made my way back to his side. I scooped out the oily concoction, rubbed it between my palms, and applied it thickly to his face. "You have to take care of yourself, Papa."

"It was easier when Imella was here to remind me."

I rubbed the soothing balm into his fingers and as far up his arms as I could reach. The white patches turned peachy again.

"Was Ambrose really adopted solely to further your renown?"

The king's eyes went wide as he laid his head back.

"That is true, yes. I purchased him for a hefty sum. But Imella took to him immediately. Like the Solnnans, the Taleery people view adoption to be as binding as a birth would be. Ambrose was hers the moment I laid him at her breast. She would nurse Cato and him simultaneously, while Aberus would toddle about and sing to them." The king's voice grew tender as he spoke. "It took *me* some time to warm up to him, but he was just as irresistible as a babe as he is today—his first words were 'pop pop.'"

"Do you realize your people see him as a farce? Even with his status as Chosen."

Snow-white eyes, as it turns out, were still capable of shedding tears.

"My plan for him was that he would be Assigned to another kingdom and then eventually rise to the top of Verus's hierarchy. I had my heir and a spare, you see, and never did I think my Kitty Cat would agree to become Protector. Septimus was supposed to fill that role—it is tradition to have one's brother installed as your supreme guard."

"That seems politically savvy—having your kin at your back is surely a boon."

The king, in a gesture that must have been second nature, stroked the beard that no longer existed. He pursed his lips and glared at his fingers.

"Perhaps in another kingdom. But my brothers, all but Septimus, I ordered to be removed from this existence."

I went icicle stiff.

"I'm sorry, but, y-you had your brothers removed? Killed?" I was sure I'd heard wrong.

The king nodded.

"Kings and queens should never be permitted to play Goddess, in my opinion."

He shrugged a shoulder to his ear.

"As firstborn, I had to ensure my throne was secure. In the game of crowns, the fiercest competitors—the most ruthless and conniving—are one's siblings. Septimus was the one I loved most and, subsequently, the only one I trusted to protect what was mine. He does not wish for the throne—he never has—but he coveted the Protectorate. I am afraid he does harbor resentment for not gaining the shield signet ring."

Cato shouldn't have been Protector?

"And how, then, did the responsibility come to rest on Cato's shoulders? Why would you allow such a thing? He-he wanted to be a scholar, you know, and read about gemstones and mining and—"

I stopped and snapped my mouth shut. Our ruse had to continue, and my feelings were escalating to a point of recklessness. I dug my fingernails into the meaty part of my palm and clenched my teeth so tightly that pain shot down my neck. The æther danced in my chest, and if I was being honest with myself, I wanted nothing more than to send His Majesty flying from his seat. How dare he? How dare he subject his child to a life of—

The king choked back a sob.

Tears eased their way down the crow's feet at the corner of his eyes. He dabbed at them with his fur-lined sleeve.

"Imella never felt secure here... Taleery Desert law gave everyone a voice, man or woman, old or young. I tried to make up for the betrayal of our marriage bed by altering the way our Council worked. At that point in time, we and our children had been living separately for a decade or more. I wanted her to see that I could change—that the kingdom was capable of change—so I introduced a policy where all men could apply for any position within the government. Cato, unbeknownst to us, had put his name forward for Protector. He was netherbent on maintaining our safety when he saw the familial unit breaking down. And you've seen him; he could persuade the dead to rise again. He easily convinced the Council to appoint him. They also hoped it would halt the long-standing, but unofficial, tradition of fratricide. And it eased my mind as well. When Imella birthed another boy after Aberus, I knew true fear."

I pulled a linen napkin from under a bowl of apples at the table's center and pressed it into Burchard's hand. My first inclination had been to accuse and berate him for meddling in the lives of others, but his own guilt seemed punishment enough.

"So many mistakes." He patted the corners of his eyes and then his nose. "And Imella, Goddess bless her, she had come to forgive my infidelity—we had begun to repair—but Catommandus's appointment was the death knell in our union. Protectors tend to die with swords in their hands." The king stared up at the moon as he continued shedding tears. A strong wind blew through the columns, ruffling the fur of his coat. Dried leaves sailed into the balcony and landed at our feet.

"How do you turn on the lamps?"

The king turned to me and smiled weakly.

"Much like how you took command of the men's bodies this morning." He sat up and rolled back his sleeves. "You will follow the lights where they take you, and then step outside of yourself. When you *become* the environment, you should be able to control the elements within it: fire, water, air, and æther. I am abysmal in my attempts to control the air, and I cannot make fire from nothing but can dim or increase its reach. Water seems to be my forte."

As if to prove his point, he pointed to an apple. It dimpled and folded in on itself, and a stream of bubbly white liquid seeped from its pores.

"Open your mouth."

I pinned him with a look from the side of my eyes.

"Go on now. My control is tenfold better than yours."

The short stream of juice twirled and spiraled an inch from my face and then raised up like a viper's head before tapping on my top lip.

My laugh was the first I'd managed all day, and when the liquid snaked into my mouth, the sour and fresh flavor of the fall's last harvest grounded me in the moment.

"Eyes closed." The king dipped his head. "I will guide you."

"Okay," I whispered faintly.

I lowered my lashes, and the flickering of the lamps caused the shadows and lights to whirl behind my lids. I struggled to focus on one spot—and then all the spots—but lost my concentration.

I tried again and again.

"How long has it been?" I said, ready to give up.

"An hour, maybe a little less. Try holding your breath and doing it again. The larger of the two tomes instructs that changing the pressure in our body can aid in the transition."

I rolled my head around and stretched my neck. My eyes drifted shut, and I took a deep breath and bared down. Quite frankly, I was growing tired and needed to pee but—

There they were.

They slid into my periphery.

I could smell the scent of apples and autumn so intensely. I could hear the batting wings of the bugs drawn to the flamelight.

In the past, my shadows had overwhelmed me, but this evening... they invited me in.

I opened my eyes.

Father Burchard was there, watching over me. His hairless face was all scrunched up, and he was holding his palm near my nose to ensure I still breathed.

I walked, or floated, rather, to the nearest light.

"Turn on, lamp."

Nope.

"Ignite."

Nothing.

I blew a strong breath of air toward the lamp nearest me.

"Go out. Do it, you silly little fireball."

The twisting flame that began blue and ended in a yellow tip crackled and flickered. I swear it mocked me. I could blow grown men back twenty feet, but I couldn't pull off a six-year-old's first conjure.

"Just die then," I hissed.

The flame turned black.

Like darkened glass, it didn't move or flicker, and I could see clearly through its entire length.

From the corner of my eye, I caught sight of the king standing and moving toward the light.

"What is this, Marmot?" He studied the non-flame flame, walking around it and assessing it from different angles. He raised his fingers to the shadow.

"Ouch!" When his hand made contact, the black flame popped and then dissipated before reverting to a yellow flame once more.

I returned to reality just in time to see the king snatch his hand backward.

"Father Burchard, are you alright?"

"I am, dear. It was not hot, but it had a fearsome sting. Did you see it turn to soot?"

"I did, and I realized something—I follow the shadows and not the lights. Do I conjure backward?"

"The shadows?"

"Mmhmm, the darkness between the light is what pulls me, not the light itself."

The king cocked his head to the side and blinked.

"Fascinating." He glanced up, and he leaned around me, looking through the double doors. "Sweetheart, I must be off. I have been located."

In a motion endearingly similar to Cato, he turned on his heels and strode into the common room. He waved at Levaunt, who stood in the door that Bem held wide.

The king swung around and fanned his fingers at me, then held out his arms to receive the shackles that were already locked by the time he faced forward.

CHAPTER 23

GREEN GOBLINS RUN AMOK

"Eira."

"Yes?"

I hunkered deeper into the bed and purposefully kept my back to him. It may have been childish of me, but I was still hurting from our earlier encounter. I leafed through the pages of a book whose title I didn't recall. I'd been staring at the parchment pages and not actually reading since returning to my room.

Cato slipped in behind me and wrapped his arm around my waist. He placed his forehead on my shoulder and breathed in deeply. He smelled of horse and sweat, and his fingernails were caked with filth.

"Will you come with me?"

I wanted to be contrite, to scold him for lashing out as he had, but even more than that, I wanted him. More than anything, we needed to discuss, share, and touch.

By the sound of his voice—heavy and hollow—I understood that he needed me too.

The wide neckline of his shirt slipped down my shoulder as I rolled over to face him.

"You still love me then?" he asked, the corner of his lip angling up.

I smoothed a limp curl back from his forehead and traced the worry line that ran alongside his mouth.

"I certainly didn't enjoy being yelled at, but it appears I can handle you at your worst." I smiled weakly, then stretched up and pressed my lips above his collar. Relief swathed me—the steady pulse in his neck was my anchor.

"My worst?" He raked his fingers through his hair, pushing the gold-streaked rings out of his eyes. "There are none among the living who have witnessed my worst."

He caught my chin between his fingers, and his lips settled against my own.

And then I cracked. I shattered into a million heartbroken pieces.

"Do you still love me? Because I'm not sure I can love myself for much longer." I choked back a sob as dread reared its nasty head again. "Cato, I sent him to his death."

"No, love, I kept him from his life." He twisted around and stood. "I cannot blame you for the consequences of my conduct—my short-sighted plans. I did exactly what he accused me of." He tossed his leather satchel onto the bed. "Put these on."

Unshed tears continued to threaten, but I rummaged through the stuffed bag and pulled out its contents one by one. A rolled-up parcel became a pair of gray leathers, the same as all the soldiers wore. Next, there was a tight, padded jacket, which was worn beneath a warrior's armor to keep the metal from pinching their skin.

"Do you have a proclivity I am unaware of, Cato?" I held the outfit in front of me. Though it smelled of a recent wash, old, rusty-red, and yellow stains covered the garment. I didn't want to think about what may have caused them.

"Not that I'm aware of, but I'll report back when your hips fill those out." The barest hint of a smile hitched up on his lips. "Now, hurry; we're gettin' outta here, ma'am." He drew out his words like one of the mountain folk.

My heart dropped to my stomach.

"Cato, I don't... where, where will we go? And what of Ambrose? Your father? We just can't—"

He came to me then. He kneeled down in front of me and wrapped his hands around my calves.

"Those are morning worries. Give me tonight." He turned my hands over and pressed kisses on my palms. His wayward curls fell over his brows, nearly concealing his gold-tipped lashes. "I thought we could take a walk in the city and leave this day behind."

Precious. He was the most precious of my treasures.

I hugged his face to my chest and shimmied with excitement.

"Move. Get out of my way." I shoved his broad shoulders backward, and he sat back on his heels. Moving as fast as I could, I hopped off of the bed and pulled the hem of my shirt over my head.

"Mmmm. A kiss for the road?"

"Of course." With the naughtiest of intentions, I bent at the waist, ensuring that my chest was front and center.

I pecked the little bump in the middle of his nose.

"One more... different locale?"

"Uh-uh. I'm ready for freedom."

I flung out the pants, working the leather up my knees. When I got to my thighs, I pulled, stretched, and wiggled, straining to get them up over my hips—buttoning them would be impossible. I fell back on the bed and shoved my stomach into the waistband. The leather had barely any stretch and smelled of hay, but for a chance at an evening free of these walls, they were going on no matter how much of me spilled out.

"I planned on more of an outing before we fucked, but if you would rather not wait..."

The crotch of his pants tightened, and I could see the outline of his erection as it filled. I ignored him and resumed grappling with the buttons.

"The anticipation," I grunted, popping the third button into place, "is part of the fun. Is it not?"

"Incorrect—the fucking is the fun part."

He stood and leaned over me, incredibly aroused.

He lowered his body to mine and hitched my leg up around his waist.

Kisses rained down on my shoulders, my bare breasts rubbed against the fleecy texture of his coat, and his hard length pressed into my low stomach. He captured my hands, twisted me up off the bed, and pulled my back to his chest.

"Your breasts are flawless." He cupped each, and gently rolled my nipples between in his fingers. "Sweetheart." He dipped a finger into my pants and skimmed the top of my curls. "Ride me before we go."

"Take me out, Protector."

I bounced my rear against him and wrestled away, but he pulled me back quickly. His hands settled on my pants, and he easily popped the last button into place as he trailed his tongue up the edge of my ear.

"Can you pull off the guise of a soldier, Lady Troth?" he asked.

"But of course... a few grunts and a well-timed scratch of the crotch, and none will be the wiser."

Cato slipped a padded jacket around my shoulders and spun me to face him. He began lacing up the front from the bottom, and with every tug of the cord, the tight canvas material pushed my breasts higher.

"Cato."

The tip of his tongue darted out to moisten his bottom lip. He reached for my—

"Caaaa-tooo," I drawled out, nodding at the front of his pants, "put that away."

"No." He caught my breast in his hand and sucked my nipple into his mouth.

"Sir!"

"Fuck off."

I shoved his shoulders the moment he opened his mouth to speak and began tying the laces while he stroked his covered length.

"*You* are taking me out as promised. Quit that." I smacked his hand and went back to lacing. If he kept it up—even through his pants—we wouldn't make it past the door.

"The state in which I find myself is no fault of my own." He scrubbed his jaws between his hands. "I have a report, Sergeant: your ass threatening to tear out of those leathers while your fat tits bounce in my face has indeed unlocked a new proclivity. To me, soldier."

Cato made quick work of armoring me.

Steel spaulders and vambraces buckled to my arms, and a pair of heavy cuisses attached to my hips and secured around my knees. Finally, a livery tabard of blue was pulled over my head, and a thick black belt was cinched around my waist.

Cato motioned for me to follow him and led me through the common room.

Bem was waiting. He crinkled his nose when he saw me and shook his head from side to side.

"Eira, stand up straight. Walk behind me and stay just to my left."

Cato produced a shining helm and lowered it over my head.

"It fits quite loosely." He eyeballed me and then lowered the helmet's visor over my face and buckled it behind my neck. "You are, without doubt, the most voluptuous guard on my staff. Avoid swaying your hips when you walk."

He turned to leave.

"I don't sway." My voice rang in my ears, and I barely caught the damn helmet before its weight pitched me forward. "I walk confidently, with purpose and regality."

Cato glanced over his shoulder. Through the narrow eye slots, I could see the lift of his skeptical brow.

"Yes, it is your *confidence* that has my hand on my cock."

"I knew it. You do prefer a proud woman." I tipped my head forward so I could see the tight-lipped smile that I knew he'd wear.

I felt the weight of a sword and scabbard settle at my left hip.

"Do *not* unsheathe that." Cato's fingers lingered on my own as he placed a spear in my right hand. "Ready, Eiric?"

Tinkling giggles were my only reply.

"Goddess, preserve us," he muttered.

I jogged behind him as we headed through Cordillaria's long corridors. We made our way to the bottom floor and headed toward the front of the palace.

"Who goes there?" barked one of the four guards stationed at the magnificent set of doors that led to the main garden.

"Captain," Cato addressed a guard who wore an ornate metal shield hanging from his chainmail, "reassign this man to armor maintenance. He cannot recognize the Protector from a distance of ten feet away—he is not fit for the duty."

"The Protector has spoken," I said in the manliest voice I could manage. I hoisted the spear in my hand and sent its butt smashing to the ground.

Four helmeted heads turned in my direction.

"A trainee. Pay the imbecile no attention."

Imbecile? It's what all of them do, asshole!

"I will be absent for the duration of this watch. Lemder is in charge until I return. Is that understood?"

"It is. Will you be needing your mount, Protector, sir?"

"No, my mission is local. Until I return, not so much as an ant is allowed to pass through unless official paperwork is in hand."

We charged out the doors and into the night.

The gardens were dimly lit, further limiting my ability to see, but the strong scent of lavender found its way through the breathing holes of the helm's grill. Immediately my mind went to Ambrose.

"Good evening, Cato."

We came to a hard stop.

I shook my head to the left in an attempt to straighten the damn helmet that twisted awkwardly around my face. Unsuccessful, I employed my spear, using it to anchor the eye holes into place.

A stunning blonde—a perfect Monwyn specimen—stood in our path. Her lips were skillfully painted a deep mauve, and her brows arched perfectly over her big, bright, brown eyes.

"It is almost time for evening prayers—care to join me on my knees?"

The fuck?

"Madam, as I have reminded you since the day I turned seventeen, I am disinterested. *Entirely*."

I tilted forward to get a better look. She stood fairly tall, with angular, squared-off shoulders. A perfect line of cleavage peeked out over the top of her neckline, revealing a set of high breasts—each a succulent handful. *Oh Cato, she may not be your type, but she's undoubtedly mine.*

She shared the same bodily structure that Evon, Greggen's sinewy companion, had—lean and finely muscled.

The woman slid close to Cato's side and placed her beautifully polished fingertips on his chest.

My chest.

"It never hurts to ask, now does it?" She trailed her fingers around his shoulder.

My shoulder.

I gritted my teeth to keep from speaking.

She walked those lithe fingertips down the path that led to *my* package.

Nope, she wasn't my type after all—ugly hag. *Saggy titted sow.*

Jealousy. White, hot, burning jealousy traversed a path through my veins.

"One day, when you cast aside that ridiculous vow of celibacy, my tight, neglected pussy will welcome you."

This woman.

She pressed herself against my man and rubbed her stupid little boobs against his pecs.

"I still remember that young man busting all over my breasts—that thick phallus jerking in my hands."

Oh, she wishes to die, I see.

I placed my hand on my sword's pommel and squeezed until I felt pain. I'd want it to be agonizing and disfiguring—maybe I'd run her over with a horse-drawn cart and then kick her entrails down a dirt road until I found a herd of hungry pigs. I'd need her bones bleached before I could mount them as my trophy... and I imagined that Father Burchard would know how to—

"Ofillia, you meant as little to me then as you do now."

The hag-bag scoffed angrily and thrust her chest out.

She snapped her head in my direction.

"And what of our recruit here? Such a big-boned boy we have."

I tightened my pectorals and sucked in my stomach as her hands found my chest. My nipples stiffened at her touch, and in spite of myself, a little shock of arousal ran through my womb as she slid her hands up and down my torso.

"Short is no bother, young man, and though you are fleshy now, a few more months under the Protector's watchful eye and you will harden right up... it would take mere seconds under my care, however." Her hand drifted between my legs.

"Leave, Ofillia," Cato's voice was cold.

"Just keep mounting your horse, then—the ladies assume you impotent any-how."

Ooooo, bitch! Nasty, shit-licking she-demon! My man is virile! In a contest of range, his load would hit the far wall!

It was a blessing that the helm hid my bared teeth.

In a wave of skirts, Ofillia flounced off.

And so did I.

"His manhood would split your pretty slit in two! He could fell a deer with his shot! He could impale a godsdamned blue whale with the spear of his spunk!"

"Eiric. At attention! Now!" Cato barked.

I halted my steps when a heavy hand landed on my shoulder.

Ooooooo!

"Fine. Fine. Lead on, sir."

Cato surged forward, and we continued down a long gravel promenade that led to the outer gate.

"So you and that one?"

He didn't spare me a glance.

"I sent her flowers for weeks—a sweet note here and there. I fancied myself in love, up until she demanded payment for her 'services.' I was a young dumbass who quickly learned his lesson."

"My poor, sweet love, jilted by a teenage handjob gone wrong. I can't say that I wouldn't have succumbed to her myself, but Cato, that must have been heartbreaking."

"You have enjoyed a woman's touch?" he asked with an expression of concern.

"Yes. Is that... does that bother you?"

"Not in theory, no. But I struggle with the thought of another's hands on you, past or present it would seem."

"What if it were both of our hands on you, Cato?"

With his wave, the gate opened and then closed behind us.

My shoulders dropped in relief. Though I hadn't been locked away by any means, being on the other side of the wrought iron filled me with a sense of giddiness.

"You are all that I need Eira, all that I desire. And how do you suppose I could pay attention to another's slit when yours was so near? Hmm?"

"Well, I would be perfectly capable of pleasuring her while you..." Cato's wide eyes settled on mine... "you truly haven't imagined the scenario have you?"

"No, I have not."

"Well, if you are imagining it now, it won't be with Ofillia, so get that out of your head."

I dropped the subject and kept walking.

The cobbled streets were fairly quiet; there was an odd couple walking here and there and a small unit of guards in the distance. Occasionally, a pub door would open, spilling out the slurred songs of an inebriated crowd.

"This way."

We turned down an alley so narrow that I had to turn sideways. We emerged into a space where a door lay recessed into the stone wall. Cato took my spear and went to work unfastening my visor. The cool air hit my sweaty face and I breathed in the night air.

I couldn't make out his features in the dark, but I could feel Cato's breath against my neck when his head neared mine.

"Your jealousy turned me rock hard."

"The green goblins got the better of me." The sound of creaking metal pierced the quiet alleyway as I circled my arms around his neck. I pulled him forward until we came up against the bricks of the building. "Shit."

"What's wrong, love?"

"It's these tight-ass pants. We can't fuck if I can't get them down." I fought the knee-length tabard trying to get to my buttons.

His low laughter surrounded me. The sound was smooth and carefree.

I stilled and let the happiness bloom within my chest.

"Cato?" He placed his forehead against mine.

"Yes?"

"When Ambrose and I Join." His arms stiffened, but his breathing remained steady. "I will be afforded the life so many only dream of—I'll have finery and can pursue my interests... and I'll have you. In the grand scheme of things, I couldn't ask for more." I kissed him once and then again. "But what of your dreams?"

"What of them?"

"Stubborn man." I twirled my fingertip in the hair at his nape. "Cato, what do you dream of?"

"You." His palms came to rest on either side of my face. "And also... well... How about I show you?"

Chapter 24

THE SHITTY SHACK

"Your dream is a shitty old shack?"

About ten minutes from the city proper, Cato and I stood in front of a rickety house that looked as if it had *barely* survived the Great War. One of its shutters swung from a single nail, and the roof was collapsed on the right side.

"Well, no, this is not *the* house I have longed for, but it is what it represents." Cato put a key into the lock, and then another, and then another, before he swung the door wide.

He charged in, but I waited a few seconds to ensure that the ancient structure didn't fall from the door being opened with such vigor.

"It's a safe house. I have used it to harbor dignitaries on the run as well as associates who needed to lie low for a period of time."

With the flick of a match, a lamp sprung to life, illuminating the single-room space.

I sucked my lips into my mouth and let them go with a surprised pop.

"Ho-lyyy snowballs."

"Yes, well, if it were between this and dangling from the end of a hangman's noose, you would find a way to cope." Cato moved about the room, lighting a few more lamps. "Have you become spoiled by the opulence of palace life?"

My mouth fell open, and my fists went to my hips.

His chuckle filled the small room, growing louder as he rounded a table and found his way back to me.

"Love." His gaze settled on mine, and the barest hint of cinnamon reflected in his eyes. "What *I* want most in my life is to"—he paused and covered my fists with his hands—"play house."

Oh fuck.

Cato bit the corner of his lower lip and my ovaries plotted out the kidnapping of his cock. The room took on a golden glow as my pupils enlarged.

"Eira... I want to play the papa. And it is my opinion that you would make the most delicious of mamas."

My mouth went dry. Desert dry.

My clitoris tightened and a deep ache took up in my pelvis. This was no slow pulse building its way to a fever pitch of arousal. This was a wallop of wantonness snapping me to bodily preparedness. My fingers tingled.

I desired my mate.

"Cato, I want sex. I want to fuck you like a godsdamned mallet tenderizing a slab of steak."

His brows jerked to his hairline while a slow, lazy smile lit up his face.

"But, wife, I have just come home from the quarry and am exhausted from working my body to the bone."

Be still my quivering vagina.

The thought of watching him take a pickaxe, or whatever the fuck they used, to a boulder... the sweat running down his broad, hair-covered chest, streaming through that dark trail that ran to his...

"You... you're going to make me playact when my passage is near to flooding my pants?"

"Yes." He nodded. "I am."

"I don't know how to treat a husband, Cato. I want dick. Is that not the wifeliest of pursuits? Wanting and getting fucked on a regular basis? Ambrose would say it was."

"Figure it out, Troth. I have faith in you."

I peeked around his chest at what was, in truth, a well-stocked, only slightly shitty hideaway. In the far right corner of the room, a copper tub sat tall, and near it was a small healer's cabinet. There was a counter that ran along the back wall that was lined with preserved foodstuffs, and below it were three stools. A modest-sized bed layered with quilts stuck out from the right wall. It had a white-washed headboard and a bedside table stacked high with books.

I thought back, trying to recall what my mother had done when my father came home from the pier in the evenings.

"Well, husband, dinner's still an hour away. There's mending to be done, and that little shit Eira got in trouble for cussing at the neighbor's boy," I said while unbuckling the armor bits on my arms.

"Did he deserve it?"

"Undoubtedly." My hands went to the ties of my heavy arming garment. I untied the cording until I was able to shrug the gambeson from my shoulders. The spaulders clattered loudly to the floor, but the vambraces fell onto the cloth that laid around my feet. "Eira is nothing if not the most honest, kind, and loving of humans." I walked around the room and looked for inspiration. "Should we... um... sit in those chairs and talk about how tired we are, or perhaps discuss the Primus's most recent announcement?" A giggle bubbled up from my throat.

"We won't make it through the conversation unless you cover your tits." He peeled his coat off and pulled a gray sweater over his head. "Take this and hang it up, sweetheart." He tossed the garment in my direction, but it sailed over my head and hit the bed.

"Your aim is impeccable." I laughed my way across the floor and snatched up the soft wool.

"*My* aim was perfect," he whispered in my ear. "Was this not the destination you had in mind after all?" The hair on his chest was like silk tickling my back. I let my head fall against his shoulder. Everything that made his body so different from mine turned me to mush—the hair on his stomach and even the dusting on his back and rear. I reveled in the bulk of his shoulders, his lean hips, and thick fingers.

"Mmhmm." I nodded. He curled his arms around me and gently rocked me from side to side. I closed my eyes and sank into the cradle of his arms.

"You have never allowed me to love you slowly, wife." His hand drifted up and settled between my breasts. "That changes tonight. But first, you will wash my hair. I'll not soil our marriage bed."

He dropped his arms and went quickly to the tub in the corner. At first, the water from the faucet ran a rusty red, but within a minute, it came out clear and steaming hot.

"Though it may sound strange, I find that I am more envious of the intimacies you share with Ambrose, compared to the time he spends within your body. Those moments of shared affection are when I entertain the notion of placing my hands around his neck."

His fingers went to the laces of his pants and my mind went to guilt.

All this time, Ambrose had been fulfilling those parts for me and I for him. We cuddled before bed. He'd have tea waiting for me in the mornings, and whenever we moved about the palace together, our hands were always linked. Cato was there at every turn, bearing witness to it all.

If I were in his shoes, were Ofillia on his arm, combing his hair, bringing him his shoes—I'd be in a constant state of fit.

"Stop," I said.

Cato's hands stilled, and his brows knit together.

"That's a wife's job, don't you think?" I glanced down at his hands. He let out the breath he was holding in a single, sharp gust. "Papa, our baby is almost one; don't you think it's time we try for number three?"

Cato chewed on the corner of his mouth and held his fingers in the air.

"Four?"

He poked out his thumb.

"Five?" I blanched. "No, sir. This mama may be in for one—maybe—and..."

"This is my dream, Mama, and we have five. All girls. Each and every one of them is the spitting image of you, except for the littlest, who has my eyes. And I have already been in seven altercations with men trying to betroth their snot-nosed little boys to our eldest, who is of course named after me."

"Catanna? Catorina?"

I sauntered my way over to him, swaying my hips as I worked the tight pants down. I stopped at the halfway point and let my leathers hit the floor before continuing to him.

"No. Catommandus. Why would we change it?"

"Catommandus? For our beautiful and soft-hearted little love?"

"The fuck do you mean 'soft'? Do you suppose *you* will raise mild-tempered babes?" Cato tossed his head back and snort-laughed. "Our girls will terrorize the kingdom. The middle child demands snacks from the courtiers and stamps her tiny feet on the ground when she doesn't get her way. His Majesty will, of course, give into her every whim."

The future he painted—the one I'd never wished for—took hold in my heart.

My hands made short work of his ties, and when I pushed his pants over his hips, his pulsing and deep-colored erection sprung free.

His soft heat brushed my shoulder as I went to my knees.

"Step out." I tossed his pants aside and then skimmed the tip of my finger from his base to tip. "One of my favorite things is having you in my mouth." I kissed his head, and his stickiness dotted warmly on the center of my lips.

Cato caught my chin and tilted my head up.

"Slow." He traced two fingers along the edge of my jaw.

"My domain," I said saucily. "Now, into the bath, Papa."

Cato threaded his fingers through mine and helped me to stand before lowering himself into the slipper-shaped tub. There were a couple of bars of soap and a stack of clean linen squares atop the healer's cabinet. The bars were unscented and would probably dry the skin from his bones, but there were an assortment of creams and oils that I would happily slather on him if the need arose.

I went to the foot of the basin and lathered my washcloth.

"Feet."

One foot popped out of the water and onto the edge of the tub.

"Creator's Tits! You're missing a toe!" My mouth fell open. Cato mimicked my face, letting his eyes go wide and dropping his jaw.

"And you have never noticed it before because..."

"Because you never take your boots off."

"Incorrect, and you know it."

I did know it.

"Well, then it's because—"

"You get distracted by parts of me that are more *firmly* attached?"

I ran the cloth over the white-colored scar where his fourth toe used to be.

"What happened to it?"

"Nothing valiant. The day Ambrose showed up for his tenure in the mines, I brought a spade down on it while showing off." Cato chuckled. "He strolled in like he does—a prince *and* Scion—with looks that made even the overseer swoon. I was jealous."

"You jealous?" Cato scrunched up his adorable face and glared. I blew him a kiss.

"Do you realize that, due to our parents separation we saw each other maybe twice before we became men? Truly, it was not until our journey to Verus that we became anything more then just Protector and citizen." Cato laid his head back against the copper edge, and his eyelids drifted shut. "Anyway, Evandr projectile vomited on the decapitated nub, so the healer refused any attempt to sew it back into place." The corner of his mouth turned up like it did every time the short Scion's name was mentioned.

"And this one?" I ran the cloth along the odd spiral of a scar that had lightened considerably since the day I held my bleeding arm to his mouth. I shuddered at the memory of his chest being shredded to ribbons.

"A minotaur's whip."

"You have to be fucking kidding me!" I slapped my hand against the water and was rewarded with a splash to the face. "Half-man and half-goat? Bull?"

"Bull, yes, and—"

"Which half was cow?" I said, exuberant in the knowledge that my most beloved of the fabled creatures existed. "Are they big and brawny? Do they have horns and indigo skin?"

Cato smiled fully and wiped the water from his eye before launching in. "This was a lady minotaur, and her head was the cow. She was very muscular, and no, she wasn't blue. Her complexion was quite unusual, though. Her ass was spotted."

"Her ass? Did you want to have sex with her? Were her boobs covered, or did they just hang out?"

"Gods, Nortia. The nether-beast was actively trying to slaughter me. I was not in a place to stop and think, 'My, my, what a unique, if deadly creature. Perhaps she will cease terrorizing me and allow me to mount her.'"

"And her boobs? Multiple, like udders, or just two?" I had to know.

"There were just two... They just hung there." He laughed in his rich and resonant tone.

I ran the cloth along one of his legs and then the other, tracing the muscles that showed distinctly on either side of his knee.

"The ink around your thigh. How did it come to be bisected?" I stood and went to the side of the tub where I could more easily scrub the rest of him. "And what is the tattoo?"

Cato ran his palm over the band of glyphs.

"When His Majesty's attacks began to increase, my mother located a wise woman who made her home near the fire mountain to the south. She supposedly wove a protective spell into the tattoo, and I honestly think it worked, though maybe I just needed to convince my mother that it did."

Cato caught my soapy hand and held it against his chest.

"This gouge was delivered by the first troll I ever met. The wound was negligible, but whatever lay under his nails made me so violently ill I nearly met Merrias."

The thought—just the mention of him losing his life—made my stomach clench.

"This one," he said, placing my hand above his hip. "The one that used to be here before you healed me, was dealt by my father." His voice was so faint I could barely hear him. "Septimus had lashed out at my mother, accusing her of coddling

Ambrose and loving him more than her natural children. I put myself in front of him when the spear—a projectile no one could see—opened my side." Cato peered out from under his lashes. "He was out of his mind with grief when I came to. He wailed and sobbed and messed himself—pissing all over the carpets of the ladies' solarium."

"My Goddess, Cato, it's no wonder you feel the way you do. But... why protect Septimus? I think I would have positioned him more accurately for the strike."

Cato raised a dripping hand to my cheek.

"Septimus was my true father, Eira. He raised me and taught me the ways of the world while mine was off kinging and conjuring. He had no son of his own and treated me as if the sun rose only when my eyes opened each morning."

"And then you became Protector?"

Cato scowled while tapping his fingers on the tub's edge.

"Father Burchard visited this evening." I looked away and scrubbed his underarms rougher than I probably should have. "I meant to tell you."

"Will you always make your own rules?"

"What would little Catommandita do?"

"Listen to her papa and never *ever* lie."

"Sit up." Cato moved forward while I stood and slid my underwear down my legs. I stepped in behind him and squished myself between the tub and his back. The water rose, spilling over the rim. "I'll clean it up when—"

"Shut up, love." He leaned back and pillowed his head on my breasts. "This is my every dream."

Protective feelings engulfed me. I wanted to keep him from all harm and make his every wish a reality. The feelings were so intense that the shadows flickered in my vision. I didn't want to see us from the outside, though, so I pushed them back, opting to stay firmly in this moment. I soaped my hands and scrubbed his hair, then rinsed the suds away. His soft sigh hung in the air.

"Cato?"

"Hmm?"

"I never want to be parted from you."

Silence stretched between us.

"Then tuck me away in your heart—exactly where you reside in mine."

I didn't care when the water turned to ice.

I didn't budge when my skin turned to prune flesh.

This was home.

I was home.

When he came to me, he was bathed in the glow of candlelight. The thin aura that glittered in his dark irises spread widely as his pupils enlarged. He settled himself heavily on top of my body.

"I wish to know you. The depth of your mind. The adorable space between your toes. This freckle on your arm." He bent his head and kissed the tiny spot above the crease of my elbow. "All of you."

A blush crept over my cheeks, and warmth spread from my chest outward. The æther knew him.

We had never shared the quiet and the peace together. At Verus, there was always the fear of intrusion or the ticking of the clock that ended our private moments too soon. After the temple, we had rushed our loving, all tangled limbs and heightened emotions.

Here it was just us.

He blew warm air around my areola.

"Your breasts are so sensitive. They draw up, and the nipples deepen to the same lush color as your lips as they stiffen." My delicate skin constricted and tightened as he spoke. "Yes, just like that." He blew again, this time more forcefully, outlining my breast and traveling down my ribcage. "The first time I claimed you with my mouth, I felt goosebumps rising on your thighs. I have been obsessed with recreating the moment ever since."

Cato pushed up to his knees and sat between my legs.

"The other day on the balcony, I had planned to lay you back on the table and take my meal hot while the cold wind filled your skirts. You would have liked that."

"Yes, I would have." I wiggled my hips, trying to find his thigh with my center.

"But then my brother intruded."

"Because you told him to come."

Cato rolled his eyes.

"He wouldn't have minded waiting... or watching."

The deep internal throbbing built, and moisture trickled down my rear.

Cato saw it. He breathed in deeply, and a smug smile played across his face.

"Just this week, my hand brushed against the softest leather hide and reminded me of you—I palmed myself in the armory's bathing chamber. And then again, when I bit into a peach, its flesh was so similar to the texture of your slit that I ducked into the chatelain's storage closet."

I spread my legs, inviting him to admire me further.

"You should never have to resort to your hand. I want to be the vessel in which you take all of your pleasure." My breathing turned rapid, and for a few seconds, my heart palpitated, beating out of its normal rhythm. "Cato, I can't wait—"

"You will."

He slid his fingers from the top of my thigh to my ankle and then lifted my foot to his shoulder. He turned his head, his tongue darting out, licking the sole of my foot.

"Cato, don't do that!" I jerked my leg back.

"No boundaries. I have made it clear that I wish to know all parts of you—the way every inch of you feels and tastes." He sucked on the pad beneath my toes and bit down on the sensitive skin of my arch. The slight sting mingled with the tickling sensation of his beard against my sole. I pulled back, but he held firm and dipped his tongue between my toes. "There they are—those tiny bumps." He placed his palm on my upper thigh. "Spread yourself for me, sweetheart. Part yourself wide."

I reached between my legs and pressed my fingers into my slit, spreading myself with one hand.

"The way your wetness glistens is... wonderful."

"Lord Vaughn thought so too." I chuckled internally as Cato gave me a side-long glance.

His eyes were riveted to my exposed sex. His light-copper skin flushed deeply across his shoulders, and he nibbled the corner of his bottom lip, content to keep staring. I was transfixed as he watched me. Slowly, I swiped my finger across the tip of my gem, tracing sensual circles around the tight bundle. I moved my hand down and dipped just the tips of two fingers into my passage. I was so aroused that my vagina contracted, trying to pull the digits in.

"More?"

His breath hitched.

"Sink them deeply."

I pushed in and pulled out slowly, coating my fingers until I was three knuckles deep.

"She clenches around me so tightly when you come. Your walls swell so thick that it's like pushing my cock through a... a... hot from the oven, clotted-cream-filled pastry."

"Do what?" I laughed.

His face cracked into a full-on beam. One of those dimple-showing, scrunched-up eyes kind of smiles that made me forget there was a world outside of these rickety walls.

"I said what I said." He winked and took my hips into his hands. Bending low, he placed a kiss on the dark curls at my apex. He breathed in deeply, inhaling my scent, and then stretched his neck from side to side as if he were preparing for rigorous exercise. "Would you like my tongue?"

I grabbed his head with both hands, but he shifted back and reached for a pillow that had fallen off the side of the bed. He shoved it under my hips, tilting up my pelvis.

"The better to see you with..."

Cato laid on his stomach between my bent knees and propped his head between his hands. With his eyes fastened to mine, he leaned in and lazily dragged the point of his tongue between my labia.

"Cato..." I breathed. He drew my bud into his mouth and sucked me unhurriedly in a steady rhythm. I laced my fingers through his short locks.

"You make such lovely sounds." He looked up, swirled two fingers into my wetness, and then pushed forward.

"Oh, gods, Cat..."

"Is it like this when you lay with him?" Cato descended again and swept his broad tongue from my penetrated entrance to the tiny spot above my clitoris.

I shook my head from side to side as he pumped his hand at a leisurely pace.

He was keeping me on the edge—just a step away from crashing like a wave on the shore. I writhed beneath him and bucked my hips, trying to coax his fingers into moving faster than the snail's pace he was subjecting me to.

"H-he's never made me... I've never clim—It's just not the same."

I heard it then—that growl—that guttural, possessive purr.

"That is because *I* am the papa."

Cato rose to his knees and removed his fingers from my passage. He ran his fist down his erection and stroked himself until his arousal was slick with my wetness.

I sat up, prepared to climb him, but he shoved me backward and then pressed my thighs wide.

He rubbed his thick tip up and down my cleft and then fed in just enough to stretch my outer ring.

"Every inch feels like living a lifetime." He wrapped an arm behind my neck and touched the tip of his nose against mine. "Love is too simple a word for what I feel." He pushed forward slowly, so slowly. My walls pushed apart until his hips were seated snugly against my pubic bone. "But you make it so simple to love you."

He rolled his hips against me, moving his spine in a wave, all the while staying tightly embedded inside me. The motion and his closeness stimulated my inner and outer pleasure centers simultaneously.

"Cat... I..."

"Tell me what you feel, love."

"I... feel... " His mouth found the space below my ear.

"Hmm." The vibration of his hum against my earlobe sent a chill down my arms.

"When you love me, I feel whole... entire."

"Like the sum of a complex equation," he whispered.

I nodded, my chin rubbing against the scratchy beard on his jaw.

His mouth sought mine, warm and unhurried.

He continued working himself methodically in and out, and when I urged him on with the tilt of my hips, he dropped a hand to my thigh and squeezed.

In the oldest of mankind's dances, we found our rhythm together. Our tongues touched, and our fingers felt.

Cato moaned into my mouth, and I drew in the sound. He pulled back and then plunged himself deeply into my passage.

"Mmm... Papa..."

Once. Twice. Three times he drove forward, grunting with every exertion.

I broke like a dam after a mighty rainstorm. My muscles contracted around him, and the spasms wracked me. My back arched high, pressing my breasts against his chest, while he rocked and thrust me to satisfaction.

"From my lips to her ears—*You* are the life of my choosing, Cato."

My blood surged, and my body jerked. I panted and cried out—moaned and hummed—speaking to him in the ancient language of physical love.

Through the haze of half-closed eyes, I watched as tears rolled down the tip of his oft-broken nose and felt them splash warmly onto the space above my heart.

"You were my beginning, Eira, and there will be only you until my final rest."

CHAPTER 25

SWEET DREAMS

"Eira, wake. We must return."

I opened my groggy eyes and stretched my arms over my head. The quilts snugged perfectly around my shoulders, and I struggled to blink away the sleep that kept lulling me back into its embrace.

Cato was dressed and sitting at the table with a ball of fiber and a wooden needle in his hands.

"Are you... Do you knit?" It was the most precious sight I'd ever laid eyes on—watching him loop the string around his thumb. "My grandmother knits, and Nan does as well, but I've never seen a brawny soldier making booties."

He glanced up under half-hooded eyes.

"No. I do not *knit*. Do you not see well?" He scoffed so hard that the hair tucked behind his ear sprang free. "I nalbind. It is the superior stitch by far. If the fibers are cut, it can easily be repaired, and the knots form so tightly that the cold winds quake in fear."

I tossed back the covers and rolled out of bed, keeping my smile to myself.

"The winds, huh? Well, my sincerest apologies, Lord Crafterton." I bowed stiffly at the waist and made to peek out a window. "Still dark."

"It *is* dark, but not that dark. The inside of the windows are blackened so the lamps won't draw unwanted company; a master artist painted the outsides to look see-through but grungy."

I nodded, understanding the sense in that.

"My clothing?" I searched the floor and looked under the bed, but came up short. "What did you do?"

He tossed his head in the direction of the far wall.

"I placed them in the corner so I could watch you walk about in the nude." Sure enough, they were folded neatly and placed in a chair as far away as possible. "The Millanderers keep you cooped up in long gowns, thwarting all of my attempts to watch your thighs quiver. Verus's Solnnan-inspired ones were better by far."

"Well played, sir." I sauntered my way across the room, swinging my hips exaggeratedly from side to side. I stopped a few feet in front of him and twirled around with my arms held above my head.

"Do not taunt me, woman—you will find yourself on your back again," he muttered while making a few more stitches on the round body of what I now could see was a blue cap.

The leathers were chilly against my skin as I fought them on again, and I wasn't looking forward to putting my feet into borrowed boots without a thick pair of protective stockings, but more than that, I didn't want to return to reality. I'd take the foot funk of a man-at-arms if it meant we could stay.

"Cato, I'm not ready to go back." I shrugged my arms into the tight-fitting, padded arming coat.

"Nor am I." He stuffed the cap and needle into the inside pocket of his satchel and walked toward the door.

"Cato." I went to his side, fumbling to tie the tight bottom set of laces near my stomach. "Time permitting, would you consider allowing me to indulge in a fantasy of my own?"

He ran his hands down my arms.

"Will you still call me Papa?" he said while wiggling his thick brows. "If it takes less than half of an hour, it would be fine, though I do hope it involves you making me breakfast."

I wrapped my arms around his middle and pulled him close. I stuck my nose into the *V* of his collar and breathed him in.

"Come outside and hold my hand, like we're not some secret to be kept."

He opened the door and then bowed at the hip.

"Allow me to oblige your request."

It was still dark out, but the birds were up, chirping their early morning tunes. The smell of pine sap wafted in the air, mixing with the scent of the leaves that crunched under our feet as we strolled out, hand in hand. We walked to the edge of the road, the one that would eventually lead us back to Cordillaria.

If only we could turn left instead of right.

Cato dropped my hand, and I turned to him. The faint light of the moon outlined his silhouette.

"Shall we watch the sunrise or take a stroll through the dew?" Cato asked while lifting a foot in the air to roll the cuff of his pants. He patted his knee, and I placed my toes on his bent leg. Cold fingers caressed my ankle before they flipped up the bottom of my leathers.

"No, I've seen many sunrises, and I hate wet feet."

"Then what?"

"Close your eyes."

"Close my eyes? It is already dark, love."

I lifted my hands to his face and drew my fingertips lightly over his lids. He complied but crossed his arms over his chest and pressed his lips thin. I took my time walking around him—I ran my hand around his waist and placed my cheek against his back. He was the finest of specimens.

"Cato?"

"Yesss?" He drew out the word.

I inhaled the scent of man and forest pine.

And then I kicked out, striking the back of his knee.

He dropped to the ground, and I spun. I ran as fast as my feet could carry me.

There *was* something I wanted, and I knew of only one way to get it.

I hit the cabin door with outstretched hands. My toes rammed the stupid helmet that I'd left near the entrance. Kicking it aside, I bolted in the direction of the bed.

Three steps. I made it exactly three steps before he hit me from behind. My arms were captured and pulled backward, half-lifting me from the floor.

The fronts of my thighs slammed into the solid edge of the wooden table.

"If you wish to be fucked by a monster, you little shit," he wrenched the top of my jacket from my shoulders, letting it hang from my hips, "that was a decent way to ensure it happens."

Cato wrapped his fingers around the back of my neck and shoved me down until my breasts mashed against the tabletop. A jar of salt went flying and shattered on the floor.

I hid my smile.

My warrior-king had returned.

Making slow, sensual love with him had been the most meaningful and expressive experience of my life... but I craved a filthy, primal mating where Cato took me and proved his ownership.

He yanked my leathers from my hips.

I danced around and kicked them aside as moisture flooded me. I was soaking—primed to receive him.

"Is this what you want, Eira, my loss of control—my dominion over your body?"

Fingers plunged into my entrance, rigid and demanding. He hooked them downward and fingered me hard, with long, fast strokes.

I inched my legs further apart and tilted up my rear.

"Use me."

He removed his fingers and, in a single slick motion, replaced them with his cock.

My strangled cry filled the small room.

"I will take what I want," he slurred.

My eyes rolled back.

Today, with reality looming, this is how I needed him—hammering and thrusting, hard and rough. Who knew when we'd be together again? I was already on the edge. From this angle, the ridge of his head popped back and forth, hitting that sacred spot. The spasms began.

"Go, love, deeper still... Don't stop, Cato, don't ever stop."

He pulled away from me.

"No!" I cried. "Cato, p-please..." I twisted my head around. "I'll beg. I'll drop to my knees and plead." I wasn't above it.

"Face forward."

"But... I..."

"Face. Forward," he gritted out between clenched teeth.

Cato's palm clutched the back of my thigh, and he lifted my knee to the table. His fingers dug into my rear, and he spread my cheeks wide.

I felt the wetness of his saliva as it hit squarely against my puckered flesh.

"This is what I desire." He inserted a finger and pushed in deeply, before pulling it free.

His tip nudged at my tightness and pressed forward. *Oh, Goddess. This is...*

"Too much. It's too much, Cato." He squeezed through my tight ring, and I squirmed below him and tried moving away. "It stings Cat, it hurts and—"

"You demanded this—the instant my knee hit the ground."

His hand came around my waist and cupped my vulva. His finger slipped into my entrance, and the meaty part of his palm pressed snuggly against my clitoris.

"Relax your muscles. You can take me."

I was frozen, but I trusted him.

I held my breath and went as slack as I could.

"The fantasies I have had of spearing your asshole would shock you." He slid forward until I was filled to a level I had never experienced. "This is how I claim you in my dreams—taking you like a beast in rut—coating your cheeks with my essence."

He inched deeper still, and moved his fingers faster until the intense pressure in my backside was accompanied by a coiling snake of pleasure.

My openings were at capacity, both filled to the point where I couldn't move. The shock and unfamiliarity of the sensations sent me into a haze.

"The night before last, I dreamt of sitting on the godsdamned throne while the courtiers watched you suck me off. You knelt so prettily between my knees. I hiked up your skirts as you bent forward, presenting them with the slit that glistens *just* for me."

I trembled in his arms. "I would go to my knees for you. I'd play servant to your body."

He growled that deep, possessive sound and abandoned all restraint. He moved in me, fingering me roughly, drawing my wetness backward to provide more lubrication.

"Look at how well you take me. You were created for my pleasure." He thrust properly now, knowing I'd grown accustomed to his width.

My toes curled, trying unsuccessfully to grip the wooden floor. I clawed out and grabbed the opposite edge of the table, shouting incoherently into the room.

My orgasm tore through me.

"CATO!"

I jerked up and snapped my head around.

"CATOMMANDUS ODELGAURD!"

A menacing growl came from the depths of his chest.

"Holy mother, holy fuck, Cato, stop!" I yelled while attempting to wrestle from his grasp.

"*Face* forward." His fingers wrapped around my neck and cheek, forcing my head to face the wall. He pumped his hips so hard that the table walked forward.

He dug his fingernails into my backside and roared his release as he came, pulsing in hot waves of euphoria.

I dropped to the floor and scrambled to find my pants.

"Catommandus! What have you done?"

Fear.

Shame.

I tried to crawl under the table to die alongside the dust mites.

"Mother, I would welcome you, but your timing is rather poor."

I found my leathers and began fumbling them on, shoving myself into the too-tight waistband.

Imella.

Wife of Burchard.

Mother to Cato and Ambrose—the Queen of Motherfucking Monwyn—stood in the threshold of the doorway.

She glared at her son with her obsidian gaze, and her mouth worked up and down, no doubt groping for the correct words.

Cato shoved his penis back into his pants, looking for all the world like he'd just strolled into the dining room for dinner.

"Mistress, I heard voices. Are you—"

Imella's lips thinned.

Her servant's eyes went wide as he took in the scene, and her armored guard tensed.

Imella yanked a dagger from the sheath at her guard's hip and then sank the blade into the soft flesh of her manservant's neck, as quick as a hawk striking its prey.

"And that one?" Cato asked. He started forward.

I shot my hand out and grabbed his ankle, but he easily pulled from my grip.

"Stop at once, child. I trust him with my life," Imella said, placing a protective arm over her guard's chest as Cato sized him up, "and more importantly, I trust him with yours." She looked in the direction of the body that was now slumped awkwardly on the ground. "Hughes, dispose of him. No trace remains."

My stomach lurched.

Another gone.

Another death added to my count.

Dry heaves wracked my body, and saliva flooded my mouth.

"Eira, it had to be done." Cato closed the space between us, dropped to my side, and pressed my face closely to his shoulder.

Armor clanged and creaked as Imella's guard pulled the dead weight out the front door.

Had to be.

"Have you ignorant children given no thought to the repercussions of what you have done? What about your brother, Catommandus?"

Imella slammed the door shut and flew into the room. She was fury incarnate.

"Mother, do not chastise me as if I am—"

"We will explain." I grabbed Cato's forearm, and he went silent. I moved from his embrace and quickly tied up my coat's closures. "My Goddess, Imella, I can't even begin to imagine how you are feel—"

"Eira, tread lightly," Cato said.

"No, sir. Your mother is concerned for her children. It's probably a constant worry considering how often Burchard conjures up disasters."

"Cato," Imella's voice dropped low, "why is she aware of our private matter?" Her hand tightened around the bloody blade she held.

"Imella, please, let us speak."

I pulled a chair out from the table, went to the other side, and took my ease.

"Mother, as Protector of this realm, I—"

Imella pushed past her son and lowered herself into the wooden seat. She laid the knife between us.

"That doesn't work on mamas, Kitten. Now leave. Go straighten yourself up."

"I will not be—"

"Cato, your mother witnessed her son ass-fucking his brother's betrothed. Turn and go." I stabbed my finger toward the door.

"Neither of you has the right to—"

"Get!" His mother spat. She shooed him away with a wave of her hand.

Cato flung open the door. It hit the wall so hard that dust fell from the rafters and settled around us.

"Start talking. Leave out no details."

COMPLICATIONS

"**D**aughter mine, I'm not at all sure I agree with Burchard. When he was cavorting with Soolie, he would never have wasted his seed in her rear."

"Can't breed without the seed," I whispered, looking off into the distance. That was certainly food for thought.

"No come in a bum." Imella smirked behind her hand.

"For fuck's sake, mother." Cato walked through the door, looking even less happy than he had when he'd left.

"Was that not what you were doing, my son? Have my poor eyes deceived me? Imagine, if you will, the shock to my heart when forced to bear witness to the stiffened stump of my own grown boy."

Cato pushed his hands through his curls and made to leave again.

"I cannot. If the two of you must continue on in this manner, I simply cannot—"

"Sit down and hush." Imella slid a chair out with her foot. "And in the future, the tissues of the anus shouldn't be treated so unkindly. You will likely have blessed Eira with a painful fissure as hefty as you are—what does that get her but a bloody bum and a world of pain? You should have thought of that. She said her sole experience had been just a finger. That is unacceptable."

Cato's mouth pulled down in the most severe of frowns, which only seemed to deepen as he stomped his way to the table. His gaze seared into mine. No words were needed for me to understand that he was mentally *willing* me to shut the fuck up.

I shrugged. *Too late for that.*

I quite liked Imella and her forward manner. Not even my own mother, with her years of experience as a midwife, had been so refreshingly open. And sharing my concerns with her did wonders to lighten the burden of my mounting fears.

Imella leaned forward, caught Cato's chin between her fingers, and turned his face about.

"Look at your eyes, Kitten. They've nearly returned to their beautiful dark brown. Speaking of the incident that led to this, I'm appalled that neither you nor your brother was considerate enough to leave me a missive upon leaving Colpass."

"That *was* unkind of you," I said in agreement.

Cato's brows shot to his forehead, but his mouth snapped shut.

"Eira saved your life, and now it seems that Monwyn is to be her refuge and *Ambrose* her protector. And rightfully so."

Cato's eyes flashed, but he remained silent. He drummed his fingers on the tabletop and stared straight ahead.

"In the desert, maintaining two husbands was commonplace, but here, my son, it will never be allowed." She placed her deeply bronzed hand over his lighter copper one, stilling his fingers. Cato's jaw worked, flickering as he clenched and released his teeth. "Eira has explained that she was your first, and I am thrilled that you have found the one who awakened your body, but I am concerned with your emotional well-being. If this *is* a Mating Bond, it will end the moment you get her with child. Has this been discussed?"

"No, we haven't known about that part for long." I reached for Cato's other hand and brought it close. "When we're alone we tend to progress to sex very quickly. I *a m* on the herbs."

"That's youth, Eira, not to worry. The young king and I were caught spearing the bearded clam in every hidey-hole Cordillaria offered. Primus Thierry discovered us in the larder once." The corner of Imella's mouth tipped up. "Butter makes an abysmal lubricant—I had yeast for the next month—anyhow, the frequency and drive to love is normal."

Cato whipped his hand free and brought his fist down on the table.

"Mother. *What.* Are. You. Doing. Here?"

She turned to him, and her eyes filled with the most tender of love.

"I've always been here." She reached out and skimmed her knuckles along his beard. "I could never walk away from you or my other children—the babes of Monwyn *and* Taleer. And your father… Though our marriage went to the nether, we spent too much life together for me to stop caring. I've used this house for decades to ensure that your lives progressed smoothly. My men know your schedule and make me well aware of the comings and goings around the capital."

"Your men?" Cato pressed his fingers to his temples. "You have men."

As if on cue, Hughes opened and closed the door. He whisked off his cloak and began wrapping it into a tight ball.

Imella's guard didn't have the typical look of a Monwyn. He was slender and of average height, with short-cropped, reddish hair and a pair of spectacles. His beard was quite handsome and full. Unlike the guards of Cordillaria, he wore no plated armor but had an assortment of hardened leather pieces that he'd concealed under the cloak that he now stuffed into a canvas bag.

"You are not the only one capable of building a network, Cato."

Hughes came to stand by Imella and bent low to whisper in her ear.

"Well done. It can be tossed on a fire when you head into town. We will stay here until the nuptials have ended. Oh, and add the Primus-King to the list of persons of interest and strike the Scion."

Hughes nodded once and resumed his post.

Cato pressed his palms flat against the table and studied his mother.

"How did you come to know of Scion Ozius's fate?" Cato asked. The tension in his voice was nearly palpable.

"If you think my reach doesn't extend to Verus, Kitty Cat, then I will reconsider the notion that you were born with your father's good looks and *my* brains. Any Obligates with even the remotest chance of Assignment to the kingdom have been vetted. Eira confirmed that the Scion no longer walked the soils of Ærta—after their run-in at the temple, it was for the better."

"Imella, will you attend the Joining?" I interrupted.

She shifted in her chair and rearranged the volume of the dark cloak she wore.

"No. No, I am not sure I'd be welcome, but I will be near for the sake of my cub. Though he never saw marriage in his future, he loved the idea of Joining—at least twice per week, I found myself fake Joining him to his stuffed bear." She covered her mouth with the side of her hand, and her eyes misted over.

"Imella." I took a deep breath and poured all of my good intentions into my next words. "I care for Ambrose, and I could see coming to love him quite fiercely as time marches on."

Cato began bouncing his leg so hard that the table rattled. I reached out, and he took my hand as if it were second nature. He rubbed his thumb back and forth over my knuckles while I continued focusing on his mother.

"I'll cherish our children and always remember the true value of the gift he has given me."

She nodded softly as tears pooled at the corners of her deep, umber eyes.

The walk back to the palace was painful.

Cato went entirely Protector on me and was moving so fast that my damned helmet was seesawing atop my head.

"You will meet with the Millanderers today and greet the Obligates on behalf of His Majesty and Ambrose. Primus Thierry has taken to his bed. If it is his usual ailment, he will be well in a few days' time."

Sweat was pouring down my back, and my leg armor slipped and was biting painfully into my thigh. I came to a quick halt, grabbed the helmet, and pulled it down to where I could see out of its eye slots.

I stomped my foot on the paved road and held my position.

Cato rotated around on his heels and crossed those damnably well-muscled arms over his chest.

"I have asked you *twice* to speak to me, and *twice* I have been ignored. What's on my daily schedule matters much less to me than what's going on in your mind."

He rubbed the material at his elbow as he looked me up and down.

"Since arriving at this Goddess-forsaken palace, the cold reality of my failure has repeatedly hit me in the face. I, as Monwyn's Protector, have been useless. Control is a farce. My kind and soft-hearted dumpling of a mother is a violent mastermind. You did see her put a knife in a man's throat, yes?" Cato walked forward and worked to re-strap my too-large helm. "The father I used to idolize is a dumbfuck, and I may only love you because of some fluke in my heredity—and you love Ambrose."

His shoulders slumped. He was so crestfallen that it seemed as if he'd aged five years in the last hour.

"I'm so sorry, my love. I am so very sorry."

I moved toward him and wrapped my arms around his waist. It was the only thing I knew to do.

"Eira." He softened his voice. "I am going to shove you to the ground as gently as possible and hurl a foul string of obscenities in your direction."

"You what? Why?"

"Do you not hear the men laughing in the gatehouse above?"

"No, but I can't hear much truthfully."

"It would never do to have them think I am coddling a new recruit."

I nodded, and the too-big helmet smacked the back of my neck as it tilted.

"I'm ready," I whispered, "go ahead."

My butt hit the ground, and my feet sailed over my weighted head.

"Drunken idiot. If you are found inebriated once more, I will string your tiny fucking testicles onto a goddamned line and go fishing for carp. Bottom-feeding maggot. Get up, soldier, move now!"

CHAPTER 27

NETHER HERE, NETHER THERE

As it turned out, the entrance to the nether was located in Cordillaria's dining hall.

"Absolutely not, Obligate Solnna. Just... I cannot believe you'd even suggest such outlandish vulgarity!"

Meachum Millanderer had been chastising me from across the dining hall table for the last hour. His nimbus of curls swayed softly as he shook his head, and his rust-colored freckles nearly blended into his anger-reddened face. Even the pulse at the base of his neck patted out a visible beat. "The very idea of white worn to a wedding—I am vomitus! Fetch me a pail, Protector, before I soil the carpets!"

Cato stood at his post near the door and made no indication whatsoever that he'd heard the tailor's request.

"Chum is right, bride Solnna, the faces of corpses are covered in white. White is the color of pus and... milk, which I find to be as foul as the place it comes from."

In all of my infinite Trothy wisdom, I recognized I was losing this battle.

"The message you would send is not one of gaiety or excitement but of decay and the macabre. Do you enjoy the macabre?"

I'd enjoy smacking both of their silly mouths.

"I'll have you know that white is the color worn by *both* spouses in Nortia. It symbolizes pure love and endless commitment."

"Rot and stank. I heard rot and stank—you husband?"

I glared at the larger of the two men.

"Skins are bleached, and the fur of white foxes line the garments. They are traditional and beautiful and reflect the ice and snow that is so much a part of our—"

"Pardon me for saying so, Obligate *Solnna*, but you are first and foremost a bride of Monwyn and—"

"Fine!" I snapped. "No white, not a fucking speck of white. I'll demand you both be drawn and quartered if so much as a *dot* of white finds its way onto my garment."

"Her mouth!" Chum flung the back of his hand to his brow and fell against Leonard's shoulder.

"Madam Nor-Solnna, we mean no offense. But these decisions are normally made by the husbands—I am sure the notion of planning such a fete is quite taxing."

"The ice upon which you stand grows thinner, master tailor." I kept my face neutral even as I imagined snipping off his massive braid with the giant shears that sat close to his hand.

"All we are saying is that your choices will convey a message. The King of Gaea himself will be present, and so too will the Primus of Solnna. The Joining is a political statement as much as it is a testament to the tenderness shared between you and His Highness."

This was literally the least important thing in my life at the moment. We were inviting our enemies into our home. That took precedence over clothing colors.

"Obligate? Hello, are you still with us?" Chum's voice infiltrated my thoughts.

"Bem, what color would you choose?" I asked.

He was tasked with being my personal guard for the day and had stood beside me the entire time, which would have been all well and good if it wasn't for the whistling sound his nose made every time he inhaled.

"Light tan."

Chum gripped the arms of his chair until his hands shook. His eyelids flickered like he'd been possessed by a netherspawn.

Grumbly laughter came from behind my shoulder. I twisted around and tilted my head back to look Allaine in the eye.

"And what, oh wise noble, would *you* wear on your Joining Day?"

"Periwinkle and pink, the most cheerful of the colors. Never white. Never."

"So Bem would have me wear the color of Leonard's dick flesh, and you would clothe me like a mother would a toddler on their naming day. That's just excellent."

I flipped back around and faced the tailors.

"Black. I'm wearing black."

Silence.

One set of eyes flashed wide. The other set began welling.

"A deep, blue-black."

Chum blinked and let the tears roll down his cheeks.

"Peacock-feather-blue. Something ridiculously feminine, with my tits hanging out and… and sparkling silver spangles."

"Gold."

"Mother*fucking* gold, then."

"And gemstones!" Leonard added.

Chum snapped his fingers in the air, and his eyes rolled back into his head.

"With gemstones!"

Leonard produced a linen and blotted the sweat on his forehead while Chum drummed out a happy hand clap.

"And your second color?"

"Two? For what?"

Leonard sat forward and reached into his breast pocket. He produced a long parchment.

"Monwyn tradition requires the bride to have two garments. One for the ceremony and another for the bedding. His Highness Ambrose will require four: one for the cleansing, another for the groom's dance, a third for the ceremony, and lastly, a garment for the bedding."

"Explain yourself. The cleansing and dance? Do I have to dance? And I've been ritualistically bathed before and quite frankly, I don't relish the thought of it happening again."

I can still smell my flesh burning.

Meachum scrubbed his face with both palms and began muttering to himself. Luckily, Leonard launched in, "In the most blessed of ceremonies, you will cleanse your beloved as the priest prays over you both. It symbolizes your willingness to care for him in times of great duress. I cried the most tears when Chum poured the fragrant waters over my feet that day. He wore plum, by the way, and I, goldenrod." Leonard smiled warmly at his spouse.

"And the dance is not for you," Meachum sneered. "His Highness will perform it as a testament to his virility. He will do so in costume. Viktos or a handsome tattooed fae are often favored choices."

Ambrose was going to dance *at* me?

All the Troth training in the world wouldn't get me through *that* with a straight face.

"I would recommend a pirate disguise, given his current whereabouts," Chum suggested.

I mulled it over briefly.

"Protector, what do pirates look like?" I asked.

"They wear whatever mismatched clothing they pillage and typically have wide-brimmed hats to shield themselves from the sun. Those I have encountered shave their faces clean to avoid buildup from constant salt spray... and they do not smell particularly good."

"That won't do then, will it? What about Lord Gammond?" I said, thinking the goddess's consort would be a solid choice.

"You think Ambrose would be satisfied holding a pile of books while decked in scholars' robes?" Cato replied.

I pictured him in the layered look. No, that wasn't right either.

"What would you suggest, Protect—"

"A horse!" Chum interjected all too excitedly. "On account of... his... impressive... mane."

"No. A minotaur!" I shouted. "With fur legs and his chest bared and—"

"—curling gold horns, and we shall paint him blue!" yelled Chum.

"Why the fuck does everyone think they are bl—" Cato snapped his mouth shut.

"You should incorporate the Solnnan cuffs the ambassadors gave him, and—Oh, Protector, my apologies for having cut you off, what was your suggestion?"

Cato crossed one ankle over the other and then leaned against the door frame.

"A fat pink pig with two rows of engorged tits... and a corkscrew tail."

Gritty little chortles sounded behind me.

The two tailors recoiled in horror, and I covered my mouth, feigning shock. In truth, I was too fatigued to continue caring. All I wanted was a nap, and giving up control was the only way to make that happen faster.

"Gentlemen, I have decided to allow you complete control over the garments. Leave me entirely out of it and bill Lord Ethens for the costs. Spare no expense."

CHAPTER 28

SHADOWS

"Y**ou look haggard!**" Allaine said. "How is it that you can snooze a full night, do nothing but talk about dresses all day, and still look like you rode a cow over the moon and back?"

It wasn't a cow. It was a Cat; that's why.

Allaine pulled down the coverlet and sheets and patted the bed while I shrugged out of the green dress I'd hastily thrown on after Cato smuggled me back into my rooms.

"I will return soon." Allaine pressed my discarded dress into the crook of her bent arm, and she inspected it closely as she did all of my garments to determine if it needed mending or washing. "I will require every moment we have to appropriately dress you. Blue or red for the occasion?"

I mulled over her question, not really coherent enough to care.

"Purple or pink. I'll greet them as Troth Solnna." My mind flashed back to the ambassador and the message he'd whispered into my ear. "And Allaine, send for the Diadem of Taleer. I would like to look upon its gloriousness once more."

She nodded and walked out.

I squished myself back into the stack of feather pillows. They cupped my body and supported my neck, but despite the comfort of my shoulders, the pressure in my posterior was fairly intolerable.

I closed my eyes and listened to the beat of my heart sounding in my ears.

Imella had turned out to be much different from the soft and tranquil mother I had first met at Colpass. She'd reacted swiftly in taking a life, as easily as she might have tossed out a threadbare garment. It was like looking in a mirror. I'd acted just as fast when Cato became the target of the bowman's arrow.

The shadows danced behind my lids.

I cracked my eyes open and groggily looked around the room, expecting danger.

There was nothing—no one.

A small, shadowy arm waved in my periphery.

Hello there, I'm not sure I should follow you without Father Burchard nearby.

Its shady little appendage flickered faster.

Where will you take me this time? Could you show me Ambrose or Momma?

My heavy lids closed, and I sank into slumber.

The darkness swirled beside me as we stood on the back lawn. It expanded, contracted, and twisted like the incense the priestesses used on the high holy days.

It moved between my ankles, slithering like a serpent, and then curled around my waist and clung to me like a babe on its mother's hip. It wound up my arm and perched on my shoulder. A chubby, semi-transparent hand reached out and patted my cheek, and then the shadow dropped to the ground and rolled into a tight ball. It grew now, taking on the shape of a—

Well, hello, little one.

A black-and-gray raccoon reached out to me with its adorable people-hands. I bent low and grasped it under its arms, surprised to find the shade-creature solid. I held the thing straight out in front of me and examined it closely. The sockets of its eyes were see-through—just swaths of darkness that made up the shape of a round eye—and I could see the light of the moon shining through them.

The oddity squirmed and wriggled, so I set it back on the ground. It stood on its hind legs and took a few steps forward before turning back to me.

Should I follow?

It dropped to all fours and ran.

The shade glided along the ground, flowing back and forth between its raccoon and shadow forms as it wove its way around hedges and discarded flowerpots.

I followed it closely, my own body seeming to move like a liquid over the rocks and divots in the ground.

We came to a cabin.

The shadow kept moving, but the warmth of a glowing taper drew me in.

I peered inside.

Maihon rocked little Mae in his lap as they sat near the fire. She played with the new little hoops in her earlobes, and her father gently removed her hand once, and then again.

I turned my attention back to the shadows who had patiently waited for me. They were swirling around the trunk of a tree, dipping in and out of a hole where a squirrel family had made their home. It solidified once more, and the raccoon scurried down the tree and shot off toward the mountain chain that rose in the north.

We came to a gate, but I walked easily through the wrought-iron barrier that surrounded the palace grounds and went completely unnoticed by the guards stationed at the perimeter tower. The shade and I continued through brambles and trees and over soft rolling hills.

In the distance, an archway materialized. It was part relief and part sculpture—the sides of the arch were stylized legs, and the keystone resembled a dog's collar. Sprouting from the arch, three sculptures depicted the three canine heads of Cynder, the protector of the goddess Merrias, and her Arbiter blade. One head was reared back in a snarl, another had its tongue lolling out, and a third lay curled up on its own shoulder, napping. Two lamps had been fixed to its paws, and as we passed through the structure, they illuminated, providing soft light.

The shade at my side reached up, beckoning me with both tiny hands. I lifted it and perched it on my hip before walking through to the other side.

The whole of Ærta's pantheon stared at me.

Stone representations of the divine lords dotted the entirety of the masterfully plotted garden. Lykksun stood out prominently in the front of the walled monument. The sunrays that projected from her crown rose nearly two feet from her brow. Viktos, his body as thin and lithe as the bolts he hurled, stood mid-throw in the far-left corner. As in lore, he was cloaked in a mantle of fireproof wyvern scales. Maressa, the guardian of the forests, watched over the far-right corner, her bow string pulled to her cheek and her hawk familiar on her shoulder.

The Goddess's form resided atop a massive square base in the center of the stone garden. Her halo of coils surrounded her head and shoulders, and her arms lay open as if she were inviting you into her embrace. Her pregnant belly protruded through her diaphanous gown, and her full breasts were displayed as well, soon to nourish the world's children. It was a marvel that a chisel and a steady hand could make rock appear soft and flowy.

"Granddaughter."

I turned my head toward the voice, and my shadow jumped from my arms and ran toward a dark figure.

"Grandmother?" I squinted, trying to make out the person in the distance.

"Dim the lights, child."

I fanned my fingers, and the lamps at my back faded.

She stood before me then—Merrias, daughter of She Who Gave Us All.

In full armor, she reclined against her own sculpted likeness. She looked nothing like the shapely and tall depiction.

Her eyes were hazel, both green and brown, and her features were strong—striking and prominent. Her top lip was markedly fuller than her bottom one, and her face was quite round. She wasn't tall or sinewy, but rather bulky in her musculature.

"Must a deity be beautiful to be considered worthy? I've had an abundance of besotted lovers—attracted by the power of my mind, more so than my body." She cocked her head to the side and laughed. The sound was rich and robust, entirely uninhibited. "Unfortunately for them, they were disappointing sparring partners, both physically and intellectually."

"My apologies, I didn't mean to—"

"I know my worth, granddaughter. I'm not offended."

She moved with the confidence of an entire army of trained men. She strode across the clipped grass and came to stand directly in front of me. My shade zigged and zagged through her ankles.

"Ask your question."

I stood stricken. Did I have a question? Did I get just one? Would she answer a million if I pressed?

She reached for the faux braid that ran down my back and brought it over my shoulder. She ran her fingers over its length and frowned.

"Wh-why am I here?"

She dropped the tail of hair, and her eyes found mine.

"Because the shadows brought you—they are as free as the light to move where and how they please."

"Am I a shadow?"

"No. But they are the dominant force within you." Merrias raised her sparse brows while she angled my chin up between her fingers. "My daughter was born of light *and* dark. Her daughter and those that followed were the same. But not you; you are the first of our line to be drawn solely by night."

"And that means what, exactly?"

She dropped her hand and rested it against her hip as she contemplated.

"I don't know, granddaughter. That has yet to be revealed. But stay the course. Trust your instincts."

"Is my mother safe? My father? Where are they?" Once the questions began, I couldn't stop them. "Will I see them again?"

Merrias blinked thoughtfully.

"Your mother is where fate led her. She shares your blood's gift, you know, but not the ability to conjure. She is much like your young man—the æther resides in them both, though they cannot use it directly. Which father do you want to know about?"

"Eira!"

I shook my head against the painful noise in my head. My vision rocked, but I refocused, trying to keep the goddess within my sight.

"Eira! Don't leave me. Not yet... no, gods. Please..."

I slapped my hands over my ringing ears.

"Go on. He's beside himself," my grandmother said.

"Wait! Can you tell me if my Bond is—"

"EIRA!"

My eyes flickered open. I blinked through the haze until my doubled vision became one.

Cato was above me. His hands were poised in the middle of my chest.

"Cat?"

He tugged my shoulders and hauled me against him. The perspiration from his forehead slicked the side of my cheek as he spoke into the crook of my neck.

"I thought you were gone, Eira. Your heart barely beat. I-I couldn't wake you."

"I'm here, Cato. I'm here. I was sleeping, I think. Dreaming."

His hot tears wetted my hair, and the shadows flew and bounced haphazardly through my field of vision.

"Cato." I wrapped my arms around him until his breathing steadied. "No dream of Merrias will take me from you."

"I would fall on her blade and follow you."

I lifted his head and coaxed him backward. He sat back on his knees and swiped his forearms across his eyes.

"My weakness disturbs me." Cato pivoted and sat on the edge of the bed. He stared at his upturned palms.

"Nothing about you is weak." I kneeled and rested my hand on his back.

He jumped to his feet and pulled at the cuffs of his jacket.

"The largest gem in the diadem contained a cipher. I have saved you the trouble of figuring out its instructions. After decoding the script, it pointed to a particular bit of hardware that had to be spun and tightened, which allowed a hinge to release and the box's false panel to drop."

He gestured to the end of the bed where the Diadem of Taleer spilled from its box.

"Clearly, your mind shows no weakness." I rolled off the bed and stood. I held my arms wide. His chest heaved and then sank. In a single step he came to me, crushing me to his chest. "What was stashed away, Protector?"

He nodded toward a parcel next to the fallen crown. I tried to break away, but he squeezed me tighter.

"There are two sets of Solnnan citizenship papers. One bears your factual information. The other was created for a woman who fits your description but was made under the name Halaya."

Clever Solnnans.

"Place them in a safe area, hide them, and tell no one where they are kept. Not even me."

I nodded. A viable method of escape had dropped right into my hands.

"And here, this was within the jewel setting. I have not read it." Cato reached into his coat pocket and handed over a tiny rectangle of parchment.

I unfolded the small bit and squinted at the minuscule writing.

Nortia, I'm good. Owe you one. Evandr

"Cato, look!" I held the thumb-sized scrap up to the light.

Cato drew me backward and popped loud kisses onto my neck and jaw.

"Thank the Goddess—thank you, Eira. You are the reason he walks above the ground."

The woman who stared back at me from the mirror had aged a half-decade in a matter of days. And not in a bad way.

Allaine put the final touches on my hair. She had taken me from a youthful maid and transformed me into a woman of the world. After meeting Merrias, the transformation felt more than superficial.

Or… or had I dreamt it all? And following the dark—the shadows—what was its significance? I knew the people of the southern lands equated the dark with evil, but not the people of the north. When the days were shorter, time was spent around the hearth, and the grueling pace of the whaling season slowed. The dark times were when we held festivals, when families were together—when the moon became our guide.

"Where are you, Eira?"

I glanced up and blinked, caught somewhere between my past and my future.

"Fetch the orca brooch. I'd like to wear a little reminder of home this evening."

Allaine walked to the drawer that housed my few jewels. She produced a cloth and began polishing the three-whale pin.

Tonight, my gown was a confection, a contrast to the Monwyn's wools and thick silks. The Millanderers had taken my specifications and created a rose hued, high-waisted sheath, that covered me from neck to bust and then flared elegantly to the floor. Over the garment, I wore an entirely sheer, lilac overdress. I felt for the tailor who'd had the task of sewing the tiny hems of light silk.

Allaine fiddled with the mass of deep burgundy and black curls that ran the length of my head and spilled over, covering one of my shaved sides. The mix of masculine and feminine styles was quite becoming.

She pinned the brooch to my dress, its dark sparkle complimented the exquisite shades of black and gray on my lids.

"I look amazing."

She crossed her arm over her chest and tucked her hand into her elbow while she appraised me.

"I perform miracles daily."

CHAPTER 29

MOTHER MONWYN

"Troth Solnna, I would introduce my father, Lord Lemder," Allaine said in a tone full of pride.

Solnnan sunshine!

The giant bowed at his waist, but his head stayed at least six feet in the air.

Lemder was massive—he'd stand a head taller than Ambrose, and I'd swear he was the width of Cato and Evandr if they stood side by side.

I dipped into a curtsy and lowered my eyes.

Ah. Fine silver closures ran from his ankle to the side of his knee. I hadn't seen his face on account of playing the submissive, but I *had* seen that footwear in the Den. Unless garish boots were a Lemder legacy item, it was Papa Lemder who prowled the secret underworld, not a brother or cousin. I tucked that bit of knowledge away. I wouldn't pass judgment on him before I understood his relationship with his wife. After all, Ambrose had frequented the establishment and even Cato had once gone, though it had ended poorly.

"It is a pleasure to make your acquaintance." His voice was as deep as a bull's bellow. With a warm and wide grin, he held out his hand.

Remembering how Ambrose reacted to my being touched, I shook my head slightly. "My apologies, Lord Lemder, it would be unseemly in my betrothed's eyes."

His mouth twitched under the mustache of his dark, bushy beard.

"Yes, well," he boomed. "I wanted to extend my thanks to you for taking pity on my elfling. I know she must present a burden, but she wished so badly to play at being a housemaid. She has my heart, my little one, and I simply could *not* deny that Goddess-blessed face."

Did he say... Did he know how he sounded? I bristled up like a porcupine and drew myself up to my full height.

"Allaine has been my saving grace, Lord Lemder."

He leaned down and popped a kiss on his daughter's cheek, and she nestled into him like the most adoring of daughters.

"Protector, old friend." Lemder waved a hand and clapped Cato on the back, as he stepped into the antechamber. "Any updates on His Highness's campaign?"

"None you would be privy to, Lemder." Cato stepped toward me, and my stomach fluttered. He was the king of the court tonight. His muted-gold over-tunic clung tightly to his chest and arms and opened just below a heavily jeweled belt revealing an under-tunic of Monwyn-blue and gold damask.

My body responded.

Of course it did.

I glanced down to gauge how much of a scene my nipples were making as they stiffened and poked proudly from behind my thin garment. *Great.* They were like two fiery beacons in the night, and of course, one was hanging lower than the other. Cato saw them too—his eyes flashed hungrily, even as his face showed disinterest. I let my gaze wander down his body.

Mmmm, is that a scepter in your pock—

"Protector," Lemder interrupted our wordless exchange. "Let us revisit the promotion of my eldest boy. He has set his eyes upon a young lady who is soon to come of age. An elevation in the ranks would do well in securing a deal with her father."

With his hands clasped behind his back, Cato faced the blue-whale-sized courtier.

"As I have stated, promotions are based on a man's merit. I am sure your boy is performing adequ—"

"Nephew."

Great. Fucking great.

Septimus strolled into the grouping that suddenly felt overcrowded. He walked directly between Cato and Lord Lemder, cutting off their conversation.

"As the highest-ranking member of this court, it falls to *me* to escort Troth Solnna. Is that not correct? Why did I not receive a missive? An oversight, I presume."

Cato peered down his nose.

"No, it is because I did not want you here, Septimus. There was no mistake."

Cool blue eyes narrowed in defiance.

"Be that as it may, *boy*, I am here now, and our laws are clear... or have you decided to usurp the will and word of your father?"

"Now you just wait a moment, Septimus. I received the honor of escorting the woman." Lord Lemder dropped his hand to the hilt of the sword at his hip.

"Draw your blade, sir. Do it," Septimus said. "I will drive my dagger through your spine if I have to sink my arm to the elbow to do it."

Allaine balked, jerking her head back and placing her hand on her fathers elbow. I stepped closer to her side.

Septimus continued to stare Lemder down.

"You will find yourselves with your blades up your *own* asses if you continue on in this way," Cato warned.

I inserted myself into the triad.

"Protector, if the law is written, then your uncle must escort me. Lord Lemder, I would be most honored to join your wife for tea in the near future." I said, trying to head off the growing conflict.

The colossus huffed loudly and threw his arms back causing Allaine to tumble from his side. I launched forward, afraid she couldn't brace herself, but Cato beat me to her. Before her knees hit the floor, he wrapped his arms around her torso and held her aloft until she was able to bring a foot under herself and regain her balance.

Lemder's eyes hardened.

"Such a bungling creature. My apologies lady Troth, I will take her home this evening. I fear she is not made for life at court—"

"Father, I am so sorry. I must have tripped over my dress," she lied.

The dress whose hem didn't reach the ground? Doubtful.

Her mouth quivered, and her eyes brimmed.

"You are wholly incorrect, sir, and you will do no such thing." Lemder's chest swelled, making his size even more impressive. "She has been my constant companion and an absolute asset to my transition to this kingdom. Allaine, are you hurt?" She shook her head but kept her eyes focused on the floor. "Then to your position. There are Obligates to greet."

She limped to her place at my back. I would have sent her immediately to a healer, but I was afraid her father would insist on removing her altogether—better she put on a brave face for now.

Lemder had the audacity to glower.

Asshole.

"Septimus. Here, now." I snapped my fingers in his direction and held out my hand. His brows shot up to his handsome forehead, and an amused smile angled up his lips.

My blood was already running warm, but now, with the diametric twins standing so close, my mind was whipping up a whole host of naughty possibilities.

Horrific. I'm actually horrific.

"Septimus, I give you permission to touch my person from elbow to hand. Those are the only areas available to you. Do not let an *inch* of you touch *any* other part of me. Do you possess the ability to comprehend what I've said?"

He proffered his arm and leaned in close.

"I possess an impressive amount of inches—I can make no promises." I hooked my hand around his elbow, and he flexed his bicep under my fingers. "Allow me to say, you look absolutely ravishing this evening." He placed his opposite hand over mine in what would be considered a most gentlemanly manner. The softest little tingles sparkled on the surface of my skin.

He raised his eyes to mine.

"Watch yourself," Cato hissed from behind us.

We turned to face the door, and Septimus used the motion to pull me closer. He opened his mouth and stifled a lazy yawn like he'd not just pressed his groin to my hip.

"Herald, begin," Septimus said.

"Was that your order to give—"

The doors flung wide.

"His Lordship, Duke Catom Mandus Lux Ahdmundus Septimus, escorting the future consort of his Most Royal Highness, Ambrose, Naval Commander of the..." The rest of the titles were lost in the swell of applause.

The grand drawing room was packed. Some in the throng shook their heads in pity. Others held their hands to their hearts.

Good Goddess, Ambrose had certainly stirred up their fervor.

"Troth Eira Verras Chulainn of Solnna, Savior of Monwyn, Obligate of Ærta, Chosen Daughter of the Goddess!" Septimus roared. His voice carried farther than the herald's previous proclamation.

"Divine creature!"

"Protect her at all costs!"

The voices rang out all around the room. They yelled, howled, and stomped their feet. Some had even donned ill-fitting armor that looked to be a century old.

"Were you my woman, I would set you above all others," murmured Septimus.

"Would you? Where is Lilium? Did you set her upon a pedestal and forget where you left her? Is that why I can't find her?"

"She is home, failing to keep my heir in her womb, yet again."

I should have spat in his face. Instead I prayed for her health as she endured a loss.

"How disgusting you are. It's rare that I am so frequently repulsed by another."

"Our child would be strong."

"*Our* child will be non-existent."

I inclined my head and smiled as we passed Evandr's father and then made a show of nodding to the healer's apprentice.

"Your bitch's mouth stirs me to violence while hardening me to stone."

"Gross."

We came to stand next to the wooden throne. A crown of sapphire-encrusted gold sat on the empty seat, flanked by two guards.

"Our time will come, Troth. I am sure of it."

"You would have to force me. That day, your brain matter meets the walls."

A low, sultry laugh met my ears as he crossed in front of the throne and stepped to its right side.

Gag me. I should have let Lemder wallop him.

Ambrose had previously explained to me that I would stand to the left of the throne and that I would neither touch nor allow my clothing to brush against the sacred seat. I was also informed that if I were to pass in front of the crown, I was required to bow and then back up two steps before turning to leave. I took my spot and turned to the assembly.

"We welcome the blessed Obligates of Monwyn to our renowned kingdom: Troth Richelle escorted by Scion Zotikos!"

The doors parted.

As fast as a surprise snow squall, tears of joy welled in the corners of my eyes.

Richelle was radiant. Her beaming smile lit up the room as brightly as the reddish-orange coils that surrounded her beautifully full face. There was no one like her—spunky, happy, and the most caring of humans. Beside her, a proud and handsome Zotikos took her arm as they strode into the room. His dark braids went clear to his backside, but where they once covered his head entirely, the sides were now shaved closely to mimic the Monwyn fashion.

"Richelle, Zotikos." I folded my hands together and nodded to each in turn. "I am pleased that your journeys were uneventful and that you have arrived in good health."

"Who told you that? My butt disagrees!" Richelle laughed and rubbed her wide bum.

"Oh?"

"The carriage ride was quite bumpy," a calm and collected Zotikos supplied.

"It was well worth the jostling!" Richelle pressed forward, and her arms went around my waist. In her exuberance she lifted my feet off the floor. I drank in her infectious laughter and inhaled her rose-scented hair.

"Zotikos, a hug is not a requirement," I squeezed out. "Have you found your apartments suitable?"

Richelle dropped me back to the floor but continued holding my hand.

"Most assuredly." He placed his fingertips on his brow. "May the Goddess bless your fast-approaching Joining."

"My sincerest tha—"

"Oh! I cannot wait to hear about the proposal! Such a man. I can scarcely imagine the attention he must have lavished upon you. And who knew he was a prince? Did you know? Can we dine together tonight?" Her questions kept coming as I looked backward. "Is it always so cold here?"

Cato nodded politely. "Dinner can be arranged. Please, Troth Richelle, back away from the throne."

"Right! Sorry, Tommand. I was just peeking at your crown jewels."

Richelle erupted into a fit of giggles, which mixed perfectly with the gruff puppy chuckling that came from behind me.

Cato flicked his fingers at Zotikos, who politely ushered my sweet friend away.

"The Chosen Children, Troth Cinden and her escort Scion Greggen, do enter!" the herald boomed.

You could have sliced the tension with a saber.

Cinden, the pink-haired beauty, held herself as regally as a queen as she walked in on the arm of Greggen. He was just as fine-looking, but in the way that demons were described in *Magika*; they drew you in with their handsome faces but slowly devoured your soul over time. Only upon your last breath were their twisted and putrid forms revealed—the last image you would see before your mortal life ended. My heart drummed against my chest wall and my shadows loomed. I held Cinden's gaze, refusing to look at the man who'd assaulted me.

"*Who* are *you?*" Greggen said.

He sailed past me.

I twirled around and watched as Allaine's eye's flew open.

"How are contracts settled in your kingdom? Does another claim rights to you?" Like a fish out of water, Allaine's mouth bobbed open and then closed.

"They would make big babies, they would!" a voice cried out.

"Hold your tongue sir! That is entirely inappropriate!" I yelled back. I twisted on my heels and saw Greggen reaching for Allaine's hand. "What the fuck is happening?"

"Naughty mouth!" crowed another in the crowd.

"Our children... Between us, we would produce the behemoths of old."

I shoved myself between the Baldorvan Scion and my maid, dislodging their clasped hands.

"You are the most stunning creature I have ever laid—"

"Nope! You will not do this, Greggen." I struck him in the chest with both hands, but he didn't step back. "Protector, your sword!" I tossed my hand out, but Cato remained still. "I will run you through before—a sword, I said!"

"This does not involve you, witch." The tall Scion took a step forward, crowding my space. His focus—his penetrating light-brown eyes—were only for Allaine. "Does she have the ability to speak for herself in this kingdom of lies and filth?"

A cold and heavy hilt slid into my palm. My fingers closed around its solidness.

"Parity? That's an odd expectation, coming from a slaver."

Greggen sneered his petulant lips.

"Our freed women choose their mates. Can you say the same?"

I swiped the dagger at his chest, fully intending to end him.

Greggen hopped back, and my blade met air.

"Thrust, do not swish!"

"Septimus, do not encourage this," Cato hissed.

"Still a shrew, I see." Greggen flicked his eyes to Cato over the top of the throne, and the corner of his mouth lifted in a demon's smile. "Ohhh, are you still fucking—"

I gave chase.

I ran the fucker backward. A courtier shot his foot out, and Greggen's ass met the ground.

"I'll tell you who I'm fucking, slaver scourge!" I lunged forward, but just as I would have met my mark, two strong arms wrapped around my waist and heaved.

Cedar and cloves—and love.

"I'm fucking the most virile, the most potent, the strongest Monwyn to walk these halls! I live for the moment that he comes between my thighs. I beg him to plant his child in my womb, and I dare you, Greggen, to let his name be more than a whisper from your lips. This is *my* home, and it is not my *man* you need to fear—it is my *men*!" I kicked out at his stupid face.

Cato's hand curled around my fist, but I shot my arm up before he could take my weapon.

"To arms, men of Monwyn! To arms!" I screamed while shaking my blade in the air.

There was a scant beat of silence.

Then all nether broke loose.

The courtiers dressed in their finery, with their paunches hanging below ill-fitting breastplates, whipped into a frenzy.

They howled their bloodlust-fueled battle cries and descended.

Cato tossed me into another pair of arms, and my knife was wrenched from my fist.

"Mother Monwyn calls!"

"To aid! To aid!"

"Death to the slaver!"

Evandr's fast-hobbling father threw his hefty body into the air and came crashing down on Greggen's face.

"To arms!"

Chaos ensued.

Literal. Fucking. Calamity.

Cato rushed in, tossing courtiers to the ground, trying to reach Greggen. Bem ran to his side, and with the verve I would have expected from a much younger man, placed himself in front of the next wave of crazed nobles.

"Let the Arbiter be his judge!" I screamed, my own blood rushing through my ears. I felt the æther collect in my chest and yanked against the grip of my captor.

"You praise Ambrose too highly. You have not known a man of worth." It was Septimus who held me tight. "If this violence excites you, I could arrange a willing, or not-so-willing, body." He drew the tip of his nose up my neck, inhaling all the while.

An absurd giggle bubbled from my throat.

"Septimus, you disgustingly strange fuck—look at them, just look at them—show me what you're made of and help end this dog pile of decrepitness. That one has to be eighty years of age."

"Most assuredly. Watch me closely."

Septimus slid into the foray like a snake—no—he crept in like a wolf.

He stayed low to the ground and dealt short, sharp blows, stunning each of his victims before fleeing quickly to his next target. His movements were calculated, strong, and perfectly timed. He whirled and twirled, his hair freeing itself from its leather thong. He was so fluid that he could kick a body from the melee while collapsing another with his fists.

"Gentlemen! GENTLEMEN!" I yelled at the top of my lungs.

Hundreds of eyes came to rest on me, some upside down, others squinting from between the legs of the men lying on top of them.

"My esteemed lords, I do believe our new Scion has come to appreciate Monwyn's aggressive hospitality." I swept back the short wisp of hair that had fallen into my eye and did my best to right the silk overdress that had torn in two. "Please resume your places. I wish to introduce you to my dear friend and Troth, Lady Cinden."

CHAPTER 30

NO REGRETS

Tall, white tapers sat in the middle of the balcony's table. With the addition of the lamps on the columns, it practically looked like daytime.

The kitchen staff proved most versatile in their abilities—instead of creating a traditional Monwyn meal for my bosom friends, they made two dishes; one Gaean and the other Solnnan.

"The mangoes aren't as sweet as they are back home, but the garlic fowl is perfection with its cream sauce and onions." Richelle polished off the last bite on her plate and chased it with a half-glass of wine. "Cinden, do the forest people get drunk off these pears?"

She swayed slightly in her seat when she turned to ask her question.

"No. Normally they're soaked in wine, removed, and then baked with sugar and dusted with cinnamon. Those, however, are still swimming." Cinden smiled, revealing her pearlescent teeth. "Still very tasty, though."

I ladled in another mouthful of the spicy, bold-flavored liquid and cozied back into my chair.

"Tell me of Verus. Ambrose and I left so quickly that my head spun on my shoulders. One minute I was dressed for dinner and the other I was whisked away in a fine carriage. The whirlwind has yet to cease."

Cinden moved her feet from my lap and squeezed her cold toes under my rear.

"Let's see. At dinner, the night you left, Evandr and Ozius departed for their homelands. Oh! And have you heard that Castor, Marcyn, and Ozius were accosted?" Richelle supplied.

I shook my head, feigning surprise.

"Scion Castor and the companion were both killed. The Mantle suspects highwaymen. We said prayers for four days, and the Obligates performed their fire rites on the front lawn. Ozius has not been found, but I'm sure the Goddess will deliver her son." Cinden said, popping another chunk of chicken into her mouth and nodding matter-of-factly.

"May Merrias see them home." I bowed my head and placed my hands over my eyes. In the brief moment of darkness, I saw her lifemate's head again, rotting in its box. A man-sized iceberg settled on my chest.

"Oh! And Evandr went to Solnna. He seemed a little glum, but he'd recently been ill. Lord Gotwig escorted him south as Emissary Tommand had already left with you." Richelle looked around, narrowing her hazel eyes dramatically. "Can this place be trusted?"

I scrunched up my face and thought for a moment.

"Maybe... maybe not?" I answered truthfully.

"Is there someplace we can go to speak in private?"

The pears must have been potent because my mind was obviously addled.

"Yes. There sure is. You go tell the guard you'll sleep here this evening, and let them know that we are ready to retire. Grab something warm."

"You leave the guards to me. I liked the look of the blonde." Cinden winked, and Richelle dissolved into laughter.

"If I looked like you, Cinden, I'd have a whole army of blondes and at least two brunettes at my beck and call. I'll go tell that Bem fellow to fetch us some drinks."

When the two Troth cleared the balcony I went to the far end and leaned over the railing.

Father Burchard, are you there?

I waited, but there was no reply.

I tiptoed to the other side. *Your Majesty, are you well?*

I stuck my head between the columns and leaned out as far as I could.

I am quite well, daughter mine. My informant mentioned that the Obligates arrived safely and that your welcome was well-received. It sounds like a most rousing afternoon was had.

My eyes darted to the left and then right. I peeked out over the darkened gardens, looking for any guards who might be on detail.

Father Burchard, do you think you could assist my friends and me? We want to leave the premises for just a little while. We'll go straight to my shed and come directly back.

Silence.

Welp. So much for having a co-conspirator.

I sat back down at the table and dunked my glass into the bowl of pears, scraping the bottom for the delicious dregs of cinnamon and ginger.

The ladder hit loudly against the stone banister.

"Come on then. Hurry."

I heard him before I saw him.

Papa Burchard's bald head popped over the ladder. He wore a wide smile and waggled the skin that used to be his brows. "You would not be the first ladies I busted out. Goddess willing, you won't be the last!"

I was still shaking my head when I caught a movement at the door.

Cinden returned wrapped up in a blanket, and Richelle wore one of Ambrose's short tunics, which became an ankle-length dress on her short self. She held a bottle in each hand, one a deep burgundy, the other pale and bubbly.

Like the experts we were not, we shimmied down the ladder that Father Burchard insisted on holding. Cinden's blanket got stuck in the rungs and had to be abandoned, and Richelle had to stop in the middle of her descent to tie the bottles up into her skirts. Luckily, the ladder was wedged into a hedge of stout bushes, which helped maintain its stability.

"To whom do we owe our thanks, Eira?"

"Oh! Of course."

Father Burchard stepped off of the ladder and joined us.

"Cinden and Richelle, I'd like you to meet His Royal Majesty Monwyn, soon to be my father-in-law."

Both Troth stood statue still. Cinden's brown eyes went saucer wide, and Richelle froze mid-drink, wine pouring down the bodice of her dress.

"Ladies, Cordillaria is now your home." He dusted his hands off on his heavy fur coat and then nodded at each of them in turn. "If you need anything, anything at all, do not hesitate to call upon me."

Cinden snapped her head to Richelle and then back to me.

Richelle performed a wobbly curtsy and let out a tinkling laugh as Cinden helped her right herself.

"I suppose if we get caught, they can't toss us in the dungeon if the king's here!" She slapped Cinden on the shoulder and then took the freezing Troth by the elbow. Together they attempted to retrieve the lost blanket.

"I will be near the shed until you return. Then I am off to the swine farm."

"Father Burchard!" he looked down at me with his stark-white eyes.

"Now, daughter, do not look at me so. And turn out the lights." His eyes flicked up toward the balcony. "Here, darling. Take my hands." He reached out with his palms facing up.

I breathed in deeply through my nose, and I placed my fingers on top of his weathered ones.

"You know the way."

I closed my eyes. I'd been able to douse the flames easily in the garden of statues, and here in the dark, I had no trouble finding and following my shadows.

I opened my incorporeal eyes on the balcony and found my chubby shade raccoon climbing a column. I pointed to each lamp, and he scurried and floated in and out of his forms, twisting through the open room and turning the lamp's knobs low. Below me, I could hear the girls trying to save their blanket. They didn't seem to notice when I leaned out and freed the red coverlet from where it had snagged on a nail. I watched it sail down and land in the bushes.

Well done, Marmot.

Father Burchard's voice brought me back to the present.

This time I didn't wake stunned or stupefied, rather the transition was smooth and comfortable.

I am so very proud of you. I was pulled into the most fatherly of hugs, and while our chests pressed closely, the less intense but still comforting tie flowed between us.

"It seems we are stuck with each other, does it not."

I nodded into his chest, and he patted my back.

"Don't kill the pigs."

"I will do my best."

I watched Father Burchard take off into the fields and send an unaware soldier to sleep. My friends and I set off the moment the man hit the ground.

Our trek across the back gardens was uneventful, and when I was finally able to turn the key after rooting around aimlessly in the dark, we cackled our way through the door.

I felt for the lamp's striker and, after fumbling for a bit, got the old wall light ignited.

"There we—oh dear."

I glanced around the small room.

Lifeless plants hung over their pots.

Dried and shriveled petals were scattered across the floor.

"Are any of them alive?"

Richelle went around assessing the damage. She clucked her tongue and shook her head while moving from pot to pot.

"One!" she snatched up a tiny clay jar, and in it, a thick-stalked, kind of lumpy bit of vegetation remained nice and green. "It's a succulent. Even a snow bunny like yourself shouldn't be able to kill it... maybe."

I touched the frond of a sad brown plant, it all but disintegrated.

"Well," I put my hands on my hips. "No use crying over frozen milk." I hoped Cato wouldn't be upset that I forgot about and killed off the gift he'd labored to give me. I let out a harsh breath, hoping my guilt would leave with it. "Richelle, I need the gossip."

We sat on the floor together, the two of them huddled under the blanket and I stretched out on my side. Cinden tucked her toes under my tummy, and I felt their chill through her thin leather slippers.

"Kol has yet to have her courses!" Richelle burst out.

My mouth fell open and then transformed into the biggest smile.

"Truly?"

"Yes! They are keeping her at the temple until they know for sure, but they say that if she is with child, it will be the first babe conceived at the rite in over two decades."

"And how is she? Is she alright? Nervous or scared?"

"She's elated, Eira. She walks around with a secretive smile and her hand is always below her belly. And Lok... he's much less hateful now. He dotes on Kol like she's the most sacred piece of poozle he's ever pumped. He even smiled once," Cinden said before breaking into peals of throaty laughter.

The thought of Lok smiling was almost disturbing. But I was glad to hear something was going well for him. Lord Henric, his companion, had mentioned Lok lost his mother right before leaving for Verus.

"*My* courses were horrific. They came on early, and they were back to being absolutely debilitating. Clotty and painful to boot," I said.

"Ugh, yes... and I went back on the herbs immediately."

"Same," agreed Cinden. "We have the herbs packed up in our rooms. Devotee Monwyn told us that they would not be accessible otherwise. But Eira, more importantly... what happened to your hair? It's absolutely awful. You have little spikes sticking out all over, and the shaved sides... Ambrose can pull it off but—"

"I wanted it this way, thank you very much, *Cinden*."

Richelle popped the cork from a bottle and took a swig before passing it to me.

"What of Mariad Keagan?" I took a sip of the dark liquid—this one was much stronger than the wine served with dinner. "I understand he was hurt."

"Yes, he sure was! He was still in the infirmary when we set out. After taking such a nasty tumble down the grand staircase, he's lucky to be alive."

"He's expected to recover then?"

"Mmhmm," said Richelle while holding the bottle to her lips.

Cinden snuggled closer and stifled a massive yawn behind her hand. I waved off Richelle when she invited me to drink more. My arms felt heavy, and my eyes were slightly out of focus.

"Eira, I'm pleased as punch that we get to attend your Joining, but I thought you were netherbent on groping for trout in the Protector's pants." Richelle slapped her hand on the floor as she lost her balance. She sank down slowly and rested her head in Cinden's lap. "Does this mean he's back on the market? His eyes are rather fetching. And what do they call him here?"

"Cato. And no, he proved infertile and has chosen a life of celibacy."

"Oh my, what a shame," she murmured, barely managing to open one eye. "His buttocks are shaped like a fine, plump pudding... delicious... round..." Richelle's bright pink mouth fell open and began emitting soft snores.

Cinden tucked the blanket closely around Richelle's neck. The Solnnan couldn't bear even a cool day atop Mount Gammond. I had no idea how she'd fare when snow fell here in earnest.

Cinden's eyes met mine.

Tears began to well in their glowy brown softness.

"Eira," she whispered.

I got up on all fours and crawled my way over to her side. Cinden was not a crier, and with her lifemate missing I worried for her mental health. Her eyes were flat, and the corners of her mouth—the ones that always tipped up in a coy slant—were at rest.

I knew the look. It was the real Cinden—not the guarded one who shielded herself behind a wall of flirtatious jests and quips. I slid in beside her and put my arm around her waist.

"He's not coming back, is he?"

I commanded my body not to stiffen, but my stomach still flipped and flopped.

Tears trailed down her slender, warm-hued face.

"I suppose even if he did, they would escort him to the coast and send him across the water. Eira, will this ache ever subside?"

She lay her cheek on my shoulder. Her pink curls smelled lightly of jasmine and honey. There were no words of comfort I could give her. Nothing that would dull the pain she felt. She was right about his fate... and I knew there was no mortal world in which he would know her love again.

"Cinden. Your lifemate was precious, and though he isn't here, we will support you and—"

"—support our child as well?"

My mind tried to deny what my ears heard.

Was the silence capable of screaming?

"The morning of the rite, you remember, I was the last Troth to arrive."

I sat her up and wiped the streaks from her face. I did remember—I would never forget a moment of that day. Cato and I loving in the dark, the pain of the rite, the horror that followed.

"They will take our baby, Eira. They will take all that remains of Ozius if they discover the truth of its conception. And they *will* find out, Eira. They will come and—"

"Cinden." I tugged her closer while I sorted through the details of the plan that began forming in my mind. "Do you trust me?"

"I-I, yes, Eira, I do."

"A man I know wants a wife. He wants a woman with rank more importantly." I grasped both her biceps and looked her in the eye. "Cinden, he is rough. He's got some odd fetish, and he's not much to look at, but I don't think he's a bad person. I would never suggest it if I thought he was. He is rich, wealthy beyond—he would stray, he would take part in activities you may find distasteful."

"Are you serious, Eira? What kind of father would he be? How could I even consider—"

"Cinden, meet him. A child that comes a month early is an everyday occurrence. The babe would bear his name, and none, including him, would be the wiser. I would handle the contract. I could write in whatever you want. He wants a high-ranking wife and an heir, and Cinden, when I said he is wealthy—he's worth more than the royal treasury. You would be safe. The baby would be safe."

"I couldn't—how could I lie with another..."

"For your babe—Cinden, you could withstand another rite—a Great War."

She shook her head from side to side while she stared at the wall.

"Would it be better to end the pregnancy?"

I felt her shift and stiffen. She took my hand in hers and dragged it under the blanket to rest on her low belly.

"I've never wanted anything more than I do this child."

"Then we must ensure its future."

The need to keep Cinden and her little unborn love safe tore through me like an avalanche through a forest.

Her sniffles stopped. She dried her eyes.

"Eira, make the introductions tomorrow—first thing in the morning." Her shield slipped back into place.

"I will arrange it. I won't leave your side and—"

A loud knock sounded at the door.

I held my finger to my lips and motioned for her to be silent.

A key turned in the lock.

"Ladies, it is time to return. Bem, escort Troth Cinden back. Levaunt, to the other." Cato said as he and a group of guards stepped over the threshold. Levaunt walked in and bent low, and like a sleep-deprived toddler, Richelle woke just long enough to wrap her arms around him before he hoisted her up.

Cinden stood and huffed her way to the door.

"Eira, are you coming?"

"Leave us," Cato snapped.

"Disgusting." She tossed her arms in the air and then walked into the night.

Cato leaned against the door and crossed one foot over his ankle.

"Am I in trouble, Protector?" I laid back down and pillowed my head against my arm. "I believe I've had too much drink. When will the fog lift?"

He walked near and I tugged his pant leg.

"I have never imbibed to excess."

"Because you're uptight?"

"Because I am uptight." He laughed and I let the sound, my favorite sound, wash over me.

"Cato, hold me?"

"My pleasure." He dropped down and laid his warm body against mine.

I breathed him in. Sweat, soap, and blood. I forced my eyes open, immediately concerned.

"Oh, Cat," I ran my fingers under his busted lip, "I cause you nothing but trouble. It's just when Greggen—"

"I beat the asshole's face in before pulling him to safety. It felt just as good as I imagined it would."

"Cato!" His handsome face turned wicked. "I'm glad you did."

He caught my hand in his and pressed my fingertips to his lips.

"My bloodthirsty queen holding a slaver at knifepoint—you stirred my soul... amongst other things."

I lifted my leg over his hip and snuggled closer.

"Is he somewhere safe now?"

"He is."

"Allaine is mortified of course, and I am sure her father will demand satisfaction." I smoothed my lips along the muscle that ran along the top of his shoulder. He shivered, and the skin along his neck went bumpy.

"Eira?"

Cato shifted to his back and crossed his arms under his head.

"Yes?"

"When I could not wake you, the rational part of me ceased to exist. In a single moment, I contemplated a life without you, and it broke me." He breathed in deeply, and my hand rode out the swell of his chest as it moved up and then down. "However, I gained a certain amount of clarity within those seconds as well."

"And you seek to enlighten me."

He glanced down his nose and grinned.

"I seek to Join with you... if you would have me."

My spirits soared.

"Wh-what?"

The æther flitted from my chest to my stomach and then out to my limbs. My fingertips tingled like they had the first time we'd touched.

"I will speak with Ambrose upon his return and to my father as well. I will give up my position, and though I have nothing beyond a small piece of land in Basilia, together, we could be happy there. I would learn to farm. Our children would have no titles, of course, no inheritance, but... what I feel in my heart would sustain us. I am sure of it."

"You would give me the perfect life, is what you're saying?" I crawled up on his chest so that I could look down upon the Goddess's perfection. His eyes reflected the color of the fertile earth, and in them, I knew he would make good on his word. He would commit himself to me. He would remain faithful until the end of our days. It was everything we longed for. It was our combined dreams come true. And it was—

"We can't go." It was the most difficult sentence I ever uttered. "You once told me that some things were more important than the both of us."

He nodded curtly but remained silent.

"But Cato, I would bind my life to yours... if you will have me." I pushed off of his chest and scrambled to stand upright. "Will you come with me?"

"To where?"

"To the Goddess's realm."

He stood and collected the blanket and stuffed it in his satchel.

"Grab the bottles. We'll need those."

Cato blinked at me but did as I asked.

"Are you coming?"

"To the ends of Ærta and after. I would follow you into the nether frost."

CHAPTER 31

IN THE NIGHT

"It's just up here, I think."

"You think?"

With our palms firmly clasped, we trekked through the bramble and briar of what must have been the forgotten grounds of Cordillaria.

Cato had been able to take us beyond the gate with an old iron key, and when the metal barrier slammed back home, we took off like two runaways in the night.

"I'm following the directions of my heart, Protector." I glanced at him shyly, and he grinned back, his full-on smile warming me despite the chill of the night. He gathered me in his arms and twirled me around in the dewy grass. The hem of my dress was already weighted with moisture, but I couldn't care less when he was looking at me like his life began and ended in my eyes. Cato bent his head and hesitated just briefly before letting his lips brush softly against mine.

"How much further? I need to make you mine, if only in the realm of make-believe—woman of my spirit, my winter queen, my nighttime... my Verus."

"We'll know it when we arrive," I breathed, "mountain of my resolve, my sun-kissed sovereign." I ran my fingers through his gold-tinted locks and smoothed his dark beard.

We ran, trampling the tall grass and twisting through the thin, pliant branches of new growth—we were the Goddess's children.

Cato pulled back a thick and twisting vine, revealing the shadowy outline of the mountains looming in the distance. At that moment, I felt it—that soft, barely discernible tug.

Near breathless, I slowed but continued forward; our destination was close.

"It wasn't like this in my dream, but this is it."

The clouds above parted.

On the ground, covered in years of vegetation, the large stones that once were the garden's archway lay scattered among bits of statuary. I looked into the eye of the tongue-lolling head of Cynder. I saw the hawk, which should have been perched on the shoulder of Meressa.

"Can you feel—"

I brought his hand to my stomach like Cinden had done to me.

"Yes," he whispered, "as if I dipped my fingers into a sun-warmed pond."

He gazed down in awe.

"The Goddess is with us—and Merrias, Lykksun, and Mossius. We need no priestess to bless our union—it is ordained from above us—around us."

We walked into what would have been the garden's center, where the partial base that used to house the statue of the Goddess lay in ruins.

"This will be our altar." I raked the leaves and vines from the stone's surface. "Pull your pants up."

"Surely you mean down." His light chuckle echoed around our ramshackle enclosure.

"You'd freeze," I said. "You're already making clouds when you speak." I made note of the goosebumps on his forearms and worked to roll his sleeves back down to his wrists. "I mean to wash you, in the Monwyn tradition."

His laugh lines disappeared, and his playful eyes turned serious. The golden shards that surrounded his pupils caught every beam from the moon's light—it was as if they glowed from within.

Cato reached out and took both my hands while I dropped slowly to kneel upon the earth. I flipped open his satchel and withdrew a bottle of spirits.

"It's not water, but is it okay if I—"

"It is."

He bent low, removed his boots, and rolled up his pant legs, pulling the cuffs up over his calves.

I poured the strong-smelling liquid into my hands and anointed his knee, taking my time to see the cleansing thoroughly carried out. I caressed his ankle and passed my fingers over his toes.

"Water is shapeless. It has no form, and yet the Goddess's gift provides health and healing like the wife to a husband."

I stilled as he spoke.

The amber liquid trailed down through the hair on his calf and disappeared into the dirt. I looked up into his eyes and was captured by the intensity I saw there.

"The husband is a strong current, a mighty river—the wife, a tea that adds flavor to an otherwise bland existence. She is the fruit that transforms drink to wine. She is the call that pulls the ocean's tide."

My fingers lingered on the serpentine scar that still wrapped lightly around his leg.

"Would you hear my vows, Eira?"

His hand came to the edge of my jaw and gently lifted.

"I would."

He joined me on his knees and his frigid fingers threaded through my wet ones.

"You are my wife—Joined to me when the Goddess birthed the world. My soul knew yours then. My love has expanded perpetually—inexorably. Through hardship and pain, I will reach for you. Through life, I will shelter you and the family we build."

The æther vibrated and knotted in my chest.

Calloused fingers swept my cheeks, wiping the tears that spilled.

My family was lost to me. But a new one formed this night.

The pulsing energy that surrounded my heart moved outward, expanding through my limbs. My fingertips throbbed; even my toes knew the flow of my life's blood.

"My words are rarely elegant, Cato, but *you* are my husband; there is no other above you—*paraem'a de meatosh amortayo vink*—love is the most profound of life's pain and its truest happiness."

He nodded, understanding the Solnnan sentiment.

I removed my hands from his and, with shaking fingers, unbuttoned the frogged fastener at his neck and worked my way down.

"Will you consummate the marriage, husband?"

"Before the bedding comes the dance." Cato pulled away. He twisted at the waist and spun, clapping a beat with his hands. "What happens in Nortia on the wedding night?" He swayed to the left and then flourished a hand and bowed.

"The men would tattoo you with symbols chosen by my family. Yours would mean virility and strength." I smiled up into his eyes. "A village elder and I would have prepared a special meal, which would be carried to our new home by the local children. Then I guess we would eat, strip, and fuck for two days straight."

"I was made to wife-up a Nortian." Cato clutched the laces of his pants. "We don't have two days. Will two hours suffice?"

I placed my hands on his, stilling his hasty fingers.

"Slow, husband. Let me love you as you have loved me."

His beautiful lips parted as he stared into my eyes, his arms dropped to his sides. I brushed the shirt from his shoulders, and it fell to the ground. Our frozen breath mingled in the night air.

"In Nortia, the lore says that if a husband and wife love atop the snow, their hearth remains lit for a lifetime. I believe your freezing form will suffice." I reached for the balled-up blanket and placed it around his shoulders.

"Yours is the only heat I need." He cast the cover aside. Though he didn't shiver, his flesh went bumpy.

Cato lowered himself to the ground, laying right upon the cold and grassy earth. He shivered then, and his nipples went taught.

I reached for him and unlaced his pants, freeing his arousal.

"You are perfection, my husband."

I traced the trail of hair on his stomach and explored the wide expanse of his chest. My body responded to the evidence of his want, but not in the way it normally did. Instead of a hot surge of molten desire, my core glowed—it tightened gently and swelled, preparing to join its mate.

I lifted my skirts and let my underwear meet his shirt on the ground. He stared at me, and without an ounce of embarrassment, I held his gaze.

I stepped over him.

He clenched his hand around the exposed root of a nearby tree.

"Eira, I need you." He shook, and his teeth chattered.

I placed my feet on either side of his hips and spread my skirts wide.

"I won't deny you, husband. Never."

The grass tickled my knees as I lowered myself over him.

His freezing head nudged at my entrance.

"Scalding." He groaned into the dark. His hips bucked beneath me. "May I die ensconced in your fire." I felt the muscles of his stomach clench against the softness of my thighs.

"Don't say such things." I moved backward and began inching him steadily into my passage. Despite having been with him, it still took time to grow accustomed to his girth. I slid down him until the ring of my entrance pulled, and then rose back up, using my moisture to take him further.

"My wife is otherworldly, yet so exquisitely real," he groaned.

My backside bottomed out. His erection was almost painfully deep, but when I sat up straight and shifted atop him, my pleasure center—that Goddess-blessed spot within—quickly became accustomed to his rigidity.

I leaned, rocking forward and then back, rubbing my clitoris against the curls on his pelvic bone. I was desperate to maintain a constant connection.

"Wife... *my* wife. *Mine.*"

I closed my eyes and braced my hands against his chest, rejoicing in the texture of his scarred skin on the sensitive pads of my fingertips.

"Husband, I, ohhh..." My words became a raspy and drawn-out moan. I tipped forward, let my covered breasts drag along his chest, and increased the pace of my grind.

His breathing changed. Over and over he sucked the air deeply into his lungs and blew it out in harsh, long streams.

"Eira, I feel... holy fuck, it's like... move... move faster, sweetheart."

I could feel it.

The tie.

The æther twisted through my womb and flowed down either side of my passage, the odd weight of the connection settling low. I wrapped my arms around Cato's neck and pillowed his head. His hands found my hips, and he rocked me harder.

"It enters me, love. I am..." His eyes rolled to the back of his head, and his lids lowered. His lips parted, and his chest arched beneath me. "Gods... Goddess..."

Cato dug his fingers into the soft flesh of my thighs.

"Fuck." He lifted his hips off the ground and I rode him still. "Eira, I love—"

He shouted and stiffened. I felt him coming—felt the æther returning to my body with his every spasm.

With each pulse of his release, the connection vibrated wildly between us.

I sat up and tipped my head back, welcoming the sensation, riding it higher and higher until my passage contracted and tremors shook me. A hot flow of moisture trickled down my thighs—his essence and mine.

Again, Cato cried beneath me. "I'm still so fucking hard," he rasped. "Receive me again." He held my hips steady and pounded into me from below. His yell caught in his throat.

"Holy fuck... I..." He poured into me again. "... ah!" He pulled me roughly against his body while taking deep and cleansing breaths. He wrapped his arms around my waist and feathered kisses over the exposed skin of my cleavage.

"Eira, look," he squinted his eyes and shifted to see between the branches overhead. I tilted my head back.

Gammond's moon showed brightly in an oval of twinkling stars.

CHAPTER 32

TROTHING

"Ow did you know where to find us, Cato?"

"Bem informed me that the Troth girls were up to no good."

Snitch.

My mouth fell open in fake astonishment. Cato grabbed me by the neckline of my gown and dragged me close. I made my eyes wide and smiled the shy smile of the innocent.

"We watched your inexpert attempts to descend the ladder and—"

"Pardon you, sir," I interrupted, "we *all* made it down without incident."

Cato shot me an expression that said otherwise. His brow furrowed until a deep *U* stood over the top of his nose and his lips pursed into a disbelieving pout.

"You were a bunch of drunken ducks, waddling and waving about. Troth Cinden was so unaware of her surroundings that she did not feel Levaunt guide her foot into the rung she missed, and he literally handed Richelle the bottle that had fallen from her skirts. Eira, he reached through the hedge in which he was ensconced and put it in her hand. She said, 'thank you, noble bush.'"

I blinked rapidly, remembering something entirely different from the tale he told.

"Well, they aren't built as sturdy or well-balanced as I am."

"Oh, did you want me to point out your—"

"—perfections? Yes, please."

We made it back to the palace in good time and came in through the kitchens. The boy who tended the fire had been so engrossed in his meal that he hadn't taken notice. As covered in dirt as I was, he likely assumed the Protector was taking up with a servant, if he'd seen us at all.

As we settled into the bathing chamber, Cato pulled his satchel over his head and placed it on the countertop. He rummaged around until, finally, he produced a jar of beige powder.

"For you."

I wiggled my fingers as he placed it in my hands.

"A Joining gift?"

"For your butt." He smacked playfully at my backside, but I leapt out of his reach and hid behind a column. "Which the Goddess has proclaimed belongs to me. I am reaching for you in your hardship and your pain, wife. Get back here." He pursued, and I scampered away, bursting into a fit of laughter.

"I am quite serious. I was in the wrong at the safehouse—my mother was right. You were not sufficiently prepared for me to take you anally, and I was—what are you doing? Are you embarrassed?"

I smacked my hand over my face, but Cato tugged it down.

"Take me anally? Cato. I just…" The giggles struck again, but I did my best to repress them—he looked so concerned. "Thank you, Kitty Cat. My… my anal region *is* rather sore."

He shook his head from side to side and took the little jar back, shaking the powder into the bath he'd drawn for me. It turned the water a murky green.

"Eira, I want you to do something before I go on the night watch." Cato led me to the chaise and motioned for me to sit. Taking a knee, he shifted around, reached into his waistband, and withdrew a small knife.

I reached for the tiny blade.

"Keep it on my person for safety?"

"No. No, surely not. You sliced Septimus in his temple while brandishing his blade in your attempt to take down Scion Greggen."

"Oops?" I set my teeth together and pulled down the corners of my mouth. "I'm learning so much about my failures today."

Cato smiled softly and placed the knife in my hand.

"You were magnificent. Even I have never inspired my men to such passion. They were foaming at the mouth the minute you took your first jab." He unbuttoned the top half of his shirt and pulled his arm free.

"Mmmm, you have my attention, Protector."

Cato froze.

"Look, you insatiable succubus, I released twice in the span of three minutes. Your æther-aided vagina owes me a break." He shivered and then leaned in to kiss the side of my lips. "It was incredible, by the way. I have never come so hard." Shrugging his shoulders, he let his shirt fall around his waist.

Heat flared across my chest and cheeks, but I tamped down my ardor.

"Eira, you will pierce me. I am unable to wear the rings in my ears, but none will be wiser if I earn another scar."

Knife still in hand, I brought my palms to his face and looked him deeply in the eyes.

"Cato, you don't have to. We will know. I am nervous to cause you—"

"The pain is of no consequence." I leaned into the hand that brushed down the edge of my jaw. Cato plucked the knife from where it lay against his cheek and put it in my fingers, blade facing down. "For me, Eira, this is real." He angled his head to the side and secured the flips of his hair with one hand. "It is enduring, like this will be."

I brushed my lips against his.

"It is real," I whispered before pressing my mouth more firmly against his. "I will mark you if it's your wish."

"My wish is to publicly proclaim our Joining and—"

"Hush. That doesn't matter. What do I do?"

"Press the tip of the blade between the two scars I bear from my original piercings. Go slowly so you do not injure yourself, but ensure the blade comes through cleanly on the other side."

I nodded and raised the tiny blade to the shell of his ear.

"Are there words for this part of the Monwyn ceremony?"

I pressed the tip of the knife slowly into his cartridge, blood welled on either side of the sharp blade—it sank in with little resistance.

Instead of the grimace I expected, he smiled a lopsided grin.

"Say them," I demanded.

His eyes went round, and he pressed his lips into a fine line.

"Cato, tell me!" I looked behind the top of his ear, and sure enough, the knife's tip showed through.

"As a husband pierces his wife's maidenhead, he ushers her into a new realm of womanhood. Let this be your reminder."

"This kingdom is disgusting." I removed the blade, easing it from the wound. When fully withdrawn, a fat drop of crimson rolled down his lobe. With a single finger, I swiped the trail and brought the red stain close to my eyes, marveling at the depth of its color.

"I have a linen prepared."

I closed my lips around the tip of my finger and tasted that which sustained him. His blood was distinctly sharp, metallic, and salty.

Cato's hand captured mine.

"*That* is disgusting."

"What happened to no boundaries? You've tasted my blood, and now I've tasted yours."

He came forward, twisted me around, and pressed me into the seat of the chaise as he crawled atop me. His lips came down on mine and his tongue swept into my mouth, teasing me until I hummed from my chest. I snaked my arms around his neck and wrapped my ankles around his knees, imprisoning him in my embrace.

He pried my fingers away and ended our kiss.

"If I am a succubus, Cato, then you are my—"

"—incubus? Mmmm, yes, I am. Already, you seduce me in my dreams. Does my semen sustain you like the demon beauties of legend?"

Through half-lidded eyes, I basked in his beauty. His broad and muscled shoulders, the mark at his ear—*my* mark.

"I should like to find out."

"When he arrives, I'll do the talking. He's smooth, Cinden, and calculating. Make note of every word he says, and together we will ensure you," I glanced at her tummy, "and yours are taken care of."

The pink-haired beauty across from me lowered her eyes. She nodded, but the faintest worry line marred the middle of her forehead.

"This is far from what I'd hoped for in life."

"Well, yes, but your other option is what? Virgin birth?"

She pulled a nasty face, peering at me through squinted eyes.

"Keep talking that way. I'll puke in your matronly shoes—who made those anyway?"

"Shut up and look regal—or innocent. They love that crap here. He's just walked in."

Cinden glanced briefly toward the solarium door while adjusting her skirts around her chair.

"That's him? The little mouse dressed in gray—my Goddess, you left out the fact that he looks as plain as bread, Eira."

"Is plain a problem? He could look like my grandmother's toenails. Would that be more to your liking?"

I rose from the table and closed the long space between Ethens and myself.

"You are luminescent." He swept into a bow and proffered his hand.

"Ethens, if you spit on me again, I'll kick you in your cow-sized stones." I smiled kindly and placed my palm into his upturned one.

"It is barely noon, and already that mouth works me into a frenzy." He smoothed my indigo sleeve up above my wrist, and his lips settled against its pulse point. "My 'stones' would relish the chance to meet your divine foot." Ethens popped up and dropped my hand like he'd touched a hot coal. "Gammond's taint, she's... It's the beauty. When I received your missive, I assumed it was the plump one. She would have been excellent, just as acceptable, but I..."

"... am at a loss for words." I didn't hold back my smile. Ethens stood up straight, and a perfectly pink blush bloomed across the bridge of his slightly upturned nose. The confidence he normally threw around faltered, revealing the person beneath the facade. "Lord Ethens, I may actually like you one day. Not today, of course, but perhaps at some juncture." I turned and took his elbow. "Take a breath, not too deep. She will exploit your insecurities so fast that your head will fall from your shoulders. She's a trained Troth, and *you've* just entered negotiations."

His thin laugh sounded between us as we made our way to the table.

"This is your last chance to reconsider taking up with the true power in this country. What say you?" Ethens said.

I batted my lashes and glanced down at the floor, like the most chaste of maidens. "I say no. But there is something I need from you."

"And that would be?"

"As a member of the Den, you are aware that His Highness's tastes tend to the submissive. I find I have not mastered the language of the dominant and would like to give him a gift of sorts upon his return... wielding power seems to be your preferred role. Will you teach me?"

"For a price."

"I expected no less."

"You will have a beginners list before the day is out... *if* you refer to me as Headmaster."

I arched a brow and then looked toward the room's massive window. The afternoon sun poured into the lady's solarium, and the rainbows bent and danced along the walls and floors.

"Goddess, Troth Solnna, her skin is the color of gleaming bronze. Her locks are..."

"... your favorite color?" Cinden did look gorgeous. He hadn't even seen her face yet, but her curls hung so beautifully over her shoulder, revealing the swan-like grace of her slender neck. The bright green dress she wore complemented her flawless skin and made her shine like a rare jewel. "Just wait until you stare into those velvety brown eyes."

As if on cue, Cinden dipped low to adjust the buckle of her leather ankle boots and turned her gaze upon us. She allowed a soft smile to flit across her lips, and she inclined her chin in greeting.

"She is fae-born," Ethens whispered.

We reached the table, and he pulled a chair for me. He turned and faced Cinden before dropping into the most exemplary of courtiers' bows.

"Madam Troth... it is my honor to—"

"Ethens, right? Do you have a first name? Hurry and sit. I'm starving, and we have serious business to discuss."

"That we do." He waved a hand in the air and hailed a servant, who hustled to the table.

"The lady requires sustenance. Procure one of everything."

Ethens dipped into his pocket and produced several gold coins that he spread conspicuously across the table. The servant shot off.

"Now, I will be acting on behalf of Troth Cinden of Monwyn, formerly of Gaea." I stacked the parchments in front of me and prepped my quill. "As an Obligate myself, I am able to oversee, create, and approve legal contracts. I cannot perform Joinings or—"

"Eira has informed me you have a certain sexual proclivity. What is it?"

A painful-sounding cough hacked out behind me. The servant chose a poor time to return. Red-faced but composed, he slid four plates in front of Cinden.

"This is... Do you have cheese? Any cheese at all?" She crossed her arms over her chest, pushing her perfectly sized bust over the squared neckline of her gown. She huffed dramatically. "Did you get lost on your way to feed the chickens?"

"We can discuss Monwyn's idiosyncrasies another day. Now, where was I?" I said, trying to keep business, *business*.

"He was about to reveal his nasty sex thing. Speak up, Ethens." Cinden pawed at a massive bunch of grapes and began sucking them off their tethers one by one and chewing noisily. "Do you... Has he suffered a stroke, Eira?"

Ethens stared at Cinden as if transfixed.

I scooted my chair forward and kicked, connecting my boot to his shin.

"I-I-It is, well, I enjoy saliva. Mouths, lips, and... saliva." A bead of sweat gathered at his temple.

"Will I need to spit on you when you attempt to fertilize me?" Cinden snagged a carrot and bit into it with a resounding crunch. "That doesn't seem nearly as awful as some of the things I was imagining. I was most concerned about poo—"

"Cinden!"

Ethens snapped his head around.

"Is this her normal level of bratty behavior?"

"Noooo, she—"

"Yes." She snapped off another bite of carrot. "Are you able to deal?"

I looked up at the ceiling and nodded while shrugging my shoulders.

"I asked if this was an issue. Ethens, should we end this negotiation?"

He sat back, crossed his legs, and draped an arm over the back of his chair. "Not. At. All."

Cinden smiled then, a full-on, bright-toothed beam. She had a massive chunk of orange carrot between her two front teeth, but the effect was still stunning.

"Cinden is on record as having retained her purity, making her a valuable asset to any man concerned with such nonsense. Here are the documents for your verification." I handed Ethens the papers that Cato had delivered to me along with a smart leather-bound notebook and shoulder bag this morning. When he dropped them off, he'd wished me a "great first day at work."

"Yuck, don't flare your nose like that. You aren't a dog. And have you not realized that one's purity, or lack thereof, is no one's business but their own?" She chastised Ethens soundly.

He worked his tongue along the inside of his cheek while he watched her.

I would have cheered her on if not for the fact that she truly *did* need to cement this relationship... and quickly.

"Eira has also mentioned that you will stray from our marriage. In Gaea, plurality is not an issue, but it's not done dishonestly or in secret. I do not like the idea of you cavorting around and spitting on others while we are trying to do the Goddess's work and bless Ærta with a new life. To that end, until I have conceived, your saliva is to remain in your mouth, and when I have conceived, you will introduce me to those you take up with and ensure they are up to date with their healing appointments. Also, I will require a monthly allowance of one thousand gold pieces. My family will need five hundred coins monthly, and the same should be sent to the Gaean treasury in my name. I prefer to orgasm twice per week to keep my nerves calm. Though I've not experienced penetration, I will need your word that you will commit yourself to learning to bring me pleasure, or I will become infuriating. Oh, and I am a deeply religious woman, and we will attend the temple together three times per week."

Ethens's hand trembled ever so slightly.

"Done. Troth Eira, how soon can we Join?"

"Do you have any requests or questions for me, Lord Ethens?" Cinden asked.

"None."

"Fine. Where do I sign?"

I blinked from one to the other. The lack of negotiation certainly took the wind from my negotiator's sails, but I passed the parchment to Cinden.

"Here, here, and... here. *Headmaster,* you do the same." Cinden scribbled her name in blue ink and then blew on the form until it dried. She passed the document to Ethens, who gazed at me through glittering eyes. I gave the document a little matter-of-fact pat.

"Troth Cinden, would you join me for a walk?" Ethens pushed back from the table and stood.

"I would be delighted; the weather looks—holy shit, Eira!" Her eyes went as round as oranges. "His appendage is the size of a three-pound sausage."

"And now, it's all yours, lucky lady. You can Join in three days if special dispensation can be arranged, five if not."

"Consider it arranged and inform the priest."

Ethens came round to a still gaping Cinden.

"I'm not sure that will fit." She pointed to his crotch.

"It will fit." He placed his hand on the small of her back and turned her in the direction of the door.

"Will you stuff it in flaccid first? I think that's the only..." Her words died on the air as they made their way to the door.

CHAPTER 33

CONJURING

I've nearly done it Papa, I just can't get the latch to fully cl-clear—ugh! "Damnit!" I yelled. I'd been trying desperately to unlock the balcony's closed door for the past two hours. Within the first hour, I had the mechanism turning, but could not, for the life of me, flick the remaining quarter of an inch I needed to fully unseat it. "Fuck, fuck, fuck!" *Am I weak? Do I need more æther?*

No, daughter, you are an endless supply. What you need is trust. Trust yourself. Follow your shadows. Tell the metal—not the lock—what you require from it. Metal, like water, is an element of the earth and therefore controllable.

Allaine beat on the glass door, unwilling to walk outside and face the cold.

Intruder. Be right back.

Personally, I was in my element. The air was crisp and clean. I could breathe in deeply and feel the refreshing coolness to the bottom of my lungs. The blanket on my lap was the perfect weight to maintain the most excellent of temperatures.

"Yes?" I opened the door and peeked my head in. The wind tossed my skirts and whipped my unbound hair around my face.

Allaine pulled her thick shawl tightly around her shoulders.

"Your itinerary is as follows: immediately after dinner, you head to the temple to meet with the priest. The Protector asks that you procure entertainment for this evening. Your guests—you have noticed the influx of guests, yes?—would like to meet their hosts. Unless you wish me to tell them you are busy sitting in the cold, talking to the walls."

She popped her brows and looked around the balcony for emphasis.

"Well, maid of mine, you just earned your spot as lead musician. Your lilting tunes will fill the... Where is this taking place?"

"Grand drawing room. And absolutely not." She leaned down and towered over me, almost touching her nose to my own.

"Absolutely, yes. Go wax your fingers or whatever your instrument requires. Oh, and Allaine, I have a rash." I pulled up my dress, exposing my knees and calves. "Can you stop by the healer's room and request something? My legs have gone all itchy."

"Josa on a jar of jam! How in the world did you get poison plant all the way up to your muffin?" Allaine bent low and surveyed my blistering skin.

"My what?"

"What you need is my family's remedy. The boys had it constantly growing up."

Allaine slammed the door in my face and then whipped it open again. "We will have to paint your legs for the bedding. Ambrose may not wish to fornicate with the plague-ridden."

Allaine slammed the door again and flew away.

Lock you little bitch!

The bolt slammed home.

"Hahahaha! Papa!" I yelled.

Silence. Right.

I ran to the spot where I had linked up with him earlier.

Father Burchard, I LOCKED THE DOOR!

I danced around merrily, tossing my hands into the air, and kicked up my heels, uncaring if a guard spied my jig through the columns.

Gracious me, Marmot. Lower your voice, dear. The Bond does not regulate—Oh, piss. I spilled my ink. I knew you could do it... Now, just reverse what you did.

"Um, open, little bitch!" I flung my arm out and pointed my finger at the door. Nothing.

Well, I probably wouldn't respond to that either.

I adjusted my stance and took a long, controlled breath. Through the shadows, I coaxed the mechanism, speaking to it like it were a person. *Unlock, precious metal.*

Click.

Elation, pure elation.

It worked! Yes, it did! I'm the queen of conjuring!

A weak mewling sounded through the connection.

Papa? Are you alright?

I gathered the leather-bound notebook and parchments from this morning's negotiations and tucked them into the bag on the table.

Burchard?

I slung the satchel over my shoulders. I needed to deliver the forms to Primus Thierry's office and pick up the dispensation. A few coins and Ethens had made the process extraordinarily expedient.

Papaaaaaa? Where are you?

H-healers greenhou—dear. I am... not feel—"

I fought with the bag's stiff closure.

Father Burchard? Papa B?

I stilled my hands. Something wasn't right. The Infinite Bond was skipping and cutting out. I peeked through the door's glass panes and saw Bem and Levaunt milling about the common room.

"Bem, I think something's wrong with His Majesty. Would you let me out?"

"Not a chance, sneaky Troth. Levaunt was just with him and the healer. I'll not chase you across the gods' green earth today."

"Fine, but please send someone to check on him. He is in the healer's shed." I sidestepped my way to the corner of the balcony and looked down.

Papa, please speak to me.

He'd gone completely silent.

Half-formed words filtered through my mind. I stilled and listened.

Dark... daught—so dark.

The barely-there tether of our connection vibrated like the plucked string of a lute.

I'm coming, Papa. Hold on.

I snatched the blanket from the wicker sofa and tied it to a column in a tight square knot. Peering over the banister, I decided the drop-off would still be too severe and yanked my dress over my head. When I tied its woolen arms to the blanket's end, it still didn't reach the ground, but it would be close enough. Squeezing my rear through the columns, I prayed for my safe descent and scooted my butt off the banister's edge.

"Shiiiiiiiit!" I dropped fast as the fibers of the wool stretched, nearly doubling their original length. "Oh, fuck. Fuck!"

My arms shook and my palms burned, but I managed a death grip on my makeshift rope. The sinking slowed, but the fibers' integrity had been compromised. It was now see-through under the strain and thinning by the second. "Fuck, fuck, nether tits!"

A jolt of nausea punched me in the gut. The æther squeezed around my stomach causing bile to rise into my throat.

D-Daughter, do not...

The connection fizzled out.

The wool rope snapped.

"Oh, oh, gods." The sharp branches of the dense hedge kept me from hitting the ground. Fear overrode the searing pain as I fought my way out of the bushes.

I ran.

My feet never moved so fast.

I covered the ground quickly, stomping down tall grass and passing the fallow fields. My lungs were on fire as the healer's greenhouse came into view.

Open, door.

Open, pretty lock.

Fucking unlock, godsdammit!

I was so near now. If I ran full-force, maybe I could bust it off its hinges. Maybe it was unlocked? I should have forced Levaunt to listen. I should have screamed for a guard. I should have...

As I ran, my eyes were drawn to the shadow that charged by my side. It seemed to flicker even in the bright light of the sun, morphing from raccoon to wolf to...

My shadow—my shade. I called to them and they came to me in the form of a winged woman whose taloned hands and feet skimmed the ground like a snow owl tracking its prey.

I stepped outside of myself.

My cheeks were flushed red, and my chemise torn. I watched as I ran, saw my feet dig into the earth.

My corporeal body dipped low and sprang.

Vanish.

Intense pain engulfed me. My shoulder and hip screamed out as they met the hard surface of the door.

I opened my eyes to a forest of greenery. The smell of dirt, medicinals, and vegetation, hung heavily in the air.

"Papa!"

The king lay on the ground. His eyelids fluttered rapidly, and his hand was tightly clenched around a quill.

"Order of his-his... maj-maj... esty." The healer lay a few feet in the distance. His mouth opened and closed, while thick pink foam spilled from between his lips.

"Order… o-of…" his neck spasmed, jerking his head to the right, and his stomach sank in on itself, "maj-esty."

Poison.

White, foamy spittle trailed from the king's mouth.

I spun around looking for a healer's bag but could see nothing of the sort. Frantically searching the large space, I found a wall crowded with small, colorful vials, various tinctures, and boxed herbs.

"Asphyxiation, arrhythmia, ague, bloody stools, blister care, boils, cough suppressant, cuts, conception control, charcoal." The palm-sized box was packed tight with the black powder. At Verus, we were told that if administered quickly enough, it could negate some of the effects of poison.

I dropped to the floor, kneeling in the king's fluids. Burchard's mouth went slack as I tilted his head. Filling the palm of my hand with charcoal, I sent up a silent prayer. *Goddess, please, he's not a bad man.* The powder poured easily into his mouth but caused him to cough and sputter. I slid my hand down the column of his throat to encourage him to swallow.

"Gentle, Papa, gentle," I said in a soft tone.

"Maj-maj-maj-maj…"

The healer.

I crawled over the king's body and administered the powder.

"Maj-maj-ma…" Just like the man in the river, he spoke the same message over and over—he'd been conjured upon. "Ma-ma." Watery, pink streaks poured from his nostrils intensifying to a viscous, dark red flow.

He strained, tensing the muscles in his neck and jaw… and then stilled.

He was gone.

Scrambling to my feet once again, I searched the greenhouse until I found a set of sharp shears. Without hesitation, I stabbed the fatty part at the base of my thumb, breaking the skin. Pink foam began to fill the king's mouth. The blood on my hand beaded but didn't fall. *Mossius, I beseech you. I implore you. Let him live. Let him heal his family before you call him home.* This time, I used the shears properly and snipped deeply into the side of my palm. Holding my hand over his mouth, I squeezed my wrist to encourage a steady trickle. I feared giving him too much *and* not enough.

The door came crashing in, shattering to splinters.

"Brother!" Septimus shouted. He ran to the king and grabbed his shoulders. He twisted and pulled until the king lay on his side. For once, his icy eyes looked human. "Hold his head. He mustn't aspirate."

I did as I was told and watched closely as Septimus held his ear to the differing parts of the king's body. As he listened, his eyes sought mine.

"How did you know he was here, and what in the Goddess's name are you?"

I stared at him.

No answer was the best answer. *Neutral, keep neutral, Eira.*

His hand shot out, and his fingers bit into my neck.

"You will not survive the methods I use to pry the answers from your lips." His grip was a vise, sealing off my ability to breathe. "Speak!"

A high-pitched scream pierced the air.

Father Burchard's torso arched, and his eyes snapped open. His head rotated on his neck, and his eerie, unblinking gaze settled on his brother.

Septimus dropped his hand.

"Burchard. Are you with us?" Septimus placed one palm on the king's jaw and used his other fingers to gently pull at the king's lids, inspecting the whites of his eyes. "What witch's trick is this? His eyes. His eyes are..."

"Septimus... Ahdmundus..." I reached out and placed my hand on his forearm, squeezing firmly. "He will live."

I was sure of it. The scream, the stare—it was exactly as it had been when I'd given Cato my blood. "He will need to rest. He will need to be bathed and watched carefully—are you hearing me?"

"I-I... yes," he whispered.

Shouts came from outside the cottage.

Cato bounded through the door, followed by a veritable battalion of armored men. He assessed the situation quickly and immediately jumped into action.

"Move them. Take both to the healer's wing—separate rooms. Comb the guest ledgers for a cult Mossius healer." With the point of his finger, the three remaining guards spread out and began searching the area, overturning pots and furniture.

"Septimus, outside," Cato said.

Septimus's eyes bore into mine, even as he nodded and then rose.

The guards moved deeper into the jungle of plants, toppling pots and trampling flowers in their haste. My eyes caught on the wall of shelved vials. When they moved far enough away, I seized the opportunity and stashed handfuls of tinctures, shoving them into the satchel that was still around my shoulders.

"Eira?"

I spun on my heels.

"Septimus said the door was locked. He said—Eira—how did you come to be in this room?" Cato asked. "You were secured when I left."

I motioned him nearer while I recalled the feeling, the sounds that surrounded me, the momentary pain. "I placed myself in the path of light... and my... my shadow just hurtled through the door."

CHAPTER 34

WELL, I FOR ONE, HAD A BALL

"He is sleeping but alive. Eira, come to me."

I walked across the floor of Ambrose's chamber and stood in front of the husband of my heart. After Cato had left me at my door and placed Bem on watch, I'd bathed under the running water of the bath's faucet, thoroughly scrubbing all manner of nastiness from my skin. Allaine had stopped and thankfully brought her family's miracle lotion for my skin. Already, the burn of the rash and the pain from some of my newer bruises were diminishing.

"Lift your shirt. I must feel you." I reached for my hem and pulled his old shirt up to my waist. Cato sucked in his breath. "Where I not aware of your recent activities, I would assume you had engaged in fisticuffs with a troll." With the most delicate touch, he encouraged me to turn and show him my backside. "I would take your pain if I could." His lips settled on the top of my rear, and he drew small circles there with his nose. "This is the only patch of you that remains unbruised or unmarred by hives. Why ever did you decide to jump?"

I swayed my hips back and forth against his clipped beard.

"I had to get to him. Part of it is our Bond, but the other part is that I care for him. I find myself reaching out to him—understanding him more. The healer was under his influence, by the way. He spoke as if in a trance. He wasn't his own man." Cato nodded his head up and down against my back. "Oh Goddess, scratch me harder." I wiggled against his rough jaw, reveling in the near orgasmic sensation of my itchy welts meeting wiry beard.

"Is that..." Cato slapped his palm against my rear. "I see how you are. Using me when I have my own patch of poison in need of nursing."

"Oh, no. Show me yours so I can be properly contrite." I stuck my bottom lip out and nodded sympathetically. Cato stood and began unlacing his pants. He turned and displayed his handsome but angrily red cheeks. I could see it climbing up his back as well.

"It's in your crack, poor love. Perhaps the next time we mate in the wilds, we should assess the terrain for vicious foliage." I smoothed my hands over the light dusting of hair on his rounded behind. He leaned into my hands. "Is your ear healing well at least?"

"Mmhmm..." He turned and then lowered his head. His lips were a whisper from my own. "Every hive is worth it. Not an hour has passed where I have not recalled the image of you atop me." He shook his head to clear his thoughts but kept going. "The way your thighs enveloped me and how your ass filled my palms." He closed his eyes and pulled his bottom lip into his mouth. "When you ground yourself against me, your chest rocked and bounced. Godsdamn, you are temptation made flesh." He sank into the cushions of the teal couch and patted his lap. "Sit with me, wife."

I happily cozied up with him and tucked my head into the crook of his neck. These were the moments I loved most—when we could exist together with no falsehoods or pretense between us.

"Septimus is aware of His Majesty's dealings."

I sat up, but Cato gently led my head back to his shoulder.

"It was time," Cato said, his lips lightly resting on my temple. "He may be exactly who I need to keep the king contained."

"And what about me? Does he—"

"I have convinced him that the king himself brought you through."

Cato tucked me deeper into the couch's corner and slid out from under me before shooting to his feet.

"Someone enters." He moved surefootedly to the door and stood to its side, staring straight ahead. I grabbed a pillow from the opposite end of the couch and tucked it under my head before closing my eyes and feigning sleep.

"Eira—oh, pardon me, Protector—Troth Solnna. I have procured the gifts for this evening's revel, and the Troths Monwyn assure me they are prepared to entertain your guests."

My mouth opened in a wide, fake yawn.

"And you? Have you prepared your song list?"

"I... Surely you jest. I am not a woman of the court and—"

"You are most assuredly a member of this court, Lady Allaine Lemder, and I will hear nothing more of it. Drop them on the table and make yourself presentable… before you make *me* look presentable." I rolled around and faced the back of the couch, pretending to fall asleep.

The wooden crate Allaine held clattered noisily on the table, and her angry little huffs punctuated the cadence of her even angrier steps as she left.

The room was filled to bursting.

Emissaries and delegates from all over Ærta had dressed in their finery and glittering jewels. Some wore thin coronets on their heads, and others had furs that dragged the ground. Gaeans, clad in greens and gold, were already kneeling in the corner atop lush carpets brought from around the palace. Their telltale shifting told me that their meditations would soon end.

Wonderful smells surrounded me as I stepped over the threshold on the arm of Lord Septimus. He'd collected me from my apartments wearing an expression of aloofness that smacked so much of Cato's that I felt an unwelcome flutter in my stomach. But not once had he made an indecent overture.

Two servants trailed behind us, carrying the small tokens I prepared for the ladies who were in attendance. They contained a few trinkets, as well as thumbnail-sized pieces of polished amethyst, among other trivialities.

Tonight, I donned my Troth mask. Septimus had informed me that the King of Gaea and his retinue would be arriving in the earliest hours of the morning, and though I knew that this was an eventuality, it still sent my nerves spiraling. Winter was closing in, and I hoped that the threat of snow would send them home faster. He would be here. He would watch my vows and become a part of my story—very much against my wishes. Would I know his face? Would he have my eyes?

I was entirely on edge and couldn't afford to let anything or anyone slip past me.

Butterflies—no, hornets—coursed through my stomach.

I'd be less inclined to worry if Cato were present, but he'd left to secure the main road and had put Lemder in charge of the palace's security. Armored guards were stationed at every door—multiple weapons hung from the chains on their steel chestplates—and I even recognized the faces of Levaunt and another handful of soldiers who mingled around the guests in plain clothes. I guarantee that their boots and pockets teemed with a variety of blades and bludgeons.

"You are a tempting sight, Troth Solnna," said Ethens, who bowed low and proffered his hand. Septimus scowled and looked away, making a show of not acknowledging his presence.

"Yes, I am, aren't I, Headmaster?" I extended my hand, and the corner of Ethens's mouth quirked up. His lips met the back of my hand, and he glanced up through half-lidded lashes.

I know what you're about. I held his gaze, and when nothing wet hit my hand, I leaned into his side, like I was having trouble hearing him in the noise-filled room.

"Good boy," I whispered. "Next time, you may take a small taste."

The lump in the column of Ethens's throat bobbed. He squinted his eyes in Septimus's direction and sniffed dismissively while he slipped a folded parchment past my hand and tucked it into my sleeve.

Septimus tugged my elbow so hard that I was required to step away.

"Greet them now. Begin this affair so I may return to my brother's side."

I nodded, and he led me to stand beside the, yet again, empty throne.

Septimus signaled, and a trumpet blared its fanfare. The crowd pressed in on me, making the space feel too small, too cramped. I could see nothing but the ornamented chests of high-ranking officials and the bosoms of well-endowed Solnnan women.

"Greetings, esteemed—wait a moment." I held my hand up to the assembled mass and then gestured for a servant. After bending his ear, he ran off quickly and returned with an upholstered chair. Supported by Septimus's steady hand, I lifted the lush pink chiffon of my skirt and stepped up on its seat. "There, much better." I looked out over the throng. "Greetings, esteemed guests! My betrothed and I welcome you as family, and tonight I implore you to accept our hospitality. Drink and eat heartily, take part in the merriment, and tomorrow, we shall do it all again." Holding my arms wide, I beamed warmly at the cheerful faces smiling back at me.

Loud guffaws and supportive cheers came from the crowd.

"Let us have music! I would introduce you to Cordillaria's own diamond, Lady Allaine, who will join our minstrels and share her musical talents." I swept my arm out and indicated the back right corner where Allaine's head rose above all but a handful in the crowd.

When I saw her, a pang of guilt stabbed my conscience.

Had I forced her to feel like a spectacle?

My intention was to showcase her talents and build her confidence. I hadn't thought of the fact that she might feel like I was putting her on stage to garner sympathy—or worse, to be seen as a charity case. *Shit.* Who was I to say she *needed* a confidence boost at all? Instead of acknowledging her experiences or asking her permission, I'd bullied her into this. *Fuck.*

I hopped down from my chair.

"Septimus, come. Get me to the corner without stopping."

There was no time like the present to make amends.

He held out his elbow, and together we walked through the crowd, inclining our heads and passing by those trying their best to pull us into conversation—vying to be seen with the guest of honor and the highest-ranking royal in the room.

"Do you want to talk about Burchard?" I asked while smiling brilliantly up into his face and then turning the grin on the crowd.

"I do not."

"Do you wish to discuss what you came upon in the shed?"

"No."

This was like speaking to an actual door.

"Are you still inclined to have sex with me?"

The corner of his mouth hitched.

"I am. It was your scent that made me give chase this morning—I meant to catch you."

A delicious pressure curled in my womb and coiled tightly at my center. Some sort of Bond had to be in play. It certainly *felt* like the Mating one.

The throng that surrounded the musicians parted, allowing us a front-row view. Allaine was resplendent in a shimmering silk dress whose right half was Monwyn blue and whose left was deep maroon. A thick woven belt embellished with intricate embroidery sat low on her hips, emphasizing her hourglass shape. The tune she played was lively—her lyre wove in and out of the rhythms provided by the drums and rebec being played behind her, and the ladies of Solnna clapped along, though the effect was slightly muffled by too many layers of linen and wool. A reed-thin fellow danced a jig in the middle of the half-circle they'd made, kicking his heels to his butt and swinging his elbows as if he were hoisting a pint in each hand. Richelle shooed the man away so she could organize the floor. Whereas *my* Trothy talent had been speaking the Solnnan tongue, hers had been dance.

"May I have the honor, Obligate Solnna?"

My stomach dropped.

"Do you bear any offensive steel?" Septimus responded for me, stepping between myself and my potential dance partner.

I stepped to his side, but, in confrontation mode as he was, Septimus forced me behind his back. Poking my head around his arm, I saw the Gaean representative who'd brought the chest bearing Ozius's head. When he noticed my face, the man dropped into a flourishing bow.

"I am Elderman Deekon, ma'am." The dignitary bowed again. "I serve the great Primus-King in the capital of Mynder, and the only steel I brought with me is my dull wit."

"Then my escort can have no objections."

A hesitant Septimus freed me from the shield of his body. He turned and stood on the outside of the dance floor, glaring at me with his arms crossed over his chest.

My Troth mask had many uses: ignoring the patriarchal implications of that stare was one, and getting information directly from the lips of my enemies was another.

The notes of a slow song floated on the air.

"A talentia. Are you familiar with the mechanics, lady?"

"But of course, my training would have been most remiss had it not included the traditional dance of your people." I took his outstretched hand, and he swept me into place beside him.

Allaine caught my eye and gave me a wink. This particular dance would resonate with my partner, giving him the benefit of familiarity while not involving a single instance of touch. *Mental note: give Allaine a raise.*

We started by taking three steps forward, and with our palms held out a few inches from each other, we circled slowly.

"If you don't mind me saying, ma'am, I was unsure of what your reaction would be to the Primus-King's gift and was concerned with the discomfort it might have caused you."

We repeated the same set of steps, but this time, we circled in the opposite direction.

I nodded my head in recognition of his concerns, but didn't betray my feelings with an answer.

"What does an Elderman do?"

A sad smile appeared on the face of the more mature gentleman. I'd place him in the middle of his sixth decade. His hair was silvery white at his temples but faded to a darker brown over the rest of his head.

"We care for the Scion who live in the palace before they go to Verus."

Oh.

"And did you—"

He knit his brows.

"Yes, I served Ozius," he answered. "Bringing him here was my last act in his service."

Gracious, that seemed morbid. But the Gaeans were nothing if not extreme.

"Your monarch took the life of a Chosen Son. Why?"

The Elderman schooled his expressions well—he'd inherited a mask from his line of work as well—but he'd not learned to slow his heart rate. A bulging vein ran across his forehead, and under his thin skin, his pulse quickened.

Uncomfortable, are we?

"I-I can't speak to his mind, ma'am. But he was distressed when Ozius returned and was outraged when he learned that Scion Castor made physical blows upon your person. Castor was not there to punish, but Ozius hadn't intervened and therefore the consequences fell to him."

Consequences.

A blood-soaked Evandr.

Mariad fallen.

Castor's dead eyes staring into nothingness.

"Ozius's fate is inconsequential. Does your king admit to resorting to violence and murder to steal me away?"

"Again, ma'am, pardon me, but I simply don't know."

"And I don't believe you. Why ask me to dance, Elderman?"

"I-I wished to ensure you weren't rattled by such a sight as—"

"No. You came with clear intentions, as I am positive all these others did. We all have motives—you, me, the man watching you so intently from the corner."

We walked in a line to the beat of the drum. He turned his head and looked to where Hughes, Imella's man, stood watching. He was dressed in the livery of a palace servant and blended in flawlessly with the group of men balancing small glasses of spirits on their trays.

"Can you get a message to your Primus-King before he reaches these walls, Elderman?"

"Ma-ma'am?"

"I think you can. Please tell him that if he dares to make another attempt to remove me from my chosen home, I will flay his wives and have their skins tanned for bookbinding. I will grind his bones into bread flour," Father Burchard's earlier threat poured from my mouth, "and I will feed the loaves to your citizens, who will praise me for my generosity."

"All things will come to pass as the Goddess wills, ma'am."

The music came to an end, as did our dance.

"I will see your message delivered." He bowed and made a hasty retreat.

I caught Hughes's eyes and made my way toward him, swimming through the dense crowd.

"Such a talent with the lyre, and what a handsome woman. She would almost be a prize if it weren't for her—"

I whipped around and interrupted some fucking lout of a Solnnan talking with his over-dressed companion.

"Say another word and I will rip out your—"

"Eira!" Richelle chirped. The wonderfully plump sister of my heart threaded her arm through the lout's elbow. The man shared her unusual shade of hair color, and the bow mouth that was so sweet on Richelle became a sensual pout under his sharp cheekbones and smoldering eyes. "I would like you to make the acquaintance of my brother, Representative—holy shit!"

I struck.

I let my fist soar.

As Cato had taught me, I swung from my hips, generating enough power that when my knuckles slammed into the flesh of the nobleman's neck, it felled him like a great oak, chopped by the woodsman's axe.

"My gods, Eira! What in Ærta have you done?" Richelle dropped to her knees, cradling her brother's head as he sputtered and coughed.

Septimus was at my side in a flash, as was Hughes.

"At the Grooming, you spoke of your kin. Is *this* the stinking shit who called you an unmountable whale?"

Richelle nodded her head in the affirmative.

"Then that was the greeting he deserved." My voice echoed around the domed ceiling above us. "Whales are fucking majestic!"

Representative Wankstain recovered enough to find his voice. "Backwoods cunt. Chosen or not, I will fucking end—" Septimus's boot struck his temple, and the threat died in his ragged throat.

Guards appeared almost instantly, and Septimus followed as they dragged the now unconscious man from the hall.

"Let the music resume." I tossed my arm in the air, and the chords struck up again. "Please continue. I love watching you dance." I offered my hand and helped Richelle to her feet. Though visibly dazed, she smoothed her gown, plastered on a lackluster smile, and returned to the crowd.

I beckoned Hughes to my side.

"Deliver this message to your mistress," I said softly as we walked toward the table where the attendants placed my crates of gifts. I pretended to direct him, while I dictated the short message. "Can you repeat that back to me?"

He removed his spectacles and polished the lenses on his sleeve.

"I guess not."

Hughes left just as Septimus caught up to me. I waited for him to creepily gloat about how he had protected my honor or how I owed him a fuck, but he remained silent.

"I wish to deliver these and leave. I have sullied this fine evening and grow tired."

"The sentiment is mutual," Lady Troth.

Septimus took my arm, and with a servant at our side, we walked from guest to guest, handing out the beautiful silk purses.

I plastered on a fake smile.

"Where is your lady?" I questioned.

He tossed his head to the side.

"Well, take me to her, shit excuse for a spouse." My mood soured rapidly.

When we approached Lilium, it was plain to see that she was even more pale than usual—she appeared weak, gaunt, and wholly unhealthy. It set me to simmering.

"Lady Septimus, you should be home recovering. Please accept a small token of appreciation. I thank you for celebrating with me on the auspicious occasion of my Joining."

I handed her the parcel, praying that I'd caused enough of a scene that Septimus, engrossed in his guard duties, had missed that the ribbon at its top was indigo instead of royal blue like the rest. Four tinctures of stolen conception control passed from my hands to hers. Let them burn me for my transgressions. I would welcome the—

The entryway door slammed open, the crashing sound echoing through the hall. Every conversation stopped and every head turned.

"NOT A MAN REMAINS ALIVE WHO ONCE PLUNDERED OUR WESTERN COASTS!"

CHAPTER 35

AHOY

Ambrose was home.

An unkempt, filthy, and snarling Ambrose.

He flung off the leather jerkin he wore and cast it on the ground with a loud snap.

"All of you, out! I require my woman."

Oh, fuck.

His hands went to the neck of his stained linen shirt, and with a full-bodied flex, he ripped the thing from his torso and let it drop to the floor. A flaky, rust-colored gash cut across the right side of his stomach and from this distance, it appeared as if a hoofed animal had sewn him back together. His long and heavily muscled form rippled as he strode forward.

Guards began herding people through the doors while Ambrose walked through the tide of people like a great leviathan, surging forth from the crests of a storm-tossed sea.

Unconcerned with the fleeing throng, he pulled at the buckle of his belt.

"Go at her, Highness!" a voice rang out.

"How much for a seat at the bedding?"

I caught sight of a bruised and battered Greggen. He was making a beeline for Allaine, and I moved to intercept.

"OUT!" Ambrose yelled.

The remaining members of the assembly went scrambling.

He whipped around, and dangerous green eyes met mine.

He marched across the floor, all shirtless, disheveled, and untamed—and when his unbound hair fell over his eyes, he shoved his fingers through the raven tresses and tossed it back over his shoulder.

My vagina flooded like the Great Nortian Thaw.

I have to be in my fertile period.

I wanted him. He was alive and home. And I wanted him bad.

"I see the look in your eyes." He bared his teeth and bit at the air. "Your pirate-punishing prince is returned. Batten your hatches and prepare to be boarded."

I pulled the long sleeves of my gown over my shoulders and then hopped up and down, trying to force the damn thing down over my chest. Dresses you couldn't get off by yourself were shit. Untying the laces at my hips, I dropped my underwear to the ground. The pink stockings and tight chemise could stay.

The doors slammed shut as he reached for me.

My heart pounded in my chest, and my core swelled and ripened.

Ambrose yanked me to his body, slid his arm low, and squeezed my backside in his massive hands. I returned his fervor and brought my hands under my breasts, offering them up like two baked pumpkins on a platter.

"Your raging libido is simply revolting." His rancid breath hit me in the face and nearly doubled me over. "I am at my worst, Eira, my lowest, and yet you *still* ogle this body like I am nothing more than a flesh sword for your insatiable skin scabbard." He pressed me backward until my knees buckled and lowered me to the floor. "Did your fresh and sparkly *first husband* not satisfy you in my stead?"

He stretched his long body out beside me, and the rank odor of a foul underarm made my eyes cross.

"For fuck's sake, Ambrose." I pushed against his chest, seeking air, but he held me captive in his vice grip.

"It was awful, Eira, ugh, gods. I have not bathed nor shaved since my departure. And it turns out that if you cut a man too deeply, his organs just fall—just slide out of his sides. And the noise it makes!" Ambrose heaved, his head shooting forward and his neck working to swallow back bile. "All squish and squelch."

He reached into the neckline of my slip and cupped my pierced breast. His normally soft finger pads felt rough as rope when he ran his thumb over my nipple. This new juxtaposition of manly and man-baby was confusing but oddly appealing. The flame between my legs sparked again when he freed my breast from the garment.

"You smell so clean, and Goddess praise, your tits are so lovely." He brought his lips to my nipple and flicked his tongue over the stiffening peak. "Mmm, yes, my dick rises. Praise her!"

Snaking pressure coiled tightly in my clitoris, and my other nipple hardened to a stiff point. I shifted it toward him, seeking the same treatment as her sister.

"There was a pirate so fat that he too had titties." Ambrose ignored my overture and grabbed my head, bringing his face close to mine. "I was haunted—HAUNTED—by the thought that I'd never fancy a pretty, peaked teat again."

"Ambr—" I gagged. "Ambrose, please."

"Are you that desperate?" he sighed. "I suppose I can spot wash." He reached up and over a table and produced someone's half-empty glass of spirits. "They sterilized my cuts with lesser quality swill. I am sure this will cleanse me adequately."

"Pl-please, I can't—" I slapped my hand over my nose.

"—wait for me? I know. There were so many sights that reminded me of your plump pussy: the open cavity of the deer Dumail took down for our dinner that first night, the wet maws of discarded fish heads, the dripping hole left after pulling my saber from some slow pirate... I missed your warmth most severely." His hand went between my legs, and two fingers dipped in to test me. "You *are* ready for me." He entered my slippery passage in a single swift motion, and I arched so hard that my freed breast smooshed against his face. "Cato regaled me with a tale wherein you conjured the very semen from his balls using some form of æther-aided snatch suction. Consider this my formal demand for the same."

His big fingers curled upward, and his thumb found my clit. He coaxed me with deep, full strokes, stretching my entrance delightfully tight.

Mounting Cato. Punching that stupid fucking brother of Richelle's. Sneaking freedom into Lilium's lithe hands. I was power-drunk, and Ambrose was working *his* magic. The funk that surrounded me was nothing compared to the thrill shooting through my soul and throughout my body.

He fingered me in a steady rhythm with a little extra nudge on the upthrust. I raised my knees and held them wide.

I am revolting.

He snatched my nipple between his teeth and ran his tongue in circles around my areola. *Revoltingly aroused.*

"Ambrose... Ambrose... As much as I fear contracting the rot from your cock, put it in." I panted while bucking my hips to meet his palm.

His face turned all mopey.

"Eira, the pirates were not nearly as bad as the women who worked the docks. My Gods, the things they shouted at me—making fun of my garments, pointing and laughing at my blue cap, asking if my mamaw knitted it."

His fingers stilled. He tucked his greasy head below my chin and made sniffling sounds.

I rocked my hips back and forth, encouraging him to continue.

"Ambrose, you looked wonderful. I'm sure of it. Now, please resume your—"

"You have not begun to hear the worst of it..."

Ambrose palmed my exposed breast and jiggled it absentmindedly.

I twisted my head to the side, unable to bear another second of his stank breath or sob story. My eyes landed on the sheet of parchment that lay next to my discarded dress. I squinted and tried to make out the list Ethens had pressed into my hand earlier.

"Ambrose! Listen to me. You have until the count of three to do what I say."

"Pardon?" He ceased his sniffles and stilled his hand.

"You will fuck me now, and if you can't do it right, I will find someone who can."

"Hmmm?"

"You heard me. Your dick exists for me to fuck, and you are my, my..." I craned my neck and squinted my eyes, trying desperately to make out the word. "Flirty? No. Oh! *Dirty* cock sucking whore!"

Ambrose moved his hand to my hip and rolled me unceremoniously onto my side. I felt him shift as he undid the laces of his pants and felt his glorious length fall against the cleft of my backside. He ran his warm tip between my legs, coating his arousal in my wetness. I lifted my top leg, reached between my thighs, and pressed his erection tightly against my vulva. My hips acted of their own accord, rubbing my most sensitive parts against his length while my hand squeezed and stroked him.

"Cato gloated about being the first to take your ass. You should have seen the smile on his face. He is besotted with this dimply rear of yours." Ambrose chuckled and smacked my cheek playfully.

"Don't touch my butt. It hurts." I squinted at the parchment again. "Do you want me to step on your cock or-or abuse your ass? If not, you'd best obey my command."

Creator's tits, how does Ethens say these things with a straight face?

"As you wish, *wifey.*"

He pressed his chest against my back and reached between my legs to part me further. "I have wanted to practice this position for when you are breeding. When I take you this way, I will be able to run my hands over your big, round belly—feel my strong son growing inside while I fuck his mother. Gods, I am getting teary-eyed."

I jerked my hips backward, and a deep groan rose from my chest.

"Breeding kink? Eira, I would not have thought it of you."

His head nudged at my entrance, and he began to work himself in and out in short strokes.

"Cato and I could take turns filling you... place wagers on who could get a babe in you the quickest. I suppose it would be a long wait for the result of who won though, and—"

"Shut up! Shut up—I, ohhh... Your slut pussy... uh, penis is mine. Do you hear me, bitch? Don't you dare fucking stop."

He thrust his hips upward and wrapped his arm around me to apply pressure on my pelvic bone.

"Oh, Goddess... fucking otherwordly cock..."

"Your Black Bear appreciates the compliment." He tossed his head back and literally cackled while he thrust. "Eira, I am afraid we have an audience at the window. Should I—"

I pushed my hips back rhythmically, meeting his every plunge, too far gone to care.

"Let them watch. Show them why you're the heir of Monwyn." I squeezed my eyes closed and relished the pounding of his hips against mine. I could feel the soft fluff of his pubic hair on my rear and the slap of his heavy sack against my thigh. The contrasting sensations drove me to near madness.

"Aye, aye," he whispered into my ear. "That's what the pirates say."

His skilled fingers found my clitoris, and he slipped the little gem between his knuckles and teased it, rocking up and down with full-fingered strokes. It felt like he was caressing my every nerve ending—my skin tingled and tightened. My breasts bounced along to the rhythm he set, and my swollen passage gripped him tightly. I writhed against him, greedily seeking my own release. I clenched my muscles around his hardness, and my climax began to build.

"Ahoy, little harpy, you've flooded your galley."

Idiot. Glorious idiot.

I shuddered and tossed my head back against his shoulder. My body wrenched, and with each of the decadent spasms that twisted through me, I dissolved into a pool of delight. My cries and his groans filled the empty room, forming a raw and sensual duet.

Ambrose yanked my leg back over his thigh. He thrust into me in smooth, long strokes, building in speed and intensity until he purred his release in my ear.

"You *do* come beautifully."

"And you satiate me quite well, *Commander*," I panted, still trying to catch my breath.

"Oh, I am well aware. And, if I may offer some notes, I think perhaps the dominant role is not for you. It just... The words were right, but the verve of your delivery fell flat."

CHAPTER 36

FUCKING MARVELOUS

Today. Today I would Join.

A team of servants descended upon me well before the sun came up. I'd been waiting all night for the light to stream into the small, colorful window above my bed, and like clockwork, the moment the rays hit the far wall, the palace woke.

Allaine had brushed my hair out and dressed me in a light gown before placing a semi-sheer veil over my face. No one was supposed to see me before the ceremony, barring Ambrose and the priests. She led me to a carriage that waited in front of the palace. The shining black vehicle with gold metal accents was stuffed to the gills with boxes and chests—so many that I was its sole passenger. It had taken Allaine and I, plus three additional servants, a full day to pack up every bit of finery and piece of clothing required for the various Joining traditions. Luckily, the task helped me focus on something other than my anxiety.

As we sped along, the townspeople lined up on either side of the road and cheered and tossed dried flowers and herbs into the horse's path. It wasn't every day that a Scion-Prince and Troth Joined, and many in the crowd had donned their best clothing and were straightening up their little ones caps and coats as the carriage rolled by.

Our destination was Cordillaria's famed Mhontarai temple—which I would've liked to have seen—but the servants rushed me in through its back entrance and left me in the chamber in which I now stood. The room was dark, lit only by the red tapers that surrounded a small pool of water sunk into the ground. The chamber's floor was the same sparkling white tile as in the palace, but the basin itself was a mosaic of blue, white, and red.

"Water is shapeless. It has no form, and yet, the Goddess's gift provides health and healing like the balm of a proper wife to a husband."

The priest emerged from a darkened doorway. He wore a cap of red and at least three layers of matching vestments that were heavily embroidered with golden floss. Two priestesses bearing baskets followed closely behind him.

"The woman enters the pool to purify."

I folded my hands, fighting the urge to wring my fingers. This felt too much like the last rite I was involved in.

The priest shot me a pointed look and repeated himself, "The woman *enters* the pool."

Right. You're the woman, Eira.

I walked to the small well and stepped down the stairs along its side. Why I ever assumed this would be *just* a foot washing was beyond me. Funny how personal experience could influence one's thoughts—there was no way in the nether this would have happened in Nortia. We would have had to chip the ice from the water and have a healer on standby.

As my hips sank into the warmed pool, my skirts lifted and floated on the water's surface. Its billowing and highly impractical sleeves weighed my arms down as they absorbed the fluid that smelled of mint and rose. Bits of herbs and dried petals drifted in the current and stuck to the gold trim sewn to my blue hems. A priestess came toward me and, without words, handed me a squishy sea sponge and a jar of soap.

"The husband is the water, a strong current, a mighty river..."

Ambrose appeared in the doorway.

The sight of his body stole my breath. Long muscular legs, lean hips, and a chest hewn by a master sculptor came together and formed what had to be Ærta's most stunning human. I didn't know where to look. How many times had I seen him naked, in both sexual encounters and otherwise?

Despite being the one in clothing, I found myself vulnerable in his supremely confident presence. His shining black hair, unbound and free, flowed around his shoulders as he walked forward. The faintest smile spread across his mouth when his eyes found mine.

My heart lurched, and I cast my lashes down. Heat bloomed over my cheeks and chest.

What a gift he was.

What a gift he was giving me—his name, his future.

Ambrose stepped down the stairs and waded in. The water lapped around his upper thighs and left the rest of him on display. I kept my gaze riveted on the dark expanse of hair that covered his chest and couldn't meet his eyes when his hands settled around my waist.

He leaned down, laying his forehead against my own.

"… the wife is the tea, adding flavor to an otherwise bland existence. She is the fruit that transforms nothingness to wine—she is the call that pulls the ocean's tide," the priest said, repeating Cato's words. I was not prepared for the sting. But there was sweetness in it, too—two incredible men had chosen me, and, though our dynamic was not simple, we were a family.

The second priestess paced around the bath's rim while pouring a pink liquid into the water. Ambrose closed his eyes and breathed deeply as an earthy aroma I couldn't place enveloped us.

"The woman cleanses her husband and cares for him, as she shall their hearth and home."

Ambrose sank to his knees and then took the jar of cleanser from my hand, removing the lid and offering up its contents. I dipped my fingers into the yellow cream and a wave of nostalgia hit me so strongly that tears flowed freely from my eyes before I even realized why.

Lemon and vanilla, the scent my mother had made for me before I left for Verus.

Her face floated into my mind's eye—the silver-streaked hair, her green eyes. And there was my father wrapping his massive arms around her, his bushy beard near engulfing the lower half of her face as he planted a kiss on her cheek.

"Ambrose? I… th-thank you," I sobbed. I flung my arms around him and hugged his head to my chest.

"Cat told me." Strong arms wrapped around my bottom, and we swayed back and forth in the water, just existing with each other while I cried. "I am truly sorry they cannot be here today. I would see their daughter happy."

He tilted his face up and I pressed my lips to his, sinking further into the tender intimacy. His parted beneath mine. My tongue shyly met his, tasting him as if it were our first time.

A lover's kiss.

I bathed us both with my tears.

Pulling away, I worked the soap into a lather, ran the sponge around his shoulders, and then kissed his swollen lips again. I scrubbed the scent into his hair, taking special care to massage the crown of his head and his temples. When he closed his eyes, falling under the spell of my touch, I feathered my lips over the corners of his mouth.

"Rinse," I whispered.

Ambrose dunked under the water and then stood—the god Derros emerging from the sea.

"I have impeccable balance." He raised one leg, and I slathered him from toe to thigh.

"Impressive for one built like a mountain troll," I murmured.

"I will remember you said—"

"Emerge, clean, untouched, and purified. Your old lives are washed away." The priest's voice rang out.

"Highness Ambrose," the priestess said, "follow me."

Ambrose climbed from the pool, and I watched the water sluice over the pronounced curve of his backside.

"Troth Eira," said the remaining priestess. She offered me a towel at arm's length. "Down this hall, you will find a room for prayer and contemplation. May the Goddess look favorably upon your womb." She motioned me forward and shut the door behind me.

My womb? Still in Monwyn. Lest you forget, Eira, lest you forget.

The short hall was bathed in the soft glow of lamplight, and paintings of the deities hung on both sides. From the ceiling, small bits of malachite and opal dangled from thin golden chains, and the strong scent of burning lavender permeated the air.

"Eira..."

My hand flew to my chest as I stifled a yelp.

"Apologies, wife." Cato stepped into the hallway. He folded his hands behind his back and slowly walked toward me. "I trust no others with your safety today. I will be near you at all times."

He was outfitted in his armor again, encased in black and gold, weapons sheathed at both sides.

"Husband," I whispered.

He halted in front of me, his body a breath away from my own. The wild flips of his hair had been braided in a tight, neat row down the center of his head—his æther-lightened streaks shone brightly amidst the rich browns.

"I am in awe of you. How strong you are. How vital and alive you remain despite the challenges placed at your feet—despite those like myself selfishly making demands upon you."

I circled my arms around his neck, touching the only sliver of skin that showed above the rolled metal edge of his gorget.

"Cato, how are *you* coping with the day? I want to know if you're—"

"Sweetheart, the moment I thought you gone—when your heart slowed—nothing and no one else mattered. Ambrose is a good man, and through him, we are allowed to have us. *Us* is what I value above all."

His gauntleted hands settled on either side of my face as he pressed me back against the wall with his metal-bound chest. He brushed his nose along my jawline.

Then he sniffed me—a long, controlled inhale.

Æther spun in tight coils around my heart.

"You smell like the first time." He chuckled and continued snuffling and sniffing my hair like a puppy dog would. "Is it possible the Goddess knew our story then?"

"I'd say it's probable." I smiled up into the depths of his dark eyes. "Do you think she knows that I long to have your mouth on mine?" I asked, seeking his lips with my own.

"Do you think she is jealous that I worship you far more fervently than I ever have her? Your claim to my soul is absolute—when I leave this world, the only reward I would seek is an eternity in your arms."

"She must hold you in high regard, as she has blessed you for your good deeds."

Cato nipped at the corner of my mouth.

"No, love, I assure you... I have been very, very bad. But when it comes to you, I will *never* repent for my transgressions against her."

A glacier slid down my spine at the intensity of his pronouncement, and I shivered against the cold metal of his armor.

His mouth took possession of mine.

Our tongues teased and intertwined. He sucked my lip into his mouth and moaned low and deep in the back of his throat. This man was my everything—the cause of my most intense pain *and* the healing balm that sustained my spirit.

The lights turned to shade.

Cato twisted and stared at the stilled black flames. His eyes flicked to one lamp and then another.

"This... this is you?"

I nodded sheepishly.

"Fucking marvelous."

His metal-covered hand wrapped around my neck, and his head descended once more.

CHAPTER 37

WEDDING, BEDDING, FRETTING

"**S**uck them in!"

"How do you propose I do that? It's not a stomach, sir; it's a tit, which you clearly forgot I owned when making such a garment."

Trapped in a sea of fabric, I looked up through the dress's bodice and met the angry eyes of Meachum Millanderer. He compressed his lips and whipped his head back angrily, causing his nimbus of curls to sway.

"Squash them! Tuck them in, roll them up, or I will slice them clean off. Stuff that lard into this masterpiece or I swear—"

I shot my arm up and snatched at his face, but he moved as quickly as the viper he was. He grabbed my hand, thrust it through the armhole, and then reached in and hauled a single boob through the garment's tight waist.

"Another reason I prefer men. Leonard, fix this now!"

From inside the gown, I felt a breeze as the big and burly Leonard joined me under my skirts.

"I swear to the Goddess—*ouch*—you son of a—" I kicked out as the whole-ass human, who had stuffed himself in the dress, grabbed my other breast and mashed it inch by painful inch to meet its skyward-facing sister.

"Meachum, grab it. Grab the bag and heave!" Another hand pawed at me, and, like the sun bursting through cloud cover, my head shot through the gown's neckline.

In the most rapid emotional about-face I'd ever witnessed, tears gathered in the eyes of the smaller tailor.

"Ohhhhh! Leonard! Have you ever seen anything more beautiful?" A high-pitched squeal pierced my ears—Meachum was as excited as a sow given her slop.

"Shoo! Shoooo! Let me out!" Leonard, still trapped in the confines of my heavy skirts, flailed about and slapped at my thighs.

"Uncover your eyes, you overly dramatic whining walrus." I smacked his head through the layers of teal silk and feathers and backed up until his hunkered body emerged.

Meachum went to his partner, helped him stand, and they embraced while staring at me like two doting uncles.

"Lady Troth, you are a vision," said Leonard, who rested his gray beard on his husband's curl-topped head.

I smoothed my hands down the gown's bodice and shifted to see my reflection in the floor-length mirror that stood in the dressing room's corner.

It *was* a work of art.

The wide neckline sat on the points of my shoulders, curved around my breasts, and dipped to my sternum in a low *V*. What I had thought to be feathers were, in actuality, bundles of looped gold floss that mimicked the resplendent outline of the eye of a peacock's plume. They covered the tight bodice and then became more sparse where my hips flared out and continued down to the floor. I twisted in the mirror and watched as the gown's fabric shifted from dark green to teal to blue. What a phenomenon that a weaver's hands could produce such finery.

"Gentlemen, out!" Allaine pounded her fist on the countertop. "I have only minutes to retouch her face and hair!"

I sat, and my maid went to work.

"Allaine, I want to apologize again for pressuring you into the concert. I just—"

"Stop apologizing. You were in the wrong. You promised to do better. Time will tell. Now face forward!"

After the fifteenth knock on the door, wherein groups of servants presented me gifts from every end of the continent, Allaine turned from maid to lioness.

"Stay the fuck out, I tell you!" She shoved a monk who had come offering us refreshment and drink back over the threshold. "And Protector! Do your job better! If one more person makes it through that door, I will sew your mouth shut with thread and needle!" she screamed.

With the tailors gone and Allaine's threats making their way around the temple, the room finally quieted.

"You look amazing." She packed up her bag of paints and combs, rested her shoulder against the nearest wall, and stared at me through the mirror. "The diadem will go on last. Sit there and think peaceful thoughts while I—"

A knock sounded at the door.

"Never fucking mind!" Allaine shouted. She hurled her bag into an open chest, marched across the room, and threw open the door. "WHAT?"

Imella stood in the entryway.

She'd come.

Wrapped in a cloak of grey, with her hair wound tightly about her head in a braided coronet, she entered the room. Hughes, thankfully, had been able to convey the importance of my missive.

"And who have they sent to disturb us now?"

"Allaine," I interrupted in a tone that was soft but firm.

"No, Eira! I have had enough. Woman, scurry back to whatever nether hole you crawled from and—"

"This is Imella of Taleer, Queen of Monwyn."

My maid snapped her head in my direction and then looked back at Imella.

"She's going down." I lunged, but Hughes, who stood behind his queen, beat me to her and lowered her to the ground. "She'll come back to us in a moment."

"Eira, daughter, I received your most urgent missive."

"Yes, I-thank-I..." I burst into earsplitting sobs. "I n-needed you." Tears streamed down my face, and I couldn't catch my breath.

She crossed the rug-strewn floor, a calm and steady presence.

"All my lovely lambs cried on their special days." Imella produced a pile of linen squares from deep within her pocket.

"Th-thank you. I just miss my m-mother so much, and Ambrose, he needs you here too."

"Oh, sweet child, I know she would tell you how beautiful you are." Imella wrapped her sturdy arms around my shoulders, and I laid my head on her ample chest. "She would hug you close and speak of the pride she feels. She would tell you about your papa, who would be standing outside beaming between bouts of bittersweet tears."

My own tears soaked through her woolen garment. The flood walls opened, and I couldn't manage to close them on my own. Imella held me and smoothed her hand along my back, making little comforting cooing noises.

What was it about a Joining that made you need your people? And how did those without parents, or those who were estranged from their loved ones, cope? At least I knew my mother was out there with my father, who loved her like no other.

The thought brought me a semblance of peace.

"Imella, I will do my best by them... I promise you, they are the most important of..."

Hughes moved to the entryway and placed his ear against the door. His hand went to the hilt of the blade at his hip.

A roar like that of an aggrieved polar bear thundered from beyond the hallway, followed by a series of heavy thumps.

Imella shifted and placed herself directly in my path, blocking me from view.

The door cracked.

"I'll wait no longer!"

It closed, cutting off the voice.

That voice.

Hughes pulled his knife and took up a defensive position, standing at the ready.

The door popped open again, but an armored hand gripped its edge, keeping it from opening fully. The sounds of the scuffle intensified.

"Settle, she-demon! All must be searched before—"

"—mule-headed mongrel! Jackass of a snollygoster!"

The door swept wide, and Hughes took a single step back.

"Another gift for you, Troth Solnna," said Cato flatly. His body filled the doorway, but his hips thrust forward as he was clearly being kicked from the other side. The perpetrator's hand shot out between his chest and arm, curled into a ball, and punched, catching him in the chin.

Cato sighed and swatted the flailing hand away from his face.

"My girl, are you in there? Move Tomwyn—fucking Cadommongus or whatever you're called—move your beast's body from my path!"

Nan.

My Nan.

"Protector, move!" I pitched myself toward him and grabbed the hand that flapped between his armored limbs. I pulled, and she pushed until Cato stumbled aside and I was in her arms. "Goddess above, Goddess, mother..."

My knees buckled.

"Now, pup, my sweet girl, dry up. Nan's here, lovey, I'm here."

My weeping began anew.

"How di-did you leave Verus so early? How did..." I sagged to the floor, no longer able to stand. "I'm so sorry, Nan, I should have—I sh-should have done more to..." My sobs cut off my words.

"That brute, Caddywampus, wrote and convinced the Mantle to shorten my tenure by a few weeks. He rode through the night to retrieve me from Colpass." Nan kneeled to the ground and hugged me tight, squeezing me into her cozy chest. "Your Nan would fight ghoulies and ghosts to be by your side."

I was safe.

She was safe.

"I would've been here sooner, but we ran into a hiccup. I was off that horse and on the damned marauder, like a wolf to his dinner, I was. The Protector scarcely made it out of the saddle before I had the miscreant pinned." Nan punched the air and dodged an imaginary attacker.

I glanced at Cato, who stood guarding the doorway. The muscle of his jaw flickered non-stop beneath his beard.

"The *miscreant* was Bem, my personal man, and we were yards from the palace."

"Bah!"

Nan mopped at my face with the hem of her dress and then peered around the room. Her eyes landed on the queen, who was fanning her hand in front of Allaine's face.

"And who are you?" Nan questioned.

"I am called Imella."

Nan nodded her head and reached out.

"Toss me a linen, Imella; she's gone to snot."

After a solid half-hour of intermittent beaming and blubbering, I was able to carry on a conversation and *mostly* rely on my wobbly legs. The shock to my system had been profound and my æther coursed and buzzed through my chest, spinning wildly to my limbs, which made me overly warm and slightly dizzy.

I sat in the chair and stared at Nan, while sipping a glass of cool water. She had clearly lost weight since we'd parted. Her sparkling black dress hung loosely around her middle, and the skin under her chin sagged just slightly—and she was the most beautiful thing in the room. I was perfectly content to sit and listen as she and Imella chatted back and forth about the state of the continent. I didn't want her out of my sight—she made my eyes too happy.

"Nan, Imella." Their heads turned in unison. "I have a request."

Both nodded up and down, and looked at me with serious expressions.

"Walk me down the aisle. Together."

Imella's mouth fell open.

"It's not wise, Eira. I am a stain on Monwyn's history, and to place a Nortian representative in such a prominent role in the ceremony—the political message could be catastrophic."

Nan squared her shoulders and sat up straight.

"You're sure this is what you want? Your Nan never minds ruffling fur, but sweet one, be sure."

I glanced between the two women, weighing my emotional needs against their collective wisdom.

"It is. I'm positive."

"And you realize your name will be synonymous with scandal, yes?" Imella asked.

"If my father can't be my escort, an emissary and a queen will surely suffice—Ambrose needs his mother today, just as much as I do."

I looked around the room, and my eyes landed on the parcel I sought.

"Allaine, bring the box with the red tie, the one from Ambrose's room…"

My poor maid, when she had come to, she had pressed herself against the far wall and remained there as if glued to the stone.

"Allaine?" I repeated myself.

Her round eyes shifted back and forth, and with a quick nod, she wordlessly complied. I removed the ribbon and set the box on the table.

Imella's dark eyes shimmered. "Daughter, I am…" She reached in and lifted out her wedding mantle, the one she and Ambrose had played with when he was a boy, the one she'd worn when she walked the very same aisle I would shortly traverse.

"I found it tucked away in the back of his closet." I took the sand-hued cape and shook it out, letting it fall to the ground. Though it bore the marks of age and a spot where it looked like a sticky hand had settled, it was still a piece of art. A multi-tonal golden sunburst had been appliquéd on its back, its pointed rays running the length of the garment.

"I want my children—your grandchildren—to know their lineage. Wear it, please."

Imella ran her fingers over the citrines that made up the center of the sun and stared off into her memories.

"No, daughter, *you* will wear the mantle as I walk by your side." She stood with some difficulty and began to unbutton her cloak. I assisted her by removing the bulky woolen garment from her shoulders. Underneath, she wore a tightly pleated skirt of muted yellow and cream. A wide cloth belt decorated with gold and silver tassels hung from her wide hips. "It is difficult to entirely give up one's culture, even in a place as frigid as Monwyn. In my former kingdom, the mother would have bared her breasts at a Joining, in remembrance of the time spent nourishing the little one she was giving away, but today I will—"

"Imella, do it. What can they do to you? You've been shunned and scorned, and if you wish to walk in as a mother of Taleer I implore you to do so."

She moved to the mirror and gazed at her reflection.

"I am not as I once was, and the years have taken their toll. Besides which, I'd freeze." Her wrinkled face broke into a wide smile.

"You are a handsome woman, Imella," Nan said, "and in this crowd, there will be many a refugee's grandchild—we all remember the sacrifice your people made."

Imella twisted the large central bead of one of the dozens of necklaces at her throat. Some clung high up on her neck, others dipped low past her breasts. I recognized topaz, amethyst, and turquoise, all separated by gold and silver beads.

She closed her eyes and bowed her head—no doubt saying a silent prayer. With age-spotted hands, she unbound her braid and let her hair fall. Her tresses reached past her hips, silver at her crown, then fading to brown and finally solid black.

"From the moment he first lay on my chest, Ambrose was my own. He has suffered the stares and the feelings of isolation. I received the same welcome when I came to Monwyn from my homeland. I will not humiliate him further with my nudity." Her hands went to her shoulders. With a few flicks of her fingers, the sleeves that had been buttoned to her top fell away. She slipped the natural-colored linen from her arms.

A blue sun, shaped like the one on her mantle, had been inked into both her biceps. Its rays reached her elbows. Within each of its points were letters and glyphs, reminiscent of the ones that wrapped around Cato's thigh. A line of crenellations, likely representing the plateaus of Taleer, circled her forearm.

She was glorious—a woman who spilled out of the boundaries set for her—a woman whose body was a work of art, a tribute to her home and her ancestors.

A knock sounded at the door and Cato poked his head in. He took in the scene before him.

"Your idea, I presume?" he said when his gaze settled on mine. "You look lovely, Mama."

"Thank you, Kitty Cat." Imella smiled at her son and made her way over to the Diadem of Taleer. She ran her fingers across its elegant arch. "I've never seen it. It is as marvelous as the storytellers said."

"You should wear it, Imella. You're the last of its line."

Imella picked up the crown and held it up to the light. Its diamonds sparkled and flared.

"I disagree, daughter; its line is just beginning."

She brought the crown to where I stood and placed the magnificent jewel atop my head. The strands of gems that fell from its temples covered my shorn sides, and its arched center stood proudly above my forehead. In my dark hair, it shone like stars in the midnight sky.

I breathed deeply and centered myself. I wouldn't walk this path alone.

"Ladies, it is time," Cato said from the doorway.

Seeing her chance, Allaine rushed out the door.

"Kitten, assist Eira with the mantle. Nan, shall we?"

"Indeed." Nan winked her silvery eye at me. "Are those two still dippin' the wick?" she whispered as they walked through the threshold, arm in arm.

The door closed.

"I only thought I knew beauty." Cato lifted the mantle from the table and draped it over my shoulders. He pinned the first golden brooch to my shoulder and then the next, before he circled me slowly. "I have never had cause to look forward to the next year, and now... now I am inspired to write poems and love songs. Would you like to hear one?" He slipped an arm over my shoulder and rested his hand in the middle of my chest.

"Mmhmm."

Cato's lips wandered up the column of my neck and skimmed across the lobe of my ear.

"Eyes the color of an angry ocean... My heart, oh how it plummets, when she wraps her legs around me... and snow settles on my summit."

I smacked my hands over my mouth and snorted.

"Do your lady parts quiver at my words?" He whipped me around and lifted my chin with the tip of his finger. "Are you overcome by my artistry—primed to throw yourself upon me? Would you reach down my back plate and scratch this fucking poison plant rash?"

"Cato?" I giggled. I squeezed my fingers between his gambeson and armor and tried to relieve his inflamed and itchy skin.

"What?"

"Stick to knitting, love." I stretched up on my toes and sought his mouth, but he pulled away with a wry smile.

"Nalbinding, wife. Get it right."

Chapter 38

Here We Go!

"Troth Solnna, Obligate of Ærta, Chosen Daughter, present yourself," the herald cried.

My stomach knotted painfully.

I may have been a partially trained Troth, but as I stared at the closed doors in front of me, all of my emotions threatened to bubble up and spill over the surface. The guards smacked the butts of their spears on the ground, and the sound jolted me from a series of anxious thoughts.

Nan slid her hand through my arm.

"Say the word, my girl, and we'll tear out of here like two thieves on the run."

I smiled at her reassuringly.

"This is the life I choose, for better or for worse."

The doors swung inward and my breath caught.

The temple's sanctuary was a monument built on the collective dreams of the devout. The ceiling arched high, and its supporting beams crisscrossed, forming a massive star at its center. Every tile that lay between the beams had been gilded and polished to such brightness that you could see the reflections of the crowd shifting on their feet below. The top quarter of the chamber walls were painted Monwyn blue, and mountainscapes and moons were stenciled onto its surface. White marble with gold and tan veins covered the lower portion of the walls and floors.

It's how I imagined the cradle—the Goddess's home beyond the stars—looked.

Nan pulled her hand away, but I held onto it tightly.

I turned back to Imella and offered her my other. As she stepped forward and wove her fingers between my own, murmurs and startled gasps echoed around the room.

"Let them talk. Let them spread the tale beyond the kingdoms and across the great ocean," I said in a volume meant to carry.

I leveled my gaze and felt Allaine at my back, straightening the mantle that trailed the ground. The diadem rested on my head, its weight a reminder of the seriousness of the commitment I was making today.

I took a step.

Cato's footfalls synced with mine as his sabaton-clad feet rattled against the stone floor.

I was surrounded—bolstered by an abundance of love.

I closed my eyes and began writing my next chapter.

The guests and courtiers lowered their heads or bowed—they were an ocean of greens, purples, and blues. Men and women were present in equal numbers for once.

Almost immediately, I caught Cinden's eye. She smiled so hard that her nose wrinkled up. I wondered if she would be able to view the ceremony as far away as she'd been placed—the multitude of dignitaries and representatives had special seating in the front rows. She tugged on Ethens's hand in her excitement, and he inclined his head in my direction as a crooked smile drew up on his mouth.

We came to the end of the aisle, and Nan and Imella went to stand amid the throng. The red-robed priest motioned me forward to stand between a group of priestesses whose faces were obscured behind veils of shimmering garnet cloth. Two of them came forward and took my hands into their gloved palms.

Cato walked around me and took up his position behind an empty throne.

"His Royal Highness Prince Ambrose, escorted by His Most Blessed Father, the revered Majesty of Monwyn! Bow down in the presence of your king!"

The masses sank to their knees—whether citizens of this kingdom or another.

At the back of the temple, the two oversized men embraced.

Burchard pulled back and placed his hands on Ambrose's shoulders. Dark, round-framed glasses perched on his nose, and as he clapped Ambrose on his chest, they slid down his straight bridge. I could see he'd recovered well from whatever poison he'd ingested. There was no tremor in his hands—his movements were steady. He spoke to his child at length, as if there weren't hundreds of kneeling guests waiting for the ceremony to begin.

With all the confidence of a king himself, Ambrose turned and faced the dais.

Holy. Fuck.

The priestesses tightened their grasps. Whether to keep me from bolting or just to keep me upright, I didn't know, but as my heart thundered in my chest, I appreciated both contingencies.

I should have known he'd be the most beautiful boy at the ball.

Ambrose wore a long coat of blue-black silk. Its collar stood tall around his neck, and fine, winged dragons were gold-worked across his chest and cuffs. From his left shoulder hung a long cape of black. It had been secured with—I squinted my eyes—my cherished three-whale brooch.

"Oh, Ambrose," I whispered. Yet another reminder of the tender blessing that was my odd but endearing new family.

A hand shot out in front of my face, startling the stars out of me. Cato dangled a fresh linen square in front of me, just in time for my never-ending supply of tears to spill.

The priestesses released me momentarily and gave me the chance to blot my cheeks, but quickly both hands returned to mine.

"Mama?"

I blinked away the blurriness until my eyes cleared once again.

Ambrose stopped in his tracks. The tears glittering in his green eyes as he drew his mother into his arms told me he appreciated his gift at least as much as I treasured mine.

"Imella, is that—he-hello, beloved—it has been so very long." The king approached his wife, reaching for her with both arms before dropping them to his sides.

Ambrose released Imella but kept his hands placed protectively on her shoulders.

"Burchard, you look well." She raised her arm in a formal gesture and offered him her hand.

Like he was cradling the most precious of gems, he held the tips of her fingers and brought them to his lips.

"Come home?" he implored in a soft tone.

She shook her head. "Not yet."

He nodded once, but was hesitant to let her go.

Imella turned and took her place, standing next to my Nan, who was positively glowing with pride. No doubt, Ambrose's nod to Nortia had won him a lifetime in her good graces.

The king walked through the ranks of the holy men and women and sat upon his throne.

That's when I saw him—the Primus-King.

The æther gathered itself into a tight knot in my stomach, and the shadows leapt into my periphery.

Ambrose eclipsed my vision, cutting off the view of my enemy.

His new piercing, a gold hoop with a sapphire embedded in its center, stood out on the top of his ear, even surrounded as it was by the pale aquamarines sewn into his black braid. His eyes swept over me from head to toe, and he nodded approvingly. The subtle praise made me uncharacteristically shy. I dropped my gaze to the floor, only to have soft fingers firmly direct my chin back up.

"Flesh is a wife's gift to her husband—to be cherished by him, to be nurtured by the sustenance he provides."

Pretty sure his servants provide me sustenance, but whatever.

The two hands that held me pressed me forward and then lifted my arms, offering me to Ambrose. He clasped both of my hands between his big palms. He dipped down and kissed my thumbs. Behind him, Allaine wept openly into her linen. Greggen watched her from a few yards away.

"The husband will love his wife's body as he loves his own. The wife will submit to his authority, and in return, he will lead her down the path of the Goddess's love."

He'd rather submit to me. I giggled to myself.

"Ambrose, you have won your consort. Love her wholly and without restraint."

Ambrose nodded his head, and again, tears pooled in the inner corners of his crinkling eyes.

"Bear witness now, all those loyal to the Goddess; may she watch over us from her throne of glory. Ambrose, do you swear yourself to be the protector and provider for this woman?"

"Yes. I do." His confident response carried throughout the room.

"Will you bless her body with strong and virtuous offspring?"

"I will."

"Do you vow to guide her through her faults and weaknesses, elevate her amongst those of the fairer sex, and to punish her in accordance with the laws of this kingdom if she strays from the one to whom she is bound?"

Ambrose placed his hand on my clavicle, and his fingers settled over my heart. "I do."

"As the Goddess as my witness—as Lord Gammond sits on his throne at her side—you are Joined."

"I say nothing?" I asked, looking around at the people who surrounded me. "How repulsively fucking Mon—"

A thunderous applause drowned out my voice.

With one arm, my *husband* hauled me securely to his side while waving to the crowd with his other. To my surprise and utter delight, he signaled the servants around the room to unleash a flurry of dried petals and white feathers from their cleverly concealed nets on the ceiling. It was a slow-motion blizzard of beauty.

Ambrose dropped to his knees and held my hands up to his lips.

And I... I stared into the eyes of the Primus-King.

He had thin, graying hair, and his eyes were partially hidden by the drooping skin above them. His crown of silver leaves stood prominently on his brow, evoking the tree sigil of Gaea. He inclined his head and smiled at me like a grandfather would his granddaughter—kind and deeply caring. The entirety of his top row of teeth were capped in gold and set with malachite, his ears were studded with the same. He placed his fingertips on his forehead and then held his hands in my direction, offering his blessing.

I bowed my head as a feather skimmed my cheek.

I've acknowledged your existence—now go back home.

Ambrose rose, blocking him again, thank Derros. I wanted to see no more of him.

"Kiss! Kiss her!"

"Do not make us wait!"

"Use your tongue!"

I leaned into Ambrose's chest and lowered my head demurely—like I wasn't the same woman who'd begged him to filth-fuck me on the floor last night.

His hands came to my cheeks, and his mouth crushed down on mine. I could feel our shared breath. He growled low in his throat, and I tilted my head, urging him on. He wasn't my growler, but it was effective all the same. The burgeoning arousal at the front of his pants lay against my stomach, and he dropped a hand to my rear and ground himself against me. My hips responded, rocking against him, seeking the pleasure they knew he would bring.

The crowd screamed its approval, and more flowers, and now coins, rained down upon us. His tongue darted past my lips, and I hummed into his mouth. He pulled back, titled my chin up, and lazily outlined my jaw with his fingertip.

"A pity neither the Scholar nor healer could attend today. May they long be an example to those who *dare* lay a hand upon *my* wife."

"Ambrose!"

He shut the door and stalked toward me with his lips pressed into a severe line.

"Look, Eira, I will be the first to admit that my second assassination did not go as smoothly as it could have, but when Cat walked me through the plans—"

My jaw dropped to the floor.

Ambrose walked right up and popped me on the bottom of my chin.

"What the fuck is wrong with you two? I'd not been permanently injured; they were assholes who needed to learn but..."

"They fucked up... and then they found out. How the nether did you get this on?" Ambrose yanked at the bodice of my gown, trying in vain to rip it in half.

"What are you...? Quit it. Get your murderer's paws off me." I batted away the big beast's fingers and retreated to the far side of the room.

"Let us fornicate, wife. You heard the priest. He said bow down—acquiesce to your husband's demands. Let me *nourish* you." He threw his head back and laughed loudly into the chamber where we were meant to reflect and pray.

Life-size paintings of Mossius healing the sick and caring for the injured surrounded us. The room's sole piece of furniture was an upholstered kneeler in the center of the room, useful for when the elderly or infirm needed stability while praying.

"I think not. We need to discuss—"

"You discuss, and I will sample your slit."

He closed the distance, snatched me around the waist and force-walked me to the kneeler.

"Ambrose! Ambrose, listen to—"

My stomach hit its padded arm, knocking the wind from my lungs. My skirts flew over my head, and I found myself in the dark.

"Listen to *me*, Eira." His palm cracked against my backside.

"Ambrose, I swear to the Goddess!"

"Are you listening?" He paused. "Answer me, wife."

Another swift and sharp smack stung my other cheek.

"Yes, I'm fucking listening. Now cut it out!"

His hands found the lacing of my underwear. I kicked back, but he caught my foot between his knees.

"Tonight. The bedding. It is *my* domain. Do you hear me? *I* will perform for our audience, and *you* will submit to me." Ambrose gripped my thighs and pulled them apart, spreading me wide. "I am going to fuck each and every one of your exquisite openings, and I want our audience to pray to their gods, begging them to be blessed with a refractory period as short as my own. Do you understand?"

"How am I supposed to respond when I'm being coerced by an admitted executioner?"

"'Yes, husband,' will suffice." He went to his knees and turned, planting his back against my thighs. His head tilted backward and his braid brushed the inside of my leg as his warm lips met mine. "Mmmm, you should consider granting me more access to your treasure trove. Once a week is fine for someone as robust as myself, but Eira, your slit is never satisfied." He drew a finger through my wetness and dipped the tip of it into my entrance. "I would savor you for hours, *wife*." His tongue slid across my clitoris, and my hips rolled against his mouth. "Something about my *wife's* slickness satisfies me like no other dick or cunt has before."

He could talk me to orgasm, I swear. My nails dug into the pillowed top of the kneeler as Ambrose squeezed my rear in his hands.

"Should I allow you to come before the big show?"

He sucked my clitoris into his mouth and tugged me hard. I bent my knees to receive him.

"Thank Derros, Cat has yet to stretch you out with that monstrosity between his legs. No matter though, I can tighten you up with seeded and split cucumber if need arises. When it warms to your temperature, my dick cannot tell the difference."

One finger, and then a second, slid into me.

"Am-Ambrose that is the most unhinged, unhygienic—"

"*Husband*. That is what you call me now."

He worked his fingers free and slowly reintroduced them while teasing me with the tip of his tongue. My legs began to shake.

"Husband," I breathed.

Ambrose stopped moving. He removed his delicious fingers and smacked his lips together in a sound of total satisfaction. I shuddered as he popped a kiss on my inner thigh.

"Now that I've brought you to the edge, you will respond even *more* beautifully this evening. Straighten up, you meet with the women—and then... I dance."

Chapter 39

DEAR GODS

"**N**o, I'm absolutely dreading it!" I chuckled.

"My girl, just imagine him up there like some virulent beastie, ready to snatch you up and ravish you in his cold, dark lair."

"I'm trying, but all I can imagine is him trotting toward me in shaggy fur pants."

Back at the palace, my womenfolk and I sat around the balcony, sipping warmed wine.

"My Ambrose would be beautiful dressed as a troll." Imella nodded curtly. "His father came to me, dancing in the guise of a double-humped camel." She giggled sedately behind her hand and recoiled in alarm when Richelle squealed out a laugh so shrill that Maihon could have heard it from his cottage.

"A camel! Di-did he chew cud and lope around on all fours? I would have died—just died!" The Troth drank deeply from her cup. Above its rim, her cheeks stood out bright red against her pale skin.

"He had no cud. His dance was one of sultry seduction, and..." Imella paused, and her shoulders began to bounce up and down. "Well, yes. Yes, he was on all fours, and his humps kept shifting back toward his bottom. But he was mine, and so I endured it." The queen raised her glass and clinked it against Nan's. "I raked my nails down my inner arm to keep from scream-laughing and later told him the lines were from the claws of a puppy. Have any of you seen a canine in the palace? No? There were none then either."

Feminine laughter surrounded me. It lifted my spirits like nothing had in weeks.

Though Imella would be leaving and heading back to Colpass this very night, I was touched that she joined both our new Troth, a very reluctant Allaine, and myself in Nan's impromptu Brooding.

"In Nortia, this is how we send a lady to her marriage bed. You've been to several, Eira, but were too young to really take part. The young'uns watch the littles while the matrons give advice to the bride." Nan speared a floret of oil-and-herb-marinated cauliflower and popped it in her mouth. "It's not like when I married my Kennt, bless his soul. We were more discerning with whom we plied our trade... if you get my meaning. Eira here, she's been plying since she fell for Gen Makerly, the butcher's daughter."

"Nan! Hush now. It wasn't like I was hawking my wares on the docks."

Nan reached over and patted me smartly on the hand.

"Don't fear your libido, love. Like I said, that was ages ago. It's much better now. I think it's healthy to thresh the wheat before you grind it. Take a turn in the cabbages..."

"Bam-bam in the yam-yam," Imella supplied. "Partake in gland-to-gland combat."

Richelle doubled over onto Cinden's lap, cackling. Allaine sang loudly to herself as she held one hand over an ear and squashed the other into her shoulder, drowning out the salacious conversation. A concerned servant popped his head in the doorway. His eyes were wide, and the color of his cheeks rivaled Richelle's. My guess was that this was his first Brooding, too. I waved him away with a smile.

"And what of you, Cinden? Do you look forward to your Joining? It's a shame you requested such a small ceremony, but I understand. Gaeans see these things in a different light—never about the fanfare, always about the reverence," said Imella.

"Ethens seems to be a good man. We'll make a solid match." Cinden sat up straight, looking like the perfect pixie, an innocent smile waving across her face.

"Do you have questions, my dear, about the wedding night?"

Cinden shook her head, and her long pink coils bobbed around her face and shoulders.

"No, but thank you. Though I remain pure, we were counseled on the ways of procreation in Gaea and then again at Verus."

"Procreation? Little lamb, take a piece of advice from your Nan. Learn how to get off... and then worry about babes."

A deep bronze blush swept its way across Cinden's cheeks.

Phenomenal Troth.

"She's not wrong, you know. It took a while for Burchard and I to get it right. Like yourself, I had not known physical love—"

"Truly?" I interrupted. "But in Taleer, the matriarchy ruled supreme. Was it not allowed?"

"It wasn't for princesses. Not for this one, anyhow. We knew that if there was a chance to rebuild, it was paramount that we cemented relationships with other kingdoms. Gaea and Monwyn *required* my purity. Solnna has always supported us, so good relations existed there without the need for mixing our bloodlines, and, no offense, daughter Eira, but the thought of stepping a single toe into the frozen north still sends me into a mild panic." Imella cinched her cloak around her neck and snuggled down into her lap blanket, emphasizing her point.

"None taken. It's not the easiest of places to exist."

Through the glass-paned doors, I saw Cato walk into the common room, heading in our direction.

"Ladies, if you will come with me, I will escort you to the—"

"Protector, you would make an alluring capybara." Richelle, who was deep in her drink, stood and ran her finger along his metal spaulder. "Would you like to engage in... the *dance*?"

Cato's brows hit his hairline, and his eyes flicked to mine.

"How much has she consumed?"

"How much can *you* consume?" Richelle fired back. She burst into another round of loud laughter and I joined in, enjoying Cato's obvious discomfort.

I stood and pressed a glass of water into her hands as the women prepared to leave.

"Protector, may I have a moment with Nan?"

Cato sighed heavily, but walked to the balcony's edge and peered over its half-wall. He raised his hand and tapped the tip of his pointer finger against his thumb and then the middle of his palm, signaling something or other to his watchmen.

"You have fourteen minutes."

The women filed out, their good-natured banter filling the air as they left.

"Thank you, *my* Protector." I smiled up into his warm eyes, astounded by the intensity of my feelings for him.

Cato winked and blew a little kiss.

I watched him go. There was nowhere I'd rather be than beside him, but I was content with the knowledge he was near.

Nan, who busied herself stacking dishes, waved me over to her side.

"Sit with me, pup. Rest your head on poor old Nan's shoulder."

I sat down beside her.

"You are neither poor nor old, Nan." I leaned my arm against hers, tilted my head, and breathed her in. I could almost smell the pure scent of freshly fallen snow.

"The time apart aged me fifteen years, I'm afraid. And there's more reason than one that these nights are called Broodings—you've flown right out from underwing, little chick."

We sat in silence, hand in hand.

The wind howled through the columns that surrounded us, and little droplets of rain pittered on their stone surfaces.

"She isn't a conjurer, is she?" I whispered, my voice barely audible to my own ears.

Nan plucked an errant leaf from the pleats of the gown I'd changed into.

"Your momma? No, but her grandmother had the gift."

I nodded, relishing the velvety texture of Nan's skin on my cheek.

"Is she safe?" I sank low and laid my head in her lap, not caring a bit if I crushed my dress or dislodged the hundreds of tiny, ruby barrettes pinned throughout my hair.

"Ulltan is with her, and never forget *her* strength."

"And my father? Do you know?"

Nan inhaled deeply through her nose and let the air flow steadily from her mouth. My stomach clenched tightly. I was worried both that I *would* and *would not* get an answer.

"She never said a word about who your sire might be, and I never asked."

"What *do* you know, Nan? What *can* you tell me? This has been like seeing the fish beneath the ice and never once catching a bite." The wetness from my eyes ran across my nose and then my temple. I was beyond thankful that the Goddess had delivered Nan to me safely, but the continued frustration surrounding my identity was crushing.

"I know this, my girl: you are deeply loved. Even by those whom you have yet to meet. Your very existence gives hope to those who keep the old ways."

I sat up and placed my palms on top of her hand.

"There are others?"

"Of course. The Solnnans have kept the conjurers safe for the last century, but our mission—your mother's and mine, and Kan's and Gotwig's—was to keep you from the hands of that Primus-King and move south. That was until you were born Troth. The Nortian king kept strict tabs on your whereabouts at all times—though Primus Adrielle was able to outwit him on some accounts. You are actually twenty and seven, love, not twenty and five. We held your fourth birthday three times, trying to buy a couple of years. Anyway, we had no choice but to sink our roots into the snow." Nan reached for her glass and sipped on it thoughtfully. "The Primus-King won't know of your abilities. It's your blood he seeks."

I didn't even blink at the differing age—I'd been dealt more significant surprises, just in the last week.

"So Cult Mossius can study me, no doubt."

"No, Eira, so that he may keep himself bound to the earth." She drained the berry-colored wine and set the glass on the table. "He would dose himself from your mother, and when she began to refuse and fight back, it would end with him bleeding her into bowls and forcing himself upon her when he ingested too mu—"

I put my hand over Nan's mouth, but it didn't stop her words from playing over and over in my head. They settled deeply in that place, where my mind tried to negotiate what was and was not reality.

My hands shook. I watched them vibrate as my shadows demanded that their presence be known. The lamps blinked to shade, and an eerie yelp, followed by a chorus of howls, took up in the back fields.

"Do you think he sleeps soundly within these walls?" The smell of burning wood inundated my nostrils as I fought to maintain control. "How dare he smile at me through his predator's teeth?" I heard shouts in the distance, but ignored them.

Nan seized both of my wrists and held them tight.

"Calm yourself at once. Your mother didn't survive for you to know evil. She is *love*, Eira. Despite it all... she is love."

A knock came all too soon.

"They can wait another minute—all of Ærta can fucking wait."

The door opened and then closed. Cato's armor clacked and clanged as he moved near.

"I'm so sorry, my girl, that we couldn't make it easier—that our plan failed. But every night I drop to my knees and thank the Goddess for the Monwyn that delivered you to safety."

I clung to her then and kissed her cheeks, just to feel her warmth.

"Nan, I can't stand the thought of you going back to Nortia."

"Oh, child, they'll have to pry this polar bear from her cub. It may take some coin passing palms, but I mean to stay in this mess of a land. You hear that, Protector? Think you can handle two Nortians on this godsforsaken rock you call home?"

"Can I interest you in Colpass? Or perhaps you would enjoy an ocean view just two days' ride from here?" Cato replied.

"Truly? Are you *truly* still bedding this loaf of dry toast?" Nan pointed directly at Cato's chest.

I blinked up at my companion and gave no reply.

"Nether it all, you never did settle on simple."

How do you prepare for the moment when a seven-foot, shaggy-legged minotaur is to prance out and perform a dance routine choreographed solely for your benefit? Gods forbid I laugh—Viktos strike me dead!

I sat in a chair, smack dab in the middle of the grand salon. Foreign courtiers and dignitaries filled the space behind and beside me. Over my left shoulder were the wives and ladies, and on my right, the men of Monwyn—there must have been an open invitation to bear witness to my mortification as I believe the entirety of the capital's population was in attendance.

Burchard and the Primus-King of Gaea sat against an elaborately painted front wall, both perched on their wooden thrones. I tried to focus on the Gaean to distract me from my pre-dance anxiety, but when I looked at him, I choked on a rage so profound that my clustering æther made it difficult to breathe.

Fine. I'm fine.

Daughter, enjoy your evening. Do not give a single thought to the fool at my side. But perhaps think less loudly. Ambrose looks adorable in his horns and shag.

Get out of my head. I narrowed my eyes at Papa Burchard, but he just looked away, all pleasant-like, at the monarch seated beside him.

I tapped my foot on the floor. I needed this to happen quickly and end just as fast. Ambrose could stick it in at the bedding, and we'd call it a day.

"Eira!" Richelle popped up over my shoulder, and I nearly jumped out of my skin. She pressed a glass into my hand.

"Drink up. It will calm your nerves."

"I'm fine!" I snapped.

"Mmhmm, so the priest has asked you twice now if you were ready to begin."

Sure enough, when I looked up, the red-capped clergyman was staring at me, his face pinched and irritated. I took a long glug of the pungent liquid, wincing as it burned a path down my throat.

"You want to trade places?" Richelle asked while waggling her thin brows.

"No, I'm resolute. All in. Gird your loins, Chelle. My husband's dance will inspire the conception of a full army of Monwyn babes—an infantry," I slurred. The liquid courage hit my limbs, numbing my fingers and face. My head felt slow—a little too slow.

"She's ready!" The bubbly little Troth yelled to the crowd.

The cheering began. They whooped, hollered, and let out sharp whistles.

Richelle flounced to her seat and flopped down so hard that her short legs sailed into the air.

The priest stepped to the middle of the room and raised his arms, spreading his expensive silks wide.

"When the Goddess birthed the world and filled it with her divine creations, she took care to sculpt the animals according to natural principles; she made the males more powerful than the female, more robust, and in many cases more beautiful," he intoned.

Fucking Monwyn.

"The peacock's plumes are vibrant and bold, and the peahen's muted and humble. The male robin's breast is a noble red, and the female's bosom a demure and mellow orange. Why... even the elephant seal has a nose ten times the size of its diminutive mate's—"

"—and looks like a freshly shit turd," I supplied, teetering in my seat. Rumbles of laughter drowned out whatever he said next. "I swear on Josa's blessed taint—Richelle, what the nether's in this?" I peered into the cup and smiled at the tiny, polka-dotted narwhal that lounged on its rim.

Richelle's ear-piercing squeal shot through my head like an arrow through a... I couldn't remember what I was thinking.

"Like the spiders who defend our vegetation and the bees who guide their mates to the most advantageous sources of pollen, so do the males of Monwyn dance in tribute to the splendor their masculinity affords them. The lamps." On the priest's signal, the room went dark.

"If he's dressed as an evil, blade-butted bumblebee, I'll..."

The drummers entered solemnly. Their mallets fell in time with their steps.

My heart took up their tempo.

They walked straight toward me, beating out a death march.

A foot from my chair, they split off to both sides, revealing a group of men painted gold from their heads to their toes. White loincloths, barely wide enough to conceal their penises, brushed the tops of their sandaled feet. They pulled two lengths of chain behind them, and the metal scraped rhythmically across the floor, lending an eerie mix to the haunting sound of the drums.

Three feet. Five feet. Ten feet of chain must have trailed by until—

Ambrose emerged.

He was glorious.

He was absolutely fucking stunning.

Each chain ended in a metal cuff that bound his wrists. Upon his head, two horns of black twisted up from his unbound mane that hung in loose rings around his shoulders and back. A shimmering indigo powder dusted his face, which highlighted and emphasized the planes of his divinely sculpted nose. His eyes, sharply outlined in black kohl, made him look animalistic, sinister, even. His lips were painted a deep burgundy, the same shade as the cloak that covered his body. As I watched him move forward, my fear and excitement melted together, transforming into a powerful fascination. I was transported to the fiery mountains of Hain, the birthplace of the bull-headed minotaurs.

The crowd dissolved into smoke around me. In this existence, there was only me... and bull Ambrose. He was my man and I was his woman, bound to him by the—

"Ambrose... who the fuck is that?"

An enchantress emerged from behind *my* spouse. She was resplendent as the sun, painted gold as the men had been. Beaten gold strands had even been twisted in her blonde—

"Is that the whore?" I looked around the room, demanding an answer, but the swirling smoke didn't respond. "I think that's the whore," I murmured, squinting and leaning forward.

Yes, that was her... Cato's whore. She who pumps dicks and scorns young love. And now, she was after my other man.

I would kill her.

I would slap around those golden titties, and spread those long legs, and—she produced a whip from behind her back and cracked it violently against the floor.

"Don't touch him, siren!" I tried to move, but my legs were like sand.

The cadence intensified. Chains rattled, and those awful drums pounded—unrelenting.

My euphoria tilted toward hysteria.

Ambrose's arms were yanked violently, again and again. They were hurting him. I had to save my husband!

He threw back his head and let out a deafening roar.

The bitch unfurled her whip again.

"Harlot, hear me!" I strained my eyes and clenched my jaw, attempting to shoot the shadows into her chest.

Nothing.

"I will eviscerate you with my brain—my brain!" I bared my teeth as a group of men blared their brass horns in my face.

Ambrose roared again, and, shocked by the sound, the golden men covered their ears, dropping the chains to the floor.

Bull Ambrose flung back his arms, and his cloak went flying.

So, too, did my vagina.

Like a harpoon slicing through water, æther shot to my core. An impassioned groan escaped my throat involuntarily. My hips ground against my chair, searching to release the pulsing pleasure that had taken over me.

I looked to the sky.

"Divine Goddess, Mother of Creation. I will bear this man's offspring if only to make the other mothers weep at their plain-faced spawn."

A mixture of indigo and dark blue powders defined his chiseled torso. His pecs were the size of platters, and my mouth watered at that disgustingly sharp V that pointed straight down to his—

"He's got the bull's limb!" A feminine voice blasted during a musical lull.

"Yes, observant friend, he does," I agreed in a voice gone thick.

There were no fluffy pants, as I had feared. Instead, tight, slick brown fur encased his legs and flared out over the tops of his gold-booted feet.

Ambrose whipped his arms around his head and let the chains fly.

His muscles rippled and expanded as he took down his would-be slavers. One by one, they fell to the ground, kicking out in their death throes.

"Feast upon their bodies, Black Bear! Rip their intestines from their assholes and wear their spleens upon your horns." Like a bull ready to charge, I stamped my foot on the ground. "No! The whore! Watch the whore!"

I could hardly stand it.

She raised her gleaming arm into the air, and the crescendo of drums reached its zenith.

The whip shot out and struck.

Ambrose reacted, twisting his body and hiding behind his arm as if it were a shield.

With a crack, the whip spiraled around his forearm from elbow to wrist. He wrenched it from the horrid woman's fingers and, with a well-placed kick, sent her rolling to the ground.

"Yes, love! Gore her. Right through the apples!" I clapped and shouted along with the audience as tears of relief pooled in the corners of my eyes.

Ambrose snapped his head in my direction and fell to the ground on all fours.

He was primed to lope.

"Dear gods..."

His knee slid out to his side and he lowered himself slowly until he was lying flat on his stomach. Palms on the floor, he pulled himself forward, reaching for me. When he was close enough that I could see the sweat beading on his body, he flexed his back and rose onto his hands, like a serpent ready to strike. Starting at his chest and then rolling through his hips, he moved like an ocean wave—like a dark, sensual god of the sea.

Oh my.

He repeated the sequence and moved forward, all the while staring into my eyes. He fucked that floor so beautifully that I grew jealous of the shine he left as he polished it to a sheen. Delicious little pulses of energy shot down through my passage, and I chewed on my lip as I watched him, overtly aware of how my nipples stiffened against the barely-there fabric of my low-necked gown.

When he was a leg's length away, he bent low, tipped his horn under my skirts, and then tossed them high enough to reveal my lower thighs. I spread my legs for him, inviting him to take me as he pleased.

I wanted my husband.

I could hear the audience panting and feel their collective sighs.

Monwyn's largest army *would* be conceived this night.

Ambrose stood slowly, allowing me to take in his god's body at my leisure. He skimmed his hands up his chest and neck and then reached above his head while he rotated his pliant hips in my face. When he turned away, his ass at eye level, I was struck by the magnificence of his meaty cheeks. A would-be lover once told me my ass reminded them of a juicy ham. I never understood that it was a compliment... until now.

I reached up and knocked.

Ambrose spun back around, grabbed the back of my chair, and straddled my thighs. My mouth went bone dry. He bent low and brought his deeply red lips a whisper away from my own.

"Husband, I would like sex now."

CHAPTER 40

THE BEDDING

The finale left steam rolling off my skin.

Ambrose had gyrated those gorgeous hips in my face, and then guided the tips of my fingers into his fur pants. After teasing me, he'd twisted around and yanked them so low that he revealed the curve of his glorious ass.

I was profoundly aroused—ferocious-horny. Like, the kind of turned-on where you needed to fuck something hard and fast, then roll over and read a good book—no cuddling, no frippery, just pull my hair, let me have it, and then leave me be.

But no, the godsdamned ceremony continued.

This fucking priest had just circled me for the fifth time while sprinkling water on my feet. I was this close to pulling off my belt and demanding *he* scratch my itch.

I fanned my face, but it did nothing to satisfy my appetites. My passage was so swollen that just pressing my thighs together made me feel wonderfully wicked—maybe if I squeezed them hard enough, he'd think he'd pontificated me to pleasure. *Hmmm.*

I crossed my arms over my chest to cover the pointed evidence of my ardor.

"You will enter the room purified and greet those who share the burden of bearing witness. Those who perform this sacred right will look upon your body and confirm that you have become woman—are you quite well? You seem to be—"

"I'm fine," I purred out, taking a step in his direction. I bit my bottom lip until I tasted blood. The combination of arousal and the desire to commit genocidal levels of atrocity against such a devout misogynist was proving too much to bear.

"Child of Ærta, enter. You will soon be made whole." I followed the priest, fastening my eyes on the train of his robe. *As I am made whole. Horseshit.* This was even more ridiculous than the idea of someone *taking* your purity. Fucking stupid Monwyn.

"Have you been made a man minister? Would you like to be?" I muttered under my breath.

We walked two flights of stairs and entered a room on the fifth floor of the palace's central tower.

"Two hundred years of Monwyn kings have been conceived upon this very bed."

Gross. Gross, gross, gross. I shuffled around the priest and looked into the dimly lit chamber. The walls, like the temple's sanctuary, were made to resemble the night sky—moons and stars shone brightly against a dark backdrop and glimmered in the light of the fire in the room's hearth.

Alright, it wasn't nasty. The bedclothes did, in fact, look to be freshly laundered.

The marital bed was not the huge monstrosity I imagined—not a sex altar at all—but it certainly was the focal point of the space. It was constructed of dark, cherry-red wood and had ornately carved posts on the sides of its tall headboard. At the foot of the bed, nearly transparent silk panels hung from the ceiling to the floor. The curtain was so thin that it floated in the air as we passed by. It was laughable that they even pretended to afford the newly joined any privacy at all.

The priest went to the bed and lifted his arms, no doubt praying to the Goddess that the ancient mattress would once again survive the weight of another big-headed Monwyn man. He dipped his hands in the vessel he carried and flicked droplets over the top of the heavily embroidered blanket. He then tipped the silver bowl to his lips and drank deeply.

I prayed he choked.

While he interceded on behalf of my not-yet-a-woman's vagina, I flipped the curtain out of my way and went to meet my audience.

Ah, yes, and there they all were. Funny how, barring Septimus, not a single one of them could meet my eye.

"Gentlemen, how kind of you to bear the *burden* of watching me absolutely destroy the most legendary cock in Monwyn."

Primus Thierry's mouth bobbed up and down.

Lemder sneered.

Dumail just stood there, looking down his proud nose.

Ethens. Ethens smiled a lecher's smile and subtly ran his hands down the crotch of his pants. *Filthy.*

I nodded at each in turn.

Both Ærtan kings sat in wooden chairs while the rest stood. The dignitaries of Solnna and the Elderman of Gaea had also gained admittance and kept watch over the monarchs, standing directly behind them. The Elderman held a platter of snacks right at the level of his king's mouth.

"Have you sampled them, Elderman? What a tragedy it would be if poison found its way into the kitchen," I said, blinking my lashes innocently.

"Yes, ma'am. I ha-have," he sputtered out while lowering his eyes. "Like any other citizen, we would lay our lives down for our leader."

"How many lives already, I wonder?"

"Consort, you are most lovely," the Primus-King said, entirely nonplussed.

I bent low. I wanted to see him up close, to look into his murderer's eyes… to see if their hue matched my own.

There came a quick knock, and Dumail leaned over and opened the door to his right.

I forgot my mission in an instant.

"Protector, thank you for joining us. The occasion of my woman-making is most auspicious indeed. Is this your first time in the deflowering chamber?"

Cato, ever the soldier, slipped into the room and stood with his back to the door. His pulse fluttered at the base of his neck, and his jaw was set so firmly that I feared for his molars. He settled his haughty gaze on my face, and it was all I could do not to saunter over and run my fingers down his magnificent chest—squeeze those pecs in my hands, rake my nails down his broad back.

"The view will be as fine as the vintage, don't you think, Lemder?" Dumail said as the Solnnans passed around a bottle of wine. Lemder punched Ethens's shoulder playfully, and Dumail clinked his glass merrily against the Primus-King's.

Disgusting. This was no sacred tradition. This was a spectacle meant to harden the dicks of those who should be at home, honoring the commitments they made to their wives or rocking their babes in their arms.

Already, Lemder and Dumail's pants tightened, and one of the dignitaries kept adjusting himself.

Cato coughed hard and then breathed in so deeply that the fine coat he wore gaped and pulled at the buttons.

I didn't want this for him.

He wasn't a Troth. He wasn't schooled in the art of accepting degradation in the name of a bigger plan—well, not since birth.

"Consort, lay upon the bed," the priest intoned in a voice most reverent.

"Do I get naked first?" I tossed my head over my shoulder and addressed him directly. "I think I should get naked."

Primus Thierry choked on his drink and shuffled back and forth, clearly looking for a way to exit.

"Consort, you *will*—"

"Calm down, cleric. I thought the question was relevant." I hissed back. "And I would like to make introductions before my defiling. If they are to bear witness to my miraculous transformation into womanhood, the least they can do is engage in the art of dialogue."

The priest flung out his arm, but I evaded his grasp easily.

"Ohhh, reverend, I really, really, wouldn't. Ambrose is quite clear in his dislike of others putting their paws upon his possessions. I don't think even your holy status would absolve you."

I turned to face my audience and caught a flash of pride in Cato's eyes. The little fire that sent his gold flecks dancing was all the fuel I needed to continue my foray into righteous dissent.

"Gentlemen." My hands went to the belt at my waist. I made quick work of unbuckling the knotwork-embellished closure. "I am sure when your daughters are Joined, you will revel in the knowledge that your closest friends will be vying for a spot to watch them be spread wide." I glared at Dumail. "Such pride in knowing she *can take it well*, am I right?"

Another bout of phlegmy coughing began, and Primus Thierry started to walk about, bumping into the other men. He ran headlong into the back wall.

"Gracious," said Burchard. "See him out, Catommandus."

"Majesty, he is needed to verify the—"

"I am here. I am the king. There is no need to worry."

Cato opened the door and snagged Thierry by his collar. He pushed the Primus into the hands of Bem, who was outside, standing guard.

"Obviously ill of mind and broken of body, and yet, he is still found competent enough to lead. Not the best for a kingdom, I would wager."

Dumail sneered. "Troth are always so willing to—"

"Papa Burchard... most *noble* King of Gaea." It took everything I had to not spit on the seated monarchs. "Did you come here to see these?" I snapped open the sides of the merlot-colored gown and let my breasts spill out.

Burchard smacked his hands over his darkened spectacles while the other king leered.

"This is... not for my eyes, I am afraid."

"Is it not, Papa?" I shook my shoulders and let my boobs bounce around.

"No, daughter, it certainly is not. Catommandus, you are in charge."

Take that piece of shit Gaean with you! With a loud slap of his hands against his thighs, Burchard hauled himself to his feet.

"Brother king, let us adjourn—this is sport for younger men."

Sport? Papa, you better prepare yourself for our next conversation. The king shrugged and then gathered his long blue robes and made his way to the door.

"May you long be fertile..." The Gaean monarch stood and bowed, his rheumy eyes lingering far too long on my chest. "I would request an audience before the Gaean contingent leaves in the morn."

"Make your request to my husband, Majesty." I stared at him, eyes locked onto his, despite my mind screaming to look away.

He inclined his head and bared his netherdemon's smile, one that I would have considered beautiful on anyone else. As he turned, the light from the nearest lamp illuminated his face.

My breath caught.

Brown.

His eyes were dark brown. Gotwig's were blue. My mother's, green.

Cato had likened my eyes to an angry ocean, a swirling mix of green and gray-blue.

The æther danced in my chest, somersaulting around my heart. A whole mountain of despair lifted from my shoulders.

The kings made their exit, and the dignitaries and Elderman filed out behind them.

I laughed aloud. The knowledge of my paternity could remain a sweet secret that just my heart would know.

Dumail looked at me askance.

I turned my attention to the tall fellow.

"My Black Bear fucks with the verve of twelve men. I imagine it is *he* whom most of you are here to see. Will you be taking notes on how to conceive strapping *sons?*"

Starting from the bottom and working its way up, Dumail's neck went cherry red. His eyes narrowed to shards.

I bent over and let my breasts dangle while I scratched roughly at my legs.

"Apologies. I once danced nude with the most decent of people in all Ærta. They live high up in the mountains, where *real* men break their backs at work. I'm not sure if it was the bathtubs or the boys that gave me this rash, but it's stuck around for some time." I shrugged the open gown off my shoulders and let it drop around my feet.

"Yeesh!" Dumail covered his mouth and took a step back.

I followed his retreat, scratching my backside at him aggressively until *his* back hit the wall. I turned and shimmied my ass up and down Dumail's legs.

"Gods almighty, do-do not touch me, diseased harlot—"

"Watch yourself, Troth," Cato growled out. I snapped my head in his direction and pinned him with a stare. He clawed at the back of his own itchy neck.

"Oh, but now you *have* to stay, Protector."

I couldn't help myself. I pulled the strings at my hips and spread my legs. When my underwear fell off, I swung them around my head and let them fly, hitting Cato square in his face. With two fingers, he plucked them from his shoulder and let them fall unceremoniously to the ground.

"He will have crotch rot in his eyeballs come morning," Lemder muttered. "Revolting, absolutely filthy!"

"Given your extracurriculars, I figured you'd have plenty of experience with this kind of thing. Do you have a go-to cream or poultice you prefer?"

Dumail smacked Lemder on the back and tossed his head toward the door.

And then there were two.

"Who is guarding my brother, Protector?" Septimus asked while keeping his eyes on mine.

"Levaunt," Cato replied.

Without another word, Septimus stood and walked himself to the door. *That's not how I thought that would go.*

"Lord Ethens, sit." I pointed to the vacant chair, but he didn't move. "It's poison plant, for Goddess's sake."

He crossed his arms and studied me intently while he sauntered to the empty seat. Still unsure, he lowered himself and sat.

"I am a woman of my word... mostly. Uncross your legs."

The corners of Ethens's nose flared, and his nondescript eyes narrowed, but he lowered his foot to the ground and parted his legs. I sank to the floor and knee-walked forward, squeezing myself between his thighs.

Cato cleared his throat. *My poor darling.*

"Sir, I'm famished and find myself in the mood for... *cake.*" I looked up through my lashes and drew out the last word.

Ethens shivered from his shoulders to his toes. I leaned forward and sat my breasts on his knees, opening my mouth wide.

"Ahem... *Ahem!*" It was the priest this time. "This is highly irregular, highly—"

Ethens plucked a morsel from the tray that sat in the chair beside his. He slipped a piece of ambrosia into my mouth—white-chocolate cream, covered in a tart raspberry sauce. I wrapped my lips around his digits and sucked while I let my eyes drift shut.

Mmmm.

"Mmmm," Ethens groaned. His wine-bottle-sized erection lifted my left breast two inches in the air. Goddess be with Cinden when she mounted this man's meat.

"Now get the fuck out of here and go convince your almost-wife to give up the goods."

Ethens nearly blacked my eye as he stood.

"You are, as ever, sublime." He bowed quickly and walked to the door.

As the final courtier left, I shook my fist in victory.

"Eira, where the fuck is my audience?"

Right.

Husband.

Chapter 41

PAPA

"**G**odsdammit! Will I never get what I want? Is this what I signed on to? A life where only *your* will matters?"

I pushed off of the chair in front of me and stood, feeling less triumphant than I had moments before. Ambrose drifted dejectedly over to the bed and sat on its edge. He tossed one leg over the other and propped his chin in his hand.

"You do the cruelest things." His eyes misted over.

"Ambrose." I went to him quickly and reached out, but he batted my hands away. "Husband, I'll make it up to you." He tossed his hair over his shoulder and pressed his lips tightly.

"No, just... here." He pulled open his matching robe and revealed his freshly oiled torso. "I was going to rip the gown from your body, but you spoiled that too. Just a moment." Ambrose ran his hand down his chest, collecting the shining slickness. He wrapped his hand around his penis and began stroking.

Oh, gods. At half mast, my mouth watered—it literally watered. The pent-up lust rushed through my veins like an avalanche cascading down a mountainside. He palmed himself hard, up and down, and tucked the bottom corner of his lip into his mouth while he worked. The defined muscles of his stomach rippled in the lamplight.

"Come here, wife. It's hard enough," he said in a morose tone.

"Ambrose, let us try to make the best of it." I stepped forward, and he grabbed my hips, spun me around, and pulled me backward. Cato became my view. He stood as stone in the corner, and though he hid the emotions on his face, there was no hiding what pressed against his pants.

"Sit," Ambrose commanded.

I bent my knees, and he sheathed himself in one long stroke.

"Thank fuck." My head dropped back. I tried to rise up and impale myself again, but Ambrose placed his hands on my hips and held firm.

"Do you see it, good priest? Do you need to measure my level of penetration? I am a solid seven inches deep. With the way her cavern feels, I could go eight, possibly nine, if she'd stop clenching." Ambrose bucked his hips below me. "Cut it out."

"God-Godsdamn," I panted.

"It... I believe that satisfies the—Protector, do you witness and verify the—"

"Yes." Cato spat. "*Leave.*"

The priest tossed his hands into the air, and Ambrose tossed my rear up and off of his cock. With an exaggerated huff, the robed man exited, slamming the door behind himself.

Cato scrubbed his face with his hands.

"This is not what we had discussed, Eira." Ambrose rolled away and curled himself into a tight ball. "This is not at all what I had imagined."

"Ambrose..." He looked over his shoulder, and ice shards shot from his eyes. "*Husband,*" I corrected. He nodded his head up and down and then scrunched his pillow under his neck. "I need to apologize to you. I acted out of my own wants and didn't take into consideration how this would affect you."

Oh Goddess, is that a sniffle?

I crawled onto the bed, and my knees sank into the million-year-old mattress.

"Your dance was one of the most enchanting sights I have ever seen." I snuggled up to his toned back and snuck my arm around his waist. There was a little smudge of blue near the hairline at the back of his neck, and somehow, seeing it there, made me feel ten times as awful as I already did.

Silence.

"What if I told you that not *only* did you inspire the basest of my womanly urges... but you also made me so undeniably jealous that I contemplated ending the lives of your captors?"

I heard Cato shuffling around the room and tried looking over my shoulder, but Ambrose reached for my arm and tucked it against his chest.

"Eira," Ambrose asked.

"Yes?"

"On the floor, you called me 'love'... Did you mean it?"

I pressed my cheek to his back and closed my eyes. I didn't remember saying it but—

The door opened.

"Cato, don't you dare walk out! Please don't leave me." I pulled free from Ambrose and flung myself around.

"I was giving Bem permission to leave his post. Are you—did something happen, Eira?"

I shook my head, unable to speak.

His eyes darkened as he crossed the floor.

"Tell me," Cato said as he kneeled down on one knee and took my palm between his warm hands.

"If someone has hurt you, wife, you *will* tell us." Ambrose sat up behind me and settled a big hand on my stomach.

"Not me, no, I just—"

Cato pushed up off his knees and captured my chin between his fingers.

"Then what?"

I leaned into his touch, closed my eyes, and breathed in his scent. I placed my palm on his hand, savoring the rough texture of his skin against my cheek.

"I can't take another person leaving when I just got Nan back."

Cato's brows knit together.

"I'm constantly swinging back and forth between feeling safe and adrift… between knowing I am a powerful being and feeling vulnerable. People have uprooted their homes and changed their life's trajectory for me. Both of you have, and Nan, my parents. And I am hiding in a palace, terrified of the moment she leaves or Ambrose goes on campaign again. Or when you finally face an adversary that…"

Ambrose's lips found my neck. He dotted soft kisses across the top of my shoulder and squeezed me around the middle.

"Do you all know when I felt the safest *and* the freest?"

Cato shook his head while listening to my every word.

"No, and I cannot say I care overly much," Ambrose said between kisses. I rolled my eyes to the ceiling.

"Do you remember the farmstead… that first night, after we'd left the cave? We slept in the back of the old smithy. You smelled so awful I could hardly draw breath, and my feet looked like they'd been mauled by a netherhound. It wasn't the most comfortable of circumstances, but, I think, if I could, I'd give this all up to be there with you again."

"Cry me an ocean, Eira. You Joined with a prince, live in a palace, and have servants for your every whim. And let us not forget the mendy blood."

"Ambrose, I swear to—"

Cato's lips found mine.

His hands were on my face and then running through my hair. Tiny ruby barrettes rained down onto my shoulders and breasts as he crawled onto the bed and pressed me back.

"I would go with you—take you back and rebuild its walls," Cato said.

Ambrose's big body halted Cato's momentum—undeterred, he straddled my legs. His hands went to my breasts as his tongue pushed through my lips.

"How do you stand him? All fuck and no finesse," Ambrose murmured.

Cato ended our kiss and worked his mouth down the column of my neck. He pressed my jaw to the side as he nipped me above my collarbone.

Green eyes met mine—the hazy, lust-filled eyes of my husband.

Ambrose's lips parted slightly, and he dipped his head in question. I ran my fingers down the line of his jaw and stretched my face up in answer. Our lips met. He shifted and slid his hand from my stomach up to my chest. He pulled me back at the same time that Cato pulled me forward.

"I have never—Ambrose, I am not acquainted with the mechanics of another trying to claim my prize." Cato glanced in his brother's direction. He took my hand in his and pressed my palm to his lips. "But I am not leaving until I have had my fill of her."

Ambrose rolled up to his knees and let his robe slide down his arms. He chucked the garment to the floor and began stretching his neck back and forth as he did before heading off to his "regimen."

"Amateurs are often oversensitive. Cato, will you be able to maintain control if I touch her? It is *my* night, after all."

"I will." He nodded curtly. "I have come to terms with that aspect."

"And when you hear her *enjoy* my touch? See her eyes roll back when I taste her?"

Cato's muscles bunched beneath the fabric of his coat and that thin gold ring danced in his dark eyes.

"When she takes *me* into her mouth, presses her sweet fingers into my ass, and I spill myself within her... will I remain your brother?" Cato sat back on his heels and drew soft lines on my thigh while he pondered. "No cunt is worth the loss of our bond," Ambrose said as he placed a hand on Cato's shoulder. "There is a chance she could bring us closer."

For fuck's sake.

"The cunt is close to leaving if she's called 'cunt' again."

Neither of the men paid attention but instead communicated with those subtle cues and movements that I couldn't comprehend.

Cat nodded once, and Ambrose mirrored the action.

"Eira, if I am being honest, the fault of his jealousy lies firmly at *your* feet. What kind of fake wife doesn't make her fake husband comfortable when he enters a room full of carnal possibilities?"

"What? Y-you are going to put his lack of emotional control on me? Not the magical fucking dick-bond between us? Not the—"

"Eira."

"Don't '*Eira*' me, Ambrose."

Ambrose's hand lashed out, catching me around the neck. In the same instant, Cato struck Ambrose's windpipe so hard his head rocked back.

"You call me what?" Ambrose looked down his perfect nose at me.

"Hus-husband," I replied in a thick and shaky voice.

"Mmm, yes you do," he purred.

Cato took deep and controlled breaths. He was coiled so tightly that the veins stood out prominently on his forearms.

"Just testing the boundaries, brother," Ambrose said.

Cato dropped his arm and shook his head rapidly.

Ambrose stretched out on the bed, propping his head up on one hand.

"Now, where was I? Yes, Eira, take Cato by the hand."

Confused, but unwilling to have them at odds again, I did as asked and linked my fingers through Cato's.

"Lead him to the middle of the room and remove his clothing. The Protector has worked hard keeping the palace safe and deserves recognition for his efforts."

Ohhh...

I climbed off the bed and pulled Cato along. He was wearing the coat he'd worn the night I was Assigned to Solnna—navy blue, patterned with gold lions sinking their teeth into their prey. He stared down at me and began to unfasten his buttons.

"Cat, can you not take instruction either? *She* is to undress you. Hands to your sides."

Cato scoffed at Ambrose, but I pushed his hands down and took over the task.

"Let me, husband," I whispered. "Allow me to unwrap *my* prize."

"Fake-husband," Ambrose sang out.

"Shut up."

I made quick work of Cato's buttons and removed his coat. I pulled his linen shirt over his head and then ran my hands up the plane of his stomach and chest. *This* is what I longed for—the broad width of him, the coarse texture of his hair and the softness of his light-copper skin under my palms.

Cato clenched his fists when I ran the tips of my breasts up his ribcage. There was no feeling quite as decadent as my nipples grazing his stomach and then gliding over his chest. The texture, the contrast—I smoothed my fingertip over the deep scar at his shoulder—he was built so perfectly imperfect. I roped my arms around his neck, pulled his head to mine, and kissed the bump at the center of his nose. My tongue slid along the crevice of his lips, and his low hum of approval raised the hair on my arms.

"Pants, Eira, pants... I'd like to get off before dawn," Ambrose said.

I refused to release Cato's mouth, but dropped my hands. I palmed his erection, squeezed its thickness, and then went to his ties. His pants fell to the ground, and so did I when I realized his boots were still on. I pulled at their leather heels and eased them off while Cato made quick work of his underwear.

His hand came to my head.

I opened my mouth to receive him, knowing precisely what he wanted.

The æther sparked and frenzied, having recognized its mate. It sank from my chest to my stomach.

I gripped the base of his arousal and guided him into my mouth until his crown hit the back of my throat. I wouldn't make him wait. I sucked him hard and pulled my head back quickly, sweeping my tongue around his tip on every upstroke. When he glistened, I kept my mouth adhered to his head and ran my fist up and down his length until I tasted his salty response.

"Stop," Ambrose commanded.

"Do not." Cato gritted out. He dug his fingers into my scalp.

"Eira, I will not ask again. Cato, beside me."

"Fine." Like a soldier obeying his superior officer, Cato freed himself from my mouth, marched across the room, and did as he was told. His cock proudly pointed toward his navel, and when he hit the mattress, it bobbed heavily against his stomach.

Holy fuck. Holy actual Goddess-given fuck. My men. My husband's. Both of them.

Behind Cato, Ambrose stared at me, his long, rigid length in his hand.

"Eira, if I bring Cato pleasure—touch him, arouse him further—will you be comfort—"

"Yes. Do it."

Cato's brows rose high as Ambrose's seductive smile spread wide.

"Cato?"

"Not sure," he huffed out. "I am absolutely not sure."

"We will start slow, Cat." Ambrose placed his fingertip in the notch below Cato's throat and he traced a line to his navel.

I was transfixed.

I could hear my breaths and feel them as they circulated through my lungs.

"He's anxious, wife, and under so much strain. He needs something to occupy his mind, and hands—you have just the thing. Place those thick thighs on either side of his head."

I clapped my hands like a fat, happy seal and then climbed up on the bed.

Cato laughed, just a single sharp sound.

"You are like no other, my love."

I straddled his waist and pushed back, teasing the head of him with my heat, before planting a kiss on his chin. Cato's hands came to my waist and directed me up to his chest.

"No. You will face me, Eira, as he delivers the Goddess's kiss," Ambrose said.

I was gonna pass out. I paused, breathing steadily through my nose and slowly out of my mouth. *One... two... three... breathe.*

"Eira, now."

I wasn't even sure who'd said it, but Cato shoved against my rear so hard that I had to move and then twist above him. He grasped the folds of my hips and led me to his face as he groaned against my thighs. His tongue flicked out against my swollen clitoris.

"Oh, gods."

"More. Eira, do not deny me." Cato lapped at my sensitive skin and sucked me into his mouth, moaning deeply. The vibrations made me weak. I could no longer support myself and sank heavily, letting my weight settle.

Ambrose kneeled. His eyes glazed over as he ran his fist up and down his erection.

"First rule of a threesome. Don't *ever* leave a lover out." He pointed to his cock and raised a brow. "Bend. Do your job, wife."

I didn't hesitate. I was in such a state of arousal that I would have done anything he asked. I bent low, bumping Cato's penis with my breasts as I slid Ambrose between my lips. Cato's hips tilted, seeking the friction of my skin.

"Your tongue has become more skilled. Practice will do that."

I traced the thick vein that ran along the bottom of his long cock and then closed my mouth over his firm tip. I sucked him hard, pumping my head steadily, loving the velvety texture of his glossy skin while it slipped between my lips.

Ambrose's hand brushed my face as he reached down past me. I heard Cato's simultaneous groan.

"Now, switch." Ambrose captured my hair and pulled my head back. He slid himself from my mouth slowly, watching every last inch of his cock emerge, and then guided my head to the thickness nudging my breasts. I wrapped my mouth around Cato's crown. Ambrose circled his fingers in a ring below my lips and in unison, we moved down until Cato was completely engulfed.

"Fuck, holy fuck," Cato grunted while thrusting his hips upward. Ambrose pushed against my mouth, and we slowly glided up. "Gods, fucking nether." Together, we stroked him until he gleamed and writhed under our combined touch. "Eira, Ambrose... I..."

"He needs a moment, wife." Ambrose swept his thumb across Cato's divot, collecting his bead of moisture. He smoothed the silky pearl across my bottom lip and bent his head to mine. His warm lips settled on my sticky ones. "Delicious. Now turn around, Eira."

I nodded and crawled off of Cato, and presented my back to Ambrose. He wedged his thighs behind my own and poised his tip at my entrance.

"Sit back slowly, Eira. I will know my wife's passage like I know my own dick."

Ambrose's arms came around me, and his hands weighed each of my breasts. He held them up high.

"Catommandus, show this bounty the attention it deserves."

My walls parted. Ambrose sank so deep into my body that I collapsed, grasping Cato's shoulders for support.

"Does he bring you pleasure, Eira?" Cato asked. "If he doesn't make you see the stars, I will put my fist into his pretty mouth."

"If I show her the stars... will you put your cock there instead?"

My eyes rolled back. Just the thought, just the mere mention...

Cato held my breasts in his hands, admiring my pierced nipple. He bent, rolled it between his lips and then bit down.

"Cato, Ambro—"

His hands came to my face, and his mouth crushed down on mine, capturing the sound. I cradled his arousal as it pushed against my belly.

"Come with me, wife. Take your pleasure from us both." Ambrose increased the pace of his hips, and Cato thrust his tongue deeply, tasting me as he pumped his hips into my hand.

Ambrose slipped his fingers into Cato's hair, and Cato closed his eyes, leaning into the touch—pressing his lips to Ambrose's forearm. My passage contracted, and tears sprang to my eyes.

I was surrounded by love.

The æther siphoned downward and flooded me.

"Ohh... my... gods," Ambrose cried out behind me, shouting as he experienced the æther. I tugged Cato closer and threw my head back against Ambrose's chest, panting loudly as my orgasm flared through me.

"Don't stop, husband, please don't—"

I soared high, and the lamps turned to shade.

Ambrose pulled from my body, his warm streams wetting my thighs.

"Take her, brother."

Cato hoisted me up by the rear and laid back. I sat above him, so incredibly slick from my first release that I sank to his pubic bone with no resistance. The ring of my opening snugged securely around him. The tingling thrill of being filled so completely, so entirely, instantly rekindled my desire, and when Cato's soft moan hit my ears, I was ready to receive my pleasure again.

Ambrose placed his hands below my backside and lifted.

Cato's chest arched. He dug his fingers into the sheets and twisted as Ambrose let me fall.

"So fucking good."

"Spread your legs Cat," Ambrose said.

Cato's eyes popped open.

"Ambrose, you will not—"

"Shut up brother. I'm fucking her ass, not yours—I'm a big man. Move."

Cato's thighs shifted beneath me.

"Ambrose, I'm not sure I—"

"You will enjoy me, Eira. I am no brute—not built like the bull's dick that impaled you prior." His hand swiped the inside of one thigh and then the other.

"Semen is an excellent lubricant," Ambrose murmured into my ear.

Unbridled lust coursed through my veins. The æther dove around my insides when Ambrose spread his essence on the tight flesh of my rear and slowly pressed a finger into me.

"Cato, you will feel me through her walls. Relax... enjoy it."

"Do not tell me what the fuck to do," Cato snapped.

"Eira, lean down."

I did as told and dropped forward. I ran my tongue over Cato's stiffened nipple until I felt Ambrose's tip press against me. He pushed his head past my rectum and then paused, sighing long and loud.

"Cato, I apologize for teasing you. Her ass is so tight I fear the strangulation of my manhood." He slipped himself further into me. "How delicious."

"I need to move. My Gods, I need to move now," I said.

"By all means."

I bounced on my knees and knew the Goddess's grace.

"You like being taken by your men, little harpy?"

I writhed against them, finding myself too full to gain the momentum I craved.

"One of you, move, please," I cried out.

Cato grabbed my hips.

"Your body is perfection, love, accommodating us both so well. I want to hear you moan, sweetheart."

He lifted me up and then thrust his hips home.

"Mmmm, that thick boy feels delightful from the inside. Would you not agree, wife?" My head lolled against Ambrose's chest. He bent and ran his teeth along my neck. "Cato's a biter, I have noticed. Loves to mark his territory. Do you think he will leave his marks on me now?"

The æther surged through me—shooting high up in my chest and then cascading downward in a hot spiral.

The lamps began to flicker between shade and flame.

"Catommandus, slow yourself and let me—"

"My woman gets what she wants, *Your Highness*... and you will take what I give you."

Cato pulled himself from my body.

I could have sobbed.

"On your back, Ambrose. Stay within her and do as *I* fucking say."

Ambrose whipped his arm around my stomach and shifted down. His thighs came under me, and he used his feet to kick my legs out.

"Eira, bear down—make me scream for the creator," Ambrose whispered.

Cato came over me and covered me with his body. He planted his arms beside Ambrose's head and brought his mouth a whisper from my own.

"Shall I mark him love? If you wish it, Eira, I will bind you both to me and never allow you your freedoms."

I couldn't breathe.

My skin turned to flame.

Cato poised himself at my entrance and quirked a brow.

"I will ensnare you profoundly—consume you entirely."

"Take from me, Cat. Take it all."

I lifted my arms over my head and circled them around Ambrose's neck. The æther shifted again and spread from my core to each of my limbs. Sweat trickled between my breasts—I was fevered, burning. Cato pushed his hips forward but paused.

"Eira, tell me if it hurts." He grabbed his erection and slowly forced himself between the walls of my swollen passage, which were made even tighter by the unyielding length in my backside. He grasped my hip with one hand and then drove forward until he was fully embedded.

And then he moved.

Relentlessly, he thrust in and out of me and sent me soaring. The æther flowed between us all—connecting us, surrounding us.

"Harder, Cato. Harder!"

Cato's eyes fluttered shut and then snapped open. He shouted and dug his fingers into my side.

"Your worst. I want your worst!" I screamed. The pressure was mounting in a way I had never felt before—my breasts, my chest, and my mind were all as stimulated as my nerve-filled gem.

Cato snatched my wrist and placed it under his nose. He drew in a breath, and I watched goosebumps break out over his shoulders and biceps. He licked the sensitive flesh beneath my palm and nipped at the skin.

"Do it, love. Let me see your worst."

His eyes seemed to glow when his teeth sank into my skin.

I couldn't move, couldn't thrash. I was paralyzed—a vessel for his pleasure.

Blood smeared across my arm as he thrust into me and rode me like a man gone mad.

The blaze in the hearth jumped from its banks, but Cato paid no attention.

My shadows came, blocking the entirety of my vision.

"There is no one above you, Eira. You are the fount that pours meaning into my existence." Cato threw his head back and roared as he released himself in waves that I could feel pulsing inside me.

"Fuck her, Ambrose."

Ambrose held me tightly and bucked his hips beneath me.

Cato pulled out, but his eyes remained wild. He was still hard as stone, and his chest heaved up and down.

"Open your mouth, brother. Taste." Cato bent my arm back, and Ambrose lapped at my broken skin.

"Cato. I-I..." Ambrose's words ended in a long and low moan. He began quivering beneath me as he rolled his hips against my rear.

"You will come for me again, wife." Cato pressed two fingers into my entrance and coaxed me toward the zenith.

I glanced down at the nodding erection that had yet to soften.

"Cato, enter him. Slake yourself. We are love, all of us together."

He bent low. Ambrose cried out as Cato's mouth slackened. I tilted my head back and kissed Ambrose on the bottom of his chin while trailing my fingers down his neck. Cato's hips rocked against me while he stroked me with his fingers.

I was encapsulated by all that I held dear. Nothing had ever felt so right.

"Fire," muttered Ambrose.

"Let it take you. Her blood is—"

"Cat... Cato. She's fucking burning me." Ambrose tried to sit up and then tried to back away, but Cato grabbed his shoulder and held firm. "Catommandus!"

"You will not retreat," Cato barked.

Brown eyes bore into mine. I ran my fingers through Cato's hair and stretched my neck up to meet him. Our tongues entwined, we sucked and tasted. I pushed my feet off the bed and rode his fingers and Ambrose's cock like it was what nourished me in this life.

"My men," I ground out between clenched teeth. I came hard, pulsing and shaking as it took me. "*Mine.*"

Cato growled into my shoulder and stiffened and spent himself. A look of pure elation spread across his face—eyes reflecting love, lips kiss-swollen. He slowed his hips and pulled back. His soft smile melted my—

Ambrose's palm cracked across Cato's jaw.

"Grab the blanket, get up!"

Spurred into action, Cato leapt, pulled the rumpled blanket from the bed, and ran to stifle the black flames that had taken hold of the rug's edge. He smothered them once, and they turned orange, again, and they extinguished entirely.

"Cato, she burned me." Ambrose brushed his hair back and exposed his neck. An angry red welt ran from his ear to his collarbone. "She got you, too. Did you not feel the sear?" Ambrose fanned his face.

Cato glanced down at his chest and ran his hand over the four marks that began at the juncture of his neck and shoulder and ended at his sternum.

He shrugged.

"Are your eyes—let me see your eyes," I said, panic setting in.

Cato looked at me. Nothing had changed—they were his beautiful dark shade with their hint of gold.

He crossed the room and gathered me into his arms.

"How do you feel?" he asked.

"I feel... I feel sated. Happy."

He smiled sweetly and laid his forehead against mine.

"And you?" I asked.

Cato breathed a calm, controlled breath.

"Inspired. In control again. Decidedly and irrevocably Joined to the most incredible human."

His lips brushed mine.

"And how am I, you ask? Oh, well, let me see." Ambrose wedged his arms in between us. "I am incredibly fucking concerned. The woman I Joined marred my skin, nearly burned down the palace, and after an incredible fuck session, both of my partners seem inclined to ignore me. I require—"

"He requires cuddles. He's a cuddler," I interrupted.

Cato mocked Ambrose, flicking his fingers dismissively.

"I refuse. I barely tolerate him. And we are *not* partners." Cato stood up and looked Ambrose squarely in the eyes. "I did what I did because *she* wanted it."

"Catommandus, how dare you? Have you no shame?" Ambrose barked while searching for his discarded robe.

Cato twisted me around and pressed his chest against my back. His arm slid under mine, and his hand rested firmly between my breasts.

"None. When it comes to Eira... I have no conscience."

Ambrose wrapped his robe around his body and secured it with the belt that I'd discarded from my own ensemble. He disappeared into the connecting room and reemerged with a bowl of steaming water and a pile of linens.

"Cat, an animal like yourself probably doesn't know that aftercare is an essential part of the sensual adventure. Am I right?" Ambrose curled his lip and narrowed his eyes in Cato's direction. "Considering your dismissal of our newly budding relationship, I suppose I do not even have to ask. Eira, sit." Ambrose pointed to the edge of the bed.

Cato's cheek pressed firmly against my own. I made to move, but he held me closer and buried his nose into the crook of my neck.

"Cato, release her at once. She is covered in semen, and your beard is streaked red."

The rumble that came from Cato's chest was feral—unhinged.

Like he controlled the very reactions of my body, my nipples tightened in response.

The hot, wet rag, smacked Cato square in the nose. He jerked back and caught the linen before it fell to the ground, and then proceeded to twist the rectangle into a rope. Ambrose's eyes went wide.

"Cat, I swear to the Goddess if you snap that..."

"Cut it out, both of you. I mate with men, not boys. I'll not have our beautiful experience devolve into a squabble. Ambrose, Cato, sit down now!"

"Yes, mommy." Ambrose caught the corner of his lip between his teeth.

"No sir, absolutely not." I pointed a finger to the middle of his chest and followed him as he sat on the bed. He raked his eyes from the top of my head to the tip of my toes. "That's not going to work for me."

I plopped down into Ambrose's lap, and his arms came around me, dipping a warm rag between my thighs. "Fine. But whether or not *you* deserve the moniker, certainly you will agree that we have finally found... *our* papa."

CHAPTER 42

EVERYTHING IS FINE

Looking back over the course of my life, I couldn't remember a time when I felt calmer and more at peace with myself or the situation I found myself in. I felt such love—an outpouring from the souls that had somehow, through the Goddess's divine grace, intertwined with mine.

My hand rose and fell with Cato's even breaths. I fought the urge to drag my fingers through the dark hair on his chest, knowing that he needed the rest. The Protector never stopped, never took time for himself, while trying to maintain the security of the realm.

Ambrose's arm tightened around my waist. He dipped a wiggling finger into my navel, causing me to scrunch my stomach tightly.

"Thank you, wife, for the most excellent bedding." His mouth settled next to my ear, and he ran his lips up its shell, tickling me with his scraggly morning beard. "It was tip-top."

I snuggled back into Ambrose, relishing the feeling of soft skin over taut muscle.

"Whether he knows it or not, he's a natural sex sovereign. Do you think he will allow us to call him that? Place a crown upon his... head," Ambrose said, keeping his voice to a whisper.

We giggled in unison—a conspirator's laugh. Ambrose swept kisses across my jaw. I turned my head, catching his mouth with mine.

"I think he would launch into a fully detailed diatribe describing exactly how he would render us *both* dead if we did—which honestly makes me want to do it even more."

"Same. And Papa suits him better anyhow." He rolled his hips into my backside, and I pushed up, settling his burgeoning erection between my cheeks. "I appreciate your kisses, wife. And your willingness to explore." Ambrose reached between our bodies and worked his arm up and down. His fingers moved rhythmically against the skin of my lower back as he glided the tip of his arousal through the crevice of my rear.

The thought of Cato lording over us while we, together, took on the obedient role was certainly appealing. There was something about the way Cato commanded in the bedroom—giving and taking his pleasure—with such a forceful degree of passion that the urge to snap to his demands was nearly irresistible.

I bit down on my lip, recalling the night Cato had played the papa to my mama. I shut my eyes and let the memory wash over me—his fingers and, oh, that tongue—where Ambrose was highly skilled and an expert at the art, Cato had no inhibitions and ate me like I was his last meal, one part reverent, the other feral.

I wouldn't have thought that my body was capable after last night's activities, but that sweet little pulse of desire found me again. We were created so beautifully.

"Mmmm, Ambrose, slip it in," I moaned while cocking my hips back.

Last night we'd unlocked a whole new realm of possibility for our sexual pursuits, and this morning I was feeling much more comfortable asserting myself. If we could love together and share intimacies while the other partner was near, managing our relationships would prove less difficult. Cato could seek me out in a free moment. I could offer Ambrose more—granted, I wasn't sure how often my body could accommodate both of them at the same time, given my current tenderness.

"No, lazy lover. I'll finish myself off in the bath. I require a decent amount of time to prepare for this morning's activities. I wish to appear in control, yet slightly disheveled at breakfast—like I tried to domesticate you... but did not *quite* succeed. Might I suggest a fine layer of gray powder under your eyes? And," he tapped his fingertip on his chin thoughtfully, "wear the same stockings as you did last night. Find a way to flash them at the assembled crowd."

Ambrose rolled over, toppling me onto my back. I huffed indignantly and crossed my arms over my breasts.

"But who will finish *me* off, rude husband? My fingers hold no appeal after—"

"My lady... The foundation of a solid relationship is built upon the concept of give and take, yes?" His palm cracked loudly against my thigh, causing Cato's eyes to flash open. "If you want me to *give* the morning dick, *take* the initiative and wake earlier... Otherwise, you are left with that." Ambrose fanned his fingers toward Cato. "Good morning." He then rose and padded across the floor.

"Fucking asshole…" I rubbed at my stinging flesh with both hands.

"No, no, I'm a *fucked* asshole. Isn't that right, Cato, lover?" Ambrose's eyes sparkled mirthfully as he tucked his bottom lip below his top.

"I will end him with no remorse." Cato raised his hands to his forehead and pressed deeply into his temples. "Last night… that will *not* be the norm in this triad. The æther and the blood—the combination was—"

"—the cause of the most monumental eruption of Mount Ambrose since that time I dipped my balls into warmed tea while all the ladies blew bubbles into it. No, it was ten times as good. Fuck, Cato, it was like she milked me with a pussy full of flapping fairies." Ambrose circled his fingers around his penis and smoothed them along his length. "Glorious."

I smacked my hands over my face. My bubble of newfound peace had popped.

"I mean, *you* Joined that, I certainly did not." The corner of Cato's mouth tipped up in amusement.

"Yes. Yes, I did. That right there, he's all mine. But… but I'll share him on occasion if you enjoyed—"

A percussive vibration thundered from the bathing chamber.

"Pardon me!" Ambrose yelled from the other room.

I laughed at the big eyes Cato made.

"Can I take it back? Can you reverse the contract, Protector?"

"Afraid not." Cato rolled over me and we sank into the mattress. He dropped his head down and captured my mouth. "Good morning, love."

"Good morn—Cato. Your eyes are—they're—one is lighter than the other. Just slightly, but I must have drawn on you, but why would the other remain?"

"Your blood, maybe?" He smoothed his lips over my collarbone, down my arm, and to my wrist. "I feel energetic, like last time I consumed it, but also like I've been involved in a high-stakes wrestling match."

"We should be more careful going forward. We don't know how the back and forth might be impacting you, and I wouldn't risk your health."

He brought my wrist to his nose and inhaled. The bite marks were bright against my skin but had already mended to nothing more than raised pink lines.

"I will decide what is good for me and denying me your body is not an option you have—æther or not."

I narrowed my eyes while squishing his lips between my fingers, effectively silencing him.

"Bu… fank you, wuv, fur your confern."

Maybe not so effectively.

Cato lifted off me and dropped to the floor. He pushed up on his arms and held himself rigid, balancing on his toes and fingers. "I am fucking famished."

Ambrose appeared in the doorway.

"Then dress for breakfast, lover. You earned a place of honor at the table after the reaming you gave me. I will treat you like the king you are meant to be, unlike Eira. She will toss you from her bed and demand you bring her sweets."

Cato bounced up out of his plank and strode over to his brother, as naked as the day he first breathed in Ærtan air.

"If you refer to me as anything but 'Protector,' 'brother,' or 'Cat' from this moment on, I will bludgeon you beyond recognition. I mean it, Ambrose."

"Will you use that thick dick to do it?" Ambrose glanced down and then let his eyes roll up to Cato's face.

I stifled my giggle to the best of my ability, but Cato swung around and glared.

"Do not encourage his behavior. I am *not* attracted to him."

Ambrose yelped like an injured animal and clutched at his chest with both hands.

"You were all I knew, Eira—all I could see." Cato was so serious and furrowed his brow so deeply that his worry line became a concern crevice. "Get the fuck out of bed and kiss me goodbye," he said over his shoulder.

"Yes, sir." I saluted him, fist to chest, and then climbed over the blankets and pillows, making my way to where he stood like a god in his glory. When our bodies met, my head swam, like I'd breathed too deeply and too quickly. "My heart, as ever, belongs to you."

"Damn right, it does." Cato brushed his palms across my nipples and ran them down my sides until they settled on my rear. I leaned into his chest, breathing him in, cedar and clove with a hint of—

Cato stiffened as another pair of arms settled around my waist, sandwiching him between us. Ambrose's head came into view above his shoulder.

"Were she not in my arms, I would drag your ass across the floor." I watched the muscles in Cato's jaw flutter as he worked to maintain his composure.

"With your dick in my—"

Like a strike of lightning, Cato twisted hard and dropped low. Ambrose's legs went flying over my head, and his big body struck the floor.

The dining room had been transformed.

Normally it was set up in a very formal fashion, with a dining table at its center and a few sideboards placed about for when a servant's hands got too full. This morning, it was far from traditional.

Stars and moons cut out of parchment hung from the ceilings. They were painted blue, gold, and cream. Long tables, placed in the shape of a horseshoe, had an array of fabric flowers, no doubt handmade by the Millanderers, placed in the vases that sat along the tables. Fat bouquets, tied with dark blue ribbons, hung from the backs of each guest's seat as well.

The room's aesthetic matched the gaiety of my mood.

Hand in hand, my contractual husband and I walked through the threshold to a resounding applause. Ambrose spun me around and dumped me backward, catching my lips in a spectacular kiss. My foot lifted into the air, and my dress flew up over my knee. Ambrose patted the hem back down as if he hadn't orchestrated the whole thing. Whistles and whoops rent the air, punctuated by kissy noises and meows—Monwyns were so strange.

"The dangling garter was a nice touch, wife." Ambrose clicked his tongue and winked an eye.

The butterflies fluttering in my stomach caught me off guard.

Ambrose righted me quickly, causing my head to spin, but it was forgotten when I saw Imella, who must have chosen to stay another night, sitting in the far corner. Burchard sat two guests away, though it didn't seem to hinder their conversation—they completely ignored the awkward expressions of the men sitting stiffly between them.

When I noticed the shy smiles, my spirits ascended to the sky.

Then I spotted my cake.

Not even eagles could have flown as high as I did!

Ethens had come through on our negotiations, and quite frankly, he could have gone with two less tiers and I would've been elated. The five-story dream dessert must have cost him a fortune. The white frosting looked as fluffy as a freshly fallen snow, and the sugared lemon wedges and dried strawberries pressed into its sides set my toes to tapping.

I stopped and tugged on Ambrose's hand.

"The cake?" he said with a smile as brilliant as a sunbeam in winter.

"Yes! On cake with cake!" I laughed.

"Do you see the polar bear and black bear atop it?" Ambrose bowed his head low, his eyes crinkling at the corners. His smile wasn't practiced, or the one he used when entertaining the court. It was lopsided and adorably genuine.

"And are you happy, husband?" I asked, my voice all airy and light.

"Kiss! Kiss him for luck!"

"Kiss, kiss, kiss!" The crowd cheered.

I tilted my head back and rose on my toes.

"I do believe I am, *wife*. I do believe that I am." He brushed his knuckles across the shaved side of my head and then twisted a finger through a stick-straight lock that had lost its coil during the night.

Soft lips met mine.

"Put your tongue in!"

"Slip it to her, Highness!"

Ambrose smiled against my mouth.

"Oh!"

He swept me up into his arms and strode into the room like a man besotted. Together, we headed toward the honorary spots at the head of the table.

The assembled masses clamored to their feet as the priest came through the door.

"Congratulations to our newly Joined. Their coupling has been validated by cloth and governance, and the bedding has been deemed successful. May her stomach swell and a babe be born within the year!" The holy man lifted his arms in benediction as he proclaimed his message to the room.

Burchard clapped his hands above his head and grinned from ear to ear.

"Hear, hear, may she be deity-blessed."

I froze—that voice was etched into my memory.

I plastered a smile on my face and turned my head, nodding respectfully as I beheld him.

The Primus-King smiled jovially as he waved his hand around in a gesture of benevolence. He stepped to my side and pulled out the empty seat. Burchard did the same for his son.

Suddenly, my excellent morning began to tarnish.

I allowed the Gaean to guide me to the table. My skin recoiled when the tips of his fingers met the small of my back. The same hand that had caused my mother pain—

Papa Burchard, how could you allow this? Playing the gracious host, I nodded my head from courtier to courtier, mouthing my thanks.

I allow this because you are now the wife of a prince, the daughter of a king. You need not cower to the likes of this malodorous leader. The king lowered his chin, pushed his dark-lensed spectacles back up on his nose, and waved in my direction.

He was right.

Yes, I am.

Get out of my head! I smiled at him, baring my teeth a little more than was necessary.

Squaring my shoulders and straightening my spine, I picked up a delicate glass filled with watered wine and raised it high in the air. The noisy room quieted.

"Though it may not be a tradition here, I feel moved to speak to those who now number among my new family." I saluted Imella, Ambrose, and even Septimus, who sat on the far right of the side table. Shifting, I tilted my glass toward Father Burchard, and then turned and found Cato at the back of the hall. I inclined my head, and his fist shot to his shoulder, the metal of his gauntlet clanging loudly against his armor. The grand gesture, carried out so publicly, nearly stole my breath.

"Family means the world to me, and there is *nothing* I wouldn't do to see my family thrive." I paused and looked pointedly at the few husbands who sat next to their wives. "I would stamp out the sun's fire—disassemble a mountain rock by rock." I smiled and nodded at Allaine, who scrunched her nose sweetly, and then looked to the man at my left. The Primus-King's eyes were unmoving and fixed upon me. "I would place myself in the avalanche's path and set the forests aflame to defend those I love."

His eyebrow quirked—just the one—and the side of his mouth drew up in a half-smile. The audience applauded, and he followed suit, tapping his hands lightly together. The green robes he wore hung heavily on his thin frame, emphasizing the skeletal appearance of his ring-covered fingers.

I held his eyes as I continued my speech—I'd win the battle of wills.

"Know that you have had a profound impact on my life, and I will *never* forget what you have done... to make my Joining so memorable." Turning, I raised my glass in a toast to the crowd. "Thank you all."

"To Lady Eira, Consort of Monwyn!" bellowed Evandr's father as he stood and leaned heavily on the table for support. He clasped his hands together and nodded his head over and over, blinking all the while. "She knows my boy. Yes, she does. Was Assigned with the lad, speaks well of him. Even now."

"To family!" I shouted.

Every last person in the room came to their feet again.

My throat constricted.

"To family!" the room replied in a chorus of voices.

Father Burchard remained standing as the rest of the room took their seats. He clacked his spoon against his glass.

"My daughter is wise, for there is nothing greater than the family you create, or the one you make amongst those you..."

"You favor her—your mother. Like yourself, she had a different sort of beauty."

I looked down at the table. I was in no way beholden to the man—I didn't owe him a response. A servant passed around thick slices of cake as Father Burchard prattled on about this noble family aligning themselves to that noble lineage. I messed with my utensils, choosing the one that would best propel the largest amount of sugary decadence into my mouth.

A fluffy lemon sponge, flavored with a hint of cardamom, made my taste buds sing out in delight. Its frosting was thick and buttery. The combination was like a full-bodied Solnnan bear hug for my soul—Kan and Mariad were both here in spirit.

"I loved her, and she loved me in return," the Primus-King whispered again.

My spoon stilled on its path to my mouth.

"A child of thirteen doesn't know love, and a man of sixty should have *known* better." I snatched a linen napkin from the table and blotted at my lips, my appetite ruined. But if he wanted to do this here and now, who was I to stand in his way?

I twisted around and gave him my undivided attention while Papa Burchard's long-winded toast continued "... in fact, when I was a man of thirty and four, my queen and I were caught in a larder *just* behind those very doors, and ah, how we..."

"You know nothing of life in Gaea, young one. Do not sit in judgment—her menses had begun, and I wooed her and paid handsomely for her hand."

"Wooed her? Was that before or after you forced her into intimacy?" I managed to keep my voice low, but my words came out serpent-tongued sharp. My grip tightened on the chair's armrest, and the shadows closed in tightly on my periphery.

He inched closer. So close that I could see the large pores on his nose and the short growth of a day-old beard.

"By the laws of Gaea, your mother is a lesser queen. You remain a citizen and under my purview as king and fath—"

"You are nothing and no one—within these walls, you have no *purview* at all."

Elderman Deekon's head slid between us, obscuring the king from my vision.

"Consort, ma'am. I would humbly request that you maintain your space."

"Or what, Elderman?" I spat.

His mouth worked up and down as he thought, revealing the glints of gold studded into his teeth. Both eyeteeth bore evidence of his commitment to his kingdom and to the man whom he shielded with his body.

He glanced down, unwilling to look me in the eye.

"Forgiveness is at times more powerful than one's hatred, ma'am." He bowed his head and looked at me thoughtfully.

"Did you advise your monarch of that before Ozius's head rolled?"

"... and now, while I have everyone's attention!" Burchard clapped his hands loudly, startling both the bored and the dozing.

I let my shoulders drop and made my face placid, centering myself before sliding my hand through Ambrose's elbow and resting my head on his shoulder. My doting husband kissed my forehead, much to the delight of the assembly, many of whom sighed longingly.

Burchard couldn't keep the smile off his face as he glanced over at Imella. Though she didn't return the grin, her eyes showed an undeniable brightness as she stared up at her husband.

"In honor of love, there will be changes in our kingdom—ones that I feel will usher us into a new golden age." The king bent and picked up his glass. He took a deep swig of the yellow liquid and then cleared his throat. "It is time that our womenfolk have the ability to find themselves an occupation. We will soon break ground on a school of midwifery in honor of my new daughter."

Ambrose wrapped his fingers around my bicep and squeezed gently. Tears pooled in my eyes, threatening to spill, and the æther flowed softly around my chest, warming me from the inside.

"Women who are interested will be encouraged to attend the classes, so long as their duties at home are adequately carried out and their husband's needs are met. They will, of course, need official documentation from their head of household permitting them to attend and will need to be above three decades of age."

I pressed my mouth against Ambrose's sleeve, hiding my bemused expression. *It's a start, Papa. It's a start.*

Burchard raised his glass in my direction and blew me a little kiss. I caught the invisible smooch in my hand and placed my palm on my cheek.

"Furthermore, though we as kings may seem omniscient—"

No, I've never thought that.

"Ahem, pardon me," Burchard sputtered as he snapped his head around and pressed his lips into a thin line. I covered my mouth and did my best to stifle my giggles. His face softened and the corners of his mouth turned up. He looked to where Imella sat, and his cheeks went rosy. "I have done wrong, and I seek to make amends."

Oh, Papa. I felt our tie tighten.

"Years ago, my actions damaged the lives of many... and to this day, it is my most profound regret."

Imella's eyes glistened as she watched Burchard, her gaze never once straying from his face. She drew a shaky breath and placed a hand on her heart.

Burchard turned to his populace. He lowered his glass to the table and laced his fingers together.

"Septimus, brother. This day, though you have not asked for it, you will take up the mantle and shield of Protector. You have always been at my back, and I was wrong to ignore tradition. Catommandus, my boy, it was *I* who stole your birthright from you, and now *I* will see it restored."

The crowd went feral, thrusting their daggers in the air and shouting battle cries. The sound was deafening.

Septimus rose. At first, his face showed utter surprise, his mouth dropping open and his eyes wide, but as he stepped toward his brother, like the visor snapping closed on a steel helm, he took on the visage of a warrior—at once severe and altogether impassive.

My head spun.

"Catommandus, the signet ring. You belong by my side—you have skulked in the shadows for too long. Take your place."

I tried to rise, to escape, but the shadows eclipsed my vision and my body fell back in a violent twist of vertigo.

"Steady, Eira, steady, it's okay—we will be okay," Ambrose murmured into my ear. He held me close and pressed my face to his chest.

The tornado in my head spun wildly out of control. The room tilted, and when I tried to focus on a single point, my eyes jerked rhythmically outside of my control.

"I credit daughter Eira for much of the recent happiness in this family—both Ambrose and myself have benefited from her wisdom and strength." Burchard glanced at Imella and back to Cato. "You will no doubt seek a wife of your own, my son. She and I will scour the kingdoms for your perfect match. And in return, you will give me a parcel of grands!"

My stomach lurched. I twisted hard, grabbed my napkin, and pitched forward as the cake I had just eaten spewed forth.

"He's got a babe on her already, he does!"

The masses crowed.

"Bets on which brother will sire a boy the fastest!"

Through the blur of my vision, I watched Cato clip a bow to his father, turn on his heel, and stride out the door.

"She needs air."

With Ambrose's aid, I stood, but then collapsed onto the floor. I grasped my head and held it tight, but nothing steadied the tumultuous swing and sway of my vision or the sick feeling of heartbreak that exacerbated my symptoms.

Strong arms lifted me as tenderly as they could and hoisted me up as I whimpered all the while.

"Highness, I have the doors."

"Thank you, Lemder."

Ambrose whisked us through the kitchen, where the smells of raw meat and fresh dairy turned my stomach even more sour than it already was. I smacked my hand over my mouth, and the impact made me see double.

Lemder held open the exterior door just in the nick of time.

The moment we hit fresh air, I heaved again while Ambrose held me over the bushes—my shadows flashed and pulsed, which added to the discomfort of what ailed me.

"Highness, the ginger root would help her. It does the trick for my wife when she is sickly."

My eyes flicked steadily back and forth, but I made out Ambrose's nod.

"Do not leave her side." He bounded back through the door.

I reached out, groping for the stone wall, and Lemder stepped nearer, offering his support.

"Th-thank you, I'm so—"

My head snapped back, and pain seared through my scalp.

Lemder clutched my hair and twisted, the pressure so intense that the tiny hairs at my nape tore from my hairline. Sunlight penetrated my eyes, making them water profusely and the sudden motion caused me to be sick again. Lemder held my head in a vice grip and the vomit rolled down my chin and into the neckline of my gown.

"You have but a single chance to heed my words, whore." Lemder brought his massive face so close that his beard pricked against my temple. "The rash you displayed so wantonly at the bedding seems identical to the one on the Protector's neck. And by my own sweet daughter's admission, she confirmed that you and he were found in His Highness's chambers while the prince was away doing the Goddess's work. Were I to make an accusation," Lemder's hand tightened in my hair, "your life would be forfeit. We have laws in this kingdom when a woman makes a cuckold of her husband... Can you imagine the scandal? Fucking your husband's brother? The Protec—Catommandus would be disgraced. And you, Chosen Daughter, would swing from the gallows. Are you listening?"

He shook my head so hard I felt faint. My legs wobbled unsteadily, but instead of letting me drop to the ground, he squeezed harder and held me upright with a single meaty hand.

"Ensure my demands are met, or face the Council. One, my daughter is to be returned to me. The outside world is no place for a person like her. Two," Lemder said, in a state of fury so intense that droplets of his spittle rained down on my cheek, "my son will receive a prestigious post and a dispensation to marry. The girl is not yet of age by our current laws, but he shall have her regardless. Secure the paperwork within two days."

"L-like fuck I will." Shadows burst into my vision, and I let them take me. I'd not sentence a child to a lifetime with any man raised by this ogre. I welcomed the darkness. My hand slapped against his temple, and I closed my eyes.

Pull little shade, siphon him until he—

My head hit the stone wall.

The force of the blow sent my vision seesawing and flipping, and I was unable to maintain my hold. Lemder flung me to the ground and then kneeled beside me.

With his sausage-sized fingers, he caressed my head like a loving father would, smoothing back my hair and tucking it behind my ears.

"Two days. A minute over, and my men deliver the parchments containing every sordid detail of your infidelity. They have their orders and now you have yours."

My mind raced in circles so fast they outstripped the horrid spin in my head.

I was far too dazed to strike back.

Ambrose walked through the door and dropped to his knees, while Lemder stood straight.

"Thank you, Lemder." The cool rim of a fragrant cup pressed against my lips. "You are okay. Everything will be fine. I'm here now."

Chapter 43

ERGO

The spinning lasted for hours, which meant the vomiting did too. I was incredibly weak and disoriented and, quite frankly, upset that I was physically unable to carry out my immediate plan to suck the æther from Lemder's body until he turned into what I'm sure would be a colossal mound of skin pulp.

Allaine would eventually reconcile the loss of her father—I'd let him die with his squeaky-clean-family-man image intact. She would continue to think of him as an honorable man, and he could go down as some great hero in the history books. I didn't give a single shit if his good name remained, as long as his end came quickly.

Knowing as many elites as I did now, I suspected that most notable Ærtan leaders were, in reality, giant assholes who had their stories censured and lionized. Regardless, I'd keep sacred the love Allaine felt for him. At home, I'm sure he seemed like a man of strong morals, but in the world of political advancement, I equated him with the stinky white goo that gathered on the back of my molars if I skipped a day of tooth care.

Ambrose carefully inserted his arm behind my neck and helped me sit up to receive the healer's diagnosis.

"Vertigo is often associated with a weakness of the ears. In most cases, it will clear up on its own, but do keep calm. Your genteel constitution requires the body to remain in harmonious balance."

"There is nothing genteel about me, *apprentice* healer Morroe. What are you doing?"

"Preparing to bleed you. The removal of excess blood will help your focus and rebalance your—"

"Husband, have him hanged." I leaned into Ambrose and hid my eyes from the harsh lamplight. "That or, or send him to some realm as backward as he is. This imbecile didn't flinch at the waterfall of blood that poured from that unfortunate mother... I daresay he will bleed me dry." I turned my head slowly, but even the slightest movement caused my vision to somersault. "We are *modern* now, healer. Join us in the *now*, or go back to peering at piss. Shall I fill a jar for you? Fetch me a vessel. Go on, sniff my waste and prescribe me your tonic of *horseshit!*"

The young man's mouth fell open as he glared at me, openly hostile. I didn't give a damn. What was another enemy added to my list?

"Insolent, serpent-tongued—"

Ambrose's palm cracked against the man's cheek so hard that he hit the bed on his way down to the floor—sending me into another bout of the spins.

"You are dismissed."

"Highness I-I—"

"—will get out." His voice dropped so low that it was as if thunder rolled outside my window. "Leave now, or *I* will bleed *you*. My mace breaks bones easier than it draws blood, but I am willing to work at it."

The healer went pale. He righted himself quickly but stood hunched over with his arms raised, shielding his face. His shaky palm went to his cheek, covering the pink splotch that bloomed quickly across his jaw. The man clipped a bow at the waist and gathered his supplies.

"Ambrose, dearest, please don't rock. Hold me, but hold very still."

He stopped immediately, nodded against my head, and then shifted slowly, positioning himself in a way that allowed me to lay my head on his chest and remain mostly upright. Together, we watched the healer leave the room.

"I was too harsh," I said. "The way to deal with willful ignorance is to re-educate, not insult."

"He'd be a stain on the carpet if I thought your stomach could withstand the sight."

Ambrose reached, practically in slow motion, toward the bedside table.

A hot mug of broth appeared under my nose. Unlike the first time he tried, the herby aroma was tempting and not seconds from setting me off like a whale's blow spout. I sipped the delicious liquid and was almost immediately rewarded with a small spark of energy.

"Where is Cato? Is he alright?"

"Around the palace, I suppose." He tilted the cup back to my lips and then took a swig of the briny comfort himself. "I would imagine he finds himself in a state of shock. My father did not make me aware of his plans, but king's prerogative and all that."

"When I can think normally again, I'm likely to spiral into a host of what-if questions." I found the comfortable spot on Ambrose's chest again and snuggled into his warmth.

"Eira?"

"Yes?"

"You are *my* wife, and that cannot be changed."

Under my ear, the beat of his heart increased in speed.

"Can... can Father Burchard force Cato to Join?"

Ambrose's silence spoke volumes.

There was no world in which I could stand watching... knowing Cato was with another woman. He was *my* mate. *Mine.* Even if the woman was a decoy, a political arrangement—the thought of the mythical woman's lips on his skin, her heat ensconcing his length in the hope of bearing his child—it made me physically ill. It was unpleasant coming to terms with my hypocrisy.

"Sleep now. I'll be here when you wake."

"Ambrose." I attempted to look up at him, but he held my head firmly to his chest. "I am your wife and have no regrets but I..."

His soft exhalation ruffled my hair as his finger settled against my lips.

When I woke, only the soft glow of a single lamp greeted me. The others burned low, and the tapers had since melted into their little glass holders.

I stared up at the ceiling, turning my head from left to right, thankful that my equilibrium had been restored. Ambrose, bless him, was fast asleep by my side, still dressed in his clothing and boots. Strands of his hair had come free from his braid and were trapped under his shoulder, pulling his head back at an awkward angle.

I closed my eyes and counted backward, but sleep wouldn't come. My pillows felt like ice bricks, and my blankets were too hot. Ambrose was sniffling and snorting without a discernible rhythm, and I... I wished he were Cato.

I needed to know he was alright. I longed to hold him and take on his pain. Selfishly, I needed him to take my pain, too. I refused to regret the life of my choosing or spend time dwelling on potential futures that would never exist, one where the piercing in his ear contained a hoop, but I still wanted him to know I was all in, no matter where destiny led us.

Ambrose mumbled in his sleep, drawing my attention.

My husband. Ordained before Goddess and government.

I studied him as he slept. I'd never noticed the itty-bitty tip of a scar that peeked out from his hairline or the endearing brown freckle at the corner of his lip. He was certainly turning out to be more husband than contract—more beloved than befriended. In all the stories of damsels in need of rescue, he could certainly play the ideal hero. Selfless. *Sort of*. Caring. *Mostly*. Confident and headstrong. *Without doubt*. I bent over him and loosened the strands that held his head hostage.

His sleepy eyes opened halfway. There was only a tiny glint of reflection in the dim room, but I could make out their color—the hue of a forest's ground cover.

"Are you better?"

"I am. Because of you." I smiled.

"Kiss?"

"Kiss."

His lips were salty and soft under mine. I trailed my knuckles down his jaw and then finger-combed his beard. He captured my hand and pressed it lightly against his chest, which made his spicy-and-sweet scent waft around me.

"Wake me if you have need. Promise?"

"I will... Black Bear," I whispered while lightly running my mouth over his temple.

His sweet chuckle made my heart smile. I drew my fingers through his hair, lightly scratching his scalp, until his soft snores returned.

In the common room, the freshly filled lamps cast enough light for me to easily navigate the furnishings and locate my satchel, which I tossed on the table. I withdrew both quill and parchment, and in my most attractive hand, I penned "Eliminating a Ranking Government Official or ERGO."

I laughed softly, wondering how common it was for a mastermind or cutthroat to make a detailed list of their nefarious deeds.

I ran the clipped feather along my chin as I pondered.

No gore.

Must be quick acting—drawn-out suffering is not attractive.

No bodily fluids if they can be avoided—especially poop.

Move humongous body to forest.

No, scratch that. He'd take too long for the local fauna to polish off. Um. Dump in the river? But would that taint the drinking water? I'd not have him seek vengeance posthumously by means of a diarrhea epidemic.

Gracious.

Verus hadn't taught us murder, though they'd often alluded to ending relationships, ending futures, and manipulating history to benefit the greater good. They'd completely skipped the "Matters of Murder Methodology: Tidy Tidbits for a Clean Execution" course.

I could see Cinden or even Ymailrys making quick work of an adversary—their brains acted fast. The others, though, not so much. It would never even occur to gentle Farai, and Amias would say please and thank you before attempting to deliver the killing blow.

Fuck.

Am I entertaining this?

Taking the life of someone actively trying to harm me, or the life of a loved one, was one thing. Premeditating the act put me into an entirely new category of ruthless—I still wasn't sure that's who I wanted to be.

Stop and think.

I needed to speak to Cato. He'd walked Ambrose through the art of assassination and could, undoubtedly, eliminate Lemder himself with little trouble. But honestly, I hoped he could present an alternative solution to my problem.

Through hardship and pain, I will reach for you. Through life, I will shelter you and the family we build.

I padded over to the door.

Before reaching for its handle, I bore down while holding my breath. The change in pressure made my vision swim, just a little, but my shadows came instantly, which bolstered my confidence tenfold. I was learning to control them.

I swung the door wide.

"Sleep, Bem," I commanded, just as I'd seen Father Burchard do.

Bem stood statue-still and blinked at me just once.

I thrust my hands forward, prepared to cushion his head as he fell.

Nothing happened.

Fuck!

Bem sucked in one of his cheeks while he pointed to his ears with both hands. Fat wads of linen stuck out of his ear holes.

"Ooo!" I huffed. I shot my fists to my sides and looked out the door to gauge the possibility of outrunning him. I'd never seen him move faster than a slow saunter.

Bem shook his head and reached for the handle.

"Amateur!" he shouted in my face.

"Ass." I pointed to my mouth. "Hole." I enunciated the words, exaggerating the movement of my lips.

"Yep." He nodded a little too enthusiastically.

The door slammed shut.

On my way across the room, I snatched up my ERGO parchment and held it to a lamp's flame. Quickly, I made my way to the balcony, where I watched the evidence of my not-so-well-planned treachery turn to ash.

"You aren't out, Eira. Solve your problem," I said out loud.

Papa, are you there?

I waited, but no response came. I walked to the other side of the balcony and stuck my head out, looking toward the healer's shed. No lights were on.

Father Burchard, I could use your advice. I need you to talk me through, or out of, a slaughter... and I'm not talking goat-level butchery.

A low rumble sounded in the distance, and a bright white bolt flashed in the sky.

And now I need a hug. Do you think the palace can withstand a storm? I mean, I am sure it's seen plenty but... Papa?

The æther sensed my trepidation and wound up tightly in my chest.

Wind raced through the columns, creating a low and eerie whistle that chilled me far more than the dropping temperature. The sound was evil and ominous—like the wail of a dreadful haint as she proclaimed your end.

A bolt shattered in the sky, illuminating the world with streaming fingers of light. In its electric luminescence, I saw a mass of rolling and coiling clouds racing in my direction. My skin crawled, and a fine sheen of sweat formed on my brow.

Papa? Papa, where are you?

"Cato, love..." I stood petrified, frozen in place.

As if they had my scent, the clouds tumbled over each other like a pack of starving netherhounds running down their prey. My heart rate soared. I could feel its fluttering pulse in my neck and chest, and I couldn't seem to catch my breath, though I drew the air deeply. My nightgown plastered itself against my knees, and rogue strands of hair caught in my mouth and whipped painfully across my eyes.

A sizzling snap split the air.

A tree, just a short distance away, exploded, its trunk splitting in two. Its dry autumn leaves smoked and then burst into flame.

Goddess, protect us.

The thunder clapped so loudly that I smacked my hands over my ears. The palace seemed to quake in fear as Viktos raged, shouting his anger at the citizens of Ærta.

Lightning sliced through the sky—I would swear its target was me.

Go, Eira. Go!

I shot through the common room and barreled through the bedroom. A startled Ambrose snapped awake wide-eyed, but I didn't slow, even as I came up against the wall.

I hit it hard.

The pain came—a full-body sear. I passed through the barrier just as I had when Papa Burchard was poisoned.

The room I found myself in was crammed full of covered furniture and smelled of harsh polish and lacquer. My feet bound up in a white sheet, and when I bent to free them, it sent the statue underneath toppling to the floor. The crowned head of Lykksun broke free from the stone body and rolled to a stop before me. Her eyes bore into mine, passing their judgment.

My panic intensified as fear overwhelmed me. The gods were angry.

Keep moving. Don't stop!

My body ripped apart again as I passed through the far wall. My knees gave out, and I hit the stone floor of a room that looked nearly identical to mine.

I scrambled to rise and—

Septimus stood on his balcony, watching the storm that raged.

My breath caught and, like it had never sped up at all, my frantic heart stilled, lulled by the power of his presence—the tie that bound us.

Water poured between the columns, puddling around his bare feet. Beyond him, the flaming tree that resembled a giant's torch, smoked, doused by the torrential downpour. A mass of glowing embers smoldered in its newly forked trunk.

He swept his long braid over his shoulder, and my eyes swept down his shirtless torso.

I dared to inch closer.

My gods.

Septimus had known pain.

From neck to waist, he was covered in thin scars that crisscrossed the wide expanse of his back. Some were raw and pink, others were healed over, whiter even than his pale skin. Many were raised and roped, others superficial. Deep furrows ran from his shoulders to his biceps on both arms as well.

Tiptoeing forward, I cloaked myself in a curtain and spied on his solitude from behind glass doors. I watched as he walked through the shifting light of a single lamp and made his way to a lone chair. *Goddess save him.* The right side of his chest was mutilated, and it didn't look accidental or like an animal attack. From his collarbone to the bottom of his chest, a strip of his flesh had been carved out, taking his nipple but leaving a small portion of his areola on one side. A similar gouge appeared next to his navel.

Lightning struck and dancing fingers cracked a path through the sky. The Protector's signet ring glinted in the light show while Septimus stared down the clouds. He sneered at the god of thunder, like he was willing Viktos to strike him dead.

Proud nose, strong jaw—his rugged beauty threw me off course.

The wind shifted. Rain spilled between the columns, pelting his magnificent yet battered body. As the water bathed him, he hung his head between his hands and, very much like Cato, rubbed his fingertips deeply into his temples.

My legs were no longer under my control—I commanded them to stop, to turn, and to leave, even as my hand reached for the handle.

He needed his mate... and I was here.

His head snapped up, and a blade was in his hand before the latch had cleared the doorframe.

Sky-blue eyes met mine.

"To me. Now," he spoke so quietly as he rose that I wasn't convinced I'd heard him. But the æther knew. It hummed in my chest, vibrating and shooting through my breasts like the lightning that brought me here. With every step I took, the storm seemed to swell. The rain came down in sheets, and the thunder yelled out a warning from above.

As I continued, the tingling in my fingertips increased steadily in its intensity. "Why have you come?"

I stood so close to him that I felt the warmth radiating off his skin. Thin streams of water ran into my eyes and over my lips as I searched his face.

I shook my head, unable to make the words come forth.

Because I need a piece of you within me—our child growing inside me—because I am in heat like a fucking animal.

"Use your words." Septimus flipped the dagger in his hand. "Speak to me of your desires, Eira."

My name on his lips stirred the rawest of emotions within me—my most basic of instincts wanted—no, demanded—I become his.

"I wish to be bred, Septimus, by a vital man, a strong man."

The thick musculature of his pecs swelled in pride. He pulled his shoulders back and shifted from one side to the other, displaying himself like a bird would his fine plumes.

I was a bee seeking a flower—a moth drawn to his forbidden flame.

The lightning flashed, and a halo of brilliance surrounded him.

Septimus brought his fingers to my mouth but didn't make contact with my skin.

"I do not sleep, knowing that you are within these walls and not under my rule."

My eyes flickered shut, and my lips parted. Though he hadn't touched me, he was so close that I could feel my breath deflect off his hand.

"I would take you from here—there are none who would find us, and if they did, their end would be swift. Perhaps then I could rest."

I gasped when the cold, hard metal of a knife's tip slipped down my wet cheek. He could end me with a flick of his wrist, and somehow, that knowledge made me want him more. "Eira, how can you please me with your eyes closed?"

My nostrils flared, seeking his scent—spearmint and cinnamon.

"I *do* wish to please you," I whispered. "I will bow my head to the ground when you take me. Your white-as-snow hair will fall around us like a veil, hiding our deceit from the world."

What was that, Eira? What am I doing?

"Your ankles bound in ropes would please me more. I could leave you splayed for hours and pump my seed into your moist folds each and every time desire takes hold of me. I fucked the dark-haired maid's fat cunt six times in one day, pretending she was you milking my staff."

Gross. How could his words turn my stomach sour and yet stoke my libido to a sinful inferno?

I swallowed hard. I hated this man. I was disgusted by how he treated his wife, his daughter, and how he encouraged pain and seemed to revel in violence.

Eira, leave now. Turn and walk the fuck out.

Septimus pinched my chin between his finger and thumb.

"You and I both know that I can have you any time I choose."

Arousal snaked through my womb and down my passage, winding tightly around the bundle of nerves between my legs. I leaned into his touch, smelled his masculine and clean scent, and knew peace.

He yanked my mouth wide.

The wet blade rested on my tongue, and he pushed the metal backward until I gagged and felt its sharp sting on my sensitive pallet. Septimus tipped his hand, showing no concern for the fact that he could have maimed me. Water pooled on the flat blade, and he forced it, sweet and fresh-tasting, down my throat.

I opened my eyes and watched the pulse beat heavily at the base of his neck. It throbbed in a slow and even tempo. His pupils didn't dilate as Cato's tended to do when he was amorous; no, his were pinpricks, tiny peppercorns in a well of icy blue.

I sucked in the air when his bare chest pressed against mine. My nipples peaked through the sodden nightgown, which had grown heavy from the rain. Its neckline stretched, revealing the swell of my breasts.

He withdrew the knife and used its razor-sharp tip to slice open the near-transparent fabric of my gown. His eyes devoured my exposed breasts.

"I will feed from you when our child is not suckling."

He grabbed my rear and jerked me forward, grinding himself into my pubic bone, hard and fully aroused.

My passage thickened. My body betrayed the will of my mind as wetness pooled heavily at my entrance.

"Ahdmundus." I reached out and traced his braid with shaking fingers. I caught its leather binding and pulled. "This attraction between us isn't natural. I don't—I don't even like you, let alone wish to—"

"Then why does it feel as if the earth itself wills it?"

His hair unraveled into dazzlingly thick waves, the color of which matched the moon that peeked in and out of the storm clouds marching through the night sky.

I didn't know how to respond—how much I could or should reveal. But I was well aware that the bravado I presented was false, and that the longer I spent in his presence, the more damage I would do.

His head lowered, and my heart hammered in my chest.

His short-clipped beard was rough against my cheek, but his lips were smooth on the lobe of my ear.

"Septimus, I'm sorry, so sorry. I feel it as well... and... I'm leaving," I said, my voice stronger than it felt.

"You do not make the rules here and you will *not* move." He jerked me so hard that my breasts smashed painfully into his chest. He sighed, contentedly, a sound of pure relief, like a profound and long-lived agony had come to an end.

Something was wrong.

The scent of the air changed, and a distinctly metallic taste filled my mouth.

"That is where you are wrong," I said in a firm tone.

Septimus's brows knit together, and his eyes flicked to the side.

He spun and lashed a protective arm out in front of me as a bolt flashed white hot, striking the corner of the balcony. Stone exploded, and gravel rained down in chunks, hitting the man who shielded me.

I ran.

My speed was panic-fueled as I raced through his apartments, seeking the exit.

The guttural snarl of the animal that pursued me sent a shiver through my limbs, and I flipped a chair behind me in an attempt to slow the beast at my back.

I tore through the common room.

The growl came again, feral and untamed, and much closer than it had been.

My core clenched, and my æther dipped low—it begged me to encourage his pursuit.

I ripped the door open and flew into the hall, picking up speed as I headed in the direction of the healer's offices. Too fast for the corner, I made the turn but couldn't stop my momentum. Pain flared in my shoulder, and I careened through another wall.

I can't breathe.

In the dark, staring up at an unfamiliar ceiling, I willed my breath to return.

Holy shit. Eira, that was—nether it all! Making a cuck of your husband two days after Joining is a new godsdamned low.

My hands started to tingle and then burn. I brought them to my face and felt an alarming amount of heat radiating from my palms.

I lay on the floor, gasping, until my temperature lowered and I regained the ability to take in air. There had to be a way to avoid Septimus in the future, and I would make the separation happen, even if I had to ask Burchard to banish his brother from my presence. I'd not jeopardize myself or the men in my life, even *if* the Goddess placed such a twisted fuck in my path.

Rolling to my side, I surveyed the room in which I found myself. No lamps were lit, but enough light streamed through the large, floor-to-ceiling window that I could see the layout. My soaked and torn clothes left a puddle on the floor when I stood, and continued dripping around my feet as I padded across the floor.

The chamber was sparsely furnished: a large wardrobe on the left wall and a small bed on the right. A wingback chair sat behind a massive desk directly in front of the window, and a row of books, color-coded and sorted by height, ran along its back, sandwiched between two dog-shaped bookends. Every surface was clean and tidy, and if it weren't for the lingering smell of recently snuffed tapers, I would have thought it a rarely used guest room. I tiptoed in the direction of the bed and hid—my back pressed snuggly against the wall and my head below its thick mattress. With the magnitude of Septimus's reaction, I wouldn't doubt that he was nearby, combing through rooms and sniffing at the air. Cato would have done the same.

In order of importance: Find Cato. Get back to my room. Form a plan to deal with Lemder. Speak to both my men about Septimus—oh, gods, that would be a conversation. Carry out the Lemder plan. Pray. Pray every minute of the hour, twice on the hour, and then perhaps thrice more for good measure.

I raised my fingertips to my brow. A preemptive prayer couldn't hurt either.

Grandmother Merrias, it's getting more difficult to stay the course. When I follow my instincts, I end up hiding in strangers' bedrooms. Stay with Cato, please. He needs your strength. Watch over Ambrose. Allow Septimus to rest... and Lemder to die... not painfully... just permanently. Please.

Resting my head against the bed's edge, I became keenly aware of my various pains. The knot that had raised above the left side of my forehead was the most troubling. Fucking Lemder. He made sure the evidence of his assault was hidden *just* enough by my unusual hairline. My knees ached from striking stone, my throat burned where the sadist had nicked me—it throbbed with the same beating pulse as the godforsaken spot in my ever-hungry twat.

Was anger-masturbating a thing? Hate-fingering?

I pulled my gown's hem to my thighs and tested out my clitoris with two fingertips. I wasn't at all surprised by how wet or sensitive I was.

Fucking Septimus—horrible ass, delicious demon.

I spread my lips and massaged myself in slow circles. Would he feel different from Cato? Would *my* fulfillment factor into his pregnancy fetish at all? It didn't seem likely. I increased the speed of my fingers, running their pads in a back-and-forth motion. Tie me up and leave me. Fuck that, unless snacks were involved. I'd tie up *his* tree-trunk-sized thighs... and... mount his girthy... what did he call it? Rod, club, mallet? *Nope, no, don't even entertain it, Eira.* He could call it what he'd like but I'd not be impaling myself on his sword.

"Bullshit. Fucking Mating Bond bullshit!"

I plunged my fingers into my passage and conjured Ambrose's face, *my husband.* Men and women alike fell at his feet, worshiping his beauty, and he was mine. I tensed around my fingers, imagining the angle of his jaw, the V that led down to what was, in all honesty, a gorgeous dick. His tip was well defined, and the most scrumptious vein ran along his underside. His testicles were a solid handful and hung evenly and—

The image of Septimus's cruel and disconcerting face filtered through my mind.

"Creator's tits." I rubbed and thrust, but couldn't relieve myself. "Fucking moody bitch."

It wouldn't be the first, or thousandth time I couldn't come. If my brain wasn't into it, neither was she. *Whatever.*

I wiped my fingers on my gown and patted my pubic bone.

"I didn't mean to call you that. I've just become accustomed to easy orgasms as of late." I chuckled at the absurdity of my current situation and tapped my toes on the carpet-strewn floor.

"You know, if he wasn't a whale-sized dicksac, Lemder would make a solid Scion," I said to the empty room. He'd kept his eyes open, seized an opportunity, and executed a plan that would benefit both him and his. He'd make a formidable henchman as well—too bad he was coming up on his expiration date.

I mustered the courage and made my way to the door. I was ready to be back in my bed and snuggled firmly between my fellows.

Godsdammit.

Two guards were posted down the hall, in the direction of my apartments. I pressed my finger to the door latch so it would close without a telltale click and tiptoed back across the floor. I made my way to the wardrobe. If I could find something that would fit and something to cover my hair, I could head left and circle back around, or possibly even walk right past the guards.

The closet door was jammed.

Of course it was.

I kicked my foot up against its side and pried until the door snapped back so violently that it smashed my fingers and busted several nails on my left hand.

A giant mound of yarn fell from the top shelf, landed on my head, and sent me tripping to the floor. Other than a million small skeins, the closet was empty.

The Goddess has a sense of humor.

I bent over and grabbed handfuls of the soft string. There was no way I could reach the top where they had been stored, so I took a few steps back and shot each of the soft rounds, one by one, onto the shadow-darkened shelf. I laughed out loud at the game I had invented and attempted to launch them from further in the room. I was a decent shot. One, two, three more in the hole. The last skein felt different, heavier and flat. I held it up to the filtered moonlight.

It was a knitted cap of blue—no, it was nalbinding, not knitting—he'd told me so himself.

My heart.

I ran to the desk, located a box of matches, and lit two tapers. All of the parchments were blank, the inkwell dry.

He'd left nothing behind.

Frantic, I shot to the dresser and jerked the drawers from their housing.

Empty.

Empty.

Empty.

A light-colored square in the middle of the bed's dark cover caught my eye.

How was it that fear could make you flee for your life one minute and then paralyze you the next?

I knew what it was even before I saw the little figures upon the parchment—he and I at Verus... the angry slashes of his brows... the leg he'd joked was his penis.

I crawled to the middle of the bed, picked up the parchment, and clutched it to my chest.

The door cracked open, and Ambrose slipped into the room. He came to the bed and laid his long body down in front of me.

"Eira," he dipped his head and tapped the tip of his nose to mine. "He needs time—do you remember what it was like, learning that you had been fed lies all your life? Afford him the period of grace and adjustment that you were not given."

Tears slipped down my cheeks and onto the pillow that should've smelled like Cato but didn't.

"Where has he gone? Will he return?"

"Basilia... to the far west of the kingdom." Ambrose offered me a sad smile.

"And will he return?" I asked again.

Silence.

"Ambrose? Answer me," I choked out.

"Who but the Goddess knows a man's future?"

CHAPTER 44

RIGHT HERE. THAT'S WHERE.

We woke to snow.

I looked out from the solarium window and watched the Joining guests scatter.

Was Cato dressed warmly enough? Had he been caught in the snow? How did horse hooves manage on the ice?

"Storms like that, this late in the year, it's no wonder the soil is frozen this morning. The light show was spectacular, though. We watched from Ethens's house. It's the sweetest little cottage, so quaint and comfy. The pink is ghastly, but he says I can paint the whole place if I'd like, or we could move. I told him I'd only consider a larger home if we worked quickly to expand the family. Otherwise, there would be no need. We also—"

"Pass me that lap blanket if you don't intend to use it, Cinden. My body is experiencing acute hypothermia, and I'll soon perish if my big bum doesn't thaw," Richelle interrupted. "That's what happened to my aunt Milla."

Cinden reached behind her chair and pulled the thick blanket over its back.

"Your aunt passed away from ass-freeze?" Cinden looked at Richelle with a dubious expression on her face.

"No, the flu, but that's how it starts. You get too cold and all of a sudden, your lungs cease working and fill with phlegm. It's all about the cold, Cinden... it's what gets us all in the end."

"That's... Richelle, I've known of maybe two in Nortia who have perished from the flu, and it's the coldest place in all—"

"That proves my point." Richelle pulled a fur-lined cap over her curls so tightly that her orangish hair stood out like a shelf from either side of her head. "This place is barbaric. It's so frigid, I can barely form words."

"Truly? Your mouth seems to be flapping just fine. Now, where was I? Right, I'd like to have a baby as—"

"Cinden, I'd like the following songs sung at my funeral. Eira, make a note. Are you listening?"

Would he return before or after the thaw? What if he made the attempt and got the hypothermic-ass-flu? He'd be alone in the middle of nowhere and a fae-beautiful woman with hair like the sun's rays would happen upon his battered body and nurse him back to health and then their babies would be born all beautiful and golden and perfect.

A red-clad servant caught my attention, pulling me momentarily out of my depressive thought process. He was running back and forth, breaking down tents in a record amount of time, while a Solnnan woman stood watching, wiping tears from her eyes. She was probably succumbing to the ass-flu as well.

As carriages rolled by, the ensconced nobles were drawing their curtains closed over the frosty windows. Others were waving for their footmen to make haste, while the men were blowing hot air into their hands between every piece of luggage they packed.

Lilium sat next to me, sharing the view. She was silent as always, but her presence was a comfort—something normal and consistent. Like myself, the normally vivacious and chatty Allaine found herself in no mood for companionship. She must have caught my case of bleakness. Her brows had been furrowed for the last quarter of an hour, and she'd been staring at the hand in her lap, fidgeting with her perfectly polished nails. Perhaps she was having a higher pain level day.

"I don't want a ceremony at all, but Penrod insists on at least a formal dinner, therefore we will dine and—"

What did she...?

"Penrod. His name is Penrod Ethens?" I interrupted.

"It is, yes, Penrod Bigyan Ethens... Do you have a problem with my betrothed's name?" Cinden's curls bounced around her head and shoulders as she glared in my direction. "Anyway, it will take place tomorrow. You and Ambrose will of course be attending, and if you could please wear something other than blue... and have your hair restored, for Goddess's sake. Eira, you look like a—chubby little cock."

"Pardon me?"

Richelle went to giggles, and even the morose Allaine looked up in amusement.

"Have you never seen one of those puffy-headed cocks? When they peck their grain, their plumes flap and flop just like that." Cinden pointed to my head.

I ran both hands through my hair. This morning, I'd been too down in my feelings to care about my appearance, even when Allaine threatened to flog me if I walked out looking like "the hairball spewed forth by a vomitous feline."

I'd removed the faux tresses and left them in a pile on the bathing chamber counter while she wailed and chastised me. She couldn't be told, of course, but I had to rid myself of the fakery after my ill-fated, or maybe Goddess-fated, encounter with Septimus.

"I rather like it shorn," I said in a bleak tone before turning back to the window. I caught Lilium's eyes briefly, and she pressed her lips together in an expression of sympathy.

She knows.

"I'm starving. Shall we? Everything smells scrumptious!" Like the love she was, Richelle had been trying for the last hour to improve the somber mood of our breakfast. Nothing about bean paste smelled appetizing.

"You go ahead; I took my meal earlier," I lied smoothly. I didn't want to eat. I didn't want to move—I didn't want to be out of bed, quite frankly.

The two Troth and my lady's maid went to the sideboard to break their fast. I watched Cinden chatter non-stop as a disinterested Allaine walked behind Richelle, absentmindedly loading up a platter as the Troth pointed to a variety of foodstuffs.

"Thank you," Lilium whispered. I didn't turn toward her. I simply nodded my head.

"If you can, don't allow him to spend in your body for a few days. The tincture will be more effective that way."

From the corner of my eye, I caught her acknowledgment in the slight inclination of her chin.

"As Protector, he will remain in the palace now... unless I am in my fertile period."

To my eternal disgust, my clitoris pulsed and tightened at the thought of *her* revolting husband popping off. The æther constricted in my chest, responding to our Bond.

"You had another loss recently, yes? Would you like a priestess to come to your home? I can arrange a—"

The exterior doors swung open, hitting the walls so hard that the prisms above our heads went dancing. Rainbows bent and shimmered on the walls and floor, taunting me with their happy beams.

Imella and Nan burst through the threshold, their voices raised and their arms locked together at the elbows. The sight was almost enough to make me feel *something* other than desolation... almost.

"The future is coffee! I'm telling you, I have *never* been this full of energy! And to think the Baldorvans sit their detritus dicks on the most massive supply! It's no wonder the Mantle opened the borders. Their priestesses will be hopped up like a husk of horny hares! They'll spread the Goddess's word across the seas before sunrise."

"I disagree, Nanetta! Wine is where the market will flourish. Do not look at me so. I'm not speaking of the heavy Gaean brews our grandmothers grew up on, but the light and crisp flavors coming from the Solnnan vintners. Mark my words, Emissary—Gammond's gonads, you're a gloomy bunch." Imella grimaced in concern.

"I'm cold." Richelle supplied from the mound of layers that ensconced her.

Imella and Nan squeezed themselves into the empty spots around the table and both laid into the bite-sized sandwiches of watercress and cucumber.

"That's vile." Nan screwed up her face and tossed the partially eaten triangle back on its platter. "My girl, you look like the regurgitated pellet of a snow owl's supper. The day is fine and covered in white. Let us venture into the elements, you and I."

I managed a half-smile.

"Perhaps later. I'm tired, Nan."

"From the bedsport?" Richelle quipped before she snipped the tip off a celery stalk. "Ooooh, did he wear his horns to bed, Eira? Please tell me you wore the fur pants!"

I did giggle then, with the rest of the ladies.

"Scion Ambrose... how he watched you at breakfast. I want a man to look at me like that, like I'm a juicy, fatty slab of sausage and he is a carnivore starved."

"You're the most succulent of sausages I know, and I appreciate your wit and humor beyond even your comely form, Chelle." I meant it too. I loved her round face and her beautiful bow-shaped mouth. You couldn't help but be happy in the glow that seemed to surround her.

"Eira, you say the sweetest things." Richelle squeezed her hands together and scrunched her shoulders up to her ears. "Oh, and speaking of breakfast, gracious Goddess's light, what of the king's proclamations? A new school, the Protector a prince again. With just a few words, the scribes will be scribbling new histories!"

And back to depression.

"It will be odd not seeing the Protect—Prince Catommandus stomping through the halls all scowly and domineering. But how exciting for him to have his birthright restored." Allaine finally found her voice—even though I wished she wouldn't have. "My father told me he saddled his steed himself and headed east to seek his fortune."

"East? I thought Basilia was to the west. I heard that was his destination," I said in the calmest voice I could.

My heart sank into my stomach, and the æther followed it, binding up my belly in an uncomfortable knot.

Under the table, Imella's hand settled on my thigh.

"Though I am saddened by his departure, Burchard, Goddess bless him, has saved our child. No longer will violence be a constant in his life—I will never again sit by his unconscious and battered body. My mother's heart knows peace after more than a decade of worry."

I covered her hand with my own and squeezed, needing to borrow from her reserve of strength.

She was right, of course. If I had to choose between seeing him again or seeing his burial shroud, the choice would be simple. My selfish heart just couldn't understand why fate had wronged me. It should have been Cato's name signed next to mine on the Joining contract—sharing his name, his babies.

Stop Eira, you have a fine husband and a committed mate. Just. Stop.

Richelle handed her plate off to a servant and dabbed the corners of her mouth with a linen.

"No less than an hour after yesterday's breakfast, my brother sent a missive to Solnna, promulgating the news of Ærta's most eligible bachelor. He told the rider the timing was undoubtedly advantageous, as Nortia would have yet to hear the news and the Gaean Primus-King would have to make it home to send the proper dignitaries to make a match. Our recently widowed princess has proven fertile twice and is renowned for her beauty and sharp wit—she would make a brilliant partner for Prince Catommandus, unless he's infertile as the rumor mill says—"

"If he was unable to breed it would make him no lesser. He would be the best of fathers to a little like my Ambrose," Imella said.

Cinden reached across the table and grabbed the remaining sandwiches from Allaine's plate before the servant could spirit her dish away.

"Yes, the new prince is *quite* the prize—if you're interested in a hulking brute who lacks personality." Cinden leaned in close and dropped her lids low as she addressed my lady's maid. "You know, he and Eira became *very* good friends at Verus, but in the end, she chose the right brother."

"Cinden!" I kicked out under the table.

"Ouch!" Nan hollered, shooting a disgruntled look in my direction.

The room filled with gruff puppy giggles.

"Well, that makes sense now—the Protector is always popping in to say hello. Even when Ambrose was away, he made sure to—"

"Ambrose!" Nan yelped. "Is there any other as, as strapping? And there was never a finer conversationalist. Mark my words, a truer gentleman there's never been."

Goddess bless Nan for trying.

Cinden pressed her lips into a thin line, thoroughly unconvinced. Richelle bobbed her head up and down in agreement.

"Cato began a much too serious occupation early in his life. Ambrose is the kindest of my children, and he is a good boy and will be the most devout husband. Eira is lucky to have claimed his heart." Imella raised her chin, and her dark eyes met mine.

"And I will do well by him, Imella." *Even with a heart this heavy.*

"Speak of the Goddess."

Ambrose swept through the solarium, commanding the attention of all in the room. Two servants trailed behind him, running to keep up with his long-legged strides.

"Wife! I have planned an adventure. Get up, put this on." He held out his hand, and when nothing appeared in his palm, he stamped his foot on the floor and whipped his head around. "Gus, how have you remained in my employ for such a long duration?"

Huffing and panting, the servant, who had just caught up, flopped a mass of brown fur over Ambrose's arm and dropped down in a sloppy bow.

Ambrose lobbed the garment.

My vision went dark.

Mariticide.

"Ambrose, I swear to the fu—"

"—*Fur*-cking Goddess?" He giggled that high-pitched giggle of his, and the ladies who surrounded us joined in, tittering right along at his ridiculous joke.

I flailed about and yanked the fluffy mass over my head, which caused the short tufts of my hair to cling to my forehead and static to shock the shit out of my cheeks.

Ambrose's mouth turned down at the corners.

"No, no, leave it—beaver is better than what currently crowns your head, and until you acquiesce to having your tresses reattached, I recommend pulling the hood more closely about the face." Ambrose blinked down innocently and smiled the sweetest of his smiles while pointing to my head and drawing circles in the air. "The beaver's fur reminded me so much of you, dearest love, for they are consistently slick on account of their wet habitats, much like your—"

I snatched the heavy coat between my fists and ripped the hood from its body in one swift motion.

"Beavers are industrious, noble creatures, my pup," Nan interjected while plucking the hood from my hands. "It is my understanding that they are handsome critters who, um, build lovely homes and… stack things neatly."

Richelle smacked her hands over her mouth, and her rounded, sloping shoulders went to shaking.

"Are they, Nan?" I slowly twisted my head in her direction. "And how many beavers do you suppose you've come across in your lifetime? Hmmm?"

"Not nearly as many as I," Ambrose smirked. Without warning, he squatted low, yanked my hands hard, and tossed me over his shoulder.

"Put me down this instant!"

"Still your splendid lips, wife." The coat found its way back over my face, obscuring my vision. "I command you to silence." The sharp point of his shoulder dug into my stomach as he turned and strode away from the group of cackling women.

"Bunch of traitorous hags!" I yelled. "Pile of… of a—oof!" The feet of the scrambling servants appeared and disappeared as the fur flopped over my eyes. "Am-brose, put—ugh! Put me down!" I groaned with each jostling step.

He ignored me entirely.

"Have you bathed?" His hand slipped under my dress and roamed up my leg, then settled on my thigh. He audibly sniffed my backside.

"Have I—yes, of course I—"

"Good, I am sensitive to the fact that one of the first signs of someone slipping into a spell of sadness is their inability to perform their hygienics." His hand strayed further still and pushed at my left cheek. A finger poked my underwear aside and then probed at my labia. "Bone dry, as I feared. Eira, I grow increasingly concerned. You were flooded when I slipped between your thighs in the night, but your current state tells me—"

"It tells you nothing, you giant jack-dick! Women aren't constantly—you did what? YOU. DID. WHAT?" I hammered my fists against his back and kicked my foot into his stomach.

"Quit your writhing. My belly is still tender from my close brush with piratical doom. You would have known that had you cared enough to inquire about my journey instead of forcing yourself upon my bulge the moment I returned home."

"Ambrooo—ahhh!"

I flew through the air and landed with a hard thud.

The snow-covered pile of leaves softened nothing—quite the opposite. The mound deflated rapidly on contact, and a shock of pain went straight through the bones of my buttocks.

"How dare you! You had no right to—"

"Oh hush, *you* forced your plump puss onto *me*. You kept whispering, 'Catom, oh, Catom, ohhhhh Catommandus.' I tried to move away on account of you interrupting my slumber, but then conceded to your endless whimpers. In the future, know that I do not mind a night fuck, but would prefer it to happen when I am not slated for an early morning meeting."

"And I'd *prefer* it *not* happen at all if I'm not awake."

"Eh." Ambrose pursed those perfect lips of his while shrugging a single shoulder.

I struck out at his face as I scrambled to my feet, but he caught my hands and tossed me back to the ground, where I landed on my knees. Mud seeped into the wool of my dress, further fueling the anger that he was so thoroughly inspiring.

"One. Two." Ambrose pulled a pair of leather gloves from his coat pocket and began to slide them over his hands. "Three. Four." He peeled out of his heavy outer garment and began stretching his arms up and over his head. "How long does Cat give you before he pursues?"

"What?"

"Five." He crossed an arm over his chest and pulled the elbow back with his opposite hand. "Today's adventure. I will chase you through the forest, rough you up a touch, and then fuck you on all fours—Catommandus assured me this was your preference." Ambrose bent at the waist and touched his fingers to his toes. "Your glum attitude is entirely unappealing, so while he is away, I will endeavor to cheer you similarly. Six—should you be running?"

Is this—is this my life? All I want when I wake up is alone time with a pastry. That's reasonable, right?

"Seven, lazy lady. When I get to ten, your skirts fly over your head and Gus over there gets a story to tell the lads. If possible, make your way toward a suitably leaf-covered patch. My knees prefer a slight cushion, but not so much that my traction suffers. Ah, and I have placed warmed bags of rice under my testes to ensure a solid rise in this temperature."

My mouth dropped open. I wasn't sure if I should thank him for his forethought or berate him for his absolute absurdity.

"Ambrose, do you not see Maihon? And there are two men standing twenty feet behind your back," I looked around and flung my arm out, pointing in the direction of the palace, "and that is no forest—it's barely a thicket!"

"Ingrate."

A soggy glob of cold mud plopped in the middle of my face and ran down the sides of my nose.

Don't. Do not cry, Eira.

I choked back a sob and slapped my palms on the hard ground, ready to relent and give in to the tears that were already stinging the backs of my eyes.

With the flick of his toe, Ambrose launched another blob, hitting me in the temple. The chunky sludge ran down my cheek and neck.

I wiped my hand down my face and looked at the shit-colored stain that came away. *Fucking. Prick.*

"ASSHOLLLEEE!" The æther surged to my toes. I lunged up and forward like the ammunition shot from a catapult's cup and called upon the harpies of ancient legend to aid me. I screeched my displeasure so shrilly that Ambrose stopped in the middle of scooping his toes into the dirt for the third time. He cocked his head to the side as the realization of his imminent demise dawned.

"You better run, fucker!"

"This isn't how—gods!"

Ambrose turned tail and took off across the yard. He hustled past his servants, heading to the sanctuary of the palace. His footman, bound to his person, took off after him, albeit at a much slower pace.

I outstripped them with ease—his help was no match for a woman scorned, and right now, I was so fucking scorned.

Ambrose zigged his way across the back lawn. I ignored my burning lungs and pushed off the balls of my feet, digging into the ground like the great snow wolves did when running from one side of Nortia to the other.

I bared my teeth when I could hear him breathe.

I curled my lips back and sniffed the air, scenting his trepidation. For once, *I* was the predator.

"This is not at all stimulating!" He yelled over his shoulder. "This practice will firmly remain in Cato's wheelhouse!"

"Don't mention his name. Don't let it pass from your lips again!"

Ambrose zigged again when he should have damn well zagged.

There it was... his failure.

His heel slipped along the snow-topped ground, and I smelled my supper. My feet knew the snow, were one with its slickness.

His knee sank low.

And I sprang.

Fingers like hawk talons and legs spread wide, I launched myself through the air and wrapped my body around his back.

"YEESH!" Ambrose went down hard and slid a solid foot before face-planting firmly on the ground. I pulled his arms behind his back and locked them with my elbow.

"We can do this in one of two ways, *husband*. I'll flip *your* pants down and—"

The two servants and Maihon hustled their way to our sides and scrambled to help Ambrose to his feet. They knocked me aside into a watery puddle.

"Yes, well, you now understand the proper technique of subduing your captive as they make to flee. The pirate I impaled never saw it coming when I leapt upon his person." Ambrose waved a grass and mud-stained hand in front of my face, offering his aid. I took it and dug my nails into the backside of his palm. He didn't flinch at all. "You performed the drill adequately, but on account of your low level of fitness, and had I not faked faltering, you would have come up empty-handed."

I glared at the oaf and clenched my teeth together to keep from biting his fingers. "Husband. You. Are. Pure. Thoughtfulness," I ground out. Flakes of dirt worked their way into my mouth, mingling with my saliva. I cleared my throat loudly and spat the contents on the toe of his shoe.

"Your aim is satisfactory."

Ambrose looked nonchalantly at the ground and then yanked me to his side.

"Onward!" He pulled me along as he paraded forward, his fist thrust in the air.

"Ambrose, please, I think I'm done with adventuring and—"

"Nonsense." He took the fur coat from the heavily winded Gus and wrapped it tightly around my shoulders. "You will enjoy this one. I am sure of it."

"Are you, though?"

"Shut up."

We strode along the—well, he strode. I ambled slowly behind the servants, watching the two jog to keep up with Ambrose.

I followed the group through a massive barn door and encountered the pungent smell of saddle leather and dung. We walked down a long row of stalls filled with ponies, many of whom were filling their faces with the grain mixture that a stable hand had just poured into their feed buckets.

"Now, you are feeling something that I myself do not understand," Ambrose pulled back the gate that closed off the furthest stall, "but I hope this will…"

My heart—my whole heart—exploded with love.

"Amb—" I flung myself at him and buried my head between his pecs. "Im camb buweave wu dib bis," I sobbed.

He pushed my shoulders back and held me at arm's length, like a stinking wet sponge that had sat out too long.

"Come along."

"No, just hold me."

"Move, wife." He forced-turned me and walked me forward.

I peered inside the cubby while my tears dropped to the hay-covered floor.

A wedge of cheese, a crusty pie, and an old, decrepit pair of boots sat in a line against the far side of the wall. Above them, there was a framed parchment with a magnificently rendered drawing of Cato, horse Ambrose, and the mountain cat that had attacked Cato while we sought refuge at the abandoned farmstead. The cat was patting Cato on the back and was rendered to have a happy, humanlike smile.

"You said it was the last place you felt at peace or some such nonsense. I do not understand it, living in a fortified castle as we do, but then again, I'm not the one wallowing in despair—"

I stuck my mud-splattered face between his lapels and let loose my pain, weeping like I had the day my father explained that my grandmother wouldn't be returning. Ambrose bound me up in his arms and swayed back and forth, cooing and making those little comforting noises of his.

"Ahem."

"Go away, for fuck's sake," Ambrose spat at the servant who dared to interrupt our moment.

"Hi-Highness, we were given direct orders by the Protect—His Highness Catommandus—that we were to escort you to all outings, functions, and events, and not allow you to linger in one place for a lengthy amount of time."

"What about when I defecate? What did he say to do for my well-being then? No doubt, it is the instance in which I take the most time and find myself most vulnerable. How will I get on without two pea-brained banana slugs flopping about as I digest the day's news while taking my morning shit?"

The servants stared at the Monwyn heir, confusion and horror vying for a place on their faces.

"It-it's when he does his deepest thinking," I supplied. The two nodded in unison. "I feel like, knowing the Protector—His other Highness, as I do, he would allow you both to stand at the barn's entrance to keep watch. There is, to my knowledge," I leaned back and looked both ways, "no other way in or out."

The taller of the two men followed the trajectory of my eyes, seeing for himself that I spoke the truth. He nodded once, and then he and his counterpart took their leave.

"Inside." He squatted below a piece of black fabric that hung from the surrounding posts, placed just high enough that I could walk in without having to bend. He sat down in the freshly scattered hay, patted his shoulder, and then held his hand out to me. I placed my smaller palm into his large one and joined him. He reached out a long leg and rolled the door shut with his foot.

"What master artist did you hire to create the portrait?" I whispered in the dark as I nestled closer to his side. My cheek met his bicep, but he shifted, dropped his arm behind me, and gently pressed my head down to rest on his chest.

"There are no artists here. Cato allowed no one to enter unless they bore the formal invitation allowing them safe passage—I drew it."

Although I couldn't see his face, his aloof but hopeful tone told me he was perhaps a little bashful about sharing it with me.

"I absolutely adore it, but there is one thing I wish you would have included."

"What? An explosion? A broken little deer in the cat's mouth? Can you not simply be—"

I slapped my hand over his mouth, ending his tirade.

"You, Ambrose. I wish you would have included yourself. I love the idea of waking up and seeing our new little family... or what remains of it." My voice caught in my throat.

"Eira, why do you act as if he has gone to his eternal rest? Can you think rationally for a moment?"

"I could think rationally if *you* would speak truthfully. I know he headed east, Ambrose, not west. Where is he?"

Silence.

I let my fingers walk over the pulse in his neck.

"That will never work on me."

"Because you're a good Scion."

"Because I am the *best* Scion—now tell me, delectably plump little wife, when did you stop putting your trust in my brother?" Ambrose deflected my question, avoiding the topic of Cato's whereabouts entirely.

Two could play that game.

I lifted my head and kissed his whiskers.

"When did you fall in love with me, husband?"

He reared his head back and scoffed.

"You have gone quite mad." His hand came to rest on my forehead. "No fever. Your æther must be out of alignment or perhaps it is gas causing you to—"

"You are a man besotted with your wife. You show all the signs, and it's okay to love me, Black Bear."

He bristled under my touch.

"I am contractually obliged to maintain you as befits your station, Eira, and... Oh, you clever Troth. I see what you're doing."

I slid my arm around his waist and held on tight.

"Why is your trust waning, Eira? Why do you not believe me when I tell you he *will* return?"

I let my shoulders sag and my full weight rest upon his powerful body.

"Because... because the pull—the Bond that we have—it's dimmed since he left. And I am so fearful that it signifies our end."

Ambrose stroked my hair like someone would a favored pet.

"Silly woman, always listening to your silly woman's brain. Do you love him any less this morning?"

"No."

"So do you imagine he loves you any less? I have never known a man so enamored."

I shook my head even though I wanted to deny the big ogre's rational counsel—I wished to be as dramatic and forlorn as I felt.

"I hardly remember my life before him, Ambrose, and don't want to think of a hereafter unless he is with me—with us."

Ambrose nuzzled the short hair on my head with his nose, pushing the longer lock into my eyes.

"Then I suggest you put your trust in him and realize that he is feeling similarly with no other there to console him."

"But where is he, Ambrose? Where?"

His heavy hand shifted down and pressed firmly against the middle of my chest.

"Tucked away and safe, right here, I would imagine."

Chapter 45

EXTREME BRUTALITY

"And so naturally, your mind went first to murder?" Ambrose laid his head back on my knees while I scrubbed the hay and mud from his hair. "Nasty netherdog," he muttered under his breath.

"I—yes, yes, it did. And coming from the man who orchestrated the deaths of an elder and a high healer, I'm surprised to see that *you* are surprised by my plan of action." I leaned over his head and looked into his thickly lashed eyes. His eyebrows rested at the top of his forehead and his lips were drawn into a severe line.

"Yes, well. Your plan presents two issues. First, Lemder is an absolute beast in battle, and despite his bluster, he is a master tactician. Second, with Cato gone and Septimus learning the law of the land, presumably *without* having been informed of the ghouls and grossness that prowl in the night, Lemder's continued presence is necessary. He has proven himself able to guard the realm in Cato's stead, and for the sake of our citizens, he must remain. More to the point, I would have all hands on deck until we know the Gaean contingent is far from here."

I shivered, even as the heat of the spice-scented water lapped around my legs.

"Not to worry. We have scouts following the Primus-King's party, and they have orders to remain with them until they reach the Gaean border. The only foreigners in these halls are the representatives scrambling to get their contracts into my father's hands for..."

Ambrose sat up and swung around. He flung his wet hair around his back, splashing water over my chest support and across the bathing chamber floor. "Spread your legs. I have the sudden urge to savor your... flavor." He wrenched my thighs apart and dropped his head.

"No, sir, finish your sentence." I placed my palms against his cheeks and struggled to pull his head up. "This is not how couples communicate."

Ambrose stuck his tongue out and pressed forward, using all the power in his muscly neck. His face stretched back, and his lips pulled comically, making him look like a sea-slicked seal. I held on until my biceps began to shake.

"Ambrose, spit it out."

With his tongue still lapping in the air, he tried unsuccessfully to roll his eyes under his elongated lids.

"Gaea and Solnna—they meet with His Majesty this evening to discuss future Joinings. My father is quite taken with finding Catommandus the perfect bride."

"Well, that simply won't do." I relaxed my death grip and rested my chin on Ambrose's shoulder. "I expect you to perform your husbandly duties when the time comes. In this instance, that means committing acts of extreme brutality against anyone who attempts to hone in on our trio. Do I make myself clear?"

"Transparent."

"Especially if it's a she."

"Derros's dick, Nortia, you jealous shit. More and more, I find myself wondering *why* you let me near him—encouraged him to take me, even. My backside *is* first rate, but with the way you carry on..."

"Ambrose... I was so aroused by the idea of being trussed up and spitroasted like a two-hundred-plus-pound beef butt, that I would have agreed to all manner of sexual escapades that night. And I figured you would enjoy being... pronged. Pitchforked? I don't know what to call it, but it was wonderful, wasn't it? Did you see his face when he came?" A powerful shudder rolled through me, and sharp-footed pixies ran the length of my arms, raising tiny bumps in their wake. "That's my *why*."

"My gods, yes, the half-closed eyes, those parted lips, and the positively carnal manner in which he took your slit—were I able to birth his short and angry spawn..."

Ambrose gnashed his teeth, and I mimicked the gesture, snapping mine back and growling a feminine little snarl. He smiled a full, beaming smile, and his eyes darkened as he leaned forward.

"Finish washing me, wife. I have gone all stiff and require—"

"—your parted lips on my clitoris?" I raised my brows and wagged them suggestively. "Don't start what you aren't willing to finish, sir." I reached out and fisted my hand into his hair, pulled his head down, and spread my legs wide.

Green eyes glittered as he slid his arms under my thighs and tugged my dark curls between his teeth. He planted a kiss in the middle of my vulva while making a low groan in the back of his throat.

"Mmmm, yes—I *always* finish. Hard or soft, wife? Fingered or fucked? Two in the conch, one in the starfish?"

I tipped my head back as two fingers slowly submerged into my passage.

"Whatever you prefer, husband mine. You've proven adept at all manner of—"

"HOLY MOTHER WHO BIRTHED THE SUN!"

Allaine walked through the door carrying a fresh stack of linens. The surprise in her eyes rivaled that of a hoot owl at hunt.

Ambrose popped up, erect as an obelisk, and whipped his business in her direction.

"Lady Allaine Lemder, you are just the person I was looking for."

"FOR WHAT FUCKING PURPOSE?" The whites of her eyes grew until they circled the entirety of her deep-blue irises.

"There is no need to curse, lady." Ambrose placed his fists on his hips and addressed her like he was clothed in his finest velvet. His lengthy appendage bobbled up and down like a fishing lure in a lake. "It is a simple task. I require a list of your father's closest friends and associates for a gathering to honor your brother. He is to receive a new rank."

She didn't move—she didn't bat an eyelash or take a breath.

"Lady Allaine? Are you able to carry out my order?"

Her left eye twitched, just a millimeter.

"A simple yes or no will suffice. Eira, is she quite alright? Is this on account of her—"

Allaine shifted to the left, looked me dead in the eyes, and mouthed, *This is how I die.*

Oh, shit.

"Ambrose, help her!"

With a one-armed vault, he jumped out of the bath and made it to her side just as she met the floor.

He checked her head for bruising and nodded satisfactorily when he found none, and then leaned over her prone body and laid his fingers across the inside of her wrist.

"She will be fine. I am sure of—"

"Ambrose, get your balls off her forehead."

CHAPTER 46

THE THOT PLICKENS

"Everyone who is anyone has been invited."

"And you think this will work?"

I sat on the edge of our big bed and let my eyes roam over Ambrose. He was dressed smartly in a mouthwateringly tailored coat of teal, whose hem stopped just above his impressive package. The white belt, adorned with gold fixtures, that he wore slung low on his hips, continually drew my eye exactly where he meant it to. Tan leathers accentuated his muscular thighs, and the dark-brown knee boots he wore curved perfectly around his sculpted calves.

"If you play your role well enough, it will." He secured the onyx-and-diamond whale brooch to his shoulder and then made his way across the floor to affix his bear-head pin to the bottommost point of my neckline. "I like this dress on you."

I slanted my shoulders from side to side, preening like a proud peahen. I'd decided to wear the blue chiffon gown that I'd bathed him in—the moment had been defining for me and it was a physical reminder of exactly how much I owed him, as once again Ambrose swooped in to solve the issues *I* had created.

A loud drumming sound came from the common room.

Ambrose sprinted to the door, his hand on the hilt of the dagger he wore at his hip.

"IT IS I, ALLAINE, ANNOUNCING MY PRESENCE. I AM ENTER-ING! I AM WALKING THROUGH THE DOOR AT THIS VERY MO-MENT."

A single brown shoe swept over the threshold, tapping its toe on the floor. "Acknowledge my presence if you will. Do it or I shall not take another step."

Ambrose pressed his fingers to his eyelids, briefly sending up a prayer.

"We acknowledge your prudish inclinations, lady. Do present us with the rest of your priggish person."

"Ambrose, don't you dare pass judgment over her," I said as I shooed him away from the door.

"It is my job to sit in judgment, as her prince." He looked down his nose dismissively and flicked his fingers in my face.

"I mean it." I grabbed his arm, held it tightly, and attempted to punch him in the guts. "She's already had to deal with the likes of Greggen and his inappropriate attempt at embarrassing her publicly. I'll not allow you to do the same. She gets to feel her feelings exactly as she wants to. Apologize."

"I will not."

I yanked his long arm as I bent my knees and tucked my shoulder into his chest like Cato had done. I'd toss the fucker and sit on him until he acquiesced.

"Yah!" I arched up fast, pushed with all the strength in my thighs, and stomped my foot on the floor, leveraging his weight against him.

"Are you... Have you finished your attempt?" Ambrose yawned behind me, standing there as straight as he had been three seconds ago.

"No." I tucked my butt more securely against his legs and then shuffled my foot, testing the grip of my shoes.

"YAH!" I arched and stomped again, this time calling upon the strength of the Seven Cyclops's.

Suddenly, he was weightless, spinning over my shoulder in a perfect arc.

Victory! I had *never* felt more powerful.

Until he landed gracefully on both feet, pulling me easily over my center of balance and gently pushing me to the ground with one hand.

"Do it, Ambrose. It doesn't matter how you or I feel—she gets to set her own boundaries."

An artfully combed brow shot up.

"Ugh. Do it, please, most handsome man to grace the Ærtan soil."

He nodded and helped me to my feet.

"I apologize, madam, that you had the honor of witnessing two of the Creator's finest works of art... and that your mind could not handle their combined splendor."

My lady's maid finally stepped into the room.

"Allaine, there is not a thing wrong with your preference. His *High-ass* is a conceited lecher."

"I accept your coerced apology, Highness." Allaine curtsied low, bowed her head, and held out a handful of parchments.

Ambrose walked to her in his most sensual of Ambrose saunters—slow and yet full of cocky confidence. He waited patiently in front of my maid until she looked up from under her lashes.

Her cheeks went the most brilliant shade of scarlet.

"You see, my lady." Ambrose reached for the papers, allowing his fingers to caress hers for a scant second. Allaine wobbled on her bent knees. "It is not the clothing or lack thereof that makes the man." He slid the missive from her hand without breaking eye contact. "It is his confidence."

"Allaine, breathe. Ambrose, cut it out."

A wolfish smile spread across his face. He straightened and moved away, giving her a reprieve from the onslaught of his overwhelming sex appeal.

"Anyone missing from the list?" asked Ambrose as he leafed through the stack.

"No, Highness, they are all accounted for. I saw to the task myself. Lord Dumail looked outright offended when he broke the seal and read your missive. Which offended me greatly on account of the party being for my brother, but he will be there regardless and—"

"Not to worry, he just recognizes that his gaggle of daughters will never rise in the ranks like your talented sibling has." Ambrose crooked his elbow and faced the door. "Wife, to my side."

Ah, yes. Dominant Ambrose would be on display at the Den this eve.

I took his arm, and the three of us proceeded out of the palace and into the waiting carriage.

Half an hour later, we arrived at the quaint little restaurant—the front for the notorious netherworld below. Allaine and I were cloaked in hooded furs, mine as white as a snow leopard's fur and hers a red fox. Ambrose tossed his full-length coat to the doorman but waved him off when the man made to remove mine.

"Wife, after a quick greeting, you will proceed to the lower level. When Lord Lemder and his sons arrive the women should be unseen. This is a matter for the men. You will find refreshments below."

"Yes, love puffin," I replied, my smile sickly sweet.

I turned and placed my hand against the small of Allaine's back, propelling her toward the bar.

The restaurant smelled of freshly baked bread and cured meats, and a massive spread of cheese and pickled vegetables accommodated the guests, many of whom had already arrived and were tipping back pints. We made our way to the woman behind the counter, who was drying copper tankards with her apron.

"Thank you for accommodating us on such short notice." I held out my hand and let a heavy purse of coins land on the polished wood. The thud drew the attention of many a man in the crowd. "My maid and I will head down. Your name?" I asked the woman as she snatched up more gold than she'd seen in a year.

"Sylva."

"Thank you for getting the door, Sylva."

The woman took off around the counter, ran across the floor, and held open the door that led to her cellar.

"Allaine, this is going to sound silly, but you will need to put this on."

I procured a length of heavy silk from my coat pocket.

"On where?" She took the thick ribbon from my hands and held it out between us.

"Over your eyes. Some royal secrets must remain just that. I hope Ambrose didn't see us pass through without it." I made a show of chewing the corner of my lip. "I know it seems ridiculous, but—"

"Not really. Aleks, my youngest brother, has told me of all manner of bizarre practices you upper-ups keep. No tiaras for the unmarried, sleeping with the finger bone under your pillow. Oh Josa... is this where you do the honey thing?" Allaine scrunched her nose up in distaste.

"Yes. Yes, it is."

"Then I'd prefer the darkness."

Mental note: find out what the nether the honey thing is and thoroughly search the bed for body parts.

On account of her height, I walked back up a few steps and pulled the red ribbon from her fingers. I tied it around her head and then pushed her heavy fur hood back up over her auburn curls. I took her hand and led my maid into Monwyn's immoral underground.

The bluish tint of the Den's lamps highlighted the bits of flesh and leather that were already on display. The hired men and women were in place, ready to welcome their customers.

A masked woman lay on a long table atop a raised platform in the middle of the room. She kicked her foot out rhythmically over the table's edge, giving off the impression that she was as bored as if she'd been in line at the healer's offices and not about to service an entire ministry's worth of officials.

Farther into the room, another woman was bound to a thin and very flexible man. Together, they had been suspended from the ceiling and tied up in an intricate system of knots that allowed his flaccid organ to hang about a hand's width from her vagina. The masked woman and the bound duo chatted animatedly about which restaurant in the city served the best beef-and-potato pie.

"This way, consort." A lush and full-figured woman with dark hair that fell past her shoulders approached us. She was just about my height and had a—*no way*!

I dropped Allaine's hand and waved for the woman to follow me.

"Are you me?" I asked while leading her away from my blindfolded, but not deaf, maid. "Are you supposed to be me?" I pointed to the obviously hand-drawn star that peeked above her sheer red pants. She laughed in a shrill and high tone, revealing two large, yellowing front teeth with a sizeable gap between them.

"Yep, and I have been since you was here the last time." She continued chuckling as she pulled down the neckline of her overgown, revealing a large breast and a glint of metal. "It ain't real." She flicked at the little gold balls that I assumed she'd glued on to her nipple. "I've fucked all the boys in this get-up—all but that angry blonde. He stares something fierce but he ain't never touched. Too bad, really—pretty one, he is."

I nodded my head rapidly in understanding. *Septimus is very pretty.*

"Well, I think you look amazing. May your night be profitable."

"Thanks, consort." She smiled happily and smoothed her hands over her hips, obviously thrilled by the compliment. "You sit there." She pointed to the same chair that Ambrose and I'd occupied, what seemed like forever ago *and* yesterday. I went to sit but remembered I'd left Allaine standing in the aisle.

Troth hat, Eira. Put it on. Goddess, there's no room for mistakes tonight.

I doubled back.

"Alright, step up... there you go. Hold on to the back to keep your balance." I placed Allaine's hand on the chair's top edge and squeezed it gently.

"A drink, consort?"

I took the bubbling glass from the slender hand of a beautiful human whose face was painted to perfection—their lips the red of late-fall apples, and their eyebrows darkened and lengthened to fine points. Unlike Eira-for-hire, when they smiled, their perfect rows of teeth formed a brilliant and dazzling crescent.

Light filtered down the steps, momentarily brightening the room. The group of musicians tucked into the corner struck up a slow and sensual song as the men descended. A number of entertainers began to move their bodies to the beat of a hand drum that tapped out a deep and resonant tattoo.

I stood, moved to Allaine's side, and flicked my eyes at Ambrose, who was leading the pack.

"Gentlemen, tonight we offer up a host of unusual delights. Help yourselves to whatever *fare* entices you."

"Dinner does smell delicious," Allaine whispered.

I watched from beneath my lashes as Ambrose made his way across the room, talking to a noble here and a well-to-do merchant there. He caught my veiled attempt at spying and let a half-smile flow across his lips as he made his way to the one-armed chair. When he sat, I ran my hand down his dark braid, tinkering with the amethyst-studded pins woven throughout, and then let my fingers find the edge of his ear. I traced the ring he wore—he was a man taken.

"Another already?" Dumail came to stand at our front and looked from Allaine to me. "I would have thought your appetites were satisfied with just the one."

"Be gone, Dumail. I saw enough of you on campaign to last a lifetime." Ambrose picked a speck of lint off of his sleeve and let it fall onto Dumail's shoes.

The courtier glared at Ambrose, then stepped back and left in a huff.

Allaine dropped her head near mine.

"That was rather rude. If His Highness wants seconds, I see no—"

"Lady Allaine, do hush." Ambrose interrupted. I gave her hand another reassuring squeeze.

"Wife. To me."

I removed my fur hood and unclasped the large hooks that kept the garment closed. Discount Eira ran over and took the cloak, and when she turned her back, Ambrose blinked up at me with a surprise-stricken eyes.

"Flattering, right?"

"Rather insulting, if you ask me. Never has anyone emulated *me*, and frankly, I would very much like to speak with the owner of this establishment to understand why." He took me by the hand and led me to his lap. "Make me feel better, wife."

I ran my hands up his chest and around his neck and then stretched my head up, exposing the column of my neck.

His lips settled below my ear.

"Reach into my pocket," he whispered. I did as was asked, and my fingers met with a thin stack of parchments. "All but two handed them over willingly. Sadly, Mikellen and Heveret are no longer with us."

I slid them out and tucked them in the neckline of my gown. On a whim, I reached back into his pocket and stroked his length with my fingertips.

"Better now?"

"My, my, that *is* delectable... and most soothing. I enjoy the unexpected delights the most." He bent his head and pressed his lips to the upper swell of one breast and then the other.

"I can have my mother's hen-and-herb soup brought to the palace if you feel poorly later—nothing soothes the soul better."

Ambrose looked at me with a deadpan expression.

"She is who she is," I murmured, running my finger down the adorable little divot in his bearded chin.

"Have I told you today how magnificent your tits are?"

"No, not today." I shook my head.

"I am drawn to your body, Eira... even more so now that it is my legal property."

"Compliment ruined," I admonished, "and to think I wanted to give you something special. That can wait now."

"A present?" His eyes lit up.

"Of sorts." I traced the lower edge of his jaw and brought my mouth a hair's breadth away from his. The tip of his tongue glided warmly across my lips.

"Give it to me, now."

"Fine." I kissed the tip of his nose and stared at him thoughtfully. "I believe I love you."

Ambrose's face remained impassive as I whispered the admission against his lips, but the surge of blood to his member told me he'd heard me... and heard me well. "I don't care if you don't feel the same, but I would've hated to have never said it to the man who has taken such care of my heart."

His pupils constricted as he looked out over my shoulder.

"Eira I—Your mark has arrived." He tipped his head just slightly to the left, indicating Lemder's location. "Do not go just yet. Let him get comfortable." Ambrose pulled me against his chest and swept back the volume of ringlets that Allaine had reattached and arranged. I'd directed her to place a forelock of light blonde at the front of the dark mass as a tribute to my homeland. It made me feel somehow stronger and, in a way, more daring.

"What do you think of our view, *consort?*" Ambrose's warm mouth skimmed across the back of my neck.

My breath caught.

The woman lying on the table was being stripped of her clothing by the four entertainers tending her. They were outfitted in matching costumes—thick straps of tan leather that circled their bodies. One belt ran over their nipples, another around their waists, and two more surrounded the tops of each thigh. Semi-sheer gold veils covered their heads and reached to their navels, and two had objects pushed into their backsides out of which protruded dangling strands of crystals and pearls.

"Would you like to be in her place?" Ambrose asked, his voice a husky rasp.

I breathed in quick gasps of air as Ambrose's hand settled on my upper thigh.

"I would watch their hands upon you, cupping those heavy breasts and holding them up to my lips. Their delicate fingers pushing into your body might be my undoing—you could easily take three after having accommodated our *third.*"

In unison, two of the women pulled open the halves of the prone woman's bodice, revealing a pair of exquisitely pert, brown-tipped breasts that wobbled beautifully before their weight settled to her sides.

My mouth went dry. I wiggled my bottom against Ambrose's lap, seeking to relieve the pressure of my hard-hitting arousal, but he held me in place.

"No, no reprieve for you yet. Let it overwhelm you. I will watch you struggle and think of nothing but how divinely wet you will become when you finally receive me—because I am the *only* relief you will receive. Isn't that right?"

I nodded and swallowed hard.

"Have you soaked through your fine silks yet? I'd wager you have, and when you stand, I will be looking. How miraculous is it that the Goddess gifted me a wife whose libido matches my own? I am eternally grateful."

I leaned into Ambrose and closed my eyes, focusing on the frustrating throb I adored.

"Now. Now is your time, wife. Watch him closely. Do not allow him to trap you mentally. If he dares to trap you physically, he will join the Scholar in his place of rest. They would make fine companions in the afterlife."

Ambrose slid his hand down my back and forced his fingers under my rear.

"By Gammond, my dove, you've soaked right through."

Behind me, I heard the smack of his lips.

Flames teemed through my limbs. The flicker in my uterus, combined with the promise of his teasing, ignited a fire that heated my flesh to a near burn. My face and neck flushed hotly, and if it weren't for him pushing me up, I would have suggested a foray to the bathing chamber.

I stood and locked in on my adversary.

Lemder was across the room, having his cock stroked through his pants by two women on their knees. He was jamming his meaty fingers into the unlucky one's mouth.

"Mmmm, so fine," Ambrose purred behind me.

I focused on my target, and like donning a favorite dress, my Troth mask slipped comfortably into place. The spot of my moisture cooled as my skirts fluttered around my legs, and as I walked around the table, the proof of the Goddess's goodness made me feel all the more potent.

"He permitted you to come without an escort? Did you beg him prettily, or was it *another* who gave the allowance?" Lemder said. I glanced between the women at his feet, but he didn't bother to ask them to cease their petting.

Instead of averting my eyes at his power-play, I let them roam openly over the raised outline of his pants. I tilted my head to the side.

"Slightly above average—not bad."

His mustache twitched, but his eyes remained static as he sat back, draping his elbows over his seat. I looked again from the redhead to the blonde, more pointedly this time, and then glanced back at the sprawled courtier.

"Oh, forgive me. Do you wish to speak to her? They know better than to open their mouths unless a prick is stuffed down their throats."

Murder. Murder is still an option.

"Anyhow, I find I am otherwise occupied at the moment, and you do have until the morning. Run along and find me then."

Lemder's hand went to the laces at his crotch. He pulled their ties, and his bulbous-headed penis sprung free. He reached for the blonde with his still-wet fingers.

"No. No, I am certain we will be speaking directly. Ladies, your techniques are excellent, but I would ask you to give myself and his lordship a moment."

"Fuck off, consort. I gave them coin. A whore like yourself should understand that payment given demands a service rendered—suck me off, slut," Lemder growled.

"You have forgotten your place, sir... and the fact that this whore has coin of her own." I tapped both women and when they looked over their shoulders, I smiled warmly.

"Ladies, go to His Highness and offer him the same treatment as Lemder here. Just hands over clothing, though. I don't want *his* filth upon my man. Don't let him come—tell him that honor belongs solely to me."

As the blonde stood, I trailed my finger down her arm.

"You are worth far more than the pittance he has coughed up." I produced two bars of gold and handed one to each, delighting in their happy laughter as they skipped away. "My good man, what would you give to have your daughter back home, ensconced within the bosom of her doting family?" Lemder's bushy brows drew down. His gaze darkened. "What would you give for her to remain... intact?"

I stepped to the side and watched his eyes widen and mouth fall.

About now, Ambrose should be removing Allaine's heavy cloak, telling her he was so very worried that it was much too hot for her to continue standing as she was.

"His Highness seeks a new playmate." I ventured a peek as I felt my wetness escape my vulva and down my inner thigh. Passion and power were a distractingly heady combination.

How beautiful Allaine was—her sense of honor and adherence to her principles exceeded that of any of the men who surrounded us.

Ambrose had set the stage well and was twirling one of her long ringlets around his finger. She was smiling and chattering happily, blissfully unaware.

I didn't feel an ounce of remorse as I turned back to face her father.

"Lord Lemder, your eldest boy, he sits above us dining with Captain Levaunt, correct?"

Lemder remained as stone.

"I've had a special meal prepared for him."

There it is.

The cheeks above his burly beard went just a shade darker.

I let my fingertips flirt with the neckline of my gown, and before he had time to form a plan, I slipped the parchments from their hiding place.

"Oh, and I'm not worried about these in the least." I held his *evidence* over his lap and let them rain down upon the flaccid lump of dough that hung out of his pants. "I do regret that two of our loyal noblewomen find themselves widows this night. I am confident I can procure them more compliant husbands, however."

Lemder's hand went to the hilt of his dagger.

"You have, I would venture, five minutes to make your decision. Walk upstairs quickly and collect your heir while he still breathes or send for your footmen. You'll need the extra hands—you do breed them rather big."

"And Allaine?" He looked over my head.

"She is *mine*, and I protect what is mine."

Lemder shot up, knocking me backward, but a strong hand came around my waist, steadying me as the giant flew by.

"Your arousal smells like freshly caught trout. I fucking love it."

The æther nearly leapt from my chest as my head fell back against the solid and familiar shoulder.

"My mouth remembers your taste, and we have only been parted for—"

"Ahdmundus," my whisper came out a prayer. "Septimus, step away from me." Thrills of desire and apprehension mingled, as a gush of wetness moistened my already slick passage. He stepped back, and the Bond screamed out in need of him. My fingertips stung, my palms turned hot, and my legs shook, barely able to keep me upright. Suddenly, the music was too loud for my ears, and the smell of bodies, food, and perfume overpowered me. Even the movements of the people around the room seemed more intense in my hypersensitive state.

I turned slowly, both hoping and fearing that Septimus would still be there. Instead, I was treated to the sight of a strapping young man framed by two shapely legs.

The masked woman on the table was being performed upon and, judging by their body language, the man was having the time of his life while she was clearly uncomfortable, but decent at faking it.

"Oh, yes. Yes. You are my master," she said in a bland, almost apathetic tone. "Skewer me. Yes. Oh, gods, yes."

I wouldn't have been surprised had she taken a timepiece from her pocket and checked to see how much longer she was on the clock.

The young man, probably in his early second decade, stood between her legs, shoving his finger into her passage like a man crazed—too fast, too forceful, and out of rhythm.

"Sir, have you no finesse? Can you not read the language of her body?"

The young man stopped his overeager plunging and stared at me as if he were caught in some crime. Which, quite frankly, he was.

"She likes it."

My hand whipped across his face, stunning him into silence.

"Did you like that? No? Okay, so now you understand."

He rubbed at his patchy brown beard and turned to leave.

"Get back here this instant."

The man hesitated briefly, but spurred on by either his curiosity or good manners, he returned to his place.

"Would it not increase your own desire to *know* that you brought her pleasure as well? Have you experienced a woman coming around your fingers? The way she swells and grows wetter, how she thrashes and arches under your touch? I'll take your blank stare to mean no. Move aside."

I sensed a shift in the room—the air became thick as the patrons closed in around us.

I stepped between the woman's legs, noting how red her labia had become—she was nearly desert-dry.

I looked at Ambrose and crooked my finger. He rose and walked toward me.

"Darling, would it be problematic if I demonstrated the proper techniques for pleasing a woman? I believe in this case, direct instruction is necessary."

His eyes went molten.

"Not if I get to watch, no." The dazzling white of his teeth flashed briefly as he tucked his bottom lip into his mouth. "By all means, continue your tutelage."

"Do I have your permission, miss?"

"You got gold?

"An abundance."

She spread her legs wider and laughed in a tinkling, yet slightly grating manner.

"Introduce your fingers slowly. Never go straight for the clitoris... it's too sensitive by far, and though it can give us great pleasure, it can also be intensely unpleasant if assaulted so aggressively." I skimmed my fingertips from her knees to her thighs and spread her lips wide, being careful not to aggravate them further. "She's made beautifully, is she not? The gradient of colors, her golden skin, darkening around the lips of her sex, then turning pink at her entrance—the Goddess's own garden."

I could hear the pulsing of my arousal in my ears.

"Ye-yes, I think it is kind of pretty—"

"Learn to give a sincere and direct compliment. It will take you far. Husband, an example if you will."

"The power in your form takes me back to the mines—the softness of youth melting, being forged in toil and flesh. Here stands a man tempered—the steel in his bones shows in his posture, the iron in his veins is displayed in the swell of his biceps, and his fine, broad back. His Monwyn virility is clearly evident in the—"

"I meant the woman, but thank you, Ambrose. Well done."

I took the young man's hand, and together we traced the woman's outer and inner lips.

"If she's not lubricating from your touch, try enticing her with your mouth to elicit a response."

"Give her more compliments?"

"Always more compliments, but no." I looked up at the ceiling and asked Derros to guide him. "*Use* your mouth."

He kneeled and I bent low and spoke over his shoulder.

"Trail that fine Monwyn man-braid down her thighs." I took a handful of my curls and ran them from her navel to her knee. "See her nipples hardening? Now, tell her what you plan to do to her; make her anticipate your tongue."

Bending my knees, I squatted, lowering myself to her level.

"Watch and learn."

I pressed the woman's thighs back, not apart, and inhaled her feminine scent.

"Mmmm, so lovely, you must wash in lilac-scented soap."

"Mmhmm," she breathed.

My own nipples hardened as I looked down upon her hooded gem. Æther clouded my mind.

"You have two main options at this point: ask her what she likes or listen to her body."

I closed my eyes, dipped my tongue between her large labia, and swirled gently into her passage, acclimating her to the sensation.

"Divine. The Goddess knew exactly what she was doing when she made us. See how her legs relax and how she has taken hold of her knees? That's encouragement. Next lesson, don't just flick your tongue back and forth. Add pressure and then back away. Pull her clitoris into your mouth and gently suck. If she responds, slowly increase the intensity until you are sucking her like a sugary Solnnan sweet."

I circled her clit with my wet lips and lavished my attention upon her until she hummed a sweet and light sound. The woman's hips rolled.

"Perfect, now you add in a finger and realize you are *not* mining for copper. This is an exploration, not an expedition."

I moved my chest to the side to accommodate his arm and watched him carefully introduce his digit.

"That *is* different." His face changed. His skin went ruddy, and he cleared his throat loudly as he glanced nervously at the gathered crowd. "I... uh... like it wet."

"So say we all," I smiled and arched my brow suggestively. "Now, feel around for a rough patch on the upper wall, but don't attack it—it's not a tiny troll."

"I cannot seem to—"

I dropped my hand and inserted my finger next to his. I pushed forward gently, adoring the texture and warmth of her passage.

"Here, miss?" asked the young man.

"Well done. When in doubt, ask."

"Yes, there, right there," the woman moaned.

The young man nodded without looking up, his concentration focused on the task at hand.

I set the tempo of our fingers and then pushed his head between her legs—he was a quick study. His broad tongue explored and caressed her until she dropped her hips and pushed off her feet, riding our combined fingers in her own rhythm.

"Don't stop or change *anything* if she's responding, which she clearly is." He looked from me to her and understanding finally dawned on his face. He dug in once again, giving it all he had: fingers, tongue, and a loud moan of his own.

Her breasts shot up and her back arched when her orgasm hit. The crowd of panting men watched us take her to the Goddess's realm.

"Ofillia is a rare beauty," someone said as the woman pinched her nipples between her fingers as she took her prize.

I froze.

Ofillia? Cato's Ofillia? I finger-fucked the enemy!

Oh, my Goddess, Cato... how would Cato see this act... where is my control?

"I have need of you." Ambrose placed his chin on my shoulder. "I have sent Allaine upstairs with Greggen. He will see her back to the—"

"You did what?" I hissed.

Ambrose dragged me by the hand, pulling me into a corner. He took my palm and placed it on his erection as he pressed me against the wall.

"Do not tell me that you are unable to detect her feelings, Eira. Her shy glances. Staring off into nothing. The fact that they can always be found within ten feet of each other. Surely you—"

I shoved him in the chest, attempting to escape, but he didn't budge.

"Wife, my kindhearted mother hen. How would you respond if someone put a blockade across the road you traveled? Told you that Cato was no longer an option in your life."

"But Ambrose, you don't understand." Tears of rage wet my eyes.

"I spent a considerable amount of time with him at Verus, and I would never allow her to walk into harm's way. And Eira, I have experience with not being allowed to live, and if you keep her from what she thinks her heart wants, the result could be catastrophic. Let her choose. Let her go."

I held his gaze, trying to find the courage to lash out. But as much as it pained me, I knew he was right. I would walk the nether to get to Cato—I would walk it for Ambrose, too. I nodded as the wetness continued to run down my cheeks.

"Let me make it up to you, softhearted harpy." Ambrose stuck out his bottom lip like a sad little toddler and closed in on me. "I'll make it better." He smoothed his hands over my hips and—

Shouts rang out overhead. A scraping sound came from the ceiling above us.

Ambrose shoved me between himself and the wall, drawing his dagger.

"Take her," he barked, and then flew through the room, gathering the rest of the men and charging up the steps.

"Consort, with me!" Septimus snatched my hand and pulled me behind him. Together, we ran to the Den's back entrance, where a guard stood at the ready, sword drawn in a bent-legged fighting stance. Septimus wrenched open the heavy iron door. "Lock it. Do not open it unless *I* give the command."

The guard clipped a bow, and we barreled into the rocky hall.

The door slammed home.

"Septimus, what's happen—"

His mouth crushed down on mine.

I parted my lips, and his tongue swept in, tasting me. He clutched my hair in his fist and wrenched my head backward, deepening his reach. Our teeth clashed, and he bit my bottom lip until I tasted iron.

"Septimus, we cannot. This pull is—"

"Tell me to stop."

He shoved his erection into my lower belly and ground himself against me roughly. My core wept for him. It knew the Bond, felt the connection that had increased exponentially since... since Cato had left me.

I conjured his face in my mind—his oft-broken nose, the planes of his cheeks, the dimples that showed happiness in its purest form.

"He's your nephew... We mustn't... Please, we—"

"Shut your mouth. Say nothing more." Septimus tore at the ties of his pants and freed his heavy length. His thick member stood proudly under a patch of golden hair, and a bead of semen tracked down his tip.

I stopped breathing.

"Do not speak."

I couldn't if I wanted to. I couldn't take in air—couldn't make my chest rise.

He wrapped my fingers around the tip of his erection, and I watched as our joined hands ran down his length, his skin pulling as we slid over the three silver bars that pierced his underside.

"Please... please..." I whispered or, perhaps, begged.

He pushed his unoccupied hand into my gown's deep V, freeing a breast and lifting it into his mouth.

"Septimus, Ahdmundus, I need you to—"

He bit down hard, clamping me between his teeth.

My shout of pain faded into a deep moan of pleasure.

"Do *not* consent." He stood, wrapped his fingers around my throat, and squeezed. "And do not speak the words that would force me to stop." He released the hand that held mine, and I continued working him up and down, enamored by the softness of his skin and the potential sensations those metal rods would bring. "I will bear the title rapist if it means having you."

He shoved my skirts around my thighs and fisted my underwear, ripping them from my hips. The ties scraped my skin raw before they snapped and gave way. He shoved his arm under my thigh and dug his fingers into my backside, nearly lifting me off the ground. He thrust himself up, cradling his length between my labia.

"Gods... gods help me." I was crazed. My mind wasn't my own. The æther pooled in my womb. The pulsing throb was a lighthouse guiding him home.

He pumped his hips, running himself through my wetness. The piercings rubbed and bounced over my inflamed gem, sending shocks of ecstasy to my every nerve ending.

"I mean to get a babe on you, and neither Ambrose nor the armies I control will stop me once I have begun. I won't cease fucking you until your stomach swells," he gritted out through clenched teeth as his shaking fingers dug painfully into my knee.

The iron door swung wide, creaking on its metal hinges.

"Brother, release her," Burchard's voice was calm but firm as he stepped through the threshold.

Septimus buried his face in the crook of my neck and bit down on the long tendon that ran down its side.

"I will bear your young... Don't listen to him—"

"Ahdmundus. End this now—there is no one stronger than you. Come with me. I know it feels like you cannot, but I—"

"You do not know!" Septimus yelled.

"I do, brother. I do." Burchard placed his hand on the side of his brother's neck, and his light-blue eyes rolled up into his head as he sank to the ground.

I dropped my skirts and pressed my chest into the cold wall, hiding my face and my shame.

"Papa..."

I couldn't meet his eyes.

"Go, daughter. This is not your fault. We cannot know the intricacies of the Goddess's will. The best we can do is fight to keep our humanity."

CHAPTER 47

SHAME

I bolted up the stairs and into the restaurant. Chairs were strewn across the room, and tables lay scattered, splintered, and broken. Ambrose, Levaunt, and a handful of others milled about the front door, sporting various injuries, an arm hanging oddly here, a hand pressed to a laceration there. I flew into the outstretched arms of my husband and buried my face in his coat, breathing in the familiar and safe scent.

"All is well. A few spooked horses ran through the establishment, netherbent on eating up Sylva's fine spread."

Levaunt nodded up and down as he held a red-soaked linen under his eye. He pointed to the horseshoe-shaped indentation located in the middle of his breastplate.

"I could have sworn the four-legged scoundrels had the eyes of a man." Dumail sat up from where he'd lain prone, rubbing his head.

I pulled away from Ambrose and ran behind the counter, where Sylva hunkered down, wide-eyed but alive.

"Towels?"

She nodded to a spot under the bar.

"Do you need a healer?"

"No, consort, just... just shaken up a bit, I'm used to all manner of funny business, but them weren't horses—"

"For your trouble... and your silence." I plucked the bear-headed brooch from my chest and placed it in her hand.

Dumail was shaking his head as if to clear his mind when I squatted down in front of him.

"Your forehead. I believe it needs stitching." I gently pressed a clean towel against his face.

"Do horses have teats?" He asked me in all seriousness, looking all for the world like a man who'd just seen a specter.

"How much did you consume, my man?" Ambrose offered a hand to the dazed Dumail and helped him to his feet.

"Not nearly enough, it would seem."

Levaunt saddled up to Dumail's side and provided him with a steady shoulder to lean on.

"The steeds were brought to heel and have been delivered to their stables. Their master was too drunk to see them back. He lies there, still snoring." Levaunt flicked his fingers toward a man, who, sure enough, was in a deep sleep, face down on the only table that remained standing.

"Inebriated fool should have taken more care." Dumail inclined his chin in acknowledgment but winced at the sudden pain the movement caused.

Ambrose went from man to man, ever the attentive leader, testing their pulses and pulling up their eyelids to check for concussion. I busied my spiraling mind by doing the same, handing each of the injured a towel and inquiring about their state of health.

"Elderman Deekon, are you well?" I assessed the representative's face for injuries. His lip was busted clean open, and the knot on his head was nearly the size of a duck's egg. He swept a few wood shards from his shoulder while blinking rapidly.

"I am... I'm quite unstable." I helped him to stand, and he leaned heavily on me while swaying from side to side. "Thank you, ma'am."

"I'm surprised to see you here while your Primus-King is hurrying home."

We walked slowly to the storefront window, where he propped his back against a wall. I maintained my hold on his shoulder, afraid he would end up face down on the hardwood floor.

"I have a new task."

I didn't have to ask. I instantly regretted having made the small talk, even if it *was* a technique to occupy him as he dealt with the shock of his injuries.

"Securing a bride for Prince Catommandus?"

He nodded, squinting gray-blue eyes that didn't want to remain fixed in one place.

"There are six daughters of Gaea, ma'am, ranging in age from a decade and three to"—the Elderman closed his eyes, trying to concentrate—"two decades and six. Any of them would make excellent matches."

Cato. My mate and life's love. He deserved a bride who didn't commit adultery the minute her æther ran wild.

"We are leaving." Ambrose came up behind me and placed my fur around my shoulders. "Elderman, my apologies for the turn the night has taken. I look forward to pursuing our conversation about eligible brides over dinner tomorrow."

"Indeed. Thank you, Highness." He made to bow, but stopped halfway to clutch his temple. "Ma'am, I appreciate the care rendered."

Once recovered, the guards ushered me out and hoisted me up into the carriage, and before my rear hit the seat, the horse's hooves met stone. Ambrose pulled me into his lap and secured me tightly in his embrace.

"Fancy a carriage fuck? The fighting made me even harder after the show you put on—and the way this vehicle rocks, you would hardly have to move at all."

For the first time, I was too shame-filled for tears. If it hadn't been for Papa Burchard, I would have broken the promises I'd made to the two men I valued more than anything in this life.

"Eira. Do not pretend you are not as aroused as—"

"Septimus," I choked out.

The arm around my shoulder tightened, and I could've sworn the temperature fell ten degrees. His fingers curled into my bicep, and his body went taut like a newly strung bow.

"Did. He. Touch. You?" Ambrose's voice dropped so low that I could hardly discern between him and the rumble of hooves.

"And I he. I deserve to be drawn and quartered."

Ambrose remained silent.

"Please speak to me," I whispered into his chest. "Please..."

He said nothing.

I focused on the steady rise and fall of his chest, but I didn't dare lay my head on his shoulder—I was undeserving of the intimacy.

When the carriage came to a halt, Ambrose exited without offering me his hand.

We walked through the halls of Cordillaria, him three steps ahead—me wishing I could bury myself under a heavy mound of dirt. I cringed as the guards' spears crashed down onto the floor, and the doors of our apartment flew wide open.

Ambrose went to the common room table and poured himself a glass of warmed wine.

"Did you fuck?"

"No," I answered honestly.

He downed the first glass and poured another to its brim.

"Good, I could never stand the thought of watering the same vessel as someone so repugnant." He popped open the buttons of his jacket and tossed it on the table.

"Y-you believe me?"

His head snapped in my direction so quickly that I flinched and held my hands up in front of my face.

"Is trust not common among the husbands and wives of Nortia?"

I cast my eyes to the ground, unable to meet his gaze as he continued wrestling with his shirt ties.

"It is," I whispered.

"Well, this is what trust feels like—looks like."

"You're not angry with me?"

"I am fucking furious." He popped the first button of his leathers and pulled his shirt from their waistband. Chair legs scraped loudly against the floor, and from the corner of my eyes, I watched him sink into the upholstered seat and prop his elbow on the table. He brought the glass to his lips again and drank deeply.

"Wrap your lips around my dick, and all will be forgiven. No, wait, fairy cunt me. I'll not take anything less."

My head spun. I was mystified by the level of faith he had in me—it was a silken balm spread across the guilt that plagued me.

Ambrose loosened his two remaining buttons with one hand while running the fingertip of his other around the rim of his cup.

"Do *not* keep me waiting. You kept me perched on the edge all evening. I would have fucked you very publicly had the godsdamned *horse men* of the nether not interrupted."

"Centaurs?" I asked in surprise. "How big were they? *Magika* says they stand up to twenty hands tall. Were they taller than you? What color were their manes?"

He crooked his finger, and I closed the distance between us.

"Knees." He pointed to the floor in front of him. "How big was his cock?" Ambrose pulled his arousal from his pants and weighed his package in his hand.

I dropped to the floor and squeezed my breasts between his legs.

"Uhm, Magika didn't cover that, but I imagine proportionate to their bodies."

"Eira…"

"Did they wear clothes or just fur? Again, hair color? It is my understanding that their hues are more akin to the colors of a flower or rainbow." I deflected.

"How big, Eira?" He lifted my chin and then applied firm pressure to the sides of my jaws.

"Like, he was like Cato… but pierced three times." My mouth opened as his fingers continued to tighten.

"Pierced? Gracious. *I* would have been hard-pressed not to mount him." Ambrose placed his palm under my chin. "Spit."

I hesitated briefly but did as he asked and spat in his open hand. He swept away the little bead that clung to my lips with the pad of his thumb.

"Ambrose—"

"Do you love him?"

"No," I said, shaking my head vehemently.

Ambrose ran his fist down his rising length and bent its tip to my lips.

"I require it rough and vigorous. My cock should hit the back of your throat with each thrust. Don't shortchange me."

"I won't." I wrapped my fingers around his head and pulled his skin down, opening the slit at his tip. I dipped my tongue into the small, salty crevice, wanting to be his perfect and willing partner. Why did it still surprise me when Ambrose turned out to be more chivalrous than many of the men who paraded around covered in metals and ribbons? More intelligent than those who call themselves scholars? More nurturing than even the highest religious authorities? He'd proven himself time and again.

As he leaned back and scooted his hips down to the edge of the chair, he caught my white-blonde lock in his hand. He ripped the pale tress from my scalp, which pulled my mouth down to the middle of his erection.

"I do not like it. No more blonde."

My lips popped over his firm ridge as I lifted my head to stare up at him.

"I'll do my hair as I please, husband."

I bent back down and sucked him hard into my mouth, lavishing my attention on him while swirling my tongue around his tip.

Ambrose dropped his head back and closed his eyes.

"Did you take him into your mouth?"

"Uh-uh," I grunted while letting my teeth skim lightly up his shaft.

"And you do not love him?" Ambrose guided my head back down until his arousal caught at the back of my throat.

"Uh-uh." I pulled back up, my broad tongue sweeping along his entire length. "I don't even like him."

"You just want to mount him?"

"Badly," I confessed, nodding my head up and down.

Ambrose chuckled and again, with both hands on the sides of my head, pushed me slowly back down his upstanding member.

"And you, by your own admission, love me?"

"Mmhmm." I worked my fist up and down, twisting my hand on the upstroke, playing off the tempo of his short thrusts.

"I see," Ambrose groaned. I was rewarded by a small spurt of his unique taste—salty and potent, not in the least bit sweet. "Eira, wife. Would you be interested in making love to me?"

My brows hit my hairline. Slow and sensual love with Ambrose? The Scion of Sensuality?

My husband.

My skin heated, its warmth spreading across my cheeks and down my neck.

"Don't grow timid on me now—not my wife who has toppled men from their tall towers, who ignites the air with her thoughts. Allow your husband to feel what you feel. Allow me a glimpse of what you share with Cato... I would like to know."

His words tugged at me and stirred within me the most profound need to protect him and keep his heart safe. I wanted to show him love, teach him what could exist between a husband and wife, and show him the kind of tenderness that could be passed on to our children. I would be honored to show him what love looked like, just as he showed me what true trust should be.

I stood, crawled into his lap, and ran my fingers down his dark-haired jaw. His heavily dilated eyes looked deep into my soul.

"Love is handing someone a map that shows them the location of your blemishes and fears," I said in a reverent tone. "And knowing that person would only use the information to protect those most vulnerable parts." My fingertip traced the bridge of his straight nose and ran down the dip in the middle of his top lip. "It is seeing obstacles as a chance to grow and not a stumbling block." I kissed the corners of his mouth while I spread my fingers and rubbed the knots at the back of his neck. "It is when you nestle up to my back at night and I can feel excitement for our future. Your scruff is delightful, husband. I love feeling it on my skin, raking my fingers through it when it becomes mussed." I found the tie at the end of his braid and freed his hair from its confines. A few of the decorative gems fell and scattered across the floor. "You are beautiful, Ambrose—otherworldly, even. When you walked into Verus the very first day, I thought you were the son of a god."

A sweet smile curved on his mouth, causing small, crescent-shaped lines to appear at its corners.

"But it is not that which has cemented your place in my heart." I massaged his scalp deeply, like he liked, paying special attention to the area where his hair pulled at the top of his head. His lips slackened and the crease in between his eyes softened. "I love you for the way you love fully. For the way you love Cato—for how you've taught me what a partnership is—"

My voice hitched in my throat.

Ambrose opened his eyes just a crack.

"I miss him too." He pressed his cheek into my wrist. "Eira?"

"Yes?"

"My calf is cramping so badly. Can we move to the bedroom?"

Oh, Ambrose. Sweet fucking husband.

"Of course." I squeezed my lips together so I didn't laugh.

"And will you grab the fruit bowl from the balcony? I forewent my snack so that my abdominals would look flattering. I am famished."

"Absolutely. I will get the fruit." I nodded.

Do not giggle, Eira. His vanity is a small price to pay for his support.

"Perfection. I will slip into something more comfortable, and you will continue loving me. I have never performed in the missionary position—always seemed too mundane for my tastes—but suddenly I am hankering to give it a go."

I rose to my feet, blinking at the confounding giant who was twisting a strand of his hair around his finger, looking as thoughtful as a priestess giving thanks.

"You never fail to... Ambrose, go... You look best in black, by the way." He jumped up, not at all self-conscious of his wildly swinging erection. I smacked his taut rear as he turned and shooed him away with the flick of my fingers.

"Scandalous Nortian... I have just the costume."

Genuine laughter filled the room for the first time since Cato walked from the dining hall.

I made my way to the balcony and pushed hard against the door that the fast-blowing wind tried to keep shut. The brisk and chilly breeze whipped my hair into my face, and I smiled at the happy reminder of home.

"Hurry! You have left me with a king-sized erection," Ambrose yelled from the other room.

Snow flurries peppered my hot cheeks as I brushed the strands from my face.

"Quit your giggling, wife. Its—"

"Ambrose..."

"What godsdammit? I'm horny. I cannot help that—"

"Ambrose..."

I fell to my knees.

"AMBROSE!" I screamed.

Blood drenched the garments of the bodies that hung suspended between the columns.

Lilium.

Imella.

Nan.

GODDESS HEAR ME

"**G**uards! To me!" Ambrose yelled behind me. "TO ME!"

He ran into the common room.

"Get them down!" I wailed. "Get them down, please!"

Stumbling as tears streamed down my face, I wrapped my hands around Nan's legs and hefted her up with all the strength in my body. She tilted forward, and her lifeless hands brushed across my forehead. Her cracked and blood-caked nails dangled in front of my eyes.

I jerked around, grabbed the fruit bowl, and smashed it against the table. Apples scattered, and glass shards flew. With the largest shard in hand, I shoved the nearest couch to the railing and leapt upon its cushioned seat.

"Nan, wake. You said you wouldn't leave me. You can't leave me."

I sawed at the rope that bit deeply into her neck as my own blood slicked my palms. Her body fell heavily and awkwardly to the couch below us and then slid off its edge, slumping to the floor. I half-fell, half-jumped to her side, jamming the glass into my wrist as I descended—I would die if she could live.

My lifeblood poured freely. I acted fast, jamming my fingers between Nan's purpled lips, praying all the while I wasn't too late.

They were sewn shut.

I dug and pried, ripping her flesh until a small opening formed at the corner of her mouth.

"Please, Grandmother Merrias, hear me. I beg you." I pressed my arm to her lips, but the thick crimson stream bubbled and ran down her chin.

There was something—an object blocked her throat. Scissoring my fingers, I pulled the item free and flung it aside.

"Nan, please. Open your eyes. It's your girl, your pup. I need you."

Ambrose and a small battalion of soldiers ran onto the balcony and flared out.

My wrist began to clot. I attacked it again, sinking my fingers into my flesh and pulling until my skin lay open. I rubbed my wound along the thin red line that ran the width of Nan's neck.

Lilium's frail body slid into my periphery—pale, departed.

My vision doubled.

"Lady, go back inside." Bem appeared, squatting down next to me. "This ain't for your eyes."

I ignored him.

"Wake up, Nan. The snow's fallen... The bath water needs thawing." I stretched out next to my companion and rested my head on her chest. Blood ran freely from my arm and absorbed into her dress. "Don't tell me you're just resting your eyes—I know better." I shook her shoulder. "Wake, Nan."

A hand touched my head.

"Eira, you must come away. You are not safe here."

"I'll not leave her, Ambrose. Not until she wakes."

"She's gone, sweet one. Merrias guides her now—may she guide them all." Ambrose's voice hitched in his throat. "I cannot protect you here, and I need you to—"

"Cato could." I snuggled closer to Nan, hugging her around the waist. "Oh, there he is. He will fix this."

Ambrose snapped his head, looking over his shoulder.

"No, Eira, that is not Cato. But Septimus *will* search the area and find those who committed this atrocity. If they survive the night, it will be to their regret."

I pushed up to my knees and crawled to Cato. My vision blurred with tears and blood—my heart followed the tie to its lifemate.

"I've missed you so much, my love." I wept into his neck. "Please, hold me. I don't understand why she won't wake."

I sank down as my vision twisted about, my chin landed hard on Cato's chest.

"Take her, Ambrose. She has lost too much blood."

"No, love. I'm fine now that you're here. Nan is napping like she does, playing one of her games."

I sat heavily on the side of my hip when Cato moved away. My hand brushed up against a red-splotched linen that was trapped under his foot.

"Do not touch it. Drop it!" he barked.

I left the cloth alone and inhaled deeply, needing to surround myself with his scent, cedar and—his smell—it wasn't right.

I blinked slowly, trying to maintain a hold on reality.

"Cato? Septimus?"

My eyes focused. Ambrose and Septimus stood, while Bem kneeled on the ground next to Imella.

"It is a missive," said Septimus. "Take her, seal her in the interior hall, and surround it with guards."

I glanced around and took in the reality of the carnage.

Nan. She was—

"I won't leave her, Ambrose. Don't take me from her. She'd never leave me." I batted weakly at his hands as I attempted to crawl back to her side. He bent low and scooped me from the ground.

"I have you, Eira. I will protect you with every breath in my body."

"No! Let me go! She needs me!" I fought against his strength, but to no avail. "Put me down, Ambrose! Now!"

"Read it, Levaunt. What does it say?"

"Yes, Protector, it reads 'Ma'am. In retribution for Monwyn's thievery, I have taken the lives of a queen and a royal mother. Until *my* queen or her daughter—my daughter—is returned to the gates of Gaea, the slaughter will continue. The servant assaulted my person and paid the price for interfering.'"

No. My gods no... he... he...

"A gift fit for a Head Queen, *ma'am*." I whispered. "Forgiveness is, at times, more powerful than one's hatred, *ma'am.*"

"Eira, what are you saying?" Ambrose asked.

"I am... I'm quite unstable... thank you, *ma'am.*"

Realization dawned in his eyes.

"'Ma'am,'" I whispered. "He walked among us this whole time."

"Who did?" Septimus and Bem moved toward us. "Consort, if you know who—"

"The Elderman... It was the Elderman... *He* is the Primus-King."

The world fell into shadow.

NO CHOICE

His. Life. Or. Mine.

CHAPTER 50

THE SHADE

The shade did not dance or flit—it did not wave or welcome me in with a twist of its smoky hand. The shade consumed... took hold entirely, integrating and seeping into my pores. No longer did I watch my actions from the outside, a bystander marveling at the confoundedness of what was occurring.

I merged with the shadows.

I *was* the darkness.

Grandmother Merrias had been wrong.

If there was light somewhere within me, I'd shuttered it off from reaching my soul. As I launched myself from the balcony, I rode a twisting wave of smoke and haze and moved with the speed of a falcon, passing through the night, sailing over, and sinking through the streets of Monwyn.

Guttural screams tore from the chests of those unfortunate enough to step in my path, but their lives were meaningless—dust motes in the grand scheme of humanity. I flowed over them, through them, and let them fall.

The restaurant doors turned to ash.

Show your coward's face.

I tore the room apart, blasting any object that might conceal him.

Everything that could burn did.

This building where his lecher's feet had walked. The Den that hid liars, sinners, and hypocrites. A whole kingdom that refused to protect its most precious and most vulnerable. It could all burn.

Where are you, Primus-King of filth and deceit?

Gongs sounded in the distance—a call to arms.

I twisted and turned, surging back through the streets, drawn by the sound of mallets crashing into metal.

I'll burn you out before a guard can run you through. You don't get to die tonight. I will sustain you, keep your feet firmly on Ærtan soil—keep you on the edge of existence while I sate my vengeance on your body. I will sand the needle dull before I pass it through your lips.

Shouts of triumph rang out as I slid through the iron gates that surrounded the palace grounds. If they took his life, I would collect theirs in exchange.

I arched up toward the moon and shot back down, gaining momentum steadily. The snow-covered ground reflected enough moonlight to illuminate the world below.

How many horrors can a night hold?

Circling down, I slowed and took in the scene, weaving in and out of the guards that had formed a tight ring around... something.

"Look what we have, fellas!" I swirled in front of the man who spoke, looking him directly in the eyes. Handsome and noble of countenance, he sported a thick, dark beard and had a dark-brown gaze to match. "This sullied beast murdered our womenfolk."

I flitted to the ground—no one concerned themselves with a shadow, even one that moved unnaturally, with no regard for the lamplight.

Goddess's mercy.

A satryress, with the beginning buds of breasts, thin and fragile arms, and a soft round face, lay in pieces upon the ground. Her face was covered in a fine, downy fur of white and lightest brown—pale-lavender irises, with strange rectangular pupils, looked out into the nothingness.

Why had they removed her head? Butchered her limbs from her body? Had the killing blow not been enough?

Poor little one, barely a life lived. I skimmed over the full cheek, still chubby from youth.

"For my wall!"

I flew up, assessing the face of the man who spoke. He was older, gray spreading from his temples in bright waves. He heaved his sword in an arc and brought it down on the top of the satryess's head, cutting clean through one of her thin horns and a section of her scalp. "That fucking *prince* never let us keep trophies. And after how many years of keeping our lips sealed about the demons that prowl our kingdom?" He spat on the lifeless body, hitting the young one on her chin.

Who are the true demons?

A chattering noise came from behind me.

I sensed another presence in the nearby thicket. Another satyr, perhaps? I drifted to the ground and floated toward the rustling. I couldn't save what was already lost, but perhaps I could defend another.

"A pint if you put your prick in it. Still warm, I bet."

I cracked—a jolt of electricity fizzled through my spectral form, and my hands materialized in front of me.

I was whole again.

I turned slowly, collecting my bearings while I adjusted to my newly corporeal limbs.

The darkly bearded guard plunged his blade between the satyress's legs and contorted his elbow, twisting into her dismembered body for nothing more than the sake of vulgarity—cruelty.

"That child was not your demon," I rasped while watching the snow melt around my feet, "but I am."

They didn't look up as they laughed and made sport of the youngling. They didn't hear me as I approached.

"I will take enjoyment in sending you to Merrias." Two of the guards pulled their swords and crouched into position, suddenly aware that they were not alone. Another flinched and fell backward, rubbing his fingers harshly against his eyes. "You will be the first on the Arbiter blade."

"Consort," said the leanest man, nodding his head up and down, trying to avert his gaze. "How did you come to be unclothed? Have you been assaulted?" He stood tall and puffed out his chest, all false propriety and boast.

"Don't avert your eyes from my body. You didn't hesitate to defile her with your gaze or your steel."

"Protector! Protector, she is here! We have located the conso—"

I launched myself at the man and snatched his throat in my hand. I sank my fingers into his flesh and began to pull, to siphon. I drew in his æther in deep glugs, stealing his energy and taking it for my own.

He stared at me, confused and fearful. I bet the little satyr had felt similarly. A line of saliva streamed down his chin. His dark-blue eyes turned gray and then white, and then became transparent—how lovely the transition was, like the lights that sometimes danced in the northern sky.

I watched him calmly as he declined.

He ceased to exist, not when his heart stopped—I could still feel the tie then—but a few seconds later, when a shifting shadow filtered from his mortal husk and took flight.

His body hit the ground with a thud.

"What in the f-fuck are you? Protector! Protector!" the bearded man shouted.

"I am of æther and shadow, descendent of Merrias and the Child. I am a conjurer and a protector in my own right. You are a criminal—a thief of innocence."

I cast my eyes down and held my arms wide open. My clothing had burned away. The æther's fire had cleansed and restored my bloodied skin—the renewal had pushed my piercing from my breast and erased the brand that marked me as Troth.

"I am a beast, I suppose—a creature, an abomination." I kneeled beside the satyress and brushed her pale-lavender hair over her exposed skull, covering the mark of violence that had caved in a portion of her head. Her body's remaining warmth had melted away the snow she lay on, leaving a thin ring of grass to surround her. "Was this a part of your oath, sir knight, to slaughter the young and desecrate their bodies?"

The guard backed away slowly, keeping his eyes fixed on mine. "We received orders to comb the land for foreigners and intruders."

Did he think I couldn't see him motioning the other two men away?

"And then to mutilate them after you brought them down? Who gave those orders? Why wasn't her death enough?"

I rose, carefully stepping around the satyress.

"No—I—Stay where you are, ma'am." He put his hand up, cautioning me.

My temperature rose—sweat beaded on my skin. My hands shook as the æther flooded my fingertips.

"What. Did. You. Call me?"

"Do not take another step, ma'am—Protector!"

Like the cowards they were, they turned and fled, shouting for their brothers-in-arms to retreat.

"That won't save you."

I rolled my head around my shoulders and breathed the cold air deeply through my nostrils, savoring the cooling effect on my scalding flesh. My eyes closed, and I filled my lungs to their capacity.

Nan's precious face appeared. Sparkling gray eyes, the color of a slick seal's fur, that soft, pink complexion, the hair gathered at the nape of her neck.

Love. How it mimics pain so perfectly. A broken heart, or one that bursts from yearning—both leave us raw.

Nan. Imella. Lilium... little nameless one.

The retreating soldiers grouped in a tight formation as they made their way toward the palace.

Funny, that. They must have missed their lesson on evasive maneuvering.

I tossed my head back and smiled up at the moon.

"You can't out swim an orca, boys, or run fast upon deep snows," I sang out loudly, my voice carrying across the grounds. "So when the polar bear's upon you, you're an offering to Derros."

My knees hit the ground.

I plunged my fingers into the hard, frozen earth, snapping the small bones of several digits.

In a line as wide as a boat's hull, black fire discharged from the snow-topped soil. It sliced and tore through armor and flesh, shooting bodies into the air before they slid down its razor-sharp edges, impaling themselves with their own weight.

Their screams were the perfect percussion for my song.

Nan. I bet she cursed the Primus-King from here unto eternity and called the gods down upon his head—it fueled my spirit to think maybe she was the one who had busted his lip wide.

Were her last moments painful?

I gagged, my throat burning.

I will be her curse embodied.

The unmoving spikes of dark flame shot higher. I could feel the heat that lay under their black coating, waiting to break loose into the world.

I shoved my fingers deeper into the soil and pushed the darkness in the direction of the palace. What an end that would be—my personal vendetta carried out in a single night. The courtiers would burn, and the wives they ignored would continue living, tucked away safe in the estates in which their husbands hid them.

Imella. No doubt she'd fought him off like the dissident she was—may her ancestors greet their warrior queen.

The earth shook, vibrating with my rage. Its rising pressure compressed the dirt around my palms.

Frail and brave Lilium, what was her offense? Protecting herself from this fucked up world? He'd ripped her away from the sanctuary she'd created for herself.

My Gods. Kairus.

Karius was now a motherless child, but she wouldn't know it until the ice thawed and the ships moved once more.

I pulled the night flames to me, shrouding myself from the world outside. I would insulate myself from the chaos of man, just as this world had forced Lilium to do.

The fucking Primus-King, he'd made both of them the victim of *his* crimes... but in doing so, he made *me* his judge.

I bore my weight down on my hands and watched the people running from the palace like ants scattering from their overturned hill.

Mine.

I pulled from them—knew their energy as it poured into my body—and watched them drop. The heaviness in my chest built, and I squeezed my hands harder and harder, gripping the earth until the ground gave way. The flames encircling me grew higher.

The soil parted, and an enormous rift snaked toward the palace.

"Eira! Sweetheart, listen to me. You cannot continue this slaughter," Ambrose yelled.

I was too far gone to turn back. I needed the æther to bring the Primus-King low.

"Daughter, you must end this now! You pull too much, you will corrupt and—"

How far is too far, Papa? Have you seen her, your beloved?

"Yes, child, and we will seek our retribution, but not at the expense of your humanity."

Humanity is a false ideology.

Burchard pushed into the night veil that encapsulated me. I could feel his presence. He pressed forward against the swirl of shade and fell to his knees.

Papa, there is no humanity, only the horrors that we create.

"Daughter, you are pulling too much. You are a vessel that is full and you will shatter if you drink too deeply." He crawled forward, placing one hand in front of the other, clawing the ground with all his strength. He wrapped his arms—his burned and charred arms—around me. "And you are wrong. Do not choose this path. Do not become the Magis in The Child's Tale. You have known love—great love."

The tie, our tie, snapped taut between us.

From his chest to my back, it blossomed like it had the first night I'd met him. I knew comfort.

Images raced through my mind as he held me. Dancing on my father's feet with my grubby child's toes. My mother laughing at my poorly timed joke, her eyes wrinkling up at their corners. A young Septimus, grinning down at the chubby little boy who sat on his lap.

"Am I the Child?" I asked, softly. "Will I bear a child? Where is my child?" I sank into his arms, trapped somewhere between delirium and another realm. The images kept pouring past. Imella placed a swaddled babe into Burchard's brawny arms. He rocked the little one while gazing into her dark eyes. And there was Cato, my heart, looking up from the ground, watching the Goddess's sign overhead, a testament of our blessed union.

"Oh, my dear, I-I did not know," Burchard whispered. "Had I known, dearest one, we could have…"

The black fire's casing dissipated, scattering its ash on the ground.

Orange and yellow flames licked the air, their surge weakening to a glow.

My fingers slipped from the ground, and another pair of arms surrounded me as Burchard's fell away.

Tears sizzled and steamed as they rolled down my blazing cheeks.

"Where is Cato, Ambrose?" I breathed, slumping against his solid body. I was weak—so incredibly weak.

"Moving Aberus to a place where Septimus cannot find him. Eira, he will return. His safety demanded discretion."

I nodded into his chest, understanding the importance of his final task as Protector.

"How I ha-have longed t-to have all my babes home…"

"Papa?"

I wrestled away from Ambrose, who laid me gently on the ground. Father Burchard's voice was faint and frail.

He laid on his side a mass of burnt and blistered flesh.

"Papa, what have I done? Ambrose, fetch the healer!"

I struggled my way to his side and lifted a hand to his face, but didn't dare touch the angry red and black holes that had burned through his skin.

"Why, why did you… why did you do this?" I stuttered, choking on the moisture that gathered in my throat. I drew the snow to me, turned it into a cool orb, and let it skate upon the surface of his skin.

"Because it is what papas do, Marmot." His lids sagged low and then opened once more. "Sometimes, the one we need to be saved from is ourself."

He lifted a single shaking finger toward Ambrose, who bent down to the level of his mouth.

"Father, please do not..." Ambrose's throat worked up and down as his eyes flicked rapidly over his father's scorched form. "I will, I swear it."

"Hush now, cub." The king's eyes grew dim as he slid his finger over the back of Ambrose's hand. "I ha-have served the Goddess's purpose and... Hello, Imella, my love... it's so good to be home."

I searched the ground with my hands, praying a stick or stone would materialize.

"Father Burchard, my blood, take it now, and—"

Ambrose took my hand, inspecting the damage that I'd done to them. He shook his head as his tears spilled.

"Ambrose, I can save him. Let me save one of them—I have—*we* have lost them all." I tried to tear away from him, but he caught my wrists and squeezed.

"Let him sleep, wife—he wishes to rest. He's not slept well without her."

Ambrose lifted me into his arms and stood. He pressed my head to his chest, shielding me from the sight of my own massacre.

A groan radiated from deep under the ground.

The temperature dropped—the air turned frigid, like the most frozen of Nortian winters. Frost raced across the windows of my shed, shattering the glass panes. The tears in Ambrose's lashes froze into tiny snowflakes.

Shivers wracked his body, as he clung to me.

A cloud of steam billowed from my chest, where the frozen air cooled the core of boiling æther that churned within me. Thunder swelled around us, drumming in our ears... but no lightning struck.

The earth shook, sending Ambrose to his knees.

"Go-goddess, p-pr-protect us," he stuttered.

A monstrous figure rose from the shattered ground.

The Goddess's netherbound twin—the god whose name was not spoken.

He inclined his horned head.

His massive arm, the length of five horses, reached past me, cooling the atmosphere another ten degrees. He collected the fragmented body of the satyress in his ice-covered hand and closed his enormous palm over her small, broken body.

When he opened his hand again, she was gone.

"Fire Walker. Nether Daughter." Shards of ice flaked from his lips as he spoke in a heavily accented voice. "You called for your children. I return them to you."

The gaunt megalith, who looked to be carved from blue-and-white stone, brought his cupped hands forward again, pressed them together, and then opened them like a clam's hinged shell.

Two gray-tinted bodies, coated in a thick glaze of frost, lay in his palm, still as death. Their knees were tucked to their chests, and their arms—one set pale, and the other deep bronze—encircled each other as twins might in the womb.

"F-fuck, holy f-fu-fucking n-nether, Eira," Ambrose whispered, his teeth chattering together. "E-Evandr and... my gods—"

I stared up at the ice giant, resolute in what I must do.

"Nether Lord, Shepherd of the Depraved, Skeletal Father... show me the daughters of Gaea. I would make my presence known."

THE OBLIGATES OF ÆRTA

EPIC ROMANCE FANTASY BY AUTHOR E.A. FORTNEAUX

AVAILABLE **AVAILABLE** **WINTER 2024**

FOLLOW THE QR CODE TO CONTINUE YOUR JOURNEY THROUGH ÆRTA

ARTWORK BY LINA GANEF